Su
B

*Summer wedding days lead to scorching
honeymoon nights!*

Praise for three bestselling authors –
Miranda Lee, Liz Fielding
and Susan Fox

About Miranda Lee:
'Ms Lee's talent for penning colourful
descriptions tantalises the imagination
to say the least!'
—*www.thebestreviews.com*

About THE BEST MAN
AND THE BRIDESMAID:
'A delightful tale with a fresh spin on a
fan-favourite storyline.'
—*Romantic Times*

About Susan Fox:
'Fans will relish Susan Fox's emotionally
charged stories.'
— *Romantic Times*

Summer Brides

THE WEDDING-NIGHT AFFAIR

by

Miranda Lee

THE BEST MAN AND THE BRIDESMAID

by

Liz Fielding

THE COWBOY WANTS A WIFE!

by

Susan Fox

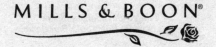

MILLS & BOON®

MILLS & BOON and MILLS & BOON with the Rose Device are registered trademarks of the publisher.
Harlequin Mills & Boon Limited,
Eton House, 18-24 Paradise Road, Richmond, Surrey, TW9 1SR

SUMMER BRIDES
© by Harlequin Enterprises II B.V., 2003

The Wedding-Night Affair, The Best Man and the Bridesmaid and *The Cowboy Wants a Wife!* were first published in Great Britain by Harlequin Mills & Boon Limited in separate, single volumes.

The Wedding-Night Affair © Miranda Lee 1999
The Best Man and the Bridesmaid © Liz Fielding 2000
The Cowboy Wants a Wife! © Susan Fox 1996

ISBN 0 263 83592 8

05-0703

Printed and bound in Spain
by Litografia Rosés S.A., Barcelona

Miranda Lee is Australian, living near Sydney. Born and raised in the bush, she was boarding-school educated and briefly pursued a career in classical music, before moving to Sydney and embracing the world of computers. Happily married, with three daughters, she began writing when family commitments kept her at home. She likes to create stories that are believable, modern, fast-paced and sexy. Her interests include meaty sagas, doing word puzzles, gambling and going to the movies.

THE WEDDING-NIGHT AFFAIR
by
Miranda Lee

CHAPTER ONE

THE door of Fiona's office burst open and Owen strode in, his round face pink with excitement. 'You've no idea who just rang and booked you for her son's wedding!' he exclaimed.

Fiona rolled her eyes, torn between exasperation and affection for her business partner. He was a dear man and a dear friend, hard-working and honest as the day was long. Mid-thirties, still a bachelor, and not at all gay as some people supposed, despite his penchant for pastel-coloured shirts and brightly coloured bow ties. Fiona thought the world of him.

He had this irritating habit, however, of accepting work on her behalf. Then he would race in to give her the details afterwards, and expect her to be thrilled to pieces.

She never was. She liked to vet all potential clients personally before accepting a job.

'You're right, Owen,' Fiona returned drily. 'I have no idea. How could I, since I didn't have the privilege of talking to this new client myself?'

As usual, Owen didn't look at all shame-faced. 'Couldn't, dear heart,' he countered breezily. 'You were on the phone when she rang, so Janey put the lady through to me.'

'Janey could have put the lady on hold for a while till I was free,' Fiona pointed out with mock sweetness.

Owen clamped a hand over his heart in horror at

such a suggestion. 'Put Mrs Kathryn Forsythe on hold? Good God, Fiona, she might have hung up!'

Fiona's own hand fluttered up to cover her own heart. 'Kathryn Forsythe?' she repeated weakly.

Owen beamed. 'I can see you're impressed. And so you should be! Do you have any idea what handling a Forsythe wedding will do for our business? Five-Star Weddings will be the toast of Sydney's social set! After everything goes off with your usual smooth and spectacular brilliance, Kathryn Forsythe will sing your praises to everyone who matters and there'll be a rush of society matrons banging on our doors to do their own daughter's wedding. Or son's, as is the case this time.'

Fiona's heart skipped another beat, before gradually returning to normal functions. What a fool she was to feel a thing after all this time—even shock!

'Well, well, well,' she mused aloud as she leant back in her black swivel chair and tapped her expertly manicured fingernails on the stainless steel armrests. 'So Philip's getting married at long last, is he?'

It was about time, she supposed. He would have been thirty last birthday. The perfect age for him to be finding a suitable bride and siring a suitable heir for his branch of the Forsythe fortune.

Owen looked slightly taken aback. 'You *know* Philip Forsythe?'

Fiona laughed a dry little laugh. '*Know* him! I was *married* to him once.' Briefly…

Owen dropped his rotund frame into one of the chairs she kept handy for clients. 'Good grief!' he gasped, then sagged, all his earlier enthusiasm swiftly abating. 'There goes our first high society gig.' Even his pink-spotted bow tie seemed to droop.

'Don't be silly. *You* can do it, can't you? Just say I'm all booked up.'

'That won't work,' Owen groaned. 'Mrs Forsythe wants the same co-ordinator who organised Craig Bateman's wedding.'

'Really? But that was hardly a society do. Just a cricketer and his childhood sweetheart. Very western suburbs, actually.'

'I know. But it was featured in one of the glossies, remember? It seems Mrs Forsythe was flipping through that particular issue at her hairdresser's and was most impressed by the photographs. The studio's name and number was printed underneath. Bill Babstock, if you recall. Anyway, when she rang to book Bill for her son's wedding, dear Bill very sensibly suggested she hire a professional wedding co-ordinator, then gave you the most glowing recommendation. When Mrs Forsythe rang just now, I did explain that you were very busy, but she promptly said that she'd heard you were the best and she wanted only the best for her son's wedding. So naturally I promised her you.'

'Naturally,' Fiona repeated in rueful tones.

Owen threw his hands up in the air. 'How was I to know you'd once been married to her infernal son? I mean…when I gave the woman your full name to jot down, she didn't react adversely. It was as though she didn't recognise it at all!'

Fiona thought about that for a moment. 'No, she wouldn't. Everyone called me Noni back then. And my surname was Stillman. Fiona Kirby wouldn't have meant a thing to her.'

Owen frowned. 'Kirby's not your maiden name?'

'No, it's my second husband's name.'

Owen gaped at her. '*Second* husband! Good grief, girl, I've known you six years, and whilst you've had more admirers than I've had bow ties you've never even got close to the altar. On top of that, you're only twenty-eight! Now I find you've got two husbands hidden in your past and the first belongs to one of Australia's richest families! Who was the other one? A famous brain surgeon? An international pop star?'

'No, a truck driver.'

'A truck driver!' he repeated disbelievingly.

'First name Kevin. Lived out at Leppington. Nice man, actually. I did him a favour when I divorced him, believe me.'

'And Philip Forsythe? Was he a nice man too?'

'Actually, yes, he was. Very.' She'd never held any real bitterness towards Philip. Or even Philip's father, who'd been surprisingly kind and gentle. It was his mother Fiona despised, his mother who'd looked down her nose at Noni and never given her brief marriage to Philip a chance.

'I suppose you did Philip Forsythe a favour when you divorced him too?' came her partner's caustic comment.

'How very perceptive of you, Owen. That's exactly what I did.' But it wasn't a divorce, she almost added. It was an annulment…

Fiona bit her tongue just in time. Such an announcement would lead to some sticky questions which she had no intention of answering.

'Let's face it, Owen,' she went on, 'I'm not good wife material. I like my own way far too much. I also hate to think we might lose this lucrative commission. Are you absolutely sure you can't convince Mrs

Forsythe to let you do it? Maybe we could say I'm ill.'

Owen sighed. 'I won't lie, Fiona. Lies always come back and bite you on the bum. Besides, I could hear the determination in her voice. She wants you for her son's wedding, and you alone.'

'That's a change,' Fiona muttered under her breath.

'What was that?'

Fiona looked up. 'I said that's a shame. As you said, this wedding would be worth a lot to us, both money-wise and reputation-wise.' She frowned and gnawed at her bottom lip. 'I wonder...'

Owen tried not to panic as he watched his partner's large brown eyes narrow into darkly determined slits. He knew that stubborn, focused look. When Fiona got the bit between the teeth, woe betide anyone who got in her way. Most times, Fiona's driven and obsessive personality didn't worry him. It was a plus, business-wise. She got things done.

This time, however, he feared getting things done might get things seriously *un*done.

'Oh, no, you don't!' he said, leaping out of the chair and jabbing a pudgy finger her way. 'Don't even *think* about it!'

'Think about what?'

'Trying to trick Kathryn Forsythe. I can see you now, putting on glasses and a blonde wig then waltz-ing in there with some funny accent, hoping your ex-mother-in-law won't recognise you.'

'But she won't recognise me, Owen,' Fiona said with blithe confidence. 'And I won't need to change a thing about my appearance. When Philip's mother knew me ten years ago I *was* a blonde. A ghastly straw colour done in a big mass of waves and curls. I also wore more make-up than a clown, carried twenty pounds too many and dressed like I was auditioning for a massage parlour. No top could be too tight; no skirt too short.'

Owen could only stare, first at the shoulder-length black hair which swung in a sleek, smooth, glossy curtain around his partner's striking but subtly made up face, then at the very slender body which was always displayed within a stylish but subtle outfit.

In appearance and dress, Fiona was the epitome of elegance and class, had been ever since he'd known her. The image she'd just painted of herself at the time of her marriage to Philip Forsythe certainly didn't match the woman she was today. Owen could not visualise her as some brassy voluptuous blonde bombshell.

Even if it was so—and he supposed it *was*—why would the likes of Philip Forsythe marry such a creature? He didn't know the man personally, but the bachelor sons of that particular family only ever married glamorous model-types, or the daughters of other equally rich families.

Unless, of course, it was for the sex.

Owen had to admit Fiona exuded a strong sexual allure which even *he* felt at times. Yet she wasn't his type at all. He fancied cuddly older women who laughed a lot, played a top game of Scrabble and cooked him casseroles. He never looked at a woman under forty, or a size fourteen.

Still, most men were madly attracted to Fiona. Once they slept with her, they became seriously smitten. She had dreadful trouble getting rid of her lovers after she tired of them.

And she always tired of them in the end.

Owen had often thought her a little cruel towards his sex, despite her always claiming that she never made a man any promises of permanency and had no idea why they presumed a deeper involvement than what was on offer. Perhaps the secret of that cruelty lay in those two marriages to those two supposedly 'nice' men.

'As for a funny accent,' Fiona was saying with a dismissive wave of her hand, 'I won't need to adopt one of those, either. The way I talk now is a lot different to the way I used to talk, believe me. I made Crocodile Dundee sound cultured back in those days. No, Owen, Mrs Forsythe won't recognise me. And Mr Forsythe senior won't have the chance. He passed away a couple of years back.'

'Did he? I didn't know that.'

'Cancer,' Fiona informed him. 'It didn't get all that much coverage in the papers. The funeral was private and closed to the public.'

There'd only been the one photo, Fiona recalled. That had been of Kathryn climbing into a big black car after the funeral was over. None of Philip.

Philip was not like his mother, or the rest of the Forsythes. He shunned publicity, and the media. Not once in the past ten years had Fiona ever caught a glimpse of him, either on television, or in the papers or magazines.

'And what was *he* like?' Owen asked.

'What?' Fiona looked up blankly. 'Who?'

'The groom's father,' Owen repeated drily.

'Actually…he was very nice.'

'Goodness, Fiona, your past seems peppered with very nice men. How is it, then, that down deep you're a man-hater?'

Fiona was startled for a moment, then defensive. 'That's a bit harsh, Owen, and not true at all. I love *you*, and you're a man.'

'I'm not talking about me, Fiona. I'm talking about the men you've dated, then discarded without so much as a backward glance. They thought you really cared for them but the truth is you just *used* them. That's not very nice, you know.'

Fiona stiffened for a moment, then shrugged. 'Sorry you think that, Owen, but they all knew the score. As for really caring for me, I doubt that very much. After an initial burst of pique at having their egos dented, they moved on to the next female swiftly enough. Now, let's get back to the subject at hand, which is that Kathryn Forsythe won't recognise me. Philip will be the only one who might. Though I stress the word *might*. Still, it's the mother who matters, isn't it? She's the one I'm meeting. Believe me when I assure you she won't know me from Adam.'

Owen stared at his partner and his friend and felt terribly sorry for her, because she *was* nice. Underneath all that delusionary and self-destructive bitterness, she was a genuine person, decent and kind, hardworking and generous. She cared about her clients and their worries. She always remembered everyone's birthday in the office, and was the softest touch when it came to charities. She never walked past one of those people selling useless badges and biros in the street, always stopping with a smile and a donation.

Goodness knows what had happened in those marriages of hers to make her hard where men were concerned, because she wasn't hard in any other department of her life. Determined, yes. And ambitious. But that was different. That was business.

Which reminded him. He had a business to protect here. He could not allow Fiona to carelessly endanger what they'd taken years to build together.

'We can't rely on Mrs Forsythe not recognising you, Fiona,' Owen said firmly. 'If you don't reveal who you are up front and it comes out later, then she's going to be furious and your name will be mud. Which means *our* name will be mud. I see no other solution than for you to keep the appointment I made for you, confess your identity with tact and diplomacy, then offer her my services once again. At least that way, even if she decides against using Five-Star Weddings, she won't be inclined to blacken our name.'

Fiona leant back even further in her chair and mulled over Owen's suggestion. It made sound business sense, she supposed. And she would still have the satisfaction of seeing Kathryn Forsythe's face when she revealed her true identity.

In a way, it would be *better* than tricking her, showing the hateful woman in person that the one-time object of her snobbish scorn was no longer as ignorant as sin and as common as muck. Philip's derided and despised first wife could pass muster in the best of circles these days!

Fiona now knew how to dress, how to talk and how to act on whatever occasion was thrown at her. She owned a half-share in a blossoming business, a beautiful flat overlooking Lavender Bay, and a wardrobe full of designer clothes. She had a vast knowledge of food and wine. She had an appreciation of art and music of all kinds. She could even ski!

But, best of all, she could have just about any man she wanted, if and when she wanted them, for as little or as long as she wanted them.

For a moment Fiona wondered ruefully what would happen if she ran into Philip again. *Would* he recognise her? If he did, what would he think of Fiona as compared to Noni? Would he want *Fiona* as he'd once wanted *Noni*?

It was an intriguing speculation.

As much as she was over her love for Philip at long last, she still felt an understandable curiosity about the man. What did he look like now? And what was the woman like he'd finally decided to marry?

'Very well, Owen,' she agreed, and snapped forward in her chair. 'I'll go and throw myself on Mrs Forsythe's mercy. But first, do tell. Why is it Kathryn's job to organise her son's wedding? Doesn't the lucky bride *have* a mother?'

Owen shrugged. 'Apparently not.'

'So who is this undoubtedly beautiful and well-brought-up creature who's to be welcomed into the bosom of the Forsythe family?'

'I have no idea. We didn't get that far.'

'So when's the appointment for?'

'Tomorrow morning at ten.'

'On a *Saturday*? You know I never see anyone on a Saturday! For pity's sake, Owen, I have a wedding on tomorrow afternoon.'

'Rebecca can handle it.'

'No,' Fiona said sharply. 'She's not ready.'

'Yes, she is. You've trained her very well, Fiona. You just don't like delegating. Much as I admire your dedication and perfectionism, the time has come to give Rebecca some added responsibility.'

'Maybe,' Fiona said, 'but not this time. The bride's mother is expecting *me*. I refuse to let her down on such an important day.'

'Maybe you could do both,' Owen suggested hopefully. 'The appointment *and* the wedding.'

'I doubt it, not if Mrs Forsythe still lives way out at Kenthurst, which by the look on your face she does. That's a good hour's drive through traffic from my place, and far too far from tomorrow's wedding down at Cronulla. You'll have to ring back and change the appointment to Sunday, Owen. Make it for eleven. I'm not getting up early on a Sunday morning for the likes of her.'

'But…but…'

'Just do it, Owen. Tell the woman the truth: that Fiona has a wedding to organise tomorrow and can't make it. She'll probably admire my…what was it you said?…my dedication and perfectionism?'

Owen groaned. 'You're a hard woman.'

'Don't be silly. I'm as soft as butter.'

'Yeah, straight out of the freezer.'

'Trust me, Owen, I know what I'm doing. The Forsythes of this world have more respect for people who don't chase or grovel. Be polite, but firm. I'll bet it works a charm.'

It did, to Owen's surprise. 'She was only too accommodating about it all,' he relayed ten minutes later, still startled. 'And she wants you to stay for Sunday lunch. Fortunately for us, her son and his bride-to-be can't make it that day. Thank heavens for that, I say. And thank heavens the groom doesn't live at home.'

Fiona already knew Philip didn't live at home. The phone book had been very informative of his whereabouts over the years. There weren't too many P. Z. Forsythes in this world, and only one in Sydney. Fifteen months after they'd broken up—around the time

he would have finished his law degree—he'd bobbed
up at an address in Paddington, only a hop, step and
a jump from the city.

The following year he'd moved further out to
Bondi. More recently he'd moved again, to an even
more salubrious address at Balmoral Beach, which,
though over the bridge on the north side, still wasn't
far from town.

Back in his Paddington days, Fiona had used to regularly ring him, just so she could hear his voice, hanging up after he answered. Once, not long after his
move to Bondi, she'd rung him on a Saturday night
and pretended to be wanting someone called Nigel,
just so she could extend the conversation for a few
seconds, then had got the shock of her life when Philip
called out to some Nigel person.

'He'll be with you in a sec, honey,' Philip had said,
before putting the phone down. The sounds of a party
in the background had been crushingly clear. Laughter. Music. Gaiety.

Fiona had hurriedly hung up and vowed never to do
that again.

And she hadn't. She had, however, never got out of
the habit of checking Philip's address every time a
new phone directory arrived, which was how she knew
about his move to Balmoral.

Fiona glanced up from her thoughts to find her partner frowning down at her. She smiled up at him. A
rather sardonic smile, but a smile all the same. 'Stop
looking so worried, Owen.'

'I want to know how you're going to handle telling
Mrs Forsythe the truth about yourself.'

'With kid gloves, I assure you. I *can* be tactful and
diplomatic, you know. I can even be sweet and charm-

ing when I want to be. Don't I always have the mother of the bride eating out of my hand?'

'Yeah. But Mrs Forsythe isn't the mother of the bride. She's the mother of the groom, and *you're* the groom's first wife!'

CHAPTER TWO

FIONA pulled over to the kerb and consulted the street directory one more time to make sure she knew the way to Kenthurst. She'd gone there only twice, after all, ten years before.

Kenthurst was not a suburb one passed through by accident, or on the way to somewhere. It was more of an 'invitation only' address.

A semi-rural and increasingly exclusive area on the northern outskirts of Sydney, Kenthurst boasted picturesque countryside with lots of trees, undulating hills and fresh air. The perfect setting for secluded properties owned by privileged people who liked peace and privacy.

Wealthy Sydney businessmen had once built summer houses up in the Blue Mountains or down in the southern highlands to escape the heat and the rat-race of the city. Now they were more inclined to build air-conditioned palaces on five to twenty-five acres out Kenthurst or Dural way, and live there most of the time.

Philip's father had done just that, though he'd also owned a huge Double Bay apartment where he'd stayed overnight when business kept him late in town, or when he'd taken his wife to the theatre or the opera. It was an enormous place, covering the whole floor of a solid pre-war three-storeyed building, lavishly furnished with antiques, and with a four-poster bed in the main bedroom which had belonged to a French countess. Fiona knew this for a fact because she'd slept in it.

Well…not exactly *slept*.

She wondered if Philip had ever 'slept' with his bride-to-be in that same bed, if he'd taken her to the same mindless raptures he'd taken her own silly self.

Now, now, don't go getting all bitter and twisted, she lectured herself sharply. Waste of time, honey. Concentrate on the job at hand, which is getting to Kathryn's house by eleven.

Fiona didn't want to be late. She didn't want to give the woman the slightest excuse for looking down her nose at her again.

Gritting her teeth, Fiona bent her head to concentrate on the directory. Once the various street turnings were memorised, she angled her freshly washed and polished Audi away from the kerb and back onto the highway.

A small wry smile lifted the corner of her mouth as she drove on. The car wasn't the only thing that had been washed and polished to perfection that morning, mocking her claim that she would not get up early on a Sunday for the likes of Kathryn Forsythe.

Pride had had her up at six. By nine there hadn't been an inch of her body which wasn't attended to, from the top of her sleekly groomed head to her perfectly pedicured toenails. Fiona had told herself that even if there was only the remotest chance of having to remove her shoes and stockings—or any other part of her clothing—she was going to be as perfect *underneath* as she was on the surface.

Oddly enough, it had been the surface clothes which had ended up causing her the most trouble. Downright perverse, in Fiona's opinion, when she had a wardrobe chock-full of the best clothes money could buy.

The fact that it was winter should have made the choice of outfit easier. But it hadn't. The black suits she favoured for work had seemed too funereal, her grey outfits a little washed out, now that her summer tan had long faded. Chocolate-brown and camel were last year's colours. She certainly wasn't going to show up in *them*! Which had left cream or taupe. Fiona never wore loud colours. Or white.

Certainly not white, had come the bitter thought.

She had dithered till a decision had simply *had* to be made. Time was beginning to run out.

In desperation, she'd settled on a three-piece trouser-suit in a lightweight cream wool. It had straight-leg trousers, a V-necked waistcoat and a long-sleeved lapelled jacket. The buttons on the waistcoat were covered, but rimmed in gold, so a necklace would have been overdone for daytime.

But she had slipped eighteen carat gold earrings into her pierced ears and a classically styled gold watch onto her wrist—both gifts from one-time admirers. Her shoes and bag were tan, and made of the softest leather. They'd cost a small fortune. Make-up had been kept to a minimum, her mouth and nails a subtle brown. Her perfume was another gift from an admirer, who'd said it was as exotic and sensual as she was.

Finally, she'd been fairly satisfied with her appearance, and just before ten had left her flat, ready to face the woman who'd almost destroyed her.

'But I rose again, Kathryn,' Fiona said aloud as she turned off the highway and headed for Kenthurst. 'Just like the phoenix.'

Fiona laughed, well aware that the likes of Noni

would not even have known what the phoenix was. 'You've come a long way, honey,' she complimented herself. 'A long, long way. Worth a few nerves to show Philip's darling mama just how far!'

The sun broke through the clouds at that point, bouncing off the shiny polished surfaces of the silver car and into her eyes. Fiona reached for the designer sunglasses which she kept tucked in the car door pocket, slipped them on, and smiled.

Fifteen minutes later she was driving slowly past the Forsythe place, her confident smile long replaced by a puzzled frown.

It had changed in ten years. And she wasn't talking about the high brick wall which now surrounded the property. Somehow, it looked smaller than she remembered, and less intimidating. Yet it was still a mansion; still very stately, with its imitation Georgian façade; still perched up on a hill high enough to have an uninterrupted three-hundred-and-sixty-degree view of the surrounding countryside.

Fiona stopped the car, stared hard at the house, then slowly nodded up and down. Of course! How silly of her! It wasn't the house which had changed but herself, and her perceptions. After all, she was no stranger to mansions these days, and no longer overawed by the evidence of wealth.

Her confident smile restored, Fiona swung the Audi around and returned to the driveway, where the iron gates were already open, despite the security camera on top of the gatepost and an intercom system built into the cement postbox.

It seemed careless to leave the gates open, but perhaps Kathryn had opened them in readiness for her arrival. Her watch did show two minutes to eleven.

Fiona drove on through, a glance in the rear-vision mirror revealing that the gates remained open behind her.

Oh, well. She shrugged. Kathryn Forsythe's security wasn't *her* problem, but it seemed silly to go to the trouble and expense of having all that put in without using it. Such rich remote properties would be a target for break-ins and burglaries. Maybe even kidnappings. You couldn't be too careful these days.

Admittedly, Philip's branch of the family wasn't as high-profile as his two uncles'. His uncle Harold was a captain of industry, owning several food and manufacturing companies as well as a string of racehorses, whilst his uncle Arnold was a major player in the media and hotels, along with expensive hobbies such as polo and wine.

Philip's father, Malcolm, had been the youngest of the three Forsythe boys and had gone into corporate law, the law firm he'd established handling all the legal transactions for his older brothers' business dealings. Philip had once told her that his father was probably richer than his two brothers, because he didn't waste money on gambling and other women.

All three Forsythe brothers had married beautiful girls from well-to-do society families, thereby increasing their wealth and securing a good gene pool for their children. Harold had sired a mixed brood of five children, and Arnold three strapping sons. Malcolm had only had the one child, Philip.

Surprisingly, none of the brothers had ever divorced, despite rumours of serious philandering by Harold and Arnold. All three Forsythe wives were regularly photographed by the Sunday papers and gossip magazines, showing off their tooth-capped smiles along with their latest face-lifts. They seemed to spend half their lives at fashion shows, charity balls and racing carnivals.

Fiona had once been impressed by it all.

Not any more, however.

Her brown eyes were cool as they swept over the groomed lawns and perfectly positioned trees, her pulse not beating one jot faster as she drew closer to the house. A little different from the first time she'd come up this driveway, her heart pounding like a jackhammer, her stomach in sickening knots. Back then she'd been as nervous as the heroine in *Rebecca*, driving up to Manderley with her wealthy new husband at her side.

Fiona could well understand that poor young bride's feelings of inadequacy and insecurity. She'd felt exactly the same way back then. Ironic that on *her* unexpected return to Manderley *she* was now the first wife.

The house grew larger on approach. But of course it *was* large. Wide, white and two-storeyed, with a huge pitched grey slate roof and long, tall, symmetrically placed windows. It looked English in design, and somewhat in setting, with its clumps of English trees and ordered gardens. Nothing, however, could disguise the Australian-ness of the bright clear blue sky, or the mountains in the distance, also blue with the haze from the millions of eucalypti which covered them.

The tarred and winding driveway finally gave way to a more formal circular section, with a red gravel surface and a Versailles-like fountain in the middle. The Audi crunched to a halt in front of the white-columned portico and almost immediately the front door opened and the lady of the house stepped out into the sunshine.

Fiona frowned as she stared over at Philip's mother.

Kathryn was still as superbly groomed as she remembered. And just as elegant, in a royal blue woollen dress, with pearls at her throat and not a blonde hair out of place.

But she looked older. *Much* older. Probably even around her real age.

She had to be coming up for sixty, Fiona supposed. Ten years ago she'd been in her late forties, though she'd looked no more than thirty-five.

She appeared frail as well now, as though the stuffing had been knocked out of her. There was a slight stoop about her shoulders and a sadness in her face which struck an annoyingly sympathetic chord in Fiona.

Her whole insides revolted at this unlikely response. *Sympathy for Kathryn Forsythe? Never!*

Steeling herself against such a heresy, Fiona pulled the keys out of the ignition, practically threw them in her handbag, climbed out and swung the door shut. Sweeping off her sunglasses, she turned to face her one-time enemy, waiting coolly to be appraised and *not* recognised.

Kathryn's lovely but faded blue eyes *did* sweep slowly over her from head to toe, but, as Fiona had predicted to Owen, there was not a hint of recognition, let alone rejection. Nothing but acceptance and approval. One could even go so far as to say…admiration.

Oddly, this did not give Fiona the satisfaction she'd hoped for. She didn't feel triumphant at all. Suddenly, she felt mean and underhand.

'You must be Fiona,' Kathryn said in a softly gentle voice, smiling warmly as she came forward and held out a welcoming hand.

Fiona found herself totally disarmed, smiling stiffly back and taking the offered hand while her mind fairly whirled. She's only being nice to you because you *look* the way you do, she warned herself. Don't ever think this woman has really changed, not down deep, where it matters. She's still a terrible snob. If she ever found out who you really were, she'd cut you dead, and, yes, she'd be furious. Make no mistake about that. So put on a good act here, darling heart, make your abject apologies and get the hell out of Manderley!

'And you must be Mrs Forsythe,' she returned in her now well-educated voice, a far cry from the rough Aussie drawl she'd once used, with slang and the odd swear-word thrown in for good measure.

'Not to you, my dear. You must call me Kathryn.' Philip's mother actually linked arms with her, gathering her to her side and giving her a little squeeze.

Fiona froze. The Kathryn Forsythe of ten years before would never have done such a thing, not even to her friends and relatives. Philip's mother had been a reserved and distant woman with an aversion to touching.

'After all,' Kathryn went on, before Fiona could recover from her shock to form a single word, 'we're going to be spending a lot of time together over the next few weeks, aren't we?'

Fiona should have put her right then and there, but she hesitated too long and the moment was lost.

'So how did your wedding go yesterday, dear?' Kathryn asked as she steered Fiona over towards the house. 'You had lovely weather for it, considering it's August.'

'It…um…it went very well,' Fiona replied truthfully, while she tried to work out how to tactfully escape this increasingly awkward situation.

'I can imagine everything you do goes very well, my dear,' Kathryn complimented her. 'I'm already impressed with your punctuality and your appearance. A lot of people these days don't seem to care how late they are for an appointment, or how they look when they get there. I've always felt that clothes reveal a lot about a man, and everything about a woman. You and I are going to get along very well, my dear. Very well indeed.'

Now *that* sounded more like the old Kathryn, Fiona thought.

To be strictly honest, however, she now shared some of those sentiments. She couldn't abide people who were late for business appointments. Neither was she impressed with the slovenly dressed, or the grunge brigade. Fiona had found that people who didn't care about their own appearance were usually not much good at their jobs.

You mean you judge a book by its cover these days, darling? an annoying inner voice pointed out drily.

The sound of a car speeding up the driveway interrupted her distracting train of thought.

'That will be my son,' Kathryn said, just as a black Jaguar with tinted windows roared into view. It braked hard inches before the gravel section, then passed sedately by them before purring to a cat-like halt on the other side of her Audi.

Panic had Fiona jamming her sunglasses back over

her suddenly terrified eyes and praying Philip wouldn't recognise her with them on.

'I thought you said Phi…your son…couldn't come today,' she pronounced tautly.

Fortunately, Kathryn didn't seem to notice her agitation. 'He rang a while back on his mobile to say that Corinne—she's his fiancée—had woken with a migraine this morning and begged off going on the harbour cruise luncheon they were supposed to attend. He didn't fancy going alone so decided to pop home for lunch instead. He rang off before I could remind him you would be here as well.'

Fiona found herself staring over at the car. From the side, she couldn't see the driver, because of the tinted windows. Several fraught seconds ticked away without Philip making an appearance, and she found herself waiting breathlessly for that moment when the driver's door would open.

Fiona began to feel sick to her stomach. It had been a dreadful mistake coming here today, she was beginning to realise. A dreadful, dreadful mistake!

As though in slow motion, the door finally opened and his dark head came into view, followed by his shoulders—his very broad shoulders. Once fully upright, he turned to glance at them over the bonnet of the car.

Was she imagining it or was he staring at her?

Surely not. She *had* to be imagining it. He couldn't have recognised her, not with her sunglasses on!

She was being paranoid. Besides, he was wearing sunglasses too. Impossible to see where his eyes were being directed, or to determine their expression with those masking shades on.

Which was a reassuring factor from her own point

of view, because the moment he strode round the front of his car and started towards them Fiona's eyes began eating him up in exactly the same way they had the very first day he'd walked into Gino's fish and chip shop ten years before.

Yet he was only wearing jeans and a grey sweater. Nothing fancy. Just casual clothes.

Philip the man, she was forced to accept, was even more impressive than Philip the youth, the promise of future perfection now fulfilled. His long, lanky frame was all filled out, his once boyishly handsome face fined down to a more mature and classical handsomeness, his thick unruly brown hair now elegantly tamed and groomed.

At twenty, Philip had been dishy.

At thirty, he was downright dangerous.

Kathryn disengaged her arm from Fiona's as Philip approached, moving forward to give her son an astonishing hug. 'It's so nice to see you, son. I hope you didn't drive too fast, now.'

'I never drive too fast, Mother dearest. Can't afford to get any blemishes on my record.'

'My son's a lawyer,' his mother proudly explained, with a smiling glance over her shoulder at Fiona.

Philip's gaze swung to Fiona as well, who felt as if there was a vice around her chest, squeezing tightly.

'So, who have we here, Mother?' he said quite nonchalantly. 'Aren't you going to introduce us?'

A little of the pressure eased, though a perverse dismay was added to the emotions besieging Fiona at that moment. So he *hadn't* recognised her! She shouldn't have been disappointed. But, stupidly, she was. He'd once claimed he would never forget her, that he would love her till the end of time.

'The end of time' apparently expired after ten years, came the pained thought. If truth be told, it had probably begun to run out the moment she'd exited his life.

Philip's father had been so right about his son's so-called love. It had had about as much substance as fairy-floss.

'Your memory for some things is appalling these days, Philip,' his mother said, blissfully unaware of the irony within those words. 'Fiona is the wedding co-ordinator from Five-Star Weddings that I was telling you about on Friday. I'm sure I mentioned I was having lunch with her today. Fiona, this is Philip, the absent-minded groom. Philip, this is Fiona. Fiona Kirby, wasn't it, dear?'

'Yes, that's right.'

'How do you do, Mrs Kirby?' he greeted her.

'Miss,' she corrected sharply, and his eyebrows lifted above the sunglasses.

'My mistake. Sorry. Ms Kirby.'

'Oh, don't call her that, Philip,' his mother said with a soft laugh. 'We're already on a first-name basis, aren't we, my dear? As I said to Fiona, we'll be spending quite a deal of time together in the near future so we might as well be friends.'

Fiona wanted to scream and make a dash for the car. *Friends?* She was no more capable of being friends with Philip and his mother than she was of being friends with a pair of serial killers.

Yet for the moment she was trapped. Owen would kill her if she alienated such an influential family as the Forsythes, thereby damaging the reputation of Five-Star Weddings. And, frankly, she wouldn't blame him. She'd been very foolish indeed to come here in person and risk all for the sake of her infernal pride.

'You've already decided on Five-Star Weddings to do the wedding?' Philip asked his mother, a frown bunching his forehead.

'I certainly have. The moment I met Fiona I knew she was the right person to do the job.'

'Did you indeed? How interesting. I, however, would like to see what she has in mind before any decisions are made and any contracts signed.'

'Lawyers!' Kathryn exclaimed, with a roll of her eyes and an apologetic glance towards Fiona. 'They see trouble at every turn.'

'Not at all,' Philip countered smoothly. 'I simply don't believe in rushing into anything, especially when it comes to business dealings. The world is full of con-artists and shysters. I know nothing of Five-Star Weddings other than what you told me over the phone. And absolutely nothing about Ms Kirby here, except what I can see for myself. As attractive as her outer package might be, in reality she might be anybody!'

Fiona stiffened, then saw red. Be damned with what Owen thought. Be damned with everything. She was not going to let Philip stand there and insult her.

Sweeping off her sunglasses, she glared up at him, her cold fury only increasing when he *still* didn't recognise her.

'Five-Star Weddings has an impeccable record and reputation, Mr Forsythe,' she stated through clenched teeth. 'As do I. Might I remind you that your mother solicited this appointment, not the other way around? Nevertheless, I can show you many personal letters of recommendation, plus extensive portfolios of weddings I have arranged. Believe it or not, I am heavily booked at the moment, and only came here as a favour for my business partner, who agreed to this appointment without consulting me.

'Under the circumstances, it would be better if you found someone else, Kathryn,' she directed at Philip's mother. 'Lovely to have met you.'

Kathryn grabbed her arm before she could make good her escape. 'Please, don't go!' she cried, before rounding on her son, her voice trembling and full of reproach. 'What on earth's got into you, Philip? I've never known you be so rude before!'

'I wasn't being rude. I was trying to be sensible. Anyway, given that Ms Kirby says she overbooked, it's better you *do* hire someone else.'

'But I don't *want* someone else! I want Fiona. She's the one who was recommended. On top of that, I *like* her. You'd do the job personally, wouldn't you, dear, if I paid you double your usual fee?'

'Well, I... I...'

'Mother, for pity's sake, you don—'

'Philip!' his mother interrupted sternly, the stubborn and autocratic Kathryn of ten years ago emerging for a few moments. 'You and Corinne asked me to organise your wedding and I am only too happy to do so. But with your proposed wedding date only ten weeks off, and your bride-to-be overseas for most of that time, I will need help. I want Fiona to be that help. Please don't be difficult about this.'

Philip stood there silently for several tense seconds, his shoulders squared, his mouth grim.

Fiona didn't know whether to laugh or cry. It really was a bizarre situation.

Suddenly, Philip swept off his sunglasses and stared deep into her eyes, his own no longer masked.

They had always been his most attractive feature, his eyes. A vivid blue and deeply set, with a dark rim around the iris which gave them an added intensity, both of colour and expression. The first time he'd looked at her all those years ago, across the shop counter, her knees had gone to jelly.

He stared at her now and she stared boldly back, her knees only marginally shaky.

His gaze raked her face, his expression puzzled and searching. For what? she thought angrily. Was he finally being bothered by a faint glimmer of familiarity? Was his subconscious teasing him with all those times he'd looked deeply into her eyes and told her she was the most incredible, adorable, irresistible girl in the world?

Quite abruptly, his eyes cooled to a bland, infuriatingly unreadable expression.

'I apologise,' he said, but insincerely, she believed. 'I didn't mean to cast aspersions on your reputation. I have to confess to a certain cynicism these days, especially in matters of business. I'm sure Five-Star Weddings is without peer in its field and I'm sure you're one of its star co-ordinators.'

'She certainly is,' his mother joined in, looking both relieved and pleased. 'You should have heard the photographer rave. He said Fiona was the very best in the business.'

'I'm sure,' Philip murmured. 'Still, perhaps Fiona could humour me a little by coming inside and telling us some more about herself. But first, I'm dying for some decent coffee, Mother dearest. Do you think you could make me some? I know it's Brenda's day off, but you make much better coffee than she does anyway.'

'Flatterer!' Kathryn returned, but she was beaming.

'What about you, Fiona?' Philip said, with the sort of suave smoothness she both desired and despised in a man. 'You look like a coffee girl to me.'

'Coffee would be nice,' she agreed, with a smooth smile of her own. She would have liked to tell him where to shove his coffee, but things had moved beyond her making any further fuss, or flouncing off in some dramatic exit. She had to see this unfortunate scenario through now, or Owen would kill her! But come tomorrow she was going to fall mysteriously ill and be unable to take on any new clients.

'I'll take Fiona through to the terrace,' Philip informed his mother.

'Oh, yes, do,' she replied. 'It's lovely out there today. I won't be long.'

Kathryn hurried off to do her son's bidding. Another vast change in the woman's character. She'd never been sweet and accommodating in the past. She'd expected everyone else to do *her* bidding.

'This way,' Philip murmured, taking Fiona's elbow rather forcefully and steering her speedily inside, across the spacious marble foyer and down the wide cool hallway which bisected the bottom floor of the house.

Fiona barely had time to scoop in a couple of steadying breaths before she was ushered through a pair of white French doors onto an enormous sun-drenched terrace which stretched the length of the house.

It was an area she'd never been, or seen before. Probably new, she decided.

As Philip directed her towards the closest grouping of outdoor furniture Fiona replaced her sunglasses and glanced around, her wedding co-ordinator's eye automatically taking over. Kathryn wouldn't need to book a special place for the reception, she realised. This setting could look magnificent, with the right kind of marquee and the right lighting.

There wasn't just the one terrace. There were two. The top one conveniently had shelter, with a pergola-style roof which had slats one could open or shut. The next terrace, much longer and wider than the first, was tiled in terracotta and incorporated a large rectangular swimming pool, lined at each end by Corinthian columns of grey marble. It reminded Fiona of a photograph she'd once seen of a pool in ancient Rome. All that was missing was the nude statues.

At each end of the terraces lay an extensive garden, which was distinctly tropical, full of ferns and palms and rich green shrubs of all kinds. Oddly, it didn't look out of place, exuding an exotic and sensual pull on the senses, making one long for the warm, balmy evenings of summer.

Fiona could easily envisage a near-naked Philip, stretched out along the edge of the pool, his eyes shut, one hand languidly trailing through the cool blue water. She could almost feel the coolness of that water on her heated skin as she imagined swimming towards him, stopping right next to him, then taking that wickedly idle hand and lifting it to her hot…wet…flesh.

Philip scraping out a chair for her on the flagstones snapped Fiona out of her erotic daydream with the abruptness of a drowning man gasping to the surface. Disorientated for a moment, she found herself staring down at the strong male hands gripping the back of the white wrought-iron chair and remembering how good he was with those hands, how well they had known her body and how completely they had been able to coerce her to his will.

Surely they couldn't *still* do that, she thought, then panicked as her body experienced a deep and violent burst of desire.

Self-disgust followed, but a fraction too late in her opinion. Clenching her teeth, Fiona wrenched her eyes away from those offending hands and swiftly sat down. She didn't watch Philip stride round to select the chair directly opposite, not looking back at him till he was seated.

'Right,' he said, his voice cut and dried as he slid his sunglasses back on. 'Now, let's stop all this pretence, Noni. What in hell are you up to?'

CHAPTER THREE

'Oh!' Fiona gasped, sitting up straight. 'You *did* recognise me.'

'Keep it down, for pity's sake,' he hissed. 'I don't want my mother to hear any of this. And, yes, of course I recognised you. How could you possibly imagine I wouldn't? I knew it was you the moment I drove up. You weren't quite quick enough putting on those sunglasses. Still, I can understand why my mother didn't twig. That's some make-over, Noni. Most impressive. But back to the point. What are you up to? Why this sick little charade?'

Any momentary elation Fiona had felt at Philip's having recognised her quickly faded at his sarcastic and accusing tone. She automatically moved back into survival mode.

'I'm not up to anything,' she defended coolly. 'It's exactly as I said earlier. My business partner made this appointment with your mother without my knowledge. I tried to get out of it. I explained to Owen that you and I had been married briefly years ago, and that I couldn't possibly do your wedding, but he still insisted I show up today in person. He said the future of Five-Star Weddings was at stake. He wanted me to apologise and recommend him instead, but when Kathryn didn't recognise me I hesitated too long, and then you showed up unexpectedly and…well…' She shrugged.

'Things got even more complicated,' Philip finished drily.

'Yes,' Fiona agreed.

There was a short, sharp silence while he just stared at her.

'You must have suspected my mother wouldn't recognise you,' he said curtly, 'looking as you look today.'

'It did briefly cross my mind.'

He laughed. 'More than briefly, I'll warrant. So…did you enjoy fooling her? Did you get a kick out of it?'

She contemplated lying, but couldn't see any point. 'I thought I would,' she confessed rufully.

He frowned. 'But you didn't?'

'No,' she confessed, still a little confused by her reaction to his mother 'No, I didn't. She's not the same woman I remember, Philip. Somehow, I couldn't find it in my heart to hold any more malice towards her.'

His frown deepened. 'What do you mean…malice?'

'Oh, Philip, don't pretend you don't know what she did all those years ago, how she made me feel.'

'I know she made things difficult for you. But, believe me, she would have made things difficult for any girl I wanted to marry back then. The bottom line is it wasn't my mother who ended our marriage, Noni. It was you.'

She opened her mouth to defend what she'd done, then stopped herself. Once again, she couldn't see the point. It was over. Philip was getting married again. No doubt to some rich, beautiful girl he loved to death and of whom his mother heartily approved.

As for herself. Well…she had her career.

'I was very young,' Fiona said flatly. 'So were you. We were from two different worlds. Our marriage

would never have worked. I did the right thing.' She
looked away from him then, afraid that she might do
something appalling like burst into tears.

When she looked back, several seconds later, she
was once again under control. 'What's done is done,'
she stated brusquely. 'Let's not hash over ancient history, Philip. Just tell me what you want me to do about
your mother and your wedding.'

He didn't answer her straight away, considering her
at length from behind his sunglasses till her irritation
table rose to dangerous levels.

'Will you be in trouble with your partner if you lose
this job?' he finally asked.

'Probably,' she snapped.

'Then do it.'

Fiona automatically shrank from the idea.

'Come now, Noni, it's no big deal. It's not as
though we mean anything to each other any more,' he
said dismissively. 'As you just said, our marriage—
such as it was—is ancient history. We don't have to
tell anyone who you really are. I've never told Corinne
about you, and Mother will never recognise you. On
top of that, you've been offered double your usual fee.
You'd be a fool to knock it back.'

His cold pragmatism put her mind—and her emotions—back on track. He was right, of course. She'd
be a fool to say no. And she was no longer a fool,
either over money or men.

'You'll have to practise calling me Fiona,' she
pointed out drily.

'No trouble. Fiona suits you better these days, anyway.'

Fiona gritted her teeth. 'And you'll have to practise
not being sarcastic.'

'I wasn't being sarcastic. I was just saying it as it was.'

Fiona bristled. 'You don't like the way I look?'

'Does it matter what *I* like? My mother thinks you're the ant's pants. That must give you great satisfaction.'

'It does, actually.'

'Then that's all that matters. She's the one you'll be working with most of the time. The groom has very little to do with wedding preparations.'

'True.' She'd *never* agree otherwise.

'Of course I *am* a little curious as to how you achieved this stunning transformation, and how you came to be a partner in a highly successful business. The last I heard of you, you were married to some truck driver.'

Fiona's mouth dropped open. 'How...how did you know about that?'

His mouth smiled, but his eyes remained a mystery behind those increasingly irritating sunglasses. Yet, at the same time, she was grateful for her own.

'Curiosity sent me looking for you after I finished university,' he explained. 'I didn't find you but I did find your father. He seemed happy to tell me about your marriage to a trucking mate of his, a man named Kevin Kirby. That's why I called you Mrs Kirby when we were introduced just now. But you soon put me straight about that! Since you're a little young to be a widow, I gather there was a divorce?'

'You gather right.'

'Your decision again, Fiona?'

'It was, actually.'

'What went wrong?' he asked. 'You certainly

couldn't say you were from two different worlds on that occasion.'

'No. I certainly couldn't,' she returned, her voice as hard as her heart. 'The bare truth is that Kevin wanted me to stay home and have children, and I didn't. Our divorce was quite amicable. He's now married again with a couple of kids.'

'And you're on your way to your first million,' he mocked.

'And what's wrong with that?' she snapped.

'Nothing, I guess. If that's all you want out of life. *Is* that all you want nowadays, Fiona? Money?'

'A little respect goes down well. But money's good. The money I earn for myself, that is.'

'Ahh. A truly independent woman. Very admirable. I dare say you live alone these days?'

'I do.'

'But you date, of course. Celibacy would not be your strong point.'

'Nor yours, Philip,' she shot back at him.

He laughed. '*Touché.* So, are you sleeping with this business partner of yours? What was his name? Owen something or other?'

'I have no intention of answering any questions about my personal life,' came her cool reply.

'You're not asking Fiona impertinent questions, are you, son?' Kathryn said wearily as she seemed to materialise beside Fiona's shoulder, bending to slide a tray onto the table. It held an elegant white coffee pot with three equally elegant white coffee mugs surrounding it. A matching jug held cream, no doubt, and the crystal sugar bowl sparkled in the sun.

'Don't take any notice of him, dear,' Kathryn went on as she sat down between them. 'Once a lawyer, always a lawyer. They like giving people the third degree, even innocent ones. I sometimes feel sorry for the witnesses Philip cross-examines.'

'You're a *criminal* lawyer?' Fiona exclaimed, taken aback. She'd presumed he'd gone into corporate law, in his father's company. That had certainly been his father's plan for him.

'Philip's beginning to make a name for himself in court, aren't you, dear?' his mother said proudly.

'I've had some modest successes recently.'

Kathryn laughed softly. 'Now who's being modest? How do you take your coffee, Fiona?'

'Oh…um…white, with one sugar, please,' she answered, a little distractedly, almost adding 'the same as Philip.' Goodness, she was a mess!

'Just to put your mind at rest, Mother,' Philip said casually while Kathryn was pouring the coffee. 'It's perfectly all right by me for Fiona to do the wedding. Now that I've had a chance to talk to her, I'm more than impressed with her credentials, but especially her professional attitude. I recognise a high achiever when I hear one. I'm sure she'll do a top job. As for her fee, and the contract, I'll take care of that personally. You live too far out of town to be bothered with that. I presume you have an office somewhere in the city, Fiona? Perhaps a business card as well?'

Fiona hated the thought of him dropping in to the office, but what could she do? She could hardly say as much in front of his mother. 'Not *in* the city exactly,' she told him, 'but not far out. We rent a suite of rooms above a couple of shops at St Leonard's, along the Pacific Highway. And, yes, of course I have a business card.'

'Of course,' he murmured, and she shot him a savage glance, which, unfortunately, he couldn't really see. But she was about to remedy that!

Taking off her sunglasses, she scooped up her handbag from where she'd dropped it beside her chair, snapped it open and dropped the glasses inside. Then she opened the side pocket where she kept her business cards and took out three, handing one to Kathryn and two to Philip.

'Perhaps you could give one to your fiancée,' she suggested with a sickly-sweet smile. 'Which reminds me, Kathryn, you said something earlier about the wedding date only being ten weeks away, and the bride going to be absent overseas for a lot of that time? Is that right?'

'Yes, Corinne does voluntary work for one of those world charities for children. Her best friend is employed by them as a nurse. Unfortunately, Corinne organised this trip to Indonesia before Philip asked her to marry him, and she doesn't want to let her friend down.'

'How very commendable,' Fiona remarked, while privately thinking it was still an odd time to be going away. 'Well, if that's the case, then there's no time to waste, is there? I should meet with the bride very soon and find out exactly what she wants. It doesn't give us much time.'

'I'll get Corinne to ring you tonight,' Philip offered. 'On which number? Your mobile?'

'No. I have a firm rule never to use my mobile on a Sunday unless I have a wedding on. Otherwise I never have any peace. Here, give me the card back and I'll jot down my home number.' She extracted a pen from her bag and added her personal number to the two already on the card.

'What time would be best for you?' Philip asked after she'd handed the card back to him.

'Any time before eight-thirty.'

'Going out, are you?'

Actually, Fiona rarely went out on a Sunday night. She liked to curl up on front of the telly and watch one of the Sunday night movies which always started at eight-thirty. During the ads she did her nails and got her clothes ready for the working week ahead. Today she'd already done her manicure, and tonight they were re-running one of her all-time favourite films.

The slightly mocking tone in Philip's voice, however, stung her into lying.

'Yes, I am, actually,' she said, and found another of those sweet smiles for him.

'Anywhere special?'

'Not really. Just visiting a friend.'

'Boyfriend?'

'I think Mark's a little old to be called a boyfriend.'

'How old is he?' Philip persisted.

'Late thirties.'

'What does he do?'

'Philip, really!' his mother exclaimed, and threw Fiona a look of helpless exasperation. 'See what I mean? Lawyers! They can't help themselves.'

'I'm just making conversation,' Philip said, sounding innocent. But Fiona knew he wasn't doing any such thing. He was deliberately trying to goad her. And he'd succeeded.

But no way was he going to know that.

'It's perfectly all right, Kathryn,' she said nonchalantly. 'I don't mind. Mark's a doctor,' she directed, straight at Philip. 'A surgeon. We met at a dinner party…oh, about six months ago. We've been dating ever since.'

Actually, it had only been three months. It just seemed like six. Mark had all the superficial qualities she found attractive in a man, being tall, dark-haired and good-looking, as well as well-read and intelligent. He was also more than adequate in bed.

But his vanity was beginning to grate and, even worse, he was starting to hint that it was time he settled down and passed on his 'perfect' genes. She'd been going to break with him this week, but now revised that decision. Mark was best kept around till Philip was safely married and out of her life once more.

Fiona felt confident she no longer loved Philip, but there was still an unfortunate chemistry there between them. She could feel it sparking away every time she looked at him. She suspected Philip could feel it too, and resented it as bitterly as she did. That was why he was taking pot-shots at her personal life.

'So where did you meet Corinne?' Fiona asked, deflecting the conversation away from her personal life and back onto Philip's.

'I can't rightly remember. At some charity do she organised, I think.'

'It sounds like she does a lot of charity work.'

'She does.'

Which meant she didn't have a real job. A rich man's daughter, obviously. Well, what had she expected? Philip moved in those kinds of circles.

'How old is she?'

'Twenty-four.'

Just as she'd thought. Young. 'Blonde?'

'Uh-huh.' Again, just as she'd thought. Philip had told her once how much he liked blonde hair.

'Pretty, I've no doubt.'

'Very.'

'She'll make a lovely bride,' Kathryn joined in warmly. 'It's a pity her mother isn't alive to see her. I went to school with her mother, would you believe? But she died when Corinne was a little girl. Corinne's father is George Latham. He's a state senator. You might have heard of him?'

Who hadn't? George Latham was not a shrinking violet, either in size or personality. He was also filthy rich. Or his family was. Yep, Fiona had this wedding tagged correctly. It would be society though and through. Owen would be so pleased.

A sudden beeping had Philip standing up and fishing an extraordinarily small mobile phone out of the back pocket of his jeans. 'Excuse me,' he said, and, flipping it open, placed it to his ear. 'Philip Forsythe,' he said as he walked off to one side.

Both women picked up their coffee cups and began to sip, but Fiona could still hear Philip's side of the conversation quite clearly.

'That's great… No, no, I wouldn't mind at all, actually… All right, Corinne… See you soon, my darling.'

He walked swiftly back to the table, but stayed standing while he snapped the phone shut and slid it back into his pocket.

'That was Corinne,' he said. 'She's feeling a bit better and wants me to come over and babysit. I couldn't really say no, given she's leaving in a week or so. Sorry about lunch, Mother, but you and Fiona will still have a lovely time together, planning the wedding of the year.'

'We certainly will, won't we?' Kathryn agreed, and smiled over at Fiona.

Fiona tried to smile back, but it wasn't easy. She was still reeling with shock over how she'd reacted to Philip calling his fiancée 'my darling.' The warmly said endearment had speared straight to her heart, evoking the memory of when he'd first made love to her and first called *her* his darling—his only darling, his most precious darling.

And now, now he was running off to his new darling, no doubt taking her to bed for the rest of the afternoon in one of those long, leisurely lovemaking sessions which he was so expert at. It had been after one of those romantic afternoons in bed ten years ago that he'd confessed to her that one of the condoms he'd used had broken, and her life had been irrevocably ruined.

Fiona's stomach suddenly clenched down hard, then swirled. A clamminess claimed her and her head began to spin. She wasn't sure if she was going to faint, or be sick. Shakily, she got to her feet, scraping the chair back on the flagstones.

Kathryn's eyes flew upwards, alarmed. 'Are you all right, Fiona? You've gone a terrible colour.'

'I... I...'

She didn't speak another word. She barely had time to blink before a blackness swept over her.

Afterwards, Fiona would wonder over the abruptness of her unconscious state. She'd never fainted before, and had always imagined one sort of drifted into it. But it wasn't like that at all. One minute she was awake, then the next...nothing!

She was totally unaware of Philip scooping her up into his arms to safety, before her head could hit the flagstones, or the look of pain which filled his face as he gathered her close and carried her swiftly into the house. She saw and felt nothing till she came to, lying on a large sofa, Philip's handsome face looming over her.

CHAPTER FOUR

'ARE you all right?' he asked worriedly.

She stared up into his beautiful blue eyes, her first woozy thought being that she was glad he'd taken those rotten sunglasses off. For one mad, delusional moment she wallowed in his concerned expression and the gentle tone of his question.

But then she came back to reality. And rationality.

A frown slowly settled on her forehead as she realised what had happened.

'I *fainted*,' she said disbelievingly.

Philip sat back on his heels and smiled a wry little smile. 'Amazing, isn't it?' he murmured. 'You're human, after all.'

His return to sarcasm sped her recovery, both emotionally and physically. Fancy getting all upset and fainting like that! What a foolish female thing to do! Futile, too.

Angry at herself, she sat up abruptly and swung her feet over the side of the sofa, Philip having to hurriedly get out of her way.

'What on earth do you think you're doing?' he said, scrambling to his feet and glaring down at her. 'You should stay lying down for a while. Mother's ringing her doctor.'

'I'm perfectly all right!' Fiona protested, and to prove it she stood up.

Unfortunately, she wasn't quite all right, and

swayed dangerously. Philip took her by the shoulders and forced her back down into a sitting position.

'For pity's sake, Fiona, do as you're told and just sit!' He plonked down in a nearby armchair and shook his head at her as though she were an idiot. 'You fainted dead at our feet, woman. You can't expect us to ignore that fact. We have to check it out.'

'I'm perfectly all right, I tell you,' she insisted. 'It was a simple faint.'

'You just intimated you've never fainted before.'

'Well, I...I've never skipped breakfast before!' she argued.

'Huh! By the feel of you, you skip breakfast a lot.'

She glared over at him. 'Are you saying I'm too thin?'

He shrugged. 'I'm not getting into an argument over a woman's weight. I'm just saying you could do with a few more pounds.'

'Oh, really? I suppose you preferred me when I was fat!'

'You were never fat. Nicely rounded, maybe, but not fat.'

'Then you were the only one in your family who thought so,' she snapped.

He went to open his mouth, but when his mother came into the room, carrying a glass of water and looking worried, he shut it again. 'The doctor's not at home,' Kathryn said as she hurried over. She handed Fiona the water, then sat next to her on the sofa and peered anxiously into her face. 'You still look pale. Would you like Philip to take you to one of those twenty-four-hour medical centres?'

'Certainly not. I'm perfectly all right,' Fiona repeated, and took a sip of the water. 'I was just confessing to Philip that I forgot to have breakfast. I'll be all right once I eat something.'

'Oh, dear, I wish you'd said something,' Kathryn said. 'I would have brought some food with the coffee instead of waiting for lunch. I'll go and make you a sandwich straight away. Brenda prepared us some lovely ham and salad. Just sit right there, dear, and don't move.'

She bustled off again, rather annoying Fiona with her solicitude. This new warm, caring Kathryn took some getting used to!

'You don't have to look so put out,' Philip said sharply. 'She's only being kind.'

Fiona sighed. 'I know. I know. It's just that…'

'You never thought she was capable of kindness?'

Fiona nodded, and Philip sighed.

'I have to admit she was once on the selfish side. And quite a snob. She'd been very spoiled, by her own father and then by mine. Dad adored her. He was a slave to her wishes. But she's changed quite a bit since you last met. She's been through a lot over the past few years. I suppose you heard about Dad dying? It was in all the papers.'

'Yes,' she admitted.

'It wasn't quite as it said in the papers. Dad didn't die peacefully at all. His fight with cancer was very prolonged, and very painful.'

Fiona's heart turned over. Philip's father had been a fair and decent man. He hadn't deserved a long, lingering death. He'd never judged her, like Kathryn had, or made her feel cheap. It was telling, she thought, that Philip called his mother 'Mother' and his father 'Dad.'

Philip seemed lost in his memories of his father for

a few moments, as she was. But then he cleared his throat. 'I guess the death of a loved one changes a person,' he said abruptly. 'Not that Mother's totally changed. She's still a stickler for manners and appearances, as I'm sure you've noticed.'

'I presume Corinne passed the manners and appearance test,' Fiona said a little tartly.

Philip winced. 'Oh, hell! Corinne! I'd forgotten all about her. I'd better give her a ring, tell her I'll be late.'

'Better still,' Fiona said swiftly, before he could flip open his mobile, 'why don't you just go, Philip? There's nothing more you can do here today.'

He hesitated, his handsome face strangely torn.

Fiona could not imagine over what. Surely he'd want to absent himself from her company as quickly as possible.

'If you're still worried about my fainting,' she said, 'then please don't. Neither my health—nor me—are your responsibility. Not till you sign me up for your wedding, that is. After that, you might like to keep me out of bed.'

His left brow arched slightly and Fiona realised what she'd said. Her eyes met his full on, and whilst her heart was racing madly her face remained superbly composed. No way was she going to let Philip rattle her any more with his sarcasm, spoken or unspoken!

'If you insist,' he said drily. 'I'll get Corinne to ring you this evening, *before* eight-thirty. And I'll drop in to your office tomorrow. Say around noon?'

'*Must* you?' she said painfully. 'I'll trust *you* over the fee if you'll trust *me* over the contract. We can see to the business side of things at some later date.'

'Is there some reason why you don't want me to visit you at your office?'

Fiona groaned silently at Philip's cynical tone and suspicious face. He didn't believe her about Owen. He probably thought she'd slept her way into her partnership at Five-Star Weddings and that she spent every second minute having sex on Owen's desk.

'I can't think of any,' she returned frostily. 'I was just trying to make things easy for you. You must be a very busy man, what with all those successful cases you've defended lately.'

'Not so busy that I can't take some time to make sure my wedding day is a resounding success. I would like to see some of those letters of recommendation you mentioned, along with that portfolio of photographs. Afterwards, if everything is as you say, then I'll take you to lunch and you can run a few ideas by me.'

Inside Fiona, everything fluttered wildly. Outside, she looked perfectly calm. 'Thank you so much,' she said coolly, 'but I don't do business that way.'

'Would Owen object if I took you to lunch?'

'No, but Corinne might.'

He laughed. 'I doubt it. We don't have that kind of relationship.'

'What kind is that?'

'Possessive. Jealous.'

'Really? What kind *do* you have?'

'The kind which will last. The kind which is soundly based on shared goals and things in common rather than some fleeting passion.'

'Sounds pretty boring to me.'

'Not at all. Corinne and I enjoy each other's company a great deal. But we're not compelled to rip each other's clothes off every time we meet.'

Fiona flinched at the reminder of just how passionate *their* relationship had once been. Whenever they'd been alone, they simply hadn't been able to keep their hands off each other. They hadn't been able to get naked quickly enough.

'Not that Corinne and I aren't very happy in bed,' Philip swept on, his blue eyes glittering angrily. 'We are. So there's really no danger in your coming to lunch with me. I promise I won't throw you back over the table and eat you up in a burst of sexual frustration.'

Now Fiona flushed, his snarled words evoking another, far more explicit memory: that of Philip doing exactly what he'd just said. It hadn't been a restaurant table, of course. It had been the richly polished walnut dining table in his father's Double Bay apartment.

She'd never felt anything like it, either before or since.

She stared at him, and her treacherous heart took off. He glared back at her, his eyes hard and narrowed.

'Noon tomorrow,' he ground out. '*Be* there!' And, whirling, he stalked from the room.

Five seconds later, the front door banged. A few seconds further on, the Jag roared into life and took off.

Fiona was sitting there, still stunned, when Kathryn came back into the room. 'Don't tell me Philip left without saying goodbye?' She sounded both puzzled and hurt.

Fiona had no idea why she spoke up to smooth over Philip's rudeness, but she did. 'He...he asked me to say goodbye to you for him. He suddenly remembered Corinne and said he had to dash.'

Kathryn looked appeased. 'Oh…oh, well, I suppose there's not much he could do here, anyway. Men are so useless when it comes to things like weddings. Just tell them what to wear and point them in the direction of the church on the day. That's about all you can do. But we wouldn't be without them, would we?' she added, smiling softly.

'Er…no, I guess not. Thank you,' she added, when Kathryn handed her a plate with a very tasty-looking sandwich on it, cut into dainty little triangles. She picked one up and took a bite, only then realising that her excuse for fainting was probably partially true. She *hadn't* bothered with breakfast. She'd been too obsessed with getting her appearance just right.

'I hope you don't think I'm prying, dear,' Kathryn said a little hesitatingly from where she'd sat down in the armchair Philip had vacated, 'but this fainting business. You…er…couldn't be in the family way, could you?'

Fiona spluttered in shock.

Finally, she gulped the mouthful of sandwich down, and tried to look calmer than she felt. 'No, Kathryn,' she managed. 'No, I'm not. Definitely not.' She'd always made sure nothing like that could ever happen to her again. Never, ever! She was secretly on the pill, as well as insisting any partner she had use protection.

Kathryn nodded. 'That's good, then. I hope you're not offended by my asking, but girls these days have babies all the time without a wedding ring on their finger. You said you had a boyfriend, so I thought…well…'

She smiled apologetically. 'Still, you did say your

friend was a doctor, didn't you? Hopefully, a doctor would know better than to get his girlfriend pregnant.'

'Hopefully,' Fiona said, thinking how Mark was no more to be trusted than any other man when it came to using a condom. She couldn't count the number of times she'd had to remind him.

'The reason pregnancy popped into my mind,' Kathryn went on, 'is because I always fainted in the early weeks of my pregnancies.'

Fiona blinked, then frowned. 'Pregnancies? But I thought…'

'Yes, Philip *is* my only child,' Kathryn admitted. 'But I had several miscarriages before I finally carried full term. My husband and I were warned not to have any more after Philip, so we didn't.

'A pity,' she added softly. 'An only child is never a good idea.'

'Why? Because they get spoiled?'

'Oh, no, Philip was never spoiled,' she denied firmly. 'Not in the slightest. Malcolm brought him up with a very firm hand. Unfortunately, my husband had a tendency to push and pressure the boy too much. Philip had to be the best at everything. School. Sport. Games. Given Philip's equally strong will, it was a recipe for disaster.'

'Disaster?' Fiona echoed weakly.

Kathryn shook her head. 'I don't like to think about that time any more. It's too distressing. Enough to say that when Philip left home to live on campus at university, he rebelled. Amongst other things, he got this most unsuitable girl pregnant, then wanted to drop out of university to marry her.'

'What…what happened?' Fiona choked out, unable to take another bite of the sandwich in her hand.

'She lost the baby. On their wedding day. Afterwards, Malcolm arranged for their marriage to be annulled. Oh, I shouldn't be telling you this, but for some strange reason I feel like I can talk to you. You don't mind, do you?'

All Fiona could do was shake her head.

Kathryn sighed. 'I tell myself everything turned out for the best, especially now that Philip's going to marry Corinne, but sometimes I wonder and worry about that poor girl. I didn't treat her very well, and I regret that now. I hope things turned out all right for her too.'

The room fell awkwardly silent, with Fiona's emotions a mess. She ached to blurt out the truth, that *she* was that poor girl, but what good would such a confession do? Kathryn would be embarrassed, and possibly distressed. Philip would be furious with her. So would Owen.

And she…she would be…what?

Healed?

The idea was laughable. Nothing would heal what had happened to her on that day. It had killed more than her baby. It had killed part of her soul.

But it was still good to hear that Kathryn was sorry for how she'd treated her. Philip was right. She *had* changed.

'It wasn't just the girl I worried about,' Kathryn went on, and Fiona stiffened. 'It was Philip. He wasn't the same afterwards. He lost interest in his studies. He just scraped through his exams that year. He even lost interest in girls. To be honest, I thought he would never fall in love again and marry. Eventually, he did start dating again. No one special, however. Or permanent…

'But then he met Corinne,' she continued, much more cheerily. 'She's just the girl for him. They get along so well. Never a cross word together. She's so sweet. No one could ever be angry with her. Best of all, she wants what *he* wants. A family. Straight away too. That's why their engagement is so short. She doesn't care about a career. She just wants to be Philip's wife and the mother of his children. She simply *adores* children.'

Fiona forced herself to eat the rest of the sandwich, though it was like lead in her stomach.

'I'm sorry, dear,' Kathryn said. 'I really shouldn't be bothering you with this.'

Fiona rallied with an effort. 'No, no, it's all right. I like to get to know the personal side of people whose weddings I work on. I suppose you'll be wanting a big wedding?'

'Oh, yes! I've waited this long to see my son happily married. Nothing's too good for him. Or for Corinne.'

'A church wedding?' Fiona asked, automatically thinking of the small non-denominational church she and Philip had been married in. She'd worn a white suit, despite Kathryn's pointedly hurtful remark about the inappropriateness of the colour.

She hadn't worn white since.

'Actually, no,' Kathryn said. 'Philip insists on a celebrant and Corinne agreed. She said whatever he wanted was okay by her. She's like that. Still, I suppose the garden here would be a nice setting for a wedding, come October,' Kathryn said. 'As long as it doesn't rain.'

'The wedding date's in October?'

'Yes, the last Sunday of the month. Corinne gets back from Indonesia the Friday night of that week.'

'She won't be jet-lagged?'

'She says not. So, as you can see, we don't have that much time.'

'You're right there. Well, first things first. The invitations.' Fiona straightened her shoulders and slipped into her working persona, all brisk efficiency. 'Have you prepared a guest list?'

'Yes. I got Corinne to do that last weekend. I'm afraid it's rather large. Just over two hundred.'

'Don't worry. They won't all come. Has Corinne told you what she wants, or do you have *carte blanche* to make all decisions?'

'I'm to make all the decisions. Corinne says she trusts my taste completely.'

Fiona couldn't make up her mind if this Corinne was clever, lazy, or just not too interested in her own wedding. She'd never known a bride like it. Still, maybe Philip's fiancée was one of those rare creatures: a society girl who wasn't vain, or spoiled, or selfish.

'Naturally, Corinne wants to choose her wedding dress,' Kathryn went on. 'Though she said she's happy to buy off-the-peg. Now you'll have to get her right onto that. She leaves in just over a week, and finding the right dress can sometimes take days.'

'I'll get her right onto that tomorrow, Kathryn. Now don't you worry. That's my job, making sure the families of the bride and groom really enjoy the wedding and don't end up having a nervous breakdown. People think of weddings as a happy time, but, believe me, they can be very stressful for those concerned. Things can get way out of hand.'

'Yes, so I've heard. But I have a feeling my son's

wedding is going to be a wonderful experience with you at the helm, Fiona. Oh, I'm so glad you were recommended. I can already tell you're going to be a godsend, and Philip's wedding is going to be the talk of the town for years to come!'

CHAPTER FIVE

FIONA closed the door of her flat, locked it, turned the air-conditioning up to warm, in deference to the approaching evening, then moved with tired steps down the hallway and into her bedroom. There, she slumped down on the side of the bed, kicked off her shoes, and fell back sideways against the pillows, her feet lifting onto the soft duvet, her eyes closing.

She'd never been so tired in all her life. It was only six o'clock, but it felt as if she'd been up for a week. Mental and emotional exhaustion, she supposed.

She could not move a muscle. She just lay there, mulling over everything that had happened that day.

Nothing, Fiona finally decided, had worked out as she'd thought it would when she'd woken that morning. Except perhaps for Kathryn not recognising her. Now *that* she'd expected!

But the woman herself had certainly come as a surprise. Fiona had found herself responding to Kathryn's new warmth, whether she'd wanted to or not.

Actually, once Philip had left, lunch and the afternoon had gone very well. If she'd been meeting his mother for the first time that day she would have liked her very much indeed. At sixty, Philip's mother had become a surprisingly sweet person, easy to talk to, very reasonable and willing to listen.

If it wasn't for Philip, Fiona would have no problems doing this wedding.

Unfortunately, Philip existed, not just in her memory now, but in reality. Worse, she was still attracted to him, whether she wanted to be or not. Circumstances and time could kill love, Fiona accepted ruefully, but it seemed sexual chemistry was not conducive to reason.

Thank heavens she didn't stir *him* the same way!

Her earlier impression that her own unwanted feelings were mutual couldn't be so, now that she thought about it. Philip had made it perfectly clear she was no longer his type. He didn't like her being a brunette, or thinner. He certainly didn't like her being a career woman. Or having a mind of her own.

Probably that was what had irritated him so much: her being so different from how he remembered.

Fiona thought about Noni for a moment, and the sort of the girl *she'd* been. A lot different from Fiona!

Noni had been curvy and cuddly, with her bottle-blonde hair worn fluffed out and wavy and feminine. She'd dressed in short skirts and tight tops to show off what she'd thought was her simply 'stunning' figure.

She shuddered now to think of it.

But it hadn't just been Noni's physical attributes Philip had been attracted to, Fiona began to see. It had been Noni herself. Naive, dumb, easily impressed Noni, who'd thought her rich, hunky, clever boyfriend was almost god-like. Noni had adored Philip so much she'd have done anything for him.

And she *had* in the end, she thought bitterly.

Fiona was Noni's opposite in every way. Smart, slimmed down and sophisticated, with sleek black hair and a not so amenable manner. She didn't dress to be provocative, or seductive. Her clothes fitted the image she wanted to project: that of a businesswoman, with her *career* at the forefront of her mind, never a man.

Fiona was willing to bet her bottom dollar that Corinne was the sweetly feminine and adoring type, who always deferred to Philip and made him feel ten feet tall. She would be on the voluptuous side, with long blonde hair. During the day she would wear flowing dresses, pink lipsticks and floral perfumes. At night she would display her curves in more glamorous gowns which, whilst not provocative, would still display her hour-glass figure and more than adequate bosom.

Philip had always had a thing for breasts.

The telephone ringing on her bedside table snapped Fiona out of her acid reverie. Frowning, she reached over to pick up the receiver, at the same time casting a quick glance at her watch. Only six-twenty. Could it be Corinne already? Hopefully, it wasn't Mark. Or…God forbid…Philip.

'Fiona Kirby,' she said, in her best business voice.

'So you're home at last!'

Fiona heaved a somewhat relieved sigh. 'Yes, Owen. I'm home.'

'I tried half an hour ago.'

'I just got in.'

'Well, how did it go? I've been dying to know. Couldn't wait till the morning.'

'It went well. I've got the job.'

'What? *You've* got the job! So Mrs Forsythe doesn't mind about…you know?'

'She doesn't mind because she didn't recognise me and she doesn't know.'

Owen's groan sounded tortured.

'Don't panic, Owen. My ex dropped in unexpectedly soon after I arrived, and, yes, he *did* recognise me. But he didn't let on to his mother, so Mum's the word, so to speak. He told me privately not to worry, to take the job and we'll pretend we only just met for the first time today.'

'Really? That was surprisingly nice of him. Still, you *did* say he was nice, didn't you?'

'I did. But, to be truthful, Philip's not quite as nice as he used to be. He's a hot-shot trial lawyer these days, with an attitude to match. Hiring me as his wedding co-ordinator is more a matter of diplomacy and expediency than niceness. For one thing, Mummy dearest was already impressed with the new me, and he didn't want to disappoint her. On top of that, the wedding's only ten weeks off, so they haven't really got much time to shop around. Mrs Forsythe offered double our usual fee, I might add.'

'My God, how did you manage *that*?'

'Accidentally, I can assure you. I was trying to worm my way out of things in the beginning, and said I was very heavily booked at the moment. Mrs Forsythe immediately jumped in with the double fee offer. You know what rich people are like. They think they can buy anything.'

'And they can, the lovely spoiled darlings!' Owen gushed enthusiastically. 'Double our usual fee! Wow, Fiona, that's simply great!'

'Don't count your chickens, Owen. Philip's dropping by the office tomorrow around noon. He wants to see my letters of recommendation and the portfolio of photographs before he puts his John Henry on the contract.'

'That'll be just a formality. No one has better credentials than you.'

'That's what I thought. Oh, and afterwards, he's taking me to lunch.'

'Oh-oh.'

'It's not like that, Owen. Believe me. It's just plain old male curiosity masquerading as politeness.'

'I hope so, dear heart. We don't want any nasty complications, do we? So try not to look too sexy tomorrow.'

'Don't be ridiculous, Owen. I *never* look sexy in my work clothes.'

Owen rolled his eyes. Was the woman blind? Why did she think she had men panting after her all the time? 'Still, I suggest you leave that darling black suit you bought recently at home,' he advised. 'In fact, leave *all* your black clothes at home. Go for grey. Or even brown. Now brown's a passion-killer, if ever there was a colour.'

Fiona laughed. 'You don't have to worry, Owen. It won't matter what I wear. I'm no longer Philip's type.'

'Yeah, but is he still *your* type?'

'Only superficially.'

'That the part I'm worried about.'

'Oh, for pity's sake,' she snapped. 'Do you or do you not want Five-Star Weddings to handle this wedding? Make up your mind!'

'A Forsythe wedding, at double our usual fee? You have to be joking! I'd turn a blind eye to just about anything for that!'

'Then do shut up, Owen, and just hang up. You're tying up the line and I'm expecting the bride to give me a call any moment.'

He hung up.

Fiona sighed irritably and flopped the receiver back

into its cradle, rolling back over and staring up at the ceiling.

'Damn you, Philip,' she muttered, after a minute or two. 'And damn you too, Owen. I'll wear black if I want to!'

Hauling herself off the bed, she scooped up her tan shoes and carried them over to the walk-in robe. There, she placed them neatly in the empty spot on the shoe-rack, then began to undress, carefully hanging up her suit on specially padded hangers. Once down to her undies, she wandered back into the bedroom and into the *en suite* bathroom. There, she stripped off totally, popped her undies and stockings into the basin and turned on the hot tap.

Hand-washing her smalls was a habit she'd got into many years before, when she'd lived in a one-room bedsit which hadn't had a laundry. She still did it that way, despite her present well-appointed apartment having an internal laundry with an excellent washing machine and dryer.

Fiona was down to the rinsing part when she caught a glimpse of her naked body in the vanity mirror, her full breasts jiggling left and right with the washing action. Philip's sneaky remark about her needing a few more pounds popped back into her mind.

He was wrong, she thought tartly. Okay, so she was a good deal lighter than when he'd known her, but she still had a decent bust, a rounded derrière and great legs. Admittedly, her arms were on the slim side, as were her neck and shoulders. Her face no longer had that rounded look, either, but she thought it suited her, with more cheekbones showing and her jawline better defined. Her mouth and eyes looked bigger as well.

Still, maybe Philip *liked* fat women. Owen did.

Maybe Corinne was fat. Or at least pleasantly plump.

No, she couldn't be. Kathryn had said she would make a lovely bride, and Kathryn definitely belonged to the *you can never be too rich or too thin* line of thinking.

No, Corinne wasn't going to be fat. Just shapely. And pretty. Very, very pretty.

The telephone rang again, catching Fiona with her hands still in the sink. Quickly drying them, she hurried, still naked, back into the bedroom, and snatched up the receiver.

'Fiona Kirby,' she answered briskly.

'It's Philip, Ms Kirby. Philip Forsythe.'

Fiona stiffened at both his relaxed drawl and at his deliberate use of both their surnames. Clearly darling Corinne was within listening distance.

Fiona immediately pictured them in bed, as naked as she was, limbs twined, their bodies still warm and sated from their lovemaking.

'Yes, Mr Forsythe?' she drawled back, but there was a brick of ice in her chest.

'Corinne wanted me to make the initial contact for her. She felt a little shy about it. Here she is now…'

Fiona could see him handing his fiancée the receiver, the cord stretching across his bare chest to reach her. His ear would still be so close that he would hear what she had to say.

'Hello? Fiona? This is Corinne.' A pleasant voice. Soft. Lilting. Sweet.

Fiona plastered a smile on her face so that she sounded happy. 'Hi, there, Corinne. Kathryn's been telling me such nice things about you.'

'Has she? How kind of her. Oh, but then, she *is* a darling, isn't she?'

'She certainly is. Now, since time is of the essence, Corinne, I think we should get together as soon as possible. I can't really make a proper plan for the wedding ceremony and reception afterwards till I know what kind of dress you'll be wearing, not to mention the colour you've chosen for the bridesmaids. Everything pivots around that.'

'Oh. Well, actually, I'm not sure what kind of wedding dress I want to wear yet. Carmel's promised to come with me when I choose. She always knows what looks best on me. Carmel's my very best friend. We do simply everything together. But I *can* tell you that there's only going to be the one bridesmaid. That'll be Carmel, of course. And she's decided to wear black.'

'Only *one* bridesmaid?' Fiona repeated, startled. The black bit didn't bother her. Bridesmaids wearing black had come into vogue over the last few years.

'Yes, that's right. Carmel's my only close girlfriend and I don't have any sisters. Neither does Philip, so it seems silly to have a big wedding party just for the sake of it.'

'I see. Well, of course you're the bride, Corinne. I'm here to do whatever you want. It's just that Kathryn implied it would be a big wedding.'

'Oh, it will be, guest-wise. Daddy's inviting all his political cronies. And the Forsythe family seems to just go on and on for ever! Oh, Philip, stop that,' she giggled. 'You know it's true. Those cousins of yours have a baby every week or so. Sorry about that, Fiona. Philip's making faces at me.'

'Really?' Fiona gritted her teeth. 'So! When would

be a convenient time for both you and Carmel to come dress-shopping this week?'

'Any day this week, really. Carmel's on holiday and staying at my place. What's that, Philip? Oh, Philip says not tomorrow, of course. *He's* coming to see you tomorrow. What, Philip?'

Fiona hung on grimly while a male voice muttered in the background. At least they weren't in bed together. Philip sounded too far away for that.

'Philip says he's going to take you out to lunch as a thank-you for dropping everything and doing our wedding. Tell you what, Fiona. Get him to take you to Moby Dick's. It's a new place down at the waterfront at The Rocks. Simply scrummy food. You'll like it.'

Fiona grimaced. Darn, but the girl *was* sweet. And with not a jealous bone in her body.

If Philip was *my* fiancé, Fiona thought savagely, I wouldn't let him within cooee of another woman, let alone some unknown female who could be anybody.

Which I am.

'Unfortunately, I simply won't have time for a long lunch, Corinne. It'll have to be a quick coffee down at the local café. So, how about Tuesday? I'll pick you and Carmel up at your place around ten?'

'That'd be great.' And she gave Fiona an address in Mosman.

'Is that where you are now?' some masochistic devil made her ask.

A light, tinkling laugh. 'Oh, no. I'm staying with Philip at his family's Double Bay apartment for the weekend.'

'Ahh. I see…' Which she did.

Fiona closed her eyes and could have wept.

It was wickedly unfair. How *could* she be this jealous over a man she no longer loved?

In desperation, she searched her heart and found a less threatening reason for her intense reactions today.

It's not really jealousy you're feeling, she decided, but envy. You envy Philip's getting over what happened ten years ago. You envy his being able to want normal things, like a wife and a family. You envy his finding someone really nice to share his life with.

And he *has* found someone nice. Clearly Corinne *was* a sweetie. Fiona wanted to hate her, but it was herself she hated, for being so screwed up.

'Philip wants to talk to you again, Fiona,' Corinne suddenly piped up, and Fiona's heart squeezed tight again. 'Here he is. I'm off to make some coffee. See you Tuesday, Fiona.'

'Looking forward to it, Corinne.'

Fiona held her breath till Philip came on the line.

'I may be a little later than noon,' he said straight away, in a businesslike voice. 'I have to be in court first thing in the morning. I shouldn't be held up, but things don't always run smoothly there. So if I'm a bit late, don't worry.'

'Fine,' she returned crisply. 'But, as I was just saying to Corinne, no lunch, thanks. I'm very busy at the moment, as I told you earlier. I haven't time to waste sitting round waiting to be served. I eat on the run most days.'

'When you eat at all, that is,' he drawled.

'What *is* this obsession with my weight?' she snapped. 'I'll have you know I'm the perfect weight for my height. Whether you believe me or not, I used to be *over*weight. If you could see me right at this moment, you would see for yourself than I'm perfectly healthy.'

'Meaning?'

'Meaning I'm standing here in my birthday suit and I have more than enough flesh on my bones to satisfy most men.'

'I'm sure you do, Fiona,' he mocked. 'I'm sure you do. But I'm not most men, and I'm really not interested in your body anymore. All I want from you, sweetheart, is closure.'

'*Closure!*' What on earth was he talking about?

'That's right. I know it's one of those irritating New Age words, but it rather covers our situation well. There's a couple of questions that I've always wanted to ask you, and a couple more that have arisen since speaking to you today. I want to hear the answers to those questions right from the horse's mouth, so to speak. So I suggest you *make* time for lunch with me tomorrow, madam. Otherwise, Five-Star Weddings won't be getting the lucrative commission for my wedding to Corinne, or the considerable kudos and publicity which will inevitably go with it. Do you get my drift?'

Fiona said nothing. She was furious, yet at the same time flustered. What questions?

'So glad you've finally seen some sense and stopped arguing,' he grated out. 'Just make sure you don't go giving me any trouble tomorrow. About lunch, that is. Oh, and make sure you come prepared to tell the truth, the whole truth and nothing but the truth.'

And he hung up.

CHAPTER SIX

OWEN was standing talking to Janey at Reception when Fiona walked in the next morning. He took one horrified look at her, grabbed her nearest arm and pulled her aside.

'You're wearing black!' he whispered. 'I thought I told you not to wear black!'

Not just any old black, either, Owen groaned silently. But that brand-new black suit of hers, with the tighter than usual skirt, and the nipped-in-at-the-waist jacket which made her bottom look bigger and gave even Owen lewd ideas. When combined with the black satin cami underneath, shiny black hose and those lethal stiletto heels, she looked all respectability on top, but with the promise of smoulder underneath.

One of Fiona's darkly winged brows lifted, and she eyed him with that don't-cross-me-or-you'll-be-sorry look. It had extra impact that morning, perhaps because she was wearing more eye make-up than usual. And more lipstick. *And* more perfume, he noted worriedly.

Her lack of jewellery wasn't a plus because its absence seemed to emphasise her striking dark beauty. Owen stared at the sleek curtain of black hair which was hooked somewhat carelessly behind an ear on one side, then at the long pale column of her throat, bare of all adornment. He thought she'd never looked more seductive.

'I'll wear whatever colour I like,' she said frostily.

'And whatever I like. Please don't go jumping to false and quite stupid conclusions here, Owen. I haven't dressed this way for Philip Forsythe. Mark is picking me up after work tonight. We're going out to dinner.'

Owen frowned. 'But I thought you said you were going to give Mark the heave-ho.'

Her smile was wry. 'I really should stop gossiping to you over my morning coffee. Still, it's a woman's privilege to change her mind, isn't it? I *am* still a woman,' she added waspishly, 'despite some people seeming to think I'm a cross between a robot and a scarecrow.

'Janey,' she rapped out, whirling to face the startled receptionist. 'Send Rebecca straight into me as soon as she arrives. Oh, and there will be a Mr Forsythe dropping by to see me around noon. When he arrives, please let me know he's here, but have him wait till I come and get him. Okay?'

Eyes like iced chocolate swung back to Owen. 'I'm afraid I won't have time for a morning tea-break this morning, Owen. I have too much work to do. My partner *will* insist on signing me up for more work than any normal human being can handle. There again, I'm not human, am I? I'm a machine!'

Owen watched her stalk off down the corridor, the premonition of doom dampening yesterday's optimism over getting the Forsythe wedding. All he could do was try to prevent anything dreadful happening, and protect the business come what may.

'Janey,' he whispered. 'Don't let Fiona know when Mr Forsythe arrives. Show him into my office first. I'll take him along to Fiona after a few minutes.'

'Okey dokey, boss,' Janey said, and smiled a conspiratorial smile.

She did just that, and shortly before noon Philip Forsythe was ushered quietly into Owen's office.

The sight of the groom instantly increased Owen's worries. The man was everything Fiona went for, only more so. Better built. Better-looking. And a better dresser.

Still, so he should be, Owen thought ruefully, with all that Forsythe money behind him.

Owen was an expert in clothing of all kinds, and he knew exactly what that sleek navy suit had cost. Combine it with the blue handmade silk shirt, designer printed tie and exclusive Italian shoes, and you had an outfit the price of which would have fed a family of four for a year.

Owen rose from behind his desk and stretched a hand across in welcome. The hand that shook his in return was firm, and strong, and unwavering. Owen hoped his love for his fiancée was just as firm and strong and unwavering.

'How do you, Mr Forsythe?' he greeted him. 'I'm Owen Simpson, Fiona's partner in Five-Star Weddings. I'll take you along to Fiona in a minute. I'd just like to have a few words before I do, if you don't mind. Do please sit down.'

A couple of minutes passed in idle chit-chat, during which they exchanged banal pleasantries and got down to first names before Owen brought up what was bothering him.

'I have to admit to some concern with this hiding of Fiona's true identity, Philip. What will happen if your mother suddenly recognises her wedding co-ordinator as her long-lost daughter-in-law?'

'Believe me,' the groom said very drily, 'that won't happen.'

'How can you be so sure? Is Fiona so very different these days?'

The corner of his client's mouth lifted into a small sardonic smile. 'As different as two people can get.'

'But *you* recognised her.'

Owen was stunned by the stark emotion which flitted across the far too handsome face. Admittedly, the flash of pain was only momentary, but it was strong, and deep.

'Ahh, yes…I recognised her,' he admitted on a raw note. 'Instantly.'

Alarm bells started ringing in Owen's brain. If ever he'd heard the sounds of a tortured soul, it had been then. Whatever had happened ten years ago, to end Philip's marriage to Fiona, it had not been due to lack of emotional involvement on this man's part. It worried Owen that Philip's one-time love for his ex-wife might be too easily revived.

Fiona's assertion that she was no longer Philip's physical type could very well be true, but he wasn't willing to risk it.

On top of that, he felt it was his male duty to warn Philip exactly what sort of girl Fiona was these days when it came to men. Owen had an old-fashioned attitude to marriage, and a strong aversion to infidelity of any kind.

Admittedly, Fiona had never tangled with a married man's affections before—or an engaged one, for that matter—but even he could see this was an unusual situation. They'd been married before, for pity's sake, already been to bed together. Fiona would know exactly what this man liked when it came to matters of the boudoir.

'You know, Philip, I was quite shocked to learn the

other day that Fiona had been married,' he piped up. 'Not once, but twice! Did you…er…know about her second marriage?'

'I did, actually,' came the taut reply.

Oh, yes, he still felt something for Fiona. Owen was sure of it. And she still felt something for him, the wicked little minx. She hadn't tarted herself up today for some dinner with Mark. Mark was on the way out. Owen knew the signs.

'Well, Fiona's certainly not the marrying kind of girl these days,' Owen said, with a knowing little laugh. 'In the six years I've known her, that girl's had more men-friends than Henry the Eighth had wives. She tires of them just as quickly too. Still…maybe she's always been like that, eh, what? Maybe after two divorces she finally learned not to promise to love, honour and cherish till death do us part—because she knew what she really meant was till six months us do part.'

Forsythe didn't say a word, but his expression was hard, his blue eyes cold.

'I doubt she'll ever marry again,' Owen added. 'She doesn't want children for starters. Not much point in marriage without children, is there?'

'Not much,' the ex bit out.

'And it's not as though a girl has to marry to have a sex-life these days. Certainly not girls who look like Fiona. She has men panting after her all the time. Pity most of them are stupid enough to fall in love with her, though. There's no future in falling in love with career girls like Fiona. They have only one use for men and it isn't to marry them.'

There was a short, sharp silence, during which Philip Forsythe just sat there, stony-faced.

Satisfied that he'd got his message across, Owen jumped to his feet. 'I'd better take you along to Fiona's office before she wonders where you are. But for pity's sake, don't tell her what I just said. She's very touchy about her private life.'

'Don't worry. I won't breathe a word. What Fiona does in her private life these days is not of the slightest interest to me.'

Despite the cold disdain in Philip's voice, Owen was not totally convinced. He'd much rather have heard indifference.

Still, he'd done his best. What more could he do?

CHAPTER SEVEN

AT FIVE minutes to twelve, Fiona sent Rebecca back to her own office, nerves finally getting the better of her.

She'd come to work this morning, fired up with resentment over Philip's high-handed attitude on the telephone. Who did he think he was, treating her like some hostile witness on the stand? No way was she going to let him grill her about the past. She'd spent ten years getting over what had happened back then and she wasn't about to relive it. Neither was she going to reexplain her actions and decisions.

She'd been steady as a rock in her resolve till around eleven, when the reality of a long lunch alone with Philip had begun to unnerve her. By eleven-thirty she'd started clock-watching and waiting for the phone to ring, announcing his arrival.

For the last twenty-five minutes, however, her phone had remained stubbornly silent, a perverse state of affairs when, on most Monday mornings, she had little peace from its infernal and eternal ringing.

Fiona glared at the darned thing, but it just sat there, mutely mocking her growing agitation. She was reminded of a scene from one of those movies where the condemned man is be executed at midnight and the camera keeps going to the clock on the wall, then to the telephone just below it. Tension builds as the audience hopes and prays for the powers that be to call with a stay of execution.

That rarely happened, and the poor fellow was duly led away.

Fiona could not imagine anything worse than knowing the exact time of one's death. The mental agony for the executee would be excruciating.

Fiona's own tension was excruciating by the time the hands on the wall-clock finally came together at noon. Yet the phone—and her office—stayed deathly silent, the double glazed windows blocking out the noise of the traffic below, the solid walls and door stopping any sounds filtering through from the adjoining rooms.

Normally, Fiona liked this aspect of the solid old building. Today she found the silence claustrophobic.

By five past twelve she felt as if she was about to burst!

Jumping to her feet, she began to pace agitatedly around the room, muttering to herself.

When the phone suddenly jangled, her stomach leapt through her chest and into her mouth. For a few seconds she froze, before launching herself back to her desk and snatching up the receiver.

'Yes?' she asked rather breathlessly.

It wasn't Janey, announcing Philip's arrival. It was one of the florists she used, wanting to check up on a few things for the following weekend's wedding.

More frustration flared, and Fiona had to fight for composure. Scooping in a deep breath, she slid up onto the corner of her somewhat battered but large desk, firmly crossed her legs, and found a cool voice from somewhere.

Experience had taught her that if she sounded and acted as though she were totally in control, soon she was. Fiona was actually idly swinging her top foot and answering the florist's questions quite calmly when there was a soft tap on her office door. Before she had time to do more than blink, the door opened and Owen popped his head inside.

'Excuse me for a sec,' she told the florist. 'What is it, Owen?'

'Er…you were on the phone, so Janey brought Philip along to me for a minute. Is it all right for him to come in now?'

An instant vice clamped around Fiona's chest, whilst a thousand fluttering butterflies invaded her stomach.

Now you just stop this, she hissed to herself. He's just a man, not some dark and dangerous nemesis. Get a grip!

'Fine,' she told Owen with seemingly blithe indifference. 'I'll just be a moment or two longer. Have him come in and sit down.'

She swung her body slightly away from the doorway so that she wasn't facing Philip when he entered the room. That way she wouldn't have to look straight at him, or smile, or do anything except pretend to be thoroughly engrossed in a discussion over what blue flowers could be substituted if forget-me-knots were still unavailable this week. Out of the corner of her eye, however, she glimpsed him coming in alone, shutting the door behind him and settling his tall, elegantly clad frame into the comfy sofa which rested against the wall not far from the door.

'So long as they're blue and not mauve, Gillian,' she was saying coolly, despite being hotly aware of Philip's gaze on her legs, and the expanse of thigh her perched position was displaying.

Still, she would look ridiculous if she hastily uncrossed her legs, yanked down her skirt and pressed her knees firmly together like some uptight virgin.

Philip had seen a lot more of her bare than her thighs, anyway.

The thought made her insides tense. Was he sitting there, looking at her legs and remembering?

Fiona had been overawed and shy with him at first, but not for long. After their first stunning time together, she'd eagerly let him remove all her clothes, plus every one of her other remaining inhibitions and misconceptions about making love.

Though not a physical virgin when they'd met, she'd been a virgin in every other way, totally ignorant of the mindless madness which overtook a girl when deeply in love, and utterly unprepared for the bitter-sweet pleasures of the flesh just waiting to enslave her.

And enslave her Philip had. With breathtaking speed and an equally breathtaking expertise. By the time they'd been going out for a month, she'd been beside herself with desire for him, blown away by an unquenchable passion which had known no taboos. She'd done everything he'd wanted, sometimes before he'd asked. She'd been his besotted love-slave, his never-say-no Noni.

Once had never been enough…for either of them.

Fiona gritted her teeth at the memory and chatted on about the flowers, feigning indifference to Philip's presence, idly swinging her foot again.

But, for all her outer nonchalance, behind her constricted ribs her heart had begun racing madly. A faint flush was wending its wicked way over the surface of her skin, bringing a prickling sensation to the erogenous zones of her body. Her breasts felt swollen, a disconcerting state of affairs since they weren't safely encased in a bra. Her nipples peaked like hot pokers against the cool black satin of her camisole. Her neck felt decidedly warm, as did her face.

The temptation to pick up a nearby writing pad and fan herself was acute. All her clothes suddenly felt far too hot and far, far too tight.

Instead, with her free hand, she reached down and popped open the waist button on her jacket, sucking in some much needed air between words. 'Yes…yes… That would be fine… Now I must go… A client… Yes, no rest for the wicked.' She gave a soft if somewhat shaky laugh. 'Bye, Gillian.'

She hung up, and without looking at Philip slipped off the corner of the desk, firmly rebuttoning her jacket as she strode round behind her desk. Only when she was safely seated in her chair did she glance up at him.

Just as well too, for he *was* staring at her. He was also looking sinfully sexy in one of those dark single-breasted suits which she simply adored on a man.

Not that Philip needed clothes to make him attractive to her. To her eye, he looked fantastic in anything. He looked extra fantastic in nothing.

Fiona gulped at this thought, having to battle to keep her mind back off *that* track. It had been bad enough imagining he was mentally undressing *her* whilst she'd been sitting on her desk. If she started stripping *him* in her mind, she would soon be *non compos mentis*.

But it was difficult *not* to look at him and wonder what he looked like now naked. He had more muscle on him now, more breadth of shoulder and overall solidity. Fiona didn't doubt that the more mature

Philip would be even more impressive in the buff than he had been at twenty.

And that was saying something.

Because he'd been pretty impressive back then.

Fiona had never seen the like, either before or since.

It was not a good thought to have in her head whilst trying to stay cool, calm and collected.

Clearing her throat, she looked down at her desk and turned some papers and a folder round to face his way.

'I have all the things ready you asked to look at,' she began brusquely. 'The letters of recommendation. The portfolio of photographs. Plus a sample contract for you to peruse at your leisure.

'If you'd like to come a little closer…' she added, glancing up again at long last.

Their eyes met. His were hard and cold. Hers were hopefully businesslike and pragmatic.

Rising abruptly, his hand reached for the nearby doorknob. 'That can wait till later,' he said curtly as he yanked open the door. 'I'm in a fifteen-minute parking spot, and my time is about to run out.'

Her mouth opened automatically to argue, but she immediately thought better of it. To argue with him was to betray emotion. Fiona didn't want Philip to know that he still had the power to affect her in any way whatsoever.

Rising, she grabbed her black handbag, hoisted the long strap over her shoulder, then, with one hand firmly on its top flap and the other swinging by her side, covered the expanse of patterned carpet between her desk and the door with confident strides.

'Where are we going?' she asked nonchalantly as she brushed past him.

His answer floored her.

'Balmoral Beach.'

She swung round and almost collided with him, momentarily putting her hand on his chest to steady herself, but swiftly snatching it away as though she'd stupidly reached out to stroke a cobra.

'If you think I'm going to go with you to your place,' she hissed, from still far too close a position, 'then you can think again!'

His eyes showed surprise at her reaction, then a measure of thoughtfulness. 'How do you know I live at Balmoral?'

Fiona thanked the Lord she could think on her feet. 'Your mother told me.'

'*Did* she?'

'Yes, she did. Why?' she challenged. Aggression was always the best defence when you were caught at a disadvantage.

He shrugged his beautifully tailored shoulders. 'I just wondered how you knew. But there's no reason to panic. I'm not taking you to my place. I've made a booking at the Watermark restaurant for lunch. It's right on Balmoral Beach.'

Fiona could not believe the irony of the situation. The Watermark was the very restaurant Mark was planning to take her to that evening after work. He'd raved over how special it was. How exclusive and expensive, with a view second to none and a clientele to match. Meaning he wanted to impress her. Maybe he'd seen the writing on the wall.

'Yes, I know of it,' she said tautly.

Philip smiled a small smile. 'I imagine you would.'

'Meaning?' she snapped.

'Meaning I presume a popular girl like you would have been there before,' he said drily.

'Who says I'm popular?'

His gaze narrowed and swept down over her tensely held body, glaring at where her breasts were throbbing beneath the confines of her jacket.

'Come now, Fiona,' he drawled. 'Much as I might prefer the old version, I'm not blind to your present-day attractions. I would imagine you're never short of a dinner date, or some eager lover, ready and willing to satisfy your no doubt still insatiable needs. His name might be Mark at the moment. But last year it was probably Roger. And next year it could be Tom, Dick, or Harry. The names don't really matter to you, do they? As long as their performance is up to scratch and they don't do the unforgivable thing of hanging around too long and wearing out their welcome.'

Fiona was momentarily stunned by his verbal attack. Fair enough that he might think her a flighty piece, incapable of any depth of feeling or love. She accepted that his low opinion of her loyalty level was the legacy of her lies ten years ago, plus that other unfortunate marriage she'd raced into.

But that didn't call for his virtually calling her a slut!

She wanted to come to her own defence, but stopped herself just in time. Why try to change his opinion of her? There was a certain safety in his misguided judgement of her present-day lifestyle.

'So what?' she flung at him offhandedly. 'What's it to you?'

'Nothing at all,' he returned coldly. 'But I pity your poor Mark.'

She laughed. 'Really? I doubt he needs it, but I'll

pass on your sentiments to him tonight. He's picking me up after work. That's why I'm all dressed up.'

'I never imagined it was for my benefit.'

'How clever of you. Now, shall we get going? You don't want to end up with a parking ticket, do you?'

CHAPTER EIGHT

THE suburb of Balmoral was only a ten-minute drive from where Fiona's office was located at St Leonard's, maybe fifteen if the local council was digging up the Pacific Highway and adjoining roads, which always seemed the case when Fiona was desperate to get somewhere quickly. She'd learnt to allow extra time, on wedding days especially.

But no workmen flagged them down during the brief journey, which was just as well. Being enclosed within a sexy black car which smelt of new leather and Philip's sexy aftershave did nothing for Fiona's state of mind. And body.

Even so, those ten minutes *seemed* like an eternity, despite Fiona taking up where she'd left off back at the office and chattering away as if she hadn't a care in the world. Not easy when, inside, she was wound up tight as a drum.

Philip made no pretence over his own mood, politeness not on his agenda, it seemed. He sat stiffly behind the wheel, his eyes fixed straight ahead, his only contribution to the conversation being one-word replies. By the time they turned down Military Road, and Balmoral was just a sea breeze away, his shoulders did loosen a little, and he stopped gripping the wheel with white-knuckled intensity. His face, however, remained without humour.

Frankly, Fiona could not understand why Philip was still so angry with her. The thought that he'd been pining for her all these years, that *she* might have been the one true love in *his* life, was far too fanciful a theory—and just too awful to contemplate—so she searched for another, more sensible, logical reason.

It dawned on her pretty quickly.

Male ego. Seriously dented at the time, and obviously still bruised.

Yes, that was the most likely cause for the sarcasm yesterday and today. Philip had always had a healthy ego. How could he not with all those God-given talents? Even at the tender age of twenty he would have already been prey to more female pursuits—and willing surrenders—than Fiona could possibly imagine. He hadn't achieved that level of skill as a lover through correspondence!

Fiona had no doubt not a single girlfriend of his had ever voluntarily broken up with him.

Till she'd come along.

Philip probably hadn't experienced rejection before and simply hadn't been able to handle it.

Most men couldn't, Fiona supposed, especially from someone like Noni. Good Lord, even *she* could excuse Philip for believing Noni would be his love-slave for life, the naive, gullible little fool!

But Noni was long gone now, she reaffirmed to herself. Fiona lived and breathed in her place, and Fiona was not naive, or gullible. She certainly wasn't about to put up with being grilled by Philip over the whys and wherefores of their break-up. Heavens, she wouldn't even *dream* of telling him the truth, the whole truth and nothing but the truth.

Masochism was not her thing at all!

She was reminding herself of this fact when the Jaguar smoothly negotiated a downhill corner, and, right before her eyes, the beach suddenly came into view.

Oddly enough, although she'd driven through Balmoral and shopped in its main street, Fiona had never been down to the actual beach before.

Its beauty quite took her breath away.

'Oh,' she gasped softly. 'Oh, how lovely.'

'Yes, it is,' Philip agreed, then slanted her a puzzled look. 'I thought you said you'd been to the Watermark before?'

'No, not actually. I've only heard of it.'

Philip stopped the car at the bottom of the hill and turned right, to drive slowly along the esplanade which hugged the cove-like beach. Fiona drank in the scene, and thought how wonderful it would be to live here and be able to walk down to this place at any time and sit on the warm golden sand, or under the shade of one of the huge trees which lined the pavement.

The water was so blue, and gentle. Not a roaring surf, just lapping waves. Relaxing. Refreshing.

An old-fashioned fenced-off pool stretched out into the bay and there wasn't a single commercial marina in sight, thank heavens, just a few boats, bobbing up and down at their private moorings.

Fiona glanced back up at the houses which hugged the hills overlooking the beach, and envied their own-ers—not so much for the houses themselves, although some of them were very grand, but for the sea view, and the position. They were close to the city yet at the same time a world away, hiding in this perfect oasis of peace and perfection.

It took a few moments before Fiona recalled Philip owned one of those houses.

'You're very lucky to live here,' she said as he directed the Jag into a parking spot facing the beach, plus the biggest Morton Bay fig tree Fiona had ever seen.

'It's not quite so ideal in the summer,' Philip returned drily, turning off the engine and pulling out his keys. 'Wall-to-wall cars, plus wall-to-wall people, all wanting their piece of paradise. But, yes, I have to agree with you. The first time I saw this place I planned to buy a house here, overlooking the ocean. But it took me quite a while to save up the money to buy the sort of house I wanted. I finally managed it last year.'

Fiona frowned over at him. 'I would have thought you could have afforded to buy any house you wanted straight away, being your father's only son and heir.'

'True. But it's a funny thing about inherited money. You don't get nearly as much pleasure and satisfaction spending it as you do the money you've earned yourself.'

'Is that the reason you went into criminal law, instead of corporate law? Because it paid more?'

'Not at all. No, I went into criminal law because corporate manoeuvrings, no matter how conniving or clever, just didn't cut it with my competitive spirit. I never *was* a team player, even when I was a boy at school. I like single-handed combat. Tennis. Judo. Fencing. They were my chosen sports. I never was one for cricket or football.

'Or boardrooms,' he added, and shot her a wry smile. 'The courtroom, however, is much more my style. A gladiatorial arena where man is pitted against man. Blood is let there, believe me. I find it an exciting challenge ensuring that the blood is not mine, or my clients'.'

The passion in his voice sent her heart doing flip-flops inside her chest. That was what separated Philip from the rest of the men she'd known in the past ten years. The intensity of his passion.

'You really love it, don't you?' she murmured.

'I suppose I do,' he said, sounding almost surprised at this self-discovery. 'But why did you say it like that?' And he fixed his intelligent blue eyes on hers. 'Don't you love *your* job?'

Fiona looked away and tried to think.

Did she? There was a certain satisfaction after a wedding of a job well done. But, in truth, it wasn't easy seeing couples so much in love all the time, radiant with joy on their special day, then going off on their honeymoons, full of optimism and happiness. It was a constant reminder of what she'd missed out on, and what she would never have.

'I like being my own boss,' she hedged. 'And it pays well.'

'Money's not everything.'

'Yes, I do know that, Philip,' she defended coolly. 'I'm not as superficial as you seem determined to believe. Even if I was, I'm at a loss to know why the way I live my life nowadays bothers you so much, or even at all!'

His eyebrows lifted and his eyes glittered beneath them. 'It shouldn't, should it?'

'No,' she said firmly.

He actually gave her remark some thought, then pursed his lips before turning cold blue eyes her way. 'You're quite right,' he said curtly. 'You have every right to live your life as you see fit and I have no right to pass judgement on it. If I've been rude, then please accept my apology. It's just that—'

He broke off as something troubling flashed across his eyes, momentarily upsetting his icy equilibrium.

'Just what?' she probed softly, and the muscles in his face stiffened.

'Nothing,' he ground out. 'I can see now that I romanticised our relationship in my memory. Maybe I even romanticised Noni. Maybe she wasn't what I thought. Ever! At the time, I found it hard to believe Noni when she said she'd only married me because of the baby, and that once the baby was gone there was no point in continuing with our marriage. I found it even harder to believe her when she claimed she wasn't really in love with me, that it was just a sexual thing, and that sooner or later it would fizzle out.'

Fiona just stared at him, afraid of where this was leading, fearful that she might have to repeat those old lies all over again.

He laughed. 'No need to look so worried, Fiona, my rose-coloured glasses have fallen away well and truly now. I finally appreciate that you *weren't* lying back then. Sex *was* the only basis of our relationship. Marriage between us would have eventually ended in divorce, as your second marriage did. *I* was the romantic fool. *You* were the sensible one. Yet at the time I could have sworn it was the other way around.'

Fiona's eyes were wide and unwavering upon him.

'In hindsight,' he raved on, 'the truth is now perfectly obvious. I'm surprised I didn't realise it before today. Hell, when did we ever do anything together except make love? We never went out. We never even talked much. We just tore each other's clothes off and did it all the time. That's not love, as you said. It's just sex.'

Fiona flinched at this harsh dismissal of what she'd

always believed the great love of her love. His cold certainty actually raised questions in her own mind. *Had* it just been sex, even on her part? Had she broken her heart over an illusion, one which would have died a natural death if she'd stuck around? Had she made the ultimate sacrifice for nothing?

Her bewildered gaze raked over Philip as she sought for answers.

There were none to be found in looking at him, only more confusion as she began to respond to his beautiful male body on that superficial sexual level which he'd just reminded her of with such perverse honesty. All that talk of how much they'd once made love didn't exactly help. She started thinking of the many times they'd made love in his car back in the old days; how steering wheels and gearsticks had been just minor hurdles to be laughingly got around, with the back seat the ultimate in decadence if they'd thought they could last long enough to climb into the back. They'd invented positions and mutual activities in that small car which the *Kama Sutra* hadn't thought of.

Her breathing grew shallow at the memories, her mouth drying, her head growing light.

A child suddenly ran past the car, laughing loudly. The sound snapped Fiona back to the reality of what was happening to her, both in her mind and body.

Action was called for. Swiftly distracting action! She dredged up her most dazzling and superficial smile, startling a grim-faced Philip with it while she reached for the doorknob.

'So glad we finally got that all sorted out!' she pronounced. 'Now we can go have lunch and sort out something far more important. Your wedding!' And she was out of the car in a flash, pulling her skirt down as far as it would go and breathing in deeply several times.

Philip was slower to alight from his side, and when he did he looked disgruntled.

'I thought we'd decided to leave all the wedding details up to you and my mother,' he said.

'In the main. But I still want to know what *you'd* like.'

'What I'd like, Fiona,' he returned sharply, 'is to simply have lunch without any talk of the wedding at all. Do you think we might leave all that till later, back at your office?'

She felt slightly perplexed by this request. And troubled. His wedding was such a *safe* subject. But she shrugged her acquiescence, determined to keep up the indifferent role she'd chosen to play with him. 'If that's what you want.'

'That's what I want,' he said firmly, and, taking her elbow, began to steer her along the pavement towards a nearby building which she presumed was the Watermark restaurant.

It was.

'Besides,' he added as he stopped abruptly at the door, 'I haven't quite sorted out what happened ten years ago to my total satisfaction. I still have one question to ask you.'

Fiona tried not to look concerned. 'Fine,' she said blithely. 'Ask away.'

'Not right now,' he returned. 'It can wait.' And he let go her arm to pull open the door, and gallantly wave her inside first.

Fiona found a smile from somewhere, and walked past him into the restaurant.

CHAPTER NINE

EVERYONE in the restaurant knew him by name. They were also given one of the best tables in the house, down in a private corner with a view to die for.

Not that the other tables didn't have lovely views. The Watermark wasn't called the Watermark for nothing. It took advantage of its position right on the beach, with huge windows facing the water and a simple, uncluttered decor which didn't distract its patrons from the beauty beyond the glass.

Fiona liked it on sight. And might have said so if she hadn't felt so distracted already. What other question could Philip possibly want to ask her, if he now accepted the things Noni had told him ten years ago? She couldn't begin to imagine what was still bothering him!

On top of that worry, she was still rattled by the questions Philip had raised in her own mind.

Had she loved him or hadn't she?

There was no doubt that her feelings *had* been superficial and strictly sexual out there in the car just now. But that was logical because she definitely no longer loved him.

That didn't mean her feelings for Philip had always been like that. Fiona simply refused to accept their past relationship had been nothing but sex.

She *had* loved him. She knew she had. No one made the kind of sacrifice she'd made except out of a deep and true love!

Satisfied at long last, she glanced up from where she'd been blankly looking at the menu which the very discreet waiter had left with her some time back.

Philip was silently studying the wine list, looking incredibly serious and incredibly handsome. She let herself admire him for a few secret moments, before glancing around again.

'What a perfect setting for a restaurant,' she said. 'I presume you come here often, Philip?'

He looked up from the wine list and she smiled over at him, determined to act naturally. His head cocked slightly to one side and she could see his mind ticking away.

Fiona wondered what he was thinking.

'Often enough,' he returned. 'It's one of the places I can have a few glasses of wine with my dinner and not have to worry about driving home afterwards. I can walk.'

'You always did like your wine,' she murmured, the comment sparking another memory, which contradicted something Philip had said earlier.

'You know, we *did* talk back then, Philip,' she pointed out, before she could think better of it. 'Especially in the beginning. Remember the first night you took me out? To that fancy restaurant in town? You ordered a bottle of wine and I was scandalised by the price. We sat at that table till the restaurant closed, just talking. You talked to me about everything under the sun. Remember?'

He smiled a rather rueful smile. 'Of course I remember. Only too well. I was trying to impress you, with the wine *and* the conversation.'

'Then you succeeded.'

'Really?'

She bristled at his cynical tone. 'Yes, Philip. *Really.*'

'I doubt it would be as easy to impress you these days. So, what would you like to drink, Fiona?' he asked when the waiter materialised once again by their table. 'I can't drink much, not if I'm going to drive afterwards. Maybe a glass or two.'

'Perhaps we could share a bottle,' she suggested.

'White or red?'

'White,' she returned firmly. 'Chardonnay. Oaked.'

One of his eyebrows arched, and he handed her the wine list. '*You* choose, then,' he commanded.

She hesitated only a fraction before dropping her eyes to the list and swiftly selecting a Tasmanian Chardonnay which she'd never tried before but which was hopefully as good as its price warranted. She ordered it in a crisp, confident voice, handing the wine list back to the waiter before returning a steady gaze to Philip.

He was watching her with a type of reluctant admiration.

'I see you really know your wines nowadays,' he said, once they were alone again.

Fiona shrugged. 'There are a lot of things I know nowadays that I didn't once.'

He leant back in his chair and gave her a long, thoughtful look. 'Yes, I can see that. And I have to admit I'm curious. How did you go from being Noni to Fiona? It's more than just a surface transformation. You do everything differently. The way you walk and talk. The way you dress and do your make-up. Everything, really. It couldn't have come easily, or cheaply.'

'It didn't.'

'So who paid for the transformation? Alimony from

your truck driver ex? Or some sugar daddy you met after your divorce?'

Fiona frowned. He really did have a low opinion of her. 'I'll have you know I paid for everything with money I earned myself. The modelling school. The elocution classes. Endless night school. Everything.'

'Doing what, exactly?'

'My Higher School Certificate, for starters. How long do you think *that* took?'

'That's not what I meant, although I'm sure it didn't take you all that long. You always were very smart, even if you didn't think so yourself. I meant how did you earn the money for all those courses? That couldn't have been easy.'

'I worked in a factory packing meat during the week and as a waitress at the weekend. At a wedding reception place. That's where I learnt a lot about the wedding business. Owen worked there, too, actually. He—'

The return of the waiter with the wine had Fiona breaking off her story mid-stream. She nodded her approval when he went through the charade of presenting the bottle to her with the label on show, then sat there silently while he opened it and poured out a small amount for her to sample.

She sipped it, said it was fine, then waited again—somewhat impatiently—while both their glasses were skilfully filled and the bottle was arranged in the portable ice bucket. She was eager to get back to telling Philip all she'd achieved on her own. She'd liked the way he'd started watching her while she spoke, with respect and admiration, much better than his thinking she was some kind of slut who had slept her way to success.

'Would you like to order yet, Mr Forsythe?' the waiter checked before he left the table.

Fiona was pleased when Philip told him to come back in a couple of minutes, then turned his attention back to her, leaning forward slightly and looking deeply into her eyes.

'Go on,' he said warmly. 'You were saying something about Owen working there as well?'

'Yes. He was responsible for the table setting and the flowers. Owen's very creative. He also worked at a formal clothes hire place during the week. His mother was a professional dressmaker and taught him a lot about clothes, especially wedding clothes. They were her specialty. We used to have coffee together after a reception was over and talk about our plans for the future. I told Owen I wanted to go into PR work and he said he was going to open a wedding consultancy. Once we realised both careers complemented each other, we started working towards going into business together. I found work at an established wedding consultancy to learn the ropes and we both started saving madly. In less than a year, Five-Star Weddings became a reality. I don't think I'm boasting when I say we've been very successful.'

'Amazing. Your dad must be very proud of you.'

'Er…not exactly. We don't see each other any more.'

'Why's that?'

Fiona sighed. 'He wasn't pleased about my leaving Kevin for starters. On top of that, he finally found himself a new wife, and Doreen doesn't care for me at all. She thinks I'm too la-di-da. So does Dad now.' She smiled a sad smile. 'Weird, isn't it? Your mother once called me cheap and common. Now my own father calls me a snob. You can't win, can you?'

'That reminds me,' Philip said, frowning and straightening up.

'Reminds you of what?'

'Of that question I wanted to ask you…'

Fiona tensed, and Philip threw her a searching look.

'The night of our wedding…'

The vice around Fiona's chest tightened further. 'What about it?'

'Remember when the doctor left and Mum sent me down the road to get the painkillers he prescribed?'

'Y…yes…'

'Did Mum say anything to you while I was gone? Put any pressure on you to give up on our marriage so quickly? I mean…from what you said yesterday, her criticisms affected you even more than I realised at the time. I've been wondering if she used some kind of emotional blackmail, or maybe even a bribe to get you to—'

'A *bribe*!' Fiona broke in, shocked and angry. 'You think I took *money* from your mother to leave you?'

His face remained unmoved. 'It crossed my mind, Fiona. It's just that you seemed to change radically while I was away. One minute you were clinging to me and crying over our lost baby. Then, half an hour later, you'd gone all cold on me. You could hardly even look at me as you told me of your decision to call it quits with our marriage and our relationship. It's only reasonable to wonder whether Mother might have got to you while I was away.'

'I didn't even *speak* to your mother that night. I couldn't bear to look at her for thinking how relieved she must be that my baby was gone.'

He nodded slowly, sadly. 'I see. Well, I just had to be sure.'

'Please, Philip,' she said shakily, eyes pleading. 'Can we close that subject once and for all?'

He frowned. 'It still upsets you?'

'Of course it still upsets me. I lost my baby that day. I don't like to think about it.'

His frown deepened. 'Is that why you decided not to have any more children? Because you're frightened that might happen again?'

Fiona could feel her emotions getting the better of her. To break down in front of Philip at this stage would be disastrous! She had to be strong. And hard. She hadn't survived this long to weaken now.

'It wasn't children I decided against so much, but marriage. And I don't believe in having children out-side of marriage. Not for any moralistic reason but because I think children need two parents, married and in love, to have the best chance of growing up to be well-adjusted adults instead of needy neurotics.'

'And is that what you think *you* are? A needy neu-rotic?'

'Sometimes. Oh, good, here's the waiter. Now, what shall I order…?'

Ordering their courses was nicely distracting. Un-fortunately, the waiter soon bustled off to do their bid-ding, leaving Fiona alone with Philip once more. She had never felt more strained in all her life. How she was going to get through the next couple of hours she had no idea!

She could not bear to talk about the past any more. She could not bear to look at him and think of all those wonderful times they'd spent together.

She was, indeed, neurotic and needy. Maybe she always had been.

'Have you chosen your best man?' she said abruptly into the awkward silence which had descended on their table.

Philip stiffened in his chair. 'Why?'

'I'll need to take both of you along to the formal wear place and order your suits soon. In fact, best we do that one day next week. There's this place in town I always recommend because they have the biggest and widest range of clothes, but they might still have to order something in your sizes. Do you want to hire or buy?'

Philip's expression was worrying.

'What is it?' she asked. 'What's wrong?'

'My best man,' he said. 'It's Steve.'

'Steve from university?'

'Uh-huh.'

Steve had been a regular at the fish and chip shop in Newtown where she'd worked ten years ago. It was popular with students because it was close to the campus and the food was cheap and filling. It had been Steve who'd brought Philip into the shop, telling his friend that the girl behind the counter was a real honey.

When Philip had left the shop with a date with Noni for that night, Steve had been a bit jealous. He'd fancied her as well.

Fiona sighed. This was getting far too complicated. 'Does he *have* to be your best man?'

'He's my best friend. And I've already asked him.'

Fiona picked up her wine and took a deep swallow.

'He probably won't recognise you,' Philip went on.

'But if he does, I'll tell him the truth. He won't let on to anyone if I ask him not to.'

'He doesn't fancy Corinne, or anything, does he?'

'Good God, no! Why do you say that?'

'Because he once fancied me, that's why?'

'Ahh, I see. Well, he doesn't fancy Corinne. Fact is, I don't think he cares for Corinne at all.'

Fiona was surprised. 'Why's that?' she asked.

'I'm not sure. Neither was Steve when I questioned him. But Steve has a narrow view of the opposite sex. He likes his women on the obvious side.'

'Well, thank you very much for the compliment!'

'Come now, Fiona, you have to admit you were once a very sexy piece of goods.'

'Not any more.'

He wiggled his hand as though that was a fifty-fifty proposition. 'Wear what you wore on Sunday for the clothes fitting next week and Steve won't take too much notice. Wear the little number you've got on today and his tongue will be on the floor.'

Fiona tried to take offence, but she couldn't. The image was too funny and she laughed. 'Maybe I will, then, if Steve's as handsome as he once was. But what about *your* tongue? I didn't notice it on the floor to-day.'

'It's not my tongue I'm worried about.'

Fiona's eyes widened. 'I thought you said you didn't find me attractive any more.'

'Don't start flirting with me, Fiona,' he warned sharply. 'Keep that side of yourself for the Marks of this world. And don't go making eyes at Steve, either. He's on the look-out for a wife, and I don't think you quite fill the bill, do you?'

'I'll try to control myself,' she said tartly.

'Do that.'

The entrée arrived, and Fiona set about spooning the spicy stir-fry concoction into her mouth and washing the dish down with great gulps of the wine. When her head started spinning, she stopped both the eating and drinking.

Philip looked up from where he'd been devouring a dozen oysters. 'Something wrong with your entrée?'

'No. I'm just not used to eating much lunch. And you make one crack about my weight and you're a dead man!'

'Wouldn't dream of it. I can see today you're not quite as thin as I thought. Maybe it's the lack of underwear.'

Fiona glanced down, horrified to see that her jacket had parted and the black satin camisole had pulled tight across her bustline, outlining her braless breasts. Gritting her teeth, she yanked the jacket closed and did the button up at the waist.

'Don't do that on my account,' Philip said drily. 'I was enjoying the view.'

'You men are all the same,' Fiona accused.

'Mark likes you without underwear, too?'

'I am *not* without underwear,' she snapped, her face flaming at this reminder of the times she hadn't worn any for him. 'Stop embarrassing me.'

'Sorry.'

'No, you're not! You're not at all! Which just shows how wrong I was about you yesterday.'

'Concerning what?'

'I thought you hadn't changed much, except that you were even better-looking. But I see now that you *have* changed. And not for the better! You've grown hard, Philip. Hard and cynical.'

'Have I indeed? Well, people do change, Fiona. You only have to look in the mirror to know that.'

'That's the kind of remark I'm beginning to expect from you.'

'Really?' He dabbed at his mouth with the white serviette and pushed away his plate. 'Then I'll try to curb my cynical tongue and be more polite in future.'

'Do that.'

One waiter arrived to whisk away their plates while another refilled their glasses.

'Shall we drink to a truce?' Philip suggested, and raised his glass towards her.

'Only if you mean to honour it. And only if it covers all my requirements of behaviour.'

He returned his glass to the table. 'Perhaps you could outline what kind of behaviour you require.'

'Very well. We will be polite to each other at al' times, even when alone. We will not bring up the past again. We will not say anything sarcastic or do anything to cause each other embarrassment from this moment till you leave on your honeymoon.'

'Mmm. A tall order.'

'Pretend we've only just met!'

He laughed. 'Now that's downright impossible.'

'*Try*. Think of it as a personal challenge.'

'A challenge, Fiona? More like a test of human endurance.' He raised his glass, his sardonic smile sending a strangely erotic shiver down her spine.

'Very well. To Fiona's truce,' he toasted.

Fiona almost reluctantly raised her glass and clinked it against his. Philip stared at her hard, put the glass to his lips and tipped the rest of the wine down his throat.

CHAPTER TEN

OWEN must have been listening for her return, because the moment Fiona walked in—alone—shortly after three, he made an appearance, his face showing some concern.

'So how did it go?' he asked anxiously as he followed her down the corridor and into her office. 'Do we still have the job?'

Fiona placed her handbag on her desk, extracted a cheque from its depths and handed it to him. 'Take a gander at that!'

Owen did, gaping. 'But that's more than *twice* what we've ever charged for a wedding before!' he exclaimed.

'Natch. This will be our most lavish wedding so far. And we're being paid double the fee, remember?'

Owen was still staring down at the cheque. 'But he's paid the lot, up front. Is the man mad? I thought he was a lawyer.'

'I don't think this money means much to him. It's probably inherited.'

'What's the difference? Money's money, isn't it?' Owen said, and kissed the cheque. 'I'm going to run down and put this in the bank straight away. You're brilliant, Fiona! Bloody brilliant!' And he raced out.

Fiona sighed deeply and walked over to close the door. Briefly, she leant against it, her eyes closing, her heart sinking.

Brilliant, was she?

More like stupid.

After the truce had been toasted to, things had relaxed a bit between them. They'd managed to chat over the main course without argument, though they'd kept to innocuous subjects like Sydney's recent water supply problems, plus the coming election.

Still, it had not been unpleasant. And quite satisfying in a way to show that she was now a well-informed woman with intelligent opinions of her own.

Of course, the absence of any sarcasm on Philip's part had helped, plus the four glasses of wine she'd downed by then. When it had come time for dessert Fiona had felt quite mellow, and she'd given in to Philip's cajolery to try the soufflé of the day, which had turned out to be butterscotch.

Fiona had always adored anything which smacked of caramel or butterscotch flavour.

The soufflé had been mouthwateringly scrumptious, Philip laughing when she'd oohed and ahhed her way all through it. The relaxed warmth of his laughter had been disarming, and charming.

By the time coffee had come Fiona had let down her guard so much that when Philip had started telling her about a murder case he'd been recently hired to defend, she'd been powerless to resist what she'd always found his most irresistible attraction.

His passion.

She had soon been engrossed, leaning her elbows on the table whilst she sipped her coffee and listened intently to his rich, male voice.

His defendant was a woman, a housewife in her late forties, who had hit her husband over the head with one of his golf clubs and killed him. Apparently, she wanted to plead guilty, but Philip had discovered a history of emotional and physical abuse which would have driven anyone to strike back eventually. He wanted her to plead temporary insanity but the poor woman had been horrified.

When Fiona had suggested that a self-defence plea might go down better, both with the defendant herself and the jury, Philip had become quite excited.

'You're right,' he'd exclaimed, blue eyes gleaming. 'Self-defence is much better. Much more real and sympathetic. You're brilliant, Fiona.'

After that, he'd become very animated, outlining the new strategies he would employ, what witnesses he had, and the arguments he would use. Fiona had just sat there, listening, and almost envying the woman, having Philip as her champion. For she knew he would never let her down.

He hadn't let *her* down ten years ago, she'd begun thinking. From the moment she'd told him of her pregnancy he'd been there for her, insisting she not worry, reassuring her that he loved her and that they would be married.

It had hit her forcibly at that moment that maybe she'd been wrong all those years ago to give Philip up. Maybe his *father* had been wrong.

Maybe her sacrifice *had* all been for nothing!

She'd suddenly felt very upset, and had had to struggle to hide her feelings, sitting up straight and trying not to look perturbed. Philip must have sensed something, because he'd stopped talking about the case and abruptly called for the bill.

Later, in the car, his voice had been brusque. 'Sorry for boring you back then. We men do like to talk about ourselves, especially when we think we've got an interested audience. I forgot you were only there under sufferance.'

Fiona had hardly been in a position to deny any of his assumptions. What could she have said? I *was* interested. *Too* interested.

'I won't have time to come up to your office when we get back,' he'd swept on. 'I'm meeting Corinne to buy the rings. I'll write you a cheque for your fee. If you still insist on a contract, then you can bring it with you next week, when we meet to order the suits. Tell me when and where for that, and Steve and I'll be there.'

She had. She'd also not argued when he'd written that outrageous cheque and given it to her, saying curtly, 'That should cover everything.'

It surely would, she thought as she levered herself away from the door and walked wearily back to her desk. And a contract was hardly necessary, once the cheque was cleared.

Fiona slumped down behind her desk, too depressed to even cry. Work was impossible.

So was going out with Mark tonight, she finally realised. How could she sit there with him in that restaurant, thinking of Philip? And how could she possibly go to bed with him afterwards, wishing he *was* Philip?

It wasn't fair to Mark, for one thing, which was something she hadn't considered much before now. She'd really become a selfish cow when it came to men. Owen was right. She used them. Not just for the sex, though she could not deny she did have strong needs in that area. Sometimes she went to bed with a man simply for a pair of strong arms to hold her through the night and take away the aching loneliness in her empty heart.

Philip's return had changed the ball game, however. Suddenly, her heart was full again. To overflowing.

Unfortunately.

Fiona reached for the phone and did what had to be done.

Mark didn't take the news well, which made her feel even worse. He demanded to know the identity of the man who was going to take his place in her bed. In a warped kind of way, he seemed to *want* there to be someone else. He could not believe she was simply breaking up with him because she didn't want to see him any more. He was so insistent that in the end Fiona cracked and gave him what he wanted.

'Oh, all right,' she bit out. 'Yes, I've met someone else. An old flame. We ran into each recently and, well…sparks just flew.'

'I knew it,' Mark muttered, still sounding very put out.

'Look, I'm sorry, Mark,' she said, because she *was*. 'I really liked you.' *Once upon a time.* 'But the truth is Philip and I were once married and we—'

'Married!' he squawked.

'Yes, married. We were very young at the time, and things just didn't work out. But from the moment I saw him again I knew I wasn't over him.'

'I see. So you're telling me you're still in love with this man. You have been all along?'

'I'm not sure I would go that far,' Fiona had to concede. 'But I could easily fall in love with him again.'

'I see,' Mark said sourly. 'I wish you'd been more honest with me sooner.'

Fiona only just refrained from telling him she'd always been honest with him. She'd never led him on to believe she loved him, or would ever marry him. But she apologised again, in deference to his obviously battered ego.

'I doubt you're sorry at all!' Mark snapped back. 'But I don't intend losing any sleep over you. If I'm brutally honest, you're not quite what I'm looking for in a wife, anyway. You're far too ambitious, Fiona. And far too selfish. A doctor's wife needs to be able to put her husband first. I can't see you ever putting any man's wishes above your own.'

Not yours anyway, she thought, without a shred of sympathy left for the man.

'So this is a permanent goodbye, I take it?' he actually had the stupidity to ask.

'Yes.' The word had a razor's edge.

'We could continue on a strictly sexual basis, if you like.'

He was lucky she didn't laugh. 'I don't think so, Mark.'

'No point in my hanging around waiting for you to change your mind, then. If nothing else, you're a decisive woman, Fiona. Maybe too decisive. You don't leave a man much room to move sometimes. And you don't leave him much damned pride.' And he slammed the phone down in her ear.

Fiona stared at the dead phone in her hand before slamming the phone down herself. How she'd gone out with such an overblown over-opinionated person in the first place she had no idea!

It was because you were lonely, you idiot, came back the brutal answer. And now you're going to be even lonelier. In fact, if you keep this up, you'll be right back to where you started ten years ago, with your heart breaking over Philip and your life in tatters.

Fiona straightened suddenly and gritted her teeth. No way, she resolved bitterly. Not again!

She wasn't in love with Philip yet, she told herself firmly. It was a sexual attraction, that was all. And admiration. The man was worth admiring.

Love, however, was something quite different. It was a huge investment of one's emotions. It wasn't something which happened overnight, or over one miserable lunch. It took much more time and much more intimacy, neither of which, thankfully, she would be investing with Philip this time.

She would only see him a couple more times before the wedding, for starters. To help with his clothes, and then for the final rehearsal. The wedding didn't count, because even though she would physically see him on that day she wouldn't be talking to him. Certainly not alone, anyway.

And then he'd be off on his honeymoon with Corinne and she could go back to living her own life as it had been before Owen forced her into this ghastly position. She would eventually find herself another man to date. One who wasn't so taken up with himself, and one who wouldn't remind her in any way whatsoever of Philip. Another truck driver perhaps!

The telephone ringing stopped her slightly hysterical self-lecture. She hadn't realised how crazy she was sounding. How darned infantile!

Because of course she only ever dated men who reminded her in some way of Philip. Sometimes it was a pair of intelligent blue eyes, or a way of walking, or talking, or dressing. Damn Philip, she thought savagely He'd ruined her for any other man!

The phone kept on jangling, demanding an answer. She swept the darned thing up, punching out her name in a crisp businesslike fashion.

'Hi, there, Fiona,' came the very breezy reply. 'It's Corinne here. Philip's just been telling me you had such a lovely lunch together, and I'm simply frightfully jealous. All that scrummy food!'

Fiona pressed her lips firmly together and breathed in and out deeply behind them. She wasn't in the mood for sweetness at that moment, or for Corinne at all!

'Yes, it was very nice,' she only just managed.

'I'm going to make him take me down to that restaurant very, very soon. He's always talking about it but we never seem to get there together.'

Fiona could not help feeling perversely glad about that. Another futile feeling, but there you are!

'He also said you'd lined up a date to fix him and Stevie up with suits for the wedding.'

Fiona winced slightly at the 'Stevie'. She was always irritated by girls who added unnecessary 'e's to the ends of names and words. In truth, she wasn't sure she could take too much of Corinne. There was only just so much sugar she could swallow.

'Have you decided what they're going to wear yet?' Corinne added brightly.

'I thought I would leave that up to Philip.'

'Well, just between us girls, Fiona, please don't let them wear one of those awful tails outfits. Those ones with the grey jackets and top hats. I would simply hate Philip in one of those silly hats. Grey is *not* a favourite colour of mine. Philip looks absolutely gorgeous in a tux, though. Black, of course. I simply adore black.'

'You're the bride, Corinne. Whatever you want. Just tell Philip.'

'Oh, he'll do whatever you suggest, Fiona. I can see he's very impressed with you. But not as impressed as his mother. She rang me this morning and simply raved some more.'

'Really?'

'I think she wanted to reassure me before I go away, but truly, I don't need reassuring. I have every faith in Philip's judgement of a person, and he says he has no doubt you won't leave a stone unturned to make our wedding a success. Now, speaking of the wedding, I was wondering if Carmel and I could meet you at the first salon you planned on taking us to tomorrow, rather than you picking us up at my place. It would be less trouble for you.'

'It's no trou'' Corinne.' Fiona had found things always went more smoothly if everyone was in one car, since they would probably be traipsing all over Sydney all day.

'Maybe, but Carmel and I want to have our own wheels, if you don't mind, Fiona. So we'll definitely be meeting you there. At ten, you said? I just need the name of the place and the address.'

Fiona was slightly taken aback by the abrupt change from the bubbly and very agreeable Corinne to this coolly assertive version.

Startled, Fiona told her the name and address of the bridal salon in question, after which the girl hung up just as abruptly, leaving Fiona feeling slightly put out. She replaced the phone with a frown on her face.

If Philip's fiancée subscribed to the theory of getting more with honey than with vinegar, then she really should learn not to let the act drop all of a sudden, even if she was only talking to a hireling.

The word 'act' just sprang into Fiona's mind, unbidden. But it immediately began to bother her.

Was this what Steve sensed about Corinne? That she was acting; that she wasn't sincere; that she didn't really love Philip?

Suddenly, meeting Corinne tomorrow took on an added aspect, rather than just getting a job done and perhaps satisfying her curiosity over what Corinne looked like. She now wanted to know what Corinne was actually *like*. Because, darn it all, she wasn't about to sit back and let Philip waste his life on anyone less than the best!

Because that was why she'd given Philip up. For him to have the best in life. And the best in life certainly wasn't some female who didn't truly really love him with every fibre of her being.

Fiona knew what such a love felt like, and if she didn't see the same kind of adoration in Corinne then she would…she would…

Do what? a cynical voice inserted.

God only knew.

But she sure as hell would do *something*!

CHAPTER ELEVEN

THE bridal salon was just off the Pacific Highway, in the northern suburb of Lindfield. It carried a wide range of wedding dresses, locally made gowns alongside those imported from Asia and America, plus every accessory imaginable, from veils to shoes, underwear to jewellery. It was a one-stop shop for busy brides, and was always Fiona's first port of call when looking for a wedding dress off the rack.

Fiona slid her Audi into the kerb outside the shop ten minutes before the allotted time for meeting Corinne and Carmel, cut the engine and just sat there, waiting. It was a fine sunny morning, but somewhat on the fresh side. Pleasant enough, though, provided you stayed in the car.

Fiona stayed in the car, thinking.

At five past ten a zappy little red sports car pulled in behind and two girls got out, laughing.

Fiona studied them in the rearview mirror for a few unobserved moments. The driver was very tall, with an athletic figure and short brown hair. The passenger had long straight blonde hair, and was of medium height, with a shapely hour-glass figure. Both girls were wearing jeans and sweaters. Both wore sunglasses, which prevented Fiona from seeing if they were really pretty or not, but from what she could see the word 'unattractive' did not spring to mind. She hadn't thought it would.

Fiona climbed out from behind the wheel and

walked over to where the two girls were standing, gaz-ing up at the bridal mannequin in the shop window and making comments.

'That would suit you, Cori,' the brunette was say-ing. 'Especially with your gorgeous boobs.'

Fiona had already noticed the gorgeous boobs her-self. And the girl was right. The dress in the window, with its low heart-shaped neckline, tight lace bodice and flouncy tulle skirt, would show the blonde's figure off to perfection.

'Hello,' she said a little stiffly from just behind them. 'You must be Corinne and Carmel. I'm Fiona.'

Corinne turned and looked Fiona up and down. She whipped off her sunglasses, and whistled. 'Wow, Fiona. Philip forgot to tell me how gorgeous you were!'

It seemed 'gorgeous' was the in word with these two.

Fiona, who'd dressed down for the occasion in brown, knew she didn't look at all gorgeous that morn-ing. Sleepless nights did that to one.

But she accepted the flattery with a polite if some-what plastic smile, told herself that she wasn't crushed that Corinne's eyes were like emerald pools, and set about trying to discover if Philip's fiancée was a gen-uine *ingénue*, or a callous, cold-blooded creature who was only marrying Philip for his money, or some such other equally superficial reason.

'Don't you think Fiona's gorgeous, Carmel?' Corinne said, and nudged her bridesmaid in the ribs.

Carmel, who'd also taken off her sunglasses, gave Fiona a sour glance and declined to comment. She wasn't nearly as pretty as her friend, her black eyes spoiled by heavy eyelids which gave her a sulky, sullen look.

Fiona decided it matched her disposition. She wondered what someone as effervescent as Corinne was doing with her, unless it was because Carmel made her look good by comparison. She'd known other stunning girls with vibrant personalities with the oddest friends.

'Shall we go inside?' Fiona suggested, uncaring and unbothered by Carmel's rudeness. It was the bride's true character she wanted to uncover.

Unfortunately, Corinne remained on her best and most delightful behaviour all morning, and, as much as Fiona hated to admit it, she didn't put a foot wrong. For once, she showed some interest in the wedding or at least in what she was going to wear—continuously asking Carmel whether she thought Philip would like her in whatever gown she was trying on at the time.

On one occasion it tartly crossed Fiona's mind that Corinne would have been better off asking *her*, Philip's ex-wife. But she could hardly say so.

Carmel gave all of the gowns the thumbs-down, except the one from the window, which she said was definitely the one. She sounded sincere too, her cold black eyes lighting up for the first time in over two hours.

Unfortunately, Fiona had to agree. Corinne looked simply delicious in that dress. Philip could not help but be turned on by the sight of her in it. Fiona knew what he liked, and that dress was definitely it—plus the curvaceous body in it.

Fiona only just stopped herself from trying to talk the girl out of buying it.

The dress decided upon, Corinne simply had to ring Philip and tell him. She even borrowed Fiona's mobile to do so.

Fiona just stood there, next to a lemon-faced Carmel, while Corinne gushed and gammered to her beloved over the dress, told him she loved him a thousand times, and how much she was going to miss him while she was away, but how it would be worth the wait when he saw her in that dress.

If it was an act, it was a darned good one. Still, when she started blowing kisses down the line Fiona knew she'd heard enough.

'Let's leave the mobile with Corinne and go find you something in black, Carmel,' she suggested brusquely to the brunette.

'Not without Corinne,' she was promptly told. 'There's no point. I'm here to do what *she* wants, not what *I* want. So are you, aren't you?'

Fiona felt duly chastened, and waited bleakly till Corinne was finished. The blushing bride finally handed back the mobile, her cheeks all pink and rosy.

Fiona gave up at that moment, admitting to herself she'd been grabbing at straws in hoping to find something shallow and nasty about Corinne. When a girl got so excited by a mere phone call then she had to be in love.

'Thanks, Fiona,' Corinne said. 'You're a doll!' She whirled around and admired herself anew in the many mirrors in the salon. 'Don't you just love me in this dress, Carmel?' she said, her face still flushed.

Carmel's mouth tightened a fraction, and it occurred to Fiona that the one and only bridesmaid might be just a little jealous of the bride's beauty. 'It's perfect, Cori,' she said, though her voice was cold.

Corinne smiled at her, then linked arms, pulling a reluctant Carmel to her side. 'Now we have to find something just as smashing for you. Something sleek and slinky and sexy, in black satin.'

Carmel looked doubtful. 'I'm not really the slinky and sexy type, Cori. I don't have the figure for it.'

'Oh, don't be silly. I simply *love* your figure. You're so tall and slim. And you have the best legs in the world. Maybe we could get you a dress which has a slit up the side to show them off. What do you think, Fiona?'

Fiona prayed for patience. She was going to need every drop she possessed, and more, to get through this day. 'Let's go and see what they have in stock in black satin, shall we?'

'Yes, let's. Oh, this is much more fun than I thought it would be!'

Fiona only just stopped herself rolling her eyes.

Thankfully, they found a black satin gown for Carmel which looked, if not sexy and slinky, then coolly elegant on the girl. It was a simple enough sheath, with a bow at the back and, yes, a slit up one of the sides. She needed it to be able to walk.

Black certainly did suit her, Fiona thought as she stood back and looked at the pair.

'The black and white does look good together,' she conceded. 'Did Kathryn tell you about the idea I had for the guests, Corinne? She said she would.'

'You mean about everyone wearing black and white? Yes, she did, and I think it's positively brilliant! Sydney's had plenty of black and white balls, but never a strictly black and white wedding that I recall. All the women guests will be rushing to the boutiques, snapping up all the black and white ball-gowns. How on earth did you think of it?'

'It just came to me,' Fiona said. She declined to tell her that with such a small wedding party and an at-home reception she'd had to think of something to make the wedding stand out in people's minds. Owen would be very disappointed if Five-Star Weddings didn't get *some* mileage out of this.

'By the way, Corinne,' Fiona went on, 'Kathryn mentioned Philip has a couple of young cousins who would make the perfect page-boy and flower girl. I know you don't want any more bridesmaids, but I didn't think you'd mind that.'

'No, I don't mind that at all. What will they do, exactly?'

'The page-boy will carry the ring cushion. He will go first, then Carmel, then the flower girl next, strew-ing rose petals in your path. Red rose petals, I thought. In fact, I was thinking red roses for both your bouquets and the men's lapels. They would look simply mag-nificent against all the black and white.'

'They certainly would. Yes.'

'I have a folder of various bouquets in the car,' Fiona told her. 'I'll go get it and you can choose what—'

'Oh, no, don't bother me with that,' Corinne inter-rupted. '*You* choose.'

Fiona stared at her. Not once, in all the weddings she'd helped with, had she had a bride who didn't want to choose her own bouquet.

Corinne must have seen the look on her face.

The girl's smile was dazzling. 'We just haven't got the time for me to choose everything personally, Fiona, darling. That's why Kathryn hired *you*. And I can understand why. You're so efficient. And you've done it all before so many times. I trust you implicitly to make me into the bride of the year. After all, that's your job, isn't it?'

'Yes,' Fiona returned, feeling a little confused. Was this girl for real or not? 'But it's *your* wedding, Corinne. Brides usually have definite ideas about what they like and don't like.'

'Oh, I have definite ideas about what I like and don't like, don't I, Carmel?' she returned, an edge creeping into her voice. 'I just don't care much about weddings as such. If society didn't dictate you should be married before you have children I wouldn't be getting married to Philip at all. I would simply have had a baby by him.'

Once again, Fiona was taken aback. 'Well…um… lots of girls do that nowadays anyway.'

Corinne laughed. 'Not with a father like mine, they don't. I—'

Carmel tapped Corinne on the arm. 'I think we'd better get out of these dresses, Cori,' she said firmly. 'We don't want to ruin anything at this stage, do we?'

For a moment Corinne looked angry with her friend, then she smiled a wry smile. 'You're right. That would never do.'

'You'd best choose your shoes before you get undressed,' Fiona said. 'And any other accessories you might want.' She could see this would possibly be her only chance to get the bride and the bridesmaid fully outfitted.

In only one added hour all purchases had been made, Corinne and Carmel had driven off together, and Fiona was on her way back to the office, feeling decidedly perturbed.

With any other bride she would have been busy with her all day. And maybe another day as well. But Corinne was clearly not the run-of-the-mill bride. She certainly wasn't the perfect 'She just wants to be Philip's wife and the mother of his children' creature which Kathryn had outlined on Sunday.

Fiona wondered if Philip knew of this unconventional and rebellious side to Corinne, if she'd confided her secret wish not to be married to him but to have his babies out of wedlock.

No, not babies, Fiona amended in her mind with a frown. 'Baby', the girl had said. Did she only want the one? Philip, Fiona was sure, would want more. He had ten years ago. Why would he have changed? Surely Kathryn had intimated as much on Sunday as well. He wanted children, not just the one child. He'd been an only child himself and hated it.

Fiona wasn't in any doubt that the girl loved Philip. But love wasn't enough when you were two totally different people, when you had different goals and different agendas.

Philip and Corinne seemed the perfect couple on the surface, but were they? Would Corinne make Philip happy if she didn't really want the constriction of marriage? Surely it was an indictment of her character that she was flitting off overseas during the weeks leading up to the wedding. Her outer gaiety might well be a cover for an inner restlessness. Why couldn't Philip see that?

Worse, what could Fiona possibly do about it?

She could hardly ring Philip up and tell him her theories about Corinne. Neither was there any point in saying anything to Kathryn when they met later this week to finalise everything for the wedding. Philip's mother thought the sun shone out of Corinne. Which it did, in a way. The girl had an irresistible and radiant charm when she chose to exercise it.

A thought suddenly crossed Fiona's mind.

Steve. The best man.

It seemed Steve didn't care for Corinne. She would be seeing Steve next Tuesday, to kit him and Philip out for the wedding.

Fiona would keep her eyes and ears open, and if an opportunity presented itself she would...she would...

Well, she wasn't sure what she would do. But she would do something! She couldn't stand by and let Philip marry the wrong girl. She'd set him free so that he could be happy. And something—some deep, inner female instinct—was warning her that he would *not* be happy with Corinne!

CHAPTER TWELVE

'AREN'T you supposed to be meeting Philip and his best man in town this morning?' Owen said to her when she walked into the office at eight-thirty the following Tuesday morning.

'Not till eleven,' she replied, her crisp tone belying the butterflies in her stomach. 'I'll catch a train around ten and still be in plenty of time.'

Owen's eyes narrowed and flicked over her mint-green linen suit. 'That's new, isn't it?'

'Yes, it is.' In actuality she'd bought it to wear to some of the spring weddings they were doing. She'd been going to wear grey or brown today, but feminine pride had had the final say that morning. 'Do you like it?'

'You look like a breath of fresh air,' he grumbled.

'And that's bad?'

'Only if you're going to meet your ex.'

'Give that a rest, will you, Owen?'

'I will...after you get back safely with the wedding still on. At least after today you won't need to see Philip again till the week of the wedding.'

Owen's very correct comment reminded Fiona that this morning was her last real opportunity to do something about Corinne.

'That bothers you, does it?' Owen said sharply.

It did, but Fiona tried to look unconcerned.

'Not really. Why?'

'Just checking. My problem antenna is still beeping. It has been ever since we took this job.'

'A job *you* insisted we take, I might add,' Fiona pointed out drily.

'Yeah. Yeah. Don't rub it in. So, how are things really going?'

'Swimmingly. Never had less trouble. What I say goes. I've never known a wedding like it. On top of that, if everything goes off as planned, it really will be something to behold.'

'What do you mean…*if*?'

Fiona didn't seriously believe she could stop this wedding. All she could do was make sure Philip knew what kind of girl he was marrying in advance.

'Oh, you know,' she said airily, then began to walk off. 'There are always things you can't control. Acts of God and such.'

'I'm not worried about acts of God,' Owen called after her. 'It's the acts of the devil which concern me.'

Fiona had to laugh. Did Owen seriously think she was about to seduce the groom? Even if she wanted to—and, yes, she did, in her darker moments—Philip wasn't in the market for seduction. Not by her, anyway.

He'd made it perfectly clear what he thought of her. Perfectly, perfectly clear!

That was why she didn't really feel guilty over wearing her new green outfit. She could stand naked before Philip and she doubted he would turn a hair.

Well…maybe a little hair…

Eleven o'clock saw her standing before the man in question, but, true to form, he was looking at her quite coldly. He was also looking heart-breakingly handsome in a dark grey suit and pale blue shirt.

Steve, however, was nowhere in sight.

'Steve's always late,' Philip said brusquely, glancing at his watch.

'Shall we wait for him?' Fiona asked. They were in the reception area of Formal Wear for Men, which occupied the first floor of a rather old building in King Street, not far from Wynyard Station.

'No, let's not. I don't have that much time. I have a meeting with a client after lunch. We can leave a message for him at Reception.'

They did, and were soon ushered inside the vast showrooms by a dapper-looking salesman who started showing Philip some of the more modern suits grooms were being decked out in these days. Philip stopped him in his tracks before he'd barely begun.

'My fiancée wants me in a black dinner suit,' he stated firmly. 'With a white dress shirt and black bow tie. She's quite adamant about that. So show me what you have in that range.'

'I see. Well, if you and your fiancée would like to come this way…' And he flashed Fiona a warm smile.

Philip shot Fiona a savage glance, which prompted her to inform the man she was *not* the fiancée in question. The salesman looked startled, then apologised for the mistake.

'And there I was, thinking what a handsome couple you would make,' he went on with an embarrassed laugh.

'Fiona's a consultant with Five-Star Weddings,' Philip said stiffly.

'Oh, yes, so she is. I recognise her now.'

After that, Fiona hung back a little while the salesman showed Philip several racks of black tuxedos, pointing out the various styles and shapes.

Philip selected an extremely elegant but traditional dinner suit, with deep black satin lapels and only one button at his waist. He matched it with a fine white shirt which had tiny black buttons and vertical pleats on each side. The bow tie was black too, as Corinne had ordered.

'I'll go try this on,' he informed the man serving him. 'When my best man arrives, I want him dressed exactly the same. And don't even *think* of suggesting one of those ghastly cummerbund things, Fiona. Neither of us would be seen dead in one.'

Philip promptly disappeared into one of the dressing cubicles, which Fiona was glad to see had proper doors. It would be bad enough waiting outside, thinking of him undressing. Much worse if she was able to glimpse bare bits and pieces of him under one of those half-doors.

Fiona sighed as she waited. This wasn't working out at all as she'd hoped. Steve wasn't here, and Philip was so cold and remote that it was impossible to bring up the subject of his bride.

Suddenly the door of the cubicle popped open and Philip leant out. 'I can't do this infernal bow tie up,' he muttered, glancing around for the salesman, who'd unfortunately been grabbed by a large man in a safari suit.

'Fiona,' he finally said in desperation. 'Come in here and do the damned thing up for me.'

Rather reluctantly, she moved into the cubicle, which, though larger than the cramped boxes some shops offered, was still far too small once the door was shut.

And it did shut behind her, operated by one of those

automatic do-dads which shut doors once they were let go.

Fiona tried to act cool, moving round to face Philip and reaching up to do what she'd done a hundred times before. When you organised weddings you learnt to do fiddly things like tie bow ties, and pin roses to lapels. Usually the people in the wedding party were all fingers and thumbs. One of Fiona's main tasks on a wedding day was to provide an unflustered mind and a steady hand.

But being this close to Philip did something to her mind and her hands. They both ceased to work properly.

Her first attempt at tying the tie was woeful. She gave a shaky laugh at the pathetic sight. 'Sorry,' she muttered, and pulled the ends undone. 'I'll try again.'

She didn't dare look up into his eyes. Instead she stared straight ahead and tried with all her might to tie a proper bow tie.

But once again it ended up all lopsided.

'I...er...think you'll have to get someone else to do this,' she said, somewhat breathlessly.

When he didn't say a single word, she looked up, then desperately wished she hadn't. He was too close. Far, far too close.

His eyes searched hers with a harsh and haunted expression, betraying in that moment that he did still feel something for her.

'Why did you leave me?' he demanded angrily. 'Why, damn you?'

Her heart tightened at the torment in his voice and face, her hand trembling as it reached up to touch his cheek. 'Oh, Philip,' was all she could manage.

He gave no warning of his intention to kiss her;

nothing, except perhaps for a moment's darkening of his eyes. Suddenly his hands shot out to grab her shoulders, she was yanked against him and his mouth crashed down hard upon hers.

Fiona gasped under his lips, an automatic air-seeking reaction which proved fateful.

Did he think she'd parted her lips deliberately, inviting him to drive his tongue deep into her mouth?

He must have, because he immediately pushed her back against the mirrored wall, holding her face captive with his hands while he did just that.

Philip had always been a hungry kisser, but this…this was something else. This was beyond hunger.

Initially, Fiona was stunned by his brutal oral onslaught. Shock, however, soon began to give way to a burst of excitement which was as dangerous as it was reckless. She began kissing him back, her tongue twining round his, her head spinning as the blood roared through her head. He pressed against her, then *rubbed* against her. She whimpered, and writhed.

When he reefed back away from her, she stared up into his flushed face and glittering eyes, then reached blindly out to touch him through his trousers, stroking him to even greater arousal.

'Oh, God,' he groaned.

The banging on the cubicle door had both of their eyes blinking wide.

'Philip! Are you in there?'

Philip stifled another groan and squeezed his eyes tightly shut.

Fiona could not believe how quickly one could go from madness to mortification. One moment she was in the grip of mindless lust, the next she just wanted to die.

Her hand whipped away from his trousers, her face going bright red.

Philip's return to reality was as quick, if a little less inclined to self-disgust. He opened his eyes and speared her with an icily accusing look.

'Yeah, Steve,' he answered curtly. 'I'm in here. Won't be a moment. Fiona's having some trouble doing up my bow tie for me.'

'Who the hell's Fiona?'

'The wedding consultant Corinne and my mother hired.'

'Oh, right. Look, I'm going into the dressing room opposite, okay? I'm trying on the suit you picked out.'

'Fine.'

All the time Philip was talking his coldly furious gaze never left Fiona. As soon as it was obvious Steve was no longer standing outside the door he rounded on her.

'What in hell did you think you were doing, touching me like that?' he demanded.

Fiona was jolted by the unfairness of the attack. 'I...I couldn't help it,' she stammered with uncharacteristic confusion, before pulling herself together. 'Hey, you kissed me first, remember?'

'Only after you touched my face and started looking at me with goo-goo eyes. And what do you mean, you couldn't help it?' he lashed out. 'What kind of lame excuse is that? What are you? Some kind of nymphomaniac that you can't keep your hands off a man once you come within three feet of him?'

'Don't be ridiculous! I'm nothing of the kind. Not normally, anyway,' she muttered.

'Oh, only with me, is that it? God, that would be funny if it wasn't so pathetic. Why don't you admit it, Fiona? You're sex-mad. You always were and you still are.'

'Sex had nothing to do with why I touched you in the beginning.'

He laughed. 'Well, believe me, honey, sex had everything to with the way you *ended* up touching me.'

'That was only after things got out of hand,' she countered, her face flaming. 'And who are you to accuse me of being sex-mad? You kissed me first. And it wasn't a polite, platonic kiss, either. So what are *you*, Philip?' she countered heatedly. 'Some kind of sex maniac that you can't keep your hands off a woman once you come within three feet of her?'

'Only with you, Fiona,' came his rueful confession. 'Only with you.

'Old memories, I guess,' he went on, before she could take any pleasure in the admission. 'But they're damned powerful old memories. Powerful and perverse. If Steve hadn't knocked when he did, I'd have let you have your wicked way with me. Yep, I admit it. I'd have joined your long line of male victims for a second sick run around your block.'

He gave a short, harsh bark of laughter. 'Hell, I'm only now beginning to appreciate why I had such trouble forgetting you, Fiona. But I'm warning you, honey. You keep well away from me. You had your chance ten years ago, and you blew it. I love Corinne now and I'm going to marry her.'

'Yes, but does *she* love *you*?' Fiona threw back at him, stung by his scorn and his anger.

Philip's eyes showed utter disbelief, then contempt. 'I want you out of here,' he muttered, low under his breath. 'Right now. And I don't want to see hide nor hair of you again till my wedding day, and then only if strictly necessary. Do I make myself clear?'

Fiona saw the bitter resolve in his face and knew she'd lost any chance she'd had. To say any more would be futile, and possibly even more disastrous.

But she simply could not leave without saying something!

'I know you won't believe this, Philip,' she tried to explain, her voice softly pleading, 'but I do care about you. I only had your best interests at heart in saying what I just said. I've only *ever* had your best interests at heart.'

His eyes stayed hard and cold. 'Then you have a funny way of showing it. Now, will you just go, please?'

She still lingered. 'What…what about your suits for the wedding? Owen will ask me, that's all.'

'Tell Owen the groom's taking care of his and the best man's clothes. He exonerates you entirely of the responsibility.'

Fiona winced at his coldness. 'I…I am truly sorry, Philip.'

His mouth tightened. 'Please, just go.'

She gave him one last despairing look, and went.

CHAPTER THIRTEEN

'OH, FIONA, how lovely you look! My, doesn't white suit you! You should wear it more often.'

Fiona's heart tightened. Kathryn had no idea of the irony within her words, or the pain she'd once given Fiona on another wedding day, ten long years ago.

'White's not a very serviceable colour for a career girl,' Fiona replied. 'Neither is this hairdo,' she added wryly, and took another peek in the mirror at the way Kathryn had talked Fiona into having her hair done that morning. Up, with wispy bits hanging down around her face and neck.

'You need a romantic hairdo to go with that romantic dress,' Kathryn had insisted.

The dress was, indeed, romantic. White chiffon, it was an elegant and close-fitting sheath in an off-the-shoulder style, with a self-made rose between her breasts, out of which chiffon scarves floated down to the hem. The neckline wasn't low enough to be vulgar, but it felt bare, so Fiona had added a pearl choker and earrings.

The dress had been an impulse buy, Kathryn steering her in its direction the day she'd taken Philip's mother shopping for her mother-of-the-groom dress. Fiona now thought wryly that she should have bought something black to signify mourning.

Instead, here she was, on Philip's wedding day, looking exquisitely soft and feminine and, yes, sort of bridal.

'I want to thank you for staying here with me last night, dear,' Kathryn was saying. 'I'd have been a bit lonely without anyone.'

Fiona snapped out of her thoughts to smile at Philip's mother. 'It was kind of you to ask me.' She'd grown to genuinely like the woman, which she supposed was perverse in the extreme. But it was true.

Staying overnight hadn't been any great hardship either, since neither Philip nor Corinne was in residence. Philip had spent his last evening of bachelorhood at his best man's place, and Corinne had stayed at home, saying she wanted to have her hair done at her usual hairdresser's in the morning. Fiona presumed Carmel had stayed with her and was going to the same hairdresser.

Both girls were due to drive out to Kenthurst after lunch, arriving around three, giving them four hours to be ready for the wedding, which was scheduled for seven. Their dresses were already hanging up in the guest suite Kathryn had allotted for the bride to use. Philip and Steve weren't due to arrive till the last minute.

Fiona had instructed the parents of the page-boy and flower girl to dress them in their respective homes and keep them there as long as possible as well. Little children, she'd found, were notorious for getting excited and having accidents on wedding days, especially where a staircase was involved, not to mention flagged steps and swimming pools.

The actual ceremony was to take place at one end of the pool, between the marble columns, with the garden as backdrop. Rows of red chairs had been set up on the two sides of the pool and down at the other end for the two-hundred-odd guests. Unfortunately, nearly all those invited had accepted. There'd even been a few last-minute additions, as Corinne's father had thought of some influential people he'd forgotten.

After the ceremony, most of the red chairs would be cleared away, leaving room for dancing around the pool. Not much room for that in the marquee, which sat on the lawn just beyond the terrace and which, though large, was chock-full of tables and chairs for the formal sit-down dinner.

'I hope everything goes smoothly,' Fiona said, giving in to a quite uncharacteristic burst of uncertainty.

Kathryn looked surprised. 'I'm sure it will,' she soothed. 'The weather's marvellous and everything looks just magnificent. The house. The marquee. The lights. Everything! You're just worried because you weren't here the other night for the rehearsal. But, truly, your partner put everyone through their paces without a hitch. Which reminds me. Are you sure you're feeling one hundred per cent better now? I must say you *look* well.'

'I'm fine. It was just one of those twenty-four-hour viruses.' Owen was the only one who knew she hadn't really been sick that day.

Other than Philip, of course.

Fiona hadn't told Owen the whole truth, just that there was a bit of tension building between her and Philip and it would be better all round if he conducted the rehearsal. Owen had been only too glad to oblige. He didn't want anything to spoil the wedding of the year!

Kathryn patted Fiona's hand. 'Corinne was worried you might not make it for the wedding, but Philip was sure you'd be here.'

Fiona winced inside. So he was still angry with her.

What was he thinking? That she might still try to spoil something?

She sighed, and Kathryn gave her a closer look. 'Come to think of it, you *are* a bit pale. How about we go downstairs and have us both a stiff brandy?'

Fiona smiled. 'Good idea, Kathryn.'

The brandy worked. So did keeping busy.

Corinne and Carmel arrived shortly after lunch, and were bustled upstairs with instructions to be ready for the photographer a good hour and a half before the ceremony.

Things really started hopping after that. The flowers were delivered. The video man arrived, keen to get set up well before mingling guests made things difficult. The official photographer, Fiona knew, would not come till five-thirty. Bill had already had a good look last week, and planned the best settings for his photographs.

The catering staff arrived, plus the parking attendants she'd hired to direct the guests' cars. Fiona kept moving and checking on things, whilst hoping and praying nothing would go wrong. Owen would kill her if it did.

At five, Kathryn went upstairs to get ready. She hadn't wanted to put her white silk suit on too early as she'd been afraid it might crush if she sat down.

Fiona didn't have to worry about that. Her dress didn't crush. Still, she had no intention of sitting down.

Bill arrived just on five-thirty, with his assistant and bevy of cameras. Fiona collected the bouquets from where they'd been resting in a cool spot in the pantry, and accompanied the photographer upstairs to collect the bride and bridesmaid for some pre-ceremony shots on the stairs.

Even Fiona had to admit that they both looked lovely. Corinne, especially. Like a fairy princess.

Bill didn't need her, so Fiona left him to it and went back downstairs to check that everything was ready for the ceremony and the reception afterwards. The sun was starting to set, throwing a spectacularly golden glow over the garden and the pool.

Everything was as ready as it was going to be. Fiona cast a final glance around the marquee, which looked superb with its elegantly draped ceiling and ultra-plush table settings. No expense had been spared, of course.

Fiona felt satisfied she'd done everything she could to make the wedding truly memorable, although there was a moment of panic when she realised the celebrant hadn't arrived. A quick call to his mobile reassured her he was on his way, in fact just around the corner.

Kathryn reappeared downstairs, looking truly lovely, but just a little strained. Weddings did that to the mothers. They did that to the consultants as well. Fiona told her she looked beautiful, pinned a delicate mauve orchid to her jacket—a red rose simply would not have done for this elegant lady—then helped her to another brandy.

'You have one too, Fiona,' she insisted.

Fiona didn't say no.

The first guests made an appearance around six-fifteen. Kathryn and Fiona both played hostess, directing everyone inside the huge front living rooms, where the pre-wedding drinks were being served and the orchestra was playing suitable music. Later on Fiona would move the musicians out onto the terrace.

'Doesn't everyone look lovely in their black and

white?' Kathryn whispered to Fiona at the door as the grandfather clock in the corner chimed six-thirty.

But Fiona wasn't listening to either Kathryn or the clock. Her ears had gone deaf as her attention focused on the car which had just purred to a stop at the front door.

A black Jaguar.

'I...I have to go check on the lights by the pool, Kathryn,' she said hurriedly, and left.

Oh, dear God, Fiona agonised as she fled through the house, her emotions in instant disarray, her control in danger of slipping. I thought I could do this but I can't! I just can't!

She moved as swiftly as her dress and high heels would allow, not stopping till she practically collided with one of the marble columns by the pool. Her hands shot out to grab at it, at first to steady herself, and then more tightly as a kind of impotent fury crashed through her. She wanted to crush the column between her hands, to topple it over, to dash it to the ground.

It took a great effort of will for Fiona to let the darned thing go. Slowly, she turned and leant her head back against the smooth marble, closing her eyes and taking a deep, deep breath.

Calm down, she ordered herself. What is this achieving? Where did you think you were running to? You have to see this through, Fiona. You have to drink from this cup.

A light tap on her shoulder sent her eyes flying open on a gasp.

'Goodness, Philip,' she exclaimed, struggling for composure. 'You...you startled me.'

'Sorry,' he said abruptly. 'You looked strange, standing there like that with your eyes shut. I thought you might be feeling unwell again. Not that you look sick,' he added in rueful tones. 'If I may say so, you look good enough to eat.'

Fiona gaped up at him and he slanted a travesty of a smile down at her.

'Not the sort of the thing the groom should be saying at this precise moment to a woman other than his bride?' he mocked. 'Perhaps not, but I can't seem to help the way you make me feel, Fiona. You seem to have a direct line to my male hormones.'

'Philip, I…I…'

'Yes, I know, you're sorry and I'm sorry,' he bit out. 'We're both sorry. Ahh…here's my best man, Steve, come to rescue me from myself. Don't worry,' he muttered under his breath, 'I haven't said anything and he won't recognise you.'

He didn't.

He'd changed a lot too, Fiona thought at first sight of the big sandy-haired man walking towards her. Better-looking and much more confident. But still not a patch on Philip.

He smiled as he looked her up and down. 'So this is the mysterious Fiona I never seem to meet. Philip didn't tell me you were a goddess when you weren't being a wedding consultant.'

'Fiona has a steady boyfriend—Mark,' Philip said drily. 'So save it.'

'Girls like Fiona always do, mate. But she's not wearing a ring, and all fair's in love and war. What are you doing after the wedding tonight, loveliness?'

Fiona might have been flattered by the jealousy on Philip's face—ten years ago. Now, she just felt sad.

'Sorry, Steve,' she responded politely. 'But Philip's right. There's another man in my life at the moment, and he's enough for me. Now I must go. You boys stay here and I'll see about getting the guests seated. No doubt Corinne will be a little late coming downstairs, Philip, but please…don't go away.'

'I'm not going anywhere, Fiona. I'm here to get married.'

'And I'm here to make sure you do.' She moved off, not looking back, even when Steve wolf-whistled at her departing figure.

Half an hour later Philip and Corinne were man and wife. Three hours later Corinne left the reception to go up and change into her going-away outfit, Carmel going with her to help. Philip started doing the rounds of thanking the guests for coming.

An increasingly depressed Fiona saw Steve making a beeline for her through the crowded marquee, so she fled into the house, where she found Kathryn standing at the bottom of the stairs, looking pale and shaken.

'Kathryn! What is it? Are you ill?'

The woman gave her a stricken look. 'Oh, Fiona, I've just had the most dreadful shock, and I…I don't know what to do!'

'What kind of a shock? Can I help?'

'I don't think anyone can help,' she said weakly.

'Let me be the judge of that,' Fiona said firmly. 'Now tell me what's happened.'

'It's Corinne,' the woman said reluctantly. 'I went upstairs to see if I could help in any way. I knocked on the door but there wasn't any answer. I…I opened the door, but the room seemed to be empty. I was puzzled and went in. It was then that I…that I…'

'That you what?' Fiona urged.

'Saw them,' Kathryn blurted out. 'In the bathroom…reflected in the mirror…'

Fiona's stomach tightened. 'What, exactly, did you see, Kathryn?'

'Corinne and Carmel... They were...hugging, and kissing.'

'Only hugging and kissing?'

'Yes, but not like friends, Fiona. Like...lovers. I do know the difference,' she said unhappily.

Fiona could only shake her head as all the pieces of the puzzle which was Corinne slotted into place. She felt absolutely furious with the girl, and dreadfully upset for Philip.

'You *have* to tell Philip,' she insisted.

'Oh, but I can't. I can't. You don't understand.'

'You can't let him go off on his honeymoon with that girl! You *can't*, Kathryn.'

Kathryn's head dropped into her hands. 'I don't know what to do!' she wailed.

'You know what you have to do. Here, come into the study and wait there. I'll get Philip and you can tell him exactly what you saw.'

Reluctantly, Kathryn agreed.

Philip didn't want to come with her, insisting on bringing Steve with him. Fiona felt sick at heart over his attitude, but nothing weakened her resolve to expose the truth about Corinne. She hadn't given Philip up all those years ago to have him betrayed by some deceitful female with a secret agenda!

'So what's all this about?' he asked impatiently, as soon as Fiona shut the door behind them.

Kathryn was sitting stiffly in the chair she was occupying, her hands twisting restlessly in her lap. Philip finally got the message that something was very badly wrong.

He looked first at his anguished mother and then at Fiona.

'What's happened?' he asked sharply. 'Is it Corinne?'

'Your mother will tell you,' Fiona said tautly.

Kathryn finally got the words out. Philip went white, while Steve swore.

'Are you absolutely sure?' he asked his mother.

'They…they were only wearing underwear,' she whispered.

Now Philip swore, then he looked hard at Fiona.

'Come with me,' he snarled.

She blinked. 'Where?'

'Upstairs. I need an eye-witness to confront Corinne with and I don't think my mother can manage right now. Steve, you stay here and get Mother a cup of tea or something.'

'I'll do that, Phil. You go sort Corinne out. I don't like to say I told you so, but I always had some misgivings about her. You know I did.'

'Yeah, I know.'

Fiona had to almost run to keep up with Philip as he took the stairs two at a time. Up on the top landing he stopped abruptly and wheeled to face her. 'Did you know about this before today?'

Fiona was taken aback. 'No! I would have said something if I had.'

'You implied Corinne didn't really love me. Why was that? Don't hedge. Just tell me the unvarnished truth. You must have known something!'

'I didn't really know anything for sure, but on the day I took her shopping for her wedding dress she said that with a father like hers she *had* to get married before she had a baby, and that was why she was marrying you. I thought it was an odd comment to make if she really loved you.'

'That's all?'

'That's all; I swear it. If you think I would deliberately let you marry Corinne, *knowing* the truth about her, then you can think again. I told you I cared about you, Philip, and I do.'

'Do you, now? In that case, then, lie for me in here. Tell Corinne you were the one who saw her with Carmel.'

Fiona's chin lifted. 'Gladly.'

Philip didn't knock. He just barged in. The bride and the bridesmaid were no longer in a compromising position— they were also fully dressed—but Philip's angry entry sent guilt leaping into their faces.

'Philip!' Corinne gasped. 'What is it? Is there anything wrong?'

'You tell me, Corinne. You tell me.'

The bride didn't look so beautiful with an ashen face and worried eyes. 'What…what do you mean?'

Carmel just looked terrified.

'Fiona came up to see if she could help you a little while ago,' Philip relayed harshly. 'She knocked, but you didn't answer, so she came in. It seems you and Carmel were…otherwise occupied,' he said mockingly. 'In the bathroom, I gather. That's right, isn't it, Fiona?'

'Yes,' she reaffirmed, and watched the two girls squirm.

'You have nothing to say, Corinne?' Philip ground out.

Guilt gradually changed to a sullen defiance. 'No,' came her sulky reply. 'There's not much point, is there, if she saw us?'

Philip looked at her bride with disgust. 'Just tell me one thing. When were you planning on leaving me? After our first baby was born, or earlier?'

'I had no intention of leaving you.'

Philip's face showed shock, and Corinne finally had the grace to look sorry.

'I did like you, Philip,' she insisted. 'Honestly. You're the only man I've ever met whom I could stand touching me. That's why it had to be you, don't you see?'

'I only see that you took my love and spat on it.'

'Oh, Philip, don't be so melodramatic. You never really loved me. I know because I know what it is to really love someone. I love Carmel and Carmel loves me. We've loved each other since we were fifteen. You liked me; that's all. I suited you. And I suited your mother. But you didn't love me.'

'You don't know what you're talking about,' he said coldly. 'Now I want you and your…girlfriend… out of this house. You have a car here, I presume?'

'Yes.'

'Then go downstairs, get in it, drive off and don't ever contact me again. You'll be hearing from me in due course. Not in person, however. I'll send the annulment papers to your father's address.'

'Don't tell him, Philip. I beg of you. He'll disinherit me. That's why I had to get married. Because he's paranoid about gays, and unmarried mothers, and just about everything else in this world.'

'I won't tell him. I won't tell anyone. Do you think I want to look that much a fool?'

'You're not a fool, Philip. You're a very nice man. You're—'

'Oh, for pity's sake, just go, will you?'

He watched over them like a vigilante till they did as he wanted. Only when their car had disappeared down the hill did he speak to Fiona, who'd stayed silently by his side all the time.

'Do you have a coat?' he asked abruptly.

'I have a jacket upstairs.'

'Get it and meet me here in two minutes. You'd better bring your handbag too, as well as anything else you might need. We're leaving.'

'Leaving!'

'You're just about to become my blushing bride. We're sneaking off early to avoid any of those 'just married' antics drunken wedding guests like to indulge in. My mother can tell Corinne's father his darling daughter and her beloved have departed prematurely.' Philip's smile was savagely sarcastic. 'He'll think she means the bride and groom. Then I'll have Steve grab a couple of selected people to run out and wave us off as we speed away in my Jag. They won't notice you're not a blonde through the tinted windows.'

'But—but…'

'Just think of the alternative, Fiona. Do you really want everyone to know this wedding turned out to be fiasco? What do you want people to remember it for? Its creativity and picture-perfect splendour? Or the fact the bride and groom never made it past the reception? Of course, I suppose I could always drive off with my mother, but I think she'd rather stay here.'

Fiona saw the sense of his idea, and sighed. 'I'll get my jacket.'

Philip's smile was chillingly hard. 'I thought you might.'

CHAPTER FOURTEEN

EVERYTHING went as Philip had planned, the Jaguar speeding off down the hill and through the open gates with no one at the wedding discovering the masquerade. The tyres squealed as Philip reefed the wheel to the right and sped up the road.

'Is there any need to go this fast?' Fiona complained.

'Yes,' he snapped, but he did slow down.

Fiona breathed a little easier, aware that Philip had to be very upset. What had just happened to him had been horrific. Whether he was deeply in love with Corinne or not was not the point. He cared for her and had committed himself to marrying her. He'd been expecting to go off on his honeymoon tonight with a beautiful girl who'd said she loved him and wanted to be his wife and the mother of his children.

Instead, he was driving into the night with a woman whom, any sexual attraction aside, he didn't particularly like anymore.

It was a drive to nowhere, for both of them.

'Where are you taking me?' Fiona asked tautly.

'Who cares?'

'I care.'

'Why? Because of your stupid bloody Mark? You don't love him,' he snarled.

'I never said I did.'

'Then why are you still sleeping with him?'

'I'm not.'

His head whipped round to stare at her.

'Watch the road,' she warned.

Philip was broodingly silent for a few seconds.

'When did you break up with him?' he asked.

'A while ago.'

'*When?*'

'I can't remember, exactly.'

He flashed her a scornful look. 'You don't care, do you, about any of us? We're all just male bodies to you, to be used and discarded at your pleasure and leisure.'

'That's not true. Not about you, anyway.'

'Oh, good. That makes me feel a whole lot better about this.'

Fiona sighed. 'Philip, I know you've been through a lot tonight. I'm truly sorry. If there was anything I could do to make you feel better, I'd do it.'

'Oh, there is, Fiona. Believe me. We're on our way there now so you can do it.'

'Pardon?'

'Don't play ignorant—or the innocent—with me. You know exactly where I'm taking you, and what we're going to do when we get there.'

'No,' she denied, her mind whirling. 'I don't.'

'In that case let me tell you. We're heading for the honeymoon suite I booked for tonight. It's just sitting there, waiting for me and my blushing bride, complete with harbour view, champagne, spa bath and satin sheets. You said you wanted to make me feel better, Fiona? Then be my blushing bride for tonight.'

Fiona's heart began to pound.

'No, I take that back,' Philip swept on caustically. 'I don't want a blushing bride. I want a female who knows exactly what she's doing and how to do it. In short, Fiona, I want you.'

'You don't mean that,' she said, shocked not only by his suggestion but by her immediate reaction to it.

A dark excitement began fizzing along her veins, tormenting her, tempting her.

'If you won't oblige me, honey, I'll find someone else who will. I won't have any trouble. I'll just cruise through some of the sleazier city bars and I'll soon find someone eminently qualified. She might even be pretty. Not that I'll care after I down a few Scotches. I nobly didn't drink much at my wedding dinner because I knew I'd have to drive, and I wanted to be right on the ball for my bride tonight. But the ball game has changed, hasn't it? Once I hand this chariot over to the hotel valet it's going to be full steam ahead in the alcohol department.'

'Philip, don't be insane! You can't go getting drunk and picking up some trampy female. You never know what diseases she might have, for one thing.'

'You're volunteering, then?'

Fiona didn't know what to do. She wanted to go with him. She couldn't deny it. Already, just thinking about being with him was turning her on.

But she also knew there was no future in it.

'You seem to be having some trouble making up your mind,' he drawled. 'What's your dilemma? Worried about catching something from *me*?'

'No…'

'It can't be pregnancy bothering you,' he ventured drily. 'A sophisticated, independent career girl like yourself would always have that base well covered.'

'I'm on the pill, yes,' she said stiffly. 'But I don't

usually tell my men-friends that. I always insist they use protection.'

'My, my, you *are* careful. Sorry, but I don't have any condoms with me. Contraception wasn't on my agenda for tonight. But I can stop at a chemist, if you like.'

'I haven't agreed to go with you yet.'

'Make up your mind, then,' he said, in a cold, hard voice. 'Once we get closer to the city it's hard to stop.'

Fiona tried to keep her cool in the face of the most appallingly corrupting thoughts.

'Fact is, Philip,' she said firmly, and tried to mean it, 'I don't go to bed with men who think I'm a slut. Or who treat me like one. Because I'm not! I'm not only discerning in my sexual partners, I demand respect from them.'

'I respect you.'

'No, you don't. You despise me for some reason. Frankly, I'm not sure why. If it's because I've been to bed with a few men for reasons other than love then you must despise yourself as well. I gathered from your mother that you haven't been in love once since we broke up—till Corinne came along, that is—yet I doubt you've been celibate all these years.'

He threw her a startled glance. 'Good grief, but you'd make a damned good defence lawyer! You have a definite skill in argument. And you *do* have a point, even if my mother could do with keeping her own counsel instead of telling a virtual stranger her son's private and personal business. Still, I stand corrected, and plead guilty to the crime of double standards. I will even apologise for any hasty judgements where you're concerned. Now will you spend the night with me?' And he flashed her a wickedly seductive smile.

Fiona felt herself wavering. 'I shouldn't,' she muttered. 'You'll probably regret it in the morning.'

He laughed. 'If you're worried that I might fall in love with you again, then don't be. I'm not a hormone-driven boy any longer. I know the difference between sex and love.'

Fiona winced. 'I just meant you might see things differently in the morning. You're acting on impulse tonight. And in anger.'

'Not entirely, Fiona,' he admitted drily. 'I've been thinking about having sex with you since I saw you leaning up against that pillar tonight. I married Corinne thinking about having sex with you. I promised to love, honour and cherish her while I was thinking how I'd like to lash you to that pillar, strip you naked, and keep you there for my pleasure for days on end.'

'Don't say things like that!' she gasped, her face flaming while her body burned with darkly answering desires.

'But it's true. That's what you do to me. You always did. You've no idea how much I used to want you, how nothing was ever enough, no matter how many times we did it, or how many ways.'

'Don't, Philip,' she choked out breathlessly.

'Yes, you're right. I have to shut up or I won't even make it to the bloody hotel. I'll pull over right here and now. And that's not what I want. Not at all. I want lots of room. I want you totally naked. And I want you more than once. The memory of you has tormented me for years, Noni,' he ground out. 'I won't be tormented tonight.'

She stared over at him and his angry face, his words echoing in her head. Masterful words. Erotic words. Exciting words.

He isn't himself, she reasoned. He's upset.

But then she thought…I don't care. I want him too, in whatever way he wants to have me. Because at least it will be Philip doing it to me, not some ghastly substitute. And when the sun comes up in the morning it will be Philip's face on the pillow beside me…

She looked over at him and caught his eye. 'How…how long till we're at the hotel?' she managed in strangled tones.

He smiled a slow, sexy, almost smug smile. They were on the same wavelength now, it said. Wanting the same things, driven by the same goals. 'Fifteen minutes, if we're lucky.'

'That's a long time.'

'You can wait, witch.'

'Maybe. Just.'

'This is going to be some night,' he muttered.

'Yes,' she agreed, and looked away from him. 'It is.'

The next fifteen minutes passed in a haze of desire the like of which Fiona had never known. It glazed her mind while it stirred her body, making the blood thrum through her veins and rush to her head till she felt dizzy and disorientated.

Perhaps she looked calm, sitting there, staring silently out at the city streets whizzing by, but she was anything but. Her head spun, and so did her thoughts. How could she do this to herself? How *could* she?

Because you *want* to, came the terrible truth.

You want to…

The Jag sped down the amazingly quiet Pacific Highway, and negotiated the Harbour Bridge with ridiculous ease. It was as though the fates were conspiring to hurry her to her doom, lest she change her mind and tell Philip to take her home. Or the devil himself making sure there was no other escape from the sexual tension which already had her in its tenacious grip; no escape but placing herself in Philip's impassioned hands once again.

Fiona feared that spending the night with Philip would break down the defences she'd built around her heart where falling in love with him again was concerned. By morning, she suspected, she wouldn't want just Philip's body but his heart as well.

But the Philip sitting beside her had a wounded heart, too wounded for anything remotely like falling in love with her in return. He wanted sex, not intimacy. Vengeance, not caring. He was being driven by lust, not love.

She was on a one-way ride to misery.

Ahh, but the wild excitement of that ride!

That was what was holding her in thrall, why she made no protest when the Jag screeched to a halt at one of Sydney's plushest inner-city hotels and Philip propelled her inside with almost indecent haste.

The honeymoon suite was on the top floor, a breathtakingly beautiful group of rooms decorated in pale blue and gold, with breathtakingly beautiful views of Sydney Harbour from every window.

Perversely, once Philip had her all to himself and the door was safely locked behind them, his sense of urgency seemed to dissipate. He walked slowly through the rooms, inspecting them for she knew not what. There seemed to be everything any honeymooner could possibly desire. A private balcony. An elegant sitting room. A cute little alcove set up for meals. A bedroom straight out of the Arabian Nights. A bathroom fit for a king, with a sunken circular spa bath, marble floors and benchtops, and the most exquisite gold taps.

'Philip,' she said at last when they'd returned to the sitting room. 'What are you doing?'

He looked up at her and smiled a wry smile. 'Calming down.'

'Oh…' Nothing was going to calm *her* down. Not inside, where her heart was racing madly and every nerve-ending she owned was on red alert

'Shall we take this into the bedroom?' he said, pointing to the bottle of champagne which was sitting in a silver ice bucket on the coffee table, along with a fresh fruit platter and two fluted crystal glasses.

'If you like,' she murmured, though all *she* wanted and needed in the bedroom was him. To use Corinne's favourite word, he looked utterly gorgeous, standing there in that beautiful black dinner suit.

Fiona couldn't wait to take it off him.

'You bring the glasses,' he told her, and scooped up the bucket.

Dropping her handbag by the table, she reefed off her jacket, picked up the glasses and hurried after him.

He opened the champagne and filled the glasses, before taking them from her hands and placing them on the bedside chest next to a very pretty gold lamp.

'What are you doing now?' she asked impatiently when Philip turned it on then walked round to turn on the matching lamp.

'Turn off the overhead light,' he ordered.

She did, and the room was immediately plunged into a romantic half-light, only the bed well lit, the blue satin quilt glowing under the golden circles of light from the lamps.

'Now, come over here.' He beckoned from where he was standing at the foot of the bed.

Her heart tripped. At last, he was going to make love to her. She felt self-conscious under the intensity of his gaze as she walked slowly towards him, and very aware of her own body: her breasts lushly full beneath her dress, her stomach tight in anticipation, her thighs trembling.

'Turn around,' he ordered when she was within an arm's distance.

She did.

She would have done anything he asked.

His fingertips brushed over her bare shoulders and she almost cried out.

She tensed even further as he took his time taking off her necklace, and then her earrings. 'I said I want you naked,' he murmured, his breath hot in her hair and over her neck.

'The…the zipper,' she told him shakily. 'It's at the back. Hidden.'

'Ahh, yes, I see.' She held her breath as he peeled it slowly down, her hands automatically clutching the dress up over her breasts when the back parted wide and threatened to fall.

'Let it go, Fiona,' he commanded.

She did, sucking in sharply when she was left standing there with nothing on but her pantyhose and high heels, a pool of white chiffon around her ankles.

'Step out of the dress carefully and walk over to the doorway,' he said in a low but firm voice. 'When you get there turn round, take off everything, then slip your shoes back on.'

Her pride screamed at her not to let him do this to her, reduce her to some kind of mindless sex object, to be displayed for his pleasure, positioned this way and that to satisfy whatever desire came into his mind.

But then she thought that maybe being a mindless sex object was safer. Maybe this way she wouldn't surrender her heart to him as well as her body. If she kept things to just sex, then she might survive this night with her self-esteem intact and her soul still her own.

So she did what he wanted, pricklingly aware of his gaze glued to her every step of the way, watching her strip naked for him, then slide her feet back into her high heels to stand there like some call girl.

'No, stay there a minute,' he rasped when she went to walk back towards him. 'I want to just look at you while I undress.' And he yanked his bow tie undone.

Fiona watched him watch her while *he* stripped. She wasn't sure which excited her the most, seeing his body slowly unfolding, or displaying her own nudity so shamelessly.

He was more beautiful than she remembered. And more awesome.

'Now you can come here,' he said, after he'd tossed all their clothes aside and sat down on the end of the bed.

She almost couldn't obey him, her legs suddenly like jelly. She forced them to move and finally made her way shakily towards him. Once she got there he directed her to straddle his thighs but to stay standing.

By this point she was beyond denying him anything, and in truth she found the position dizzyingly exciting, with her legs wide apart, his hands gripping her thighs and his mouth on a level with her fluttering stomach, so close she could feel the heat of his breath in her navel.

His hands released their firm grip to run with tantalising slowness over her body, starting at the back of her knees. Up her legs they travelled, taking their time on her taut buttocks before finding the small of her back. Once there, he trickled his fingertips around her waist, skimmed up over her ribs, then briefly over the tips of her breasts, before trailing back down across her tensing stomach.

Fiona sucked in a sharp breath as he drew close to the curls at the apex of her thighs. But he bypassed that area and finally returned to her knees, touching her everywhere but where she desperately wanted to be touched. By the time he'd repeated this torture several times, her stomach was like a rock, and her nipples like nails.

But, inside, she was a melting, quivering mess.

When his hands finally slipped between her legs her gravelly moan told of the intensity of her arousal and frustration. When his thumbs brushed against the bursting bud of flesh which was burning in erotic anticipation for any kind of touch at all, she gasped, and her knees began to go.

'Don't move,' he commanded sharply, and she really tried not to. But when he started further serious exploration of everything which made her a woman, she wanted to scream and writhe and beg him to stop. She bit her bottom lip and willed herself to be silent and still. But it was becoming unbearable. She was going to come. She had to. She…

He stopped, and a tormented sob broke from her lips.

Philip made a similar sound as he grabbed hold of her already wobbly knees and yanked them down onto the bed on either side of him, the tip of his stunning erection perfectly positioned to probe at the heated heart of her. Fiona could not wait a moment longer, sinking down onto him with a long, low moan of pleasure. When she also presented one of her aching nipples to his lips, he willingly obliged, suckling on it like a starving infant.

Wrapping her arms around his head, she began to ride him, feeling all primal woman with her man both at her breast and deep inside her body, his exquisitely swollen flesh stroking her insides as she rocked up and down.

She'd hardly started when she came with a rush, gasping as the spasms hit. Philip groaned and bit down on her nipple, grabbing her hips and urging her to continue moving all through her orgasm, and further.

Fiona was astonished to find the pleasure not draining away as it usually did when she climaxed. The rapture rolled onto another level, where the sensations became even more addictive and electric. When Philip finally exploded within her, she came again. Violently.

Afterwards, they collapsed together back onto the bed, Philip clasping her to him, muttering something into her hair which she could not make out.

For ages she lay sprawled across him, feeling dazed and disorientated. She could not remember ever having come twice like that, even back in the old days.

Of course, Philip was an even more skilled lover now. She could see that. And maybe she was a little more needy. In the last decade no man had ever really fulfilled her in a sexual sense. She'd held herself much too distant from them emotionally to really let go in the bedroom. Only with Philip did she feel this abandon, this total lack of pretence.

Which was why he was so dangerous to her.

Suddenly he opened his eyes, and smiled up at her. 'Recovered yet?' he said, before abruptly rolling over and scooping her under him. 'God, but you're so incredibly sexy,' he muttered, stroking her hair out of her face and planting a kiss on her mouth. 'I could just eat you up. But not right now. Right now I'm going to go run us a spa bath. And fix us up with some refreshment. I'd forgotten how making love to a goddess took it out of a guy. Now don't go away!' he commanded as he withdrew and clambered off the bed.

Fiona's glazed eyes followed him lustfully. She was beyond going anywhere. She was beyond anything except blind obedience to his will.

'I feel very decadent,' she murmured ten minutes later, leaning back against the bath, sipping champagne and eating a strawberry from the fruit platter Philip had brought in from the sitting room.

He grinned from his position opposite her.

'You *look* very decadent,' he said, his eyes raking over her breasts which were just on show above the bubbles.

She didn't blush. She was way beyond blushing too.

'How's your murder case going?' she asked, and he shot her a disbelieving look.

'You want to talk about my work? *Now?*'

'Just curious. What happened?'

'We won. The jury acquitted her.'

'I knew you would,' she said, and his eyebrows arched.

'Such confidence! To what do I owe that?'

She sipped some more champagne. 'To my having faith in your abilities. And your passion.'

'My *passion*? What do you mean by that?'

'You are the only man I've met who feels things as strongly as you do. You don't let anything or anyone sway you from doing what you want to do.'

'You could be right. But I'm not sure if that's a good thing or a bad thing.'

'It can't be a *bad* thing.'

'That depends. But let's not get serious. I haven't come here tonight to be serious. Drink up.' He slid over and topped up her glass, then slid back again. 'I want you nice and tipsy by the time we get out of this bath.'

'Why's that?'

'I seem to recall you're wonderfully willing to please when you're tipsy.'

Fiona drank up, telling herself that getting drunk was good. Drunk was unthinking and uncaring. Drunk had nothing to with depth and everything to do with superficiality.

'Fill 'er up again,' she said, and held out the empty glass for restocking. To be honest, she was already on the way to a nicely intoxicated state. She hadn't eaten much all night, and was probably a bit dehydrated as well. The champagne was certainly hitting her blood-stream hard, making her light-headed and just a tad reckless.

Which was a pretty funny thought. How much more reckless could she get? A giggle escaped, and Philip frowned at her.

'I want you tipsy,' he warned, 'not paralytic.'

'I'm a long way from being paralytic, Philip. Trust me.'

'That's usually the man's line.'

'If you want me to stop, then just say so,' she said. 'I'm yours to command tonight.'

'Only tonight?'

Her eyes danced at him over the rim of the glass.
'Let's take one night at a time, shall we?'

'In that case, I think it's time we got *this* night on
the road again, don't you?'

Getting out the sunken spa bath and getting dry was
a true test of Fiona's level of intoxication. Not nearly
drunk enough, she decided when Philip took one the
huge fluffy blue towels and gently dried every inch of
her.

His unexpected tenderness started things happening
inside her which were worryingly emotional as opposed to strictly sexual. Her heart contracted when he
told her how beautiful she was—*and* when he stroked
the towel softly down her back, kissing her spine from
top to bottom. By the time he handed her the towel
and asked her to reciprocate she was in a state of tur-
moil.

She simply *had* to change things back to just sex.

The trouble was, the moment she sank boldly to her
knees in front of him, she was overcome with such
feeling for him, such…caring…that she lost the plot.
Before she knew it she was making love to him with
her mouth and her hands with a passion and a commitment that could only come from a woman in love.
She prayed for him to stop her, but he didn't, and in
the end she couldn't.

Afterwards, he gave her another glass of champagne
and looked at her with thoughtful eyes.

'You always were good at that,' he murmured. 'But
you're even better now.'

'So are you,' she returned, desperate to cling to the
illusion that it was still only lust directing her actions.

'Is that a compliment, or a request? No matter,' he

laughed, and scooped her up into his arms. 'Either will get you what you want,' he said, and carried her back to bed.

She tried to hold herself distant from him. But how could she when he started kissing her all over again with such thoroughness? Her mouth, her neck, her breasts, her stomach. By the time he moved beyond her stomach she moaned her total surrender and let her legs fall wantonly apart.

He started doing what he'd done on his father's dining room table, his large strong hands holding her firmly captive so that she was powerless to twist away from the devastating forays of his wickedly knowing tongue. It tormented her for ages, flicking lightly over electrified nerve-endings before sliding slowly inside, then all too swiftly withdrawing to start the teasing process all over again. When she actually began to beg, he lifted her bottom higher and drove his tongue deep, finding a spot which brought a scream to her throat.

Her back arched violently from the bed, then stayed that way as she came and came and came.

Finally, the terrifyingly endless contractions did end, and he let her go.

With a death-rattling sigh, her spine gradually unkinked and sank back down onto the bed, her arms flopping wide. Her eyelids felt so heavy she was sure any second she would fall asleep.

Philip sat up between her leaden thighs, his eyes glittering with dark triumph as he stared down at her spreadeagled body. 'I love you like this,' he muttered. 'You haven't the energy to stop me doing whatever I want.' Leaning forward, he slid his hands under her bottom again, and eased her forward, up onto his lap and onto him.

Her groan of protest was laughingly ignored.

'See what I mean?' he mocked, his hands reaching down to play with her breasts. He plucked at their still erect nipples and she groaned in protest again, this time not at all convincingly.

His eyes flashed almost angrily at the sound.

'Time to tell you the score, my sweetly insatiable Fiona,' he growled as he began to move slowly within her. 'First, you're not going to have any other men-friends from now on except me. I'm going to be your only lover. Yes, the one and only,' he repeated as his rhythm quickened. 'You'll come out with me when I want you to; stay the night with me when I want you to; *do* what I want you to. Do I make myself clear?'

Fiona wanted to tell him to go to hell. But she could not seem to find the words, or the will. Oh, she was weak where he was concerned! Horribly, horribly weak.

'Do…I…make…myself…clear?' he repeated, his thrusting becoming almost manic, his face contorting.

'Yes,' she cried out as her body began to betray her one more time. 'Yes!'

You've made yourself very clear.

Very, very clear.

CHAPTER FIFTEEN

FIONA found some character in the morning, as well as a strong surge of anger. Mostly directed at herself. How *could* she have let Philip treat her so disgracefully, as if she was some kind of sex toy!

It was immaterial that she'd woken feeling physically fantastic, with clear eyes, glowing skin and not a trace of a hangover. Sexual ecstasy was no excuse for the disgusting way she'd behaved!

As for falling in love with Philip again...

That was her most unforgivable sin of all!

She would not entertain the thought of it. Neither would she put up with that ridiculous love-slave relationship Philip had made her agree to when she'd been incapable of thinking straight, let alone telling him where he could stick his typically male ego-driven demands.

The man must be insane to think that any intelligent, independent woman would put up with such a masochistic and one-sided relationship! She hadn't become the person she was today to revert to the sort of behaviour that that silly ninny named Noni had indulged in! Good grief. The very idea!

Once Fiona was showered and dressed, with her hair brushed, her jacket on and two good strong cups of coffee inside her, she carried a cup into a still sleeping Philip and sat down on the bed.

Her eyes were firm when they moved to Philip, but the moment she made eye contact with his sleeping form Fiona wavered again. Oh, God. He looked so beautiful and sexy lying there, with his long eyelashes resting on his tanned cheek and his lovely mouth softly parted in sleep. She groaned as her gaze travelled slowly over his naked body—what there was of it on display, that was—and she thought of the intense pleasure that body could bring her.

Was she prepared to risk losing that pleasure for the sake of pride?

Her spine straightened, her chin lifting proudly. Yes, she told herself. Her answer had to be yes!

Of course, it was incredibly easy to come to that valiant resolve with Philip unconscious. A bit like walking into a lion's cage when the lion was drugged, or dead, then bragging afterwards of one's bravery.

Not much of a challenge, that.

What if, when she awakened Philip, he grabbed her and dragged her into bed with him? What if he wouldn't take her no for an answer and proceeded to coerce and corrupt her with more fantastic sex till she begged him to use her any way he wanted, as often as he wanted?

The possibility appalled her.

Jumping up from the bed, she swiftly plonked the dangerously rattling cup and saucer on the bedside table and was about to flee when Philip stirred, yawned and rolled over, the blue satin sheet shifting to a level around his hips just short of indecent.

Before Fiona could do more than blink, two beautiful blue eyes popped open and looked straight up into hers.

They flicked over her, frowning.

Their owner immediately sat bolt-upright, the sheet slipping down to his thighs.

'Fiona?'

'Yes?' she choked out, feeling decidedly flustered as she forcibly dragged her eyes back up to his face.

He glanced at his watch and frowned some more. 'It's seven in the morning. Why are you up and dressed?'

Fiona pulled herself together. 'It's Monday. I have to go home and change, then go to work.'

'But I'm on holiday for the next week. I was hoping you might have some time off and spend it with me.'

Oh, God, she thought. A whole week of the same as last night. Seven days and seven nights.

'Then you thought wrong, Philip,' she said coolly, even while her face felt hot.

'But you're your own boss, aren't you?'

'Yes,' she said meaningfully. 'I am.'

He ignored that one. 'Is this for me?' he asked, picking up the coffee cup.

'Yes.'

'Thanks.' He took a couple of sips. 'It's perfect,' he complimented warmly. 'Just the way I like it.'

'I know.'

He smiled up at her. 'You know everything I like, don't you?'

She wanted to slap his beautifully arrogant face.

'Philip,' she said sternly.

'Yes, darling?'

Oh, that was low, she thought mutinously. And downright sarcastic.

'We have to talk about last night.'

'What about it?'

'What I agreed to...'

'Yes?'

'I misled you, I'm afraid.'

The cup stilled halfway to his mouth. He lowered

it very, very slowly and gave her a long, terrifyingly hard look. 'In what way?' he finally asked.

She swallowed. 'The thing is, Philip, I want more from a relationship than just sex.'

His eyebrows shot upwards, as though she'd genuinely surprised him. 'Really?'

'Yes, really. I won't play sex-slave for any man, not even you.'

'You did a pretty good job last night.'

'I indulged you, because I knew you were hurting.'

'*Indulged* me?'

'Yes.'

He laughed. 'You indulged *yourself*, Fiona. You loved every minute of it.'

Fiona could not deny he'd given her great pleasure.

'I know exactly what you want from a relationship with a man, sweetheart,' he went on, his tone mocking and cynical. 'And that's what I gave you last night. I'm also well aware your men-friends have a use-by date, but I wouldn't have thought mine had run out just yet. I gather from Owen your lovers last a little longer than one night.'

Fiona was truly taken aback. Owen? What had Owen been telling Philip about her and her lovers?

She might have said something, but was distracted by Philip throwing back the sheet and climbing from the bed.

'I can see, however,' he stated as he strutted towards her, stark naked, 'that you *do* have your priorities. Work still comes first, if you'll pardon the pun. So!' He chucked her under the chin, shutting her startled mouth in time for a swift peck on the lips. 'How about after work tonight? We could go out to dinner somewhere. Then you can have me for afters,' he added, with the sort of smile which would have seduced a nun.

She would have had him then and there, if she hadn't been so spitting mad!

'What did Owen say to you about me?' she persisted heatedly.

'Nothing but the truth, so don't go getting all hot under the collar. Look, it suits me very well that you don't want to get married or have children. I've given up on both those fronts. Frankly, I don't seem to be too lucky in the love and marriage arena.'

Fiona didn't know whether to scream, or to cry. She felt simultaneously angry and despairing.

'For pity's sake, don't make a fuss when you get to work,' Philip said wearily, 'Poor Owen only thought he was doing the right thing, warning me of your love 'em and leave 'em nature. He couldn't possibly have anticipated that what you offer a man is exactly what I'm looking for at this moment, to get over Corinne. So calm down and stop acting like a self-righteous little hypocrite.'

Fiona found some comfort in fury. '*You* ought to talk,' she snapped. 'You told me you didn't fancy me. You said I was too skinny, for one thing.'

'I lied.'

She just stared at him, and he shrugged.

'The truth is I've been lying ever since you walked into my life again. I should never have gone through with that sham of a marriage to Corinne. She was right when she said I didn't truly love her. How could I have, when all I could think of was you?'

Fiona stared up at him, hope bursting into flower in her heart. What was he saying? That he was in love with *her*? It didn't seem possible, but surely this couldn't be just lust looking back down at her with such hot passion in his eyes. Surely not.

Her heart lurched, then flipped right over. 'Philip,' she groaned aloud, and those blazing blue eyes suddenly went cold.

'You don't have to worry, darling,' he said with a sardonic smile, crushing that flower of hope as surely as if he'd slipped it under his foot and stomped on it. 'I'm not about to declare my undying devotion. I'm merely stating that a man truly in love with one woman doesn't spend all his waking hours wanting to have sex with another. And believe me, I've wanted to have sex with you these past ten weeks like there was no tomorrow. Old flames perhaps. But damned stubborn ones. From your responses last night, I suspect you've been suffering from the same old smoulder. But we're on the way to a cure now, aren't we? In six months or so, with a bit of luck, we'll have burnt out the fires once and for all. Meanwhile, at least I'll be able to get a good night's sleep. So, what time do you want me to pick you up tonight?'

Fiona could barely function under the weight of her despair. 'What?'

'Tonight. Do you want me to pick you up from work or at your place? I thought I'd go spend the day with my mother, since I haven't anything else to do, and I think the old dear might be wanting some company after last night's fiasco.'

'But...but I have to come out there this afternoon myself,' she protested. 'I have to see that everything has been cleared away properly.'

'Perfect. I'll see you out there, then.'

Fiona could think of nothing worse! 'But...but...'

'Fiona, darling, what is it?' he said, taking her into

his arms and giving her an almost concerned look. 'Have I upset you in some way? Look, of course there'll be more to our relationship than just sex. We'll go out together. We'll spend time together. We'll even talk sometimes. We just won't make plans for a future together. There's no point, is there?'

'I…I guess not.' Not unless he loved her.

'Good. We've got that settled, then.'

'But…'

'Now what time will you be at Kenthurst?'

'Around two.'

'Two it is, then.'

'But what about your mother?' she finally managed to blurt out.

'What about her?'

'I don't want her to know about…about *us*!'

'Why not?'

'Because…because I like her and she likes me and I…I wouldn't want her to look at me like she's ashamed of me or something.'

Philip just stared at her. 'You mean you *care* about what she thinks of you?'

'Yes. Yes, I do.'

'I see. Surprising. Well, all right, I won't tell her about us. I probably wasn't going to, anyway. I'll see you around two, then.' And, with a parting peck, he turned and walked into the bathroom.

CHAPTER SIXTEEN

'How dare you say such things to Philip about me?' Fiona ranted and raved to Owen as she thumped his desk with angry fists. 'You had no right. It was unforgivable. In fact, I will *never* forgive you!'

Oh-oh, Owen thought sheepishly. She's found out I gave Philip a résumé of her recent love life.

But how? he puzzled. Why? *When?*

She certainly hadn't known anything last evening, when he'd spoken to her on her mobile, halfway through the reception.

She'd sounded very calm, if a little subdued, as she'd told him that the ceremony had gone off very well and the reception was proceeding smoothly. What on earth had happened between Fiona and the groom after that?

Still, given the intensity of her rage, Owen thought it wise to try the low-level approach of enquiry. 'Er… I'm not sure I know what you're referring to, Fiona,' he tried.

'Oh, yes, you do, you selfish, conniving, manipulative bastard! You were worried something might spring up again between Philip and myself and spoil your chance to have your name on a fancy society wedding, so you told him I was some kind of good-time girl who slept around and had absolutely no interest in marriage and children.'

'I never said you slept around!' Owen protested. 'I merely pointed out that your admirers didn't have a good track record of going the long haul with you. As for your attitude to marriage and children, you hardly made that a secret, Fiona.'

'You have no idea what you've done!' she wailed.

'No. I have to admit I don't. What does it really matter what I said, now that the groom is safely married and off on his honeymoon? You'll never see him again.'

There was something about the way she groaned which alarmed Owen.

'What is there here that I don't know?' he said worriedly.

When Fiona slumped in a chair in front of his desk and buried her face in her hands, Owen began to panic.

'Fiona! I demand you tell me what's going on!'

Fiona's face burst out of her hands and she looked quite manic, with her brown eyes very big in her pale face. 'You want to know what's going on? I'll tell you what's going on—although what's *gone* on is infinitely more titillating!'

Titillating?

Owen didn't know whether to be intrigued or unnerved.

Fiona jumped to her feet again and began to pace agitatedly around the room. 'Where shall I start?' She tossed the words with patently false flippancy. 'The moment the mother of the groom discovered that her new daughter-in-law was in love with the bridesmaid, and not her son?'

Owen gaped.

'Or should I go back to Philip's first wedding day? To me! The day I lost his baby, then gave him up because I was told I wasn't good enough for him and I couldn't bear the thought that he would one day look at me and hate me, even though I loved him more than life itself!'

Now Owen grimaced, his sympathetic heart squeezing tight. Oh, the poor darling…

'No, that sounds far too melodramatic,' Fiona swept on. 'Not to mention dead and gone. So I shall move on to Philip asking me to pretend to be Corinne last night, after Corinne and Carmel drove off together. Just to fool the guests, mind. He didn't want anyone to know that his bride preferred the bridesmaid to him. Which was understandable, I thought, and why I agreed. As well as to protect our wonderful business, of course!' she threw at Owen with a savage glance.

'Good thinking,' Owen praised, trying to make light in the face of whatever coming disaster Fiona was about to recount.

'Only *then* darling Philip wanted me to pretend to be Corinne in a more personal way, didn't he? And I—silly, weak fool that I am—couldn't say no. So we spent the night together and now I've fallen in love with him again, only this time he doesn't love me at all! He thinks I'm just good for sex and he can use me till he gets over his broken heart, or bruised ego, or whatever he's feeling at the moment. And what really kills me, Owen, what I just can't handle in the cold light of day, is that I'm going to *let* him!'

With that, Fiona's face crumpled and she burst into tears. Owen leapt to his feet and raced around to lead her over to the cosy two-seater which he kept for visiting brides and grooms. Fiona fell into it, still weeping. Owen perched on the coffee table in front of it and patted her knees.

'There, there,' he said soothingly. 'Cry it out. You can probably do with a good cry. You don't cry enough for a female. And when you're finished, I'm going to tell you how it *really* is.'

Fiona didn't quite take in Owen's words for a minute or two as she blubbered uncontrollably. But gradually his last remark *did* sink in and her tear-stained face slowly lifted. She took the spotted handkerchief Owen was holding out to her and wiped her nose, then frowned up at him.

'What do you mean? How it *really* is?'

'Why do you think I told Philip what I did?' He explained. 'Because he was showing signs of *real* feelings towards you. And I'm not talking about sexual feelings. I'm talking deep emotional involvement, here. Believe me, I've been around enough couples in love to see the signs.'

Fiona's whole insides tightened as she tried not to hope too much. 'You…you think Philip's in love with me?' she asked.

'Let's just say I think he's still emotionally involved with you.'

'Why didn't you *say* something?' she burst out.

'Hell, Fiona, why would I? I thought you felt Philip was as much an unwanted complication in your life as *I* did. The man was marrying someone else, for pity's sake. It wasn't my place to open my big bib and claim he hadn't gotten over you.'

'Are you sure about this, Owen? I mean…are you *sure* he still cares about me?' She didn't dare use the word 'love.' If she started believing Philip loved her, only to find out he didn't, she would surely go mad!

Owen took her hands in his. 'How can I be absolutely sure?' he said. 'He's never actually said anything to me. I'm going on instinct. But you're the one who spent the night with the man. If he loves you, there must have been some moments when he told you of that love. Maybe not in so many words, but in his actions.'

Fiona wished that had been the case. Oh, yes, he'd been tender a couple of times. Tender and gentle and complimentary. But he'd also been cynical and kinky, and even cruel at other times. Would a man in love deliberately get his beloved drunk, so he could have his wicked way with her?

'I don't think it's love he feels for me,' she said unhappily.

'Why don't you ask him?' Owen suggested.

Fiona's eyes blinked wide.

'And, while you're at it, why don't you tell him you love him? And then tell him the truth about why you left him all those years ago. I'll bet you never have.'

'I... I...'

'Time for the truth, dear friend,' Owen said firmly. 'You'll never have a better chance, or a better reason.'

The truth...

Yes, she realised, even while the thought of exposing her soul brought nausea to her throat. Owen was right.

It was time for the truth, the whole truth and nothing but the truth!

So help me God, she prayed.

CHAPTER SEVENTEEN

FIONA sat in her car by the side of the road outside the gates of Kathryn's house, and watched the toing and froing of trucks as the marquee and everything which had been shipped in for the wedding was removed.

She felt sick with nerves. And sick with hope.

If only Owen was right...

But even if he was, that didn't mean everything would turn out all right. Because Philip might not believe *her* about why she'd left him ten years ago, and about what she felt for him now. His opinion of her present-day character was awfully low.

Still, she *had* to try. Owen was right. She'd never have a better chance. If she left it, things would only get more complicated, and more confusing.

Gathering her courage, she turned on the engine, then drove in through the open gates and on up to the house. It was just on noon.

High Noon, she thought, her stomach churning.

The front door was wide open and a team of carpet cleaners were still busy, putting the living room carpets back in order after some inevitable spills and stains. Fiona had arranged for them to come in the morning after the wedding, as she'd arranged everything else.

She made her way through the house and finally found Kathryn and Philip sitting together at a table on the thankfully empty and restored back terrace. There were no workmen or cleaners hovering around to disturb or overhear what Fiona had to say.

Philip rose from his seat on seeing her, his expression surprised, whispering, 'You're early,' as he held out a seat for her.

Kathryn, who was looking tired, gave her a wan smile. 'I'm glad you're here, Fiona,' she said. 'I wanted to thank you for what you did for Philip last night.'

Fiona's eyes met Philip's wry ones.

No sign of love there, she thought unhappily.

'It saved everyone a lot of embarrassment,' Kathryn went on. 'You know, I still can't get over Corinne's abysmal behaviour. I have no problem with gay people, but what she did was quite wicked—pretending to love Philip and tricking him into marrying her just so she could have a legitimate child. I'm truly amazed you've taken it as well as you have, Philip.'

'Fiona made me realise I had a lucky escape,' he returned drily. 'I might not have found out till after it was too late.'

'I shudder to think about it!' his mother exclaimed.

'Speaking of finding out things,' Fiona began, before her courage failed her.

Philip flashed her a puzzled glance, but Fiona didn't look at him, knowing in her heart that it was now or never.

'I have something to say to you, Kathryn, which Philip knows about but which we've kept from you.'

'*Fiona,*' Philip warned sharply.

'No, Philip. I've decided I want your mother to know.'

'Know what?' Kathryn looked bewildered.

Fiona gave her a pleading smile. 'Please don't be

angry with me, Kathryn. I…I really didn't mean any harm. I can see now, however, that it was wrong of me not to tell you the truth up front, and I regret it sincerely.'

'The truth? What truth?'

'About my true identity.' Fiona swallowed, then plunged on. 'You see, ten years ago people didn't know me as Fiona Kirby. Back then I was called Noni Stillman.'

Kathryn gasped while Philip groaned.

'For pity's sake, Fiona,' he ground out. 'Did you have to blurt it out like that?'

She turned surprisingly steady eyes his way. 'There *was* no easy way, Philip. The truth, I'm beginning to understand, is never easy.'

Kathryn's colour gradually came back to normal and her eyes washed disbelievingly over Fiona. 'I would *never* have recognised you.'

'Yes, I know.'

'You've changed so much!'

'Yes, she has,' Philip bit out, and his mother twisted round to frown at her son.

'But *you* recognised her?'

'Of course,' he said drily.

'Yes,' she murmured, nodding. 'Yes, of course. Yes, I see.'

Her gaze swung back to Fiona, who was astonished to see the woman's eyes fill with tears. And something else.

'I *do* see,' Kathryn told her softly, and Fiona suddenly recognised what that 'something else' was.

Sympathy, and understanding.

Emotion crashed through Fiona. Kathryn *knew*. She didn't have to explain a word to her. Not a single word. Philip was the one who didn't see, or understand. He was blind to her reasons for doing this. He just sat there, his face tight with fury and frustration that Fiona had chosen to go over his head and tell his mother who she was.

'Happy now?' he snapped. 'Maybe you'd like to confess all, while you're at it. Maybe you'd like to tell my mother where we spent last night and what we did most of the night.'

When Fiona looked crushed, an amazingly unshocked Kathryn turned to her son again and just shook her head at him. 'Oh, Philip, don't,' she reproached. 'You don't know what you're doing to her.'

'What *I'm* doing to *her*?' He exploded onto his feet. 'What about what *she's* done to *me*? What she did ten years ago? What she's been doing ever since she showed up in my life again? I've been in hell, I tell you. She's the devil in disguise, pretending to be sweet and nice when all the while she takes men's souls and destroys them. Well, she's not going to destroy me a second time. This time it's *her* who's going to be destroyed. You liked last night, Fiona?' he jeered nastily. 'Well, savour the memories, honey, because it was our swansong. I won't be seeing you again. Or touching you again. *Ever!*'

Kathryn was gaping up at him while Fiona desperately tried to cling on to the slim hope that the hatred blazing down at her was not really hatred but the other side of love.

She rose shakily to her feet and looked him straight in the eye. 'But I love you, Philip,' she said bravely. 'And I loved you ten years ago.'

'You're a damned liar! You didn't love me ten years ago. You told me you didn't. And you *showed* me you didn't. You left me, without a backward glance. Was that the action of someone in love?'

'Yes!' Kathryn pronounced, and stood up as well.

Fiona stared at her. And so did Philip.

'Sit down, the pair of you!' she ordered.

Startled, they did.

Kathryn sat down last, leaning over briefly to pat Fiona's nearest arm before turning her attention to her son.

'I never said anything to you about this before, Philip, because I didn't see any point. On top of that, I didn't *know* anything of this till just before your father died. But the situation's changed now. Noni—I mean Fiona—has come back into your life and you *have* to know the truth about what happened that night ten years ago.'

Bewilderment held Fiona silent as Kathryn gave her a warmly apologetic glance.

'This sweet child didn't want to leave you. She loved you very, very much. But losing the baby had upset and depressed her a great deal, making her very susceptible to suggestion. When you were out of the house, your father took deliberate advantage of her emotional state to talk her into giving you up. For *your* sake, he insisted. And for her own, he pretended.'

'No, just *listen*!' Kathryn insisted when Philip went to open his mouth. 'He told her you were too immature to know your own mind, that you'd fancied yourself in love many times before and that it was a common flaw in young men to confuse sex and love. He told her that one day you'd wake up and realise you weren't in love with her, and then you'd hate her for trapping you into an unsuitable marriage. He played on her own vulnerability and insecurities, making her think she wasn't good enough for you, that she'd drag you down and make you unhappy. And in this I bear a great amount of blame. I was very unkind in my criticism of you back then, Fiona. I didn't realise till after you'd long gone how mean and snobbish I was. I've always wanted the opportunity to say how sorry I am.'

'It's all right, Kathryn,' Fiona mumbled.

'No, it's *not* all right. What I did was very wrong. And what your father did, Philip, was very wrong too. And he knew it. It played on his conscience at the end, which is why he confessed his unhappy part in all this to me.'

'It didn't take him long to convince her, though, did it?' Philip said sharply. 'I was only gone half an hour.'

'You know what a clever talker he was. A brilliant negotiator. He could make black seem white once he got going. Still, he had a great weapon to use. Fiona's love for you. He made her believe she was doing the right thing, giving you up.'

'But *why*?' Philip cried, clearly anguished by this amazing revelation. 'Why would he do such a thing? He *knew* how much I loved her. He *knew*!'

'Oh, Philip, he was your father, and he wanted so much for you. *Too* much. He thought he was being cruel to be kind. He thought *he* was doing the right thing too.'

'The right thing!' Philip groaned. 'Oh, God, if only he'd known what he put me through.'

'He put Fiona through a lot as well, son,' Kathryn reminded him gently.

Fiona watched, dry-mouthed, as Philip's shocked eyes turned back to hers.

'Is this true, what my mother's saying?' he asked her. 'Is that the way it really happened?'

Fiona was in shock herself. She hadn't realised how devious Philip's father had been. She'd thought he was being kind and gentle with her that night, when all the while he'd…he'd…

Tears pricked her eyes as the reality of the man's perfidy struck home.

'Yes,' she choked out.

Philip's face struggled for composure. 'Why didn't you tell me all this when we met up again?'

'How could I when you were marrying someone else?'

'Yes, just nine years after *you* did,' he said accusingly.

Fiona dashed away the threatening tears and tried to remain strong. 'I should never have married Kevin. I admit it. I didn't love him. But I was lonely and he was nice to me. At the time I needed…someone… something. I was very wrong to marry him. As soon as I realised that I set him free, and then set about relying on myself alone in the future. I didn't want to hurt anyone else. And, yes, I didn't want to be hurt myself. I grew hard. I can see that now. Hard and tough. And I *did* hurt people. Men who liked me. Maybe some of them even loved me. I'm not proud of that. When we met up again, I truly believed I was over you. Fiona was nothing like Noni, I told myself. She didn't fall helplessly in love, certainly not with the same man.'

Fiona stiffened her spine for the ultimate confession. 'But I *have* fallen helplessly in love with you again, Philip, and there's nothing I can do about it. I'm yours…if you want me.'

He was speechless. But his eyes spoke volumes. Emotion melted their earlier hardness and love washed over her in warm, wonderful waves.

Kathryn cleared her throat and stood up. 'I think it's time I went to see about the carpet cleaners.'

'It…it never occurred to me that you might have given me up for love,' he said thickly.

'Believe me, I regretted it later.'

'I never forgot you,' he told her, and reached for her hands across the table.

She took them, and her heart almost burst with happiness. 'Nor I you.'

Their fingers entwined.

'I used to go into every fish and chip shop I saw, thinking you might be there, behind the counter.'

'I used to ring your phone number, just so I could hear your voice.'

'I hated thinking of you with someone else's child.'

'I would never have *had* anyone else's child. I only ever wanted yours, Philip,' she said, and squeezed his hands even more tightly.

'Will you try to have my child again, Fiona?'

'If you want me to.'

'If I want you to. My God, do you know how much I love you?'

Her smile was soft and warm. 'You can tell me if you like.'

His mouth twisted wryly. 'All I can think of are clichés, like how wide is the ocean, and how deep is the sea?'

Her smile widened. 'They'll do for now. I'll let you show me in person later.'

'You're a wicked woman.'

'If I am, then you're entirely responsible. Till I met

you, I didn't even *like* sex. I thought it was highly overrated and very icky.'

He smiled. 'I see you've gotten over your revulsion.'

'Philip,' she said, and he shot her a worried look. 'What?'

'I have only one thing to ask.'

'Anything.'

'Promise me you won't ask me to marry you?'

'Why ever not? I thought you loved me.'

'I do. But…we haven't been lucky with marriage and wedding days. Do you think we could leave marriage till after we've had a couple of babies?'

'You want to have children *first*?'

'Mmm, yes. Do you mind?'

'Not at all. When do you want to start?'

He smiled at her, and she smiled back.

'Do those wonderful smiles mean what I think they mean?' his mother said as she rejoined them at the table. 'Could we be planning another wedding soon?'

''Fraid not, Mother dearest. Fiona wants to make you a grandmother before she makes you a mother-in-law.'

Kathryn looked surprised, then smiled herself. 'Really?'

'I'm a little superstitious,' Fiona explained sheepishly. 'Philip's been married twice already, and disasters come in threes.'

Kathryn nodded. 'I understand perfectly. And a marriage certificate is unimportant, really, so long as you really, truly love each other.'

'We really, truly love each other,' Philip repeated, and stood up. 'Which is why we're leaving. I want to show my house to the future mother of my children.

You did say you would like to live in Balmoral, didn't you?'

'I certainly did!' Fiona jumped to her feet, hardly believing the joy she was feeling.

'Bye, Kathryn.'

'Bye, Fiona, dear. Bye, son. Drive carefully.'

'Does this mean you want me to live with you?' Fiona asked him as he ushered her through the house and out to his car.

'But of course! Don't you want to?'

Fiona reached up to kiss him on the cheek. 'I want to more than anything else in the world.'

'So that's a yes?'

'Yes.'

'Great. We can start moving your things in today. Do you rent or own?'

'I'm paying off a unit.'

'Then sell it.'

'No, I'll rent it out,' she said, and he scowled.

'It's a good investment, Philip,' she insisted, then smiled. 'And a good place to stay if you ever get sick of me.'

'I'll never get sick of you.'

'You might. You don't know the new me all that well.'

'I *love* the new you.'

'Do you, now? Well, might I point out that the new me came here in her own car and she's going to drive it back?'

Again he scowled, and she felt a moment's worry.

'Philip…I'm not Noni any more. I have a career, and a mind of my own. And I won't be giving either up.'

'And you think I want that?'

'I don't know. Maybe.'

'I want *you*, Fiona. The you you are today.'

'Are you sure you don't mean the me I was last night?'

His smile was rueful. 'Her, too,' he said, and swept her into his arms. His kiss was long and hungry, yet at the same time tender and loving.

'I love you, Fiona Kirby,' he insisted afterwards as he held her close. 'I love your spirit of independence and your strength of character. I love your ambition and your commitment to perfection. I love your sophisticated beauty and your not-too-skinny body. And, yes, I admit it, I love the way you make love. But sex is only a part of what I feel for you. You must believe that.'

'Yes, Philip,' she agreed, her heart overflowing with love for him.

'God, when you say yes to me like that I just dissolve inside. Practise saying yes just like that, even when you don't mean it.'

'Yes, Philip,' she repeated huskily, and stretched up to kiss him on the mouth.

'Not *now*,' he protested. 'Later!'

'Yes, Philip.'

She said it later. A lot. And she finally said it five years later, to the question Philip had been asking her since their first child had been born.

Four-year-old Zachary and two-year-old Rebecca attended their parents' simple wedding ceremony on Balmoral Beach, their high spirits kept in line by their grandmother. Steve and his pretty new wife, Linda, were the two official witnesses.

Owen stood on the sidelines, trying not to complain

too much at the missed opportunity for Five-Star Weddings to shine once more at a Forsythe wedding.

'But she looks so beautiful in white,' he grumbled to Kathryn next to him. 'I wonder where she found that delicious dress. Do you know, I've never seen Fiona wear white before, let alone white chiffon.'

'I chose it for her,' Kathryn said, with a strange little smile.

'Really? Then you have excellent taste for bridal wear. You wouldn't be looking for a job, would you, Mrs Forsythe?'

Kathryn laughed. 'I have my work cut out for me looking after these little darlings two days a week, don't you think?'

'They're a handful, all right. But what can you expect with Philip and Fiona as parents? Talk about strong-willed! But they're a great match, aren't they?'

'Indeed they are. Shush, now, Owen, the big moment has arrived.'

The celebrant cleared his throat. 'Do you, Philip, take Fiona as your lawfully wedded wife, to love and to cherish, for richer for poorer, in sickness and in health, for as long as you both shall live?'

'I do,' Philip said strongly, and smiled warmly over at Fiona.

Fiona tried to smile back, but couldn't. She'd put this moment off for years. Not because she hadn't wanted to marry Philip, but because she'd been afraid, she supposed. Afraid of wedding days and wearing white and…and…

'And do you, Fiona,' the celebrant said firmly, 'take Philip as your lawfully wedded husband, for richer for poorer, in sickness and in health, for as long as you both shall live?'

She hesitated as the simple but beautiful vow sank in. Suddenly she realised what a coward she'd been, saying no to Philip's proposals all these years, being afraid to stand up and tell the world how much she loved this man, how she would love him till the end of her days.

What on earth was she afraid of? At thirty-three, she wasn't superstitious any more. She didn't believe in luck, or fate. She believed in forging one's own destiny, in actively choosing rather than letting things happen, in working hard and keeping faith with one's dreams.

For heaven's sake, she *wanted* to be Philip's wife more than anything else in the world. She always had. What was she waiting for?

'I certainly do,' she said, her smile dazzling.

Philip's handsome face burst into a wide smile. Their eyes met and they both kept smiling at each other as the celebrant said the all-important words.

'I now pronounce you man and wife!'

Born and raised in Berkshire, **Liz Fielding** started writing at the age of twelve when she won a hymn-writing competition at her convent school. After a gap of more years than she is prepared to admit to, during which she worked as a secretary in Africa and the Middle East, got married and had two children, she was finally able to realise her ambition and turn to full-time writing in 1992.

She now lives with her husband, John, in West Wales, surrounded by mystical countryside and romantic, crumbling castles, content to leave the travelling to her grown-up children and keeping in touch with the rest of the world via the Internet.

Don't miss Liz Fielding's brand-new novel:
THE BILLIONAIRE TAKES A BRIDE
On sale September, in Tender Romance™!

THE BEST MAN AND THE BRIDESMAID
by
Liz Fielding

CHAPTER ONE

WEDNESDAY, 22 March. Dress fitting. Me, in frills, as a bridesmaid. It's my worst nightmare come true. The self-assertiveness course was a complete waste of time; it was utterly impossible to be assertive in the face of Ginny's sweet pleading. Lunch with Robert first, though. The lovely (and very clever) Janine has dumped him and I am, as usual, the nearest shoulder available. Crocodile tears, of course…but interesting to see how he takes being on the receiving end of the boot for a change.

'Yellow velvet? What's wrong with yellow velvet?'

'Nothing. Probably.' In its place. Wherever that might be.

'If being a bridesmaid was high on my list of ambitions.' It came five hundred and twenty-seventh on hers: right after having her teeth extracted without anaesthetic. 'Nothing, if I enjoyed the idea of being fitted into a dress that will display all my shortcomings in the figure department.' She glanced down at her chest, which she suspected would be six inches short of the desired circumference. 'Or, in my case, not display them.' Robert's gaze had followed hers and he was regarding her lack of curves with a thoughtful expression. 'Nothing,' she added quickly, to distract him, 'if I relished the prospect of walking behind a girl who is going to be the prettiest bride this century, alongside a posse of her equally beautiful and raven-haired cousins, all of whom will look ravishing in yellow.'

Was she being petty?

Oh, yes.

'Maybe you'll look ravishing in yellow,' Robert offered. He didn't sound convinced. Well, he didn't have to. Just so long as he stopped talking about Janine. She'd heard quite enough about how wonderful Janine was. If she was that wonderful, he should have married the girl.

Her boyish chest clenched painfully at the thought.

'I'll look like a duck,' she said, more to distract herself than because it mattered very much. It was Ginny's day and no one would be looking at her.

'Probably.' Robert, primed to offer at least a token contradiction, instead grinned broadly. Well, that was why he'd asked her to lunch, to cheer him up.

The best man had it so easy, she thought irritably. Robert would be in morning dress and the biggest decision he'd have to make was whether to wear a grey morning coat or a black one. Or maybe not. Ginny's mother was stage-managing this wedding like the director of some Hollywood epic, and everything was being colour co-ordinated down to the last button, so it was unlikely he'd even have to worry about that.

No. All Robert would have to do was make sure her brother arrived in time for the wedding, produce the rings at the appropriate moment and make a short but witty speech at the reception. She'd seen it all before. Robert was very good at weddings... particularly at ensuring they weren't his own.

He'd arrange a stupendous stag night for Michael and still deliver him immaculately dressed and sober as a judge at the church in plenty of time for the wedding. He'd produce the rings dead on cue, make the wedding guests chuckle appreciatively with his wit and probably have the prettiest bridesmaid for breakfast.

By the time they'd left the church every female heart would be aflutter and the eyelashes would be following suit. Well, not the bride's eyelashes, perhaps. And the bride's mother could be forgiven for being distracted. But the bride's sister, the bride's cousins, the bride's aunts...

Not that Robert needed morning dress for that. Women fell for him wherever he went, whatever he was wearing. Beautiful women. Sophisticated women. Sexy women. And he didn't have to do a damned thing except smile.

Bridesmaids, on the other hand, were at the whim of the bride's mother. She sighed. Frills. Ribbons. Velvet. That was bad enough. But why on earth did Ginny's mother have to choose *yellow* velvet? You'd have thought filling the church with daffodils would be enough yellow for anyone... 'You aren't supposed to agree with me, you know,' she scolded. 'I went to great lengths to avoid being a bridesmaid. I made Ginny swear that no matter what my mother did or said, she wouldn't make me follow her up the aisle.'

'The best-laid plans...'

'The best-laid plans be blowed. I can't believe

Ginny's mother permitted such a vital member of her cast to go skiing so close to the wedding.'

'I don't suppose anyone told her about it or she'd have done her best.' He smiled. 'Poor Daisy.' She would do almost anything to have Robert smile at her like that. Even suffer the indignity of yellow velvet. He leaned forward and gently ruffled the springy mop of curls fighting their way out of the confines of an elastic band. 'And actually, you're quite wrong about looking like a duck. Ducks waddle, you don't.' As compliments went, it wouldn't ring a fairground bell, but still Daisy had to work hard to stem a flush of pleasure. 'Definitely not a duck.'

'Really?' The flush materialised; she just couldn't help it.

He grinned. 'No. You're thinking of ducklings.'

Well, that would teach her to be vain. 'Exactly,' she said. '*Fluffy* and yellow.'

'Fluffy and yellow and—'

'Don't even think the word *cute*, Robert.'

'I wouldn't dream of it,' he said, but his eyes betrayed him. Warm, toffee-brown eyes that were quite definitely laughing at her. 'Your nose is too big for cute.'

'Thanks.'

'And your mouth.'

'Okay, I get the picture. I'd crack a mirror at twenty paces—'

'Thirty,' he amended kindly. 'Honestly, I don't know why you're making such a fuss. You'll look sweet.'

Aaargh! 'I'm not cut out for velvet and tulle,' she said tersely. Beautifully tailored suits, severely cut coat dresses and sleek silk shirts were more her style; they flattered her wide shoulders and disguised her lack of curves. 'I certainly don't want to stuff my feet into a pair of satin Mary Janes and have rosebuds entwined in my hair. I'll look about six years old.'

'What are Mary Janes?'

'Those little-girl shoes with the strap over the in-step. Why grown women wear them beats me; I hated them even when I *was* a little girl.'

'Oh, I see.' She waited, knowing there was more. 'I have to agree, six does sound about right.'

'Robert!' Well, a girl could only take so much.

He caught her hand, held it, and Daisy decided that he could insult her all day if he just kept doing that. 'Heavens, you're trembling. I've never seen you in such a state.' The trembling had nothing whatever to do with being a bridesmaid, but hey... 'This isn't compulsory, sweetheart. Just tell Ginny that you can't do it.' As if. 'She can manage with three little maids, can't she?'

Of course she could. But this wasn't about managing. This was about having the perfect wedding, and Daisy couldn't, wouldn't let her future sister-in-law down. And there just wasn't anyone else. She'd asked.

Robert, of course, could not be expected to understand. All his life people had been falling over themselves to let him do whatever he wanted. Most men with his advantages would be absolute monsters, she knew. That apart from being the most desirable man she was ever likely to meet he was also good-natured and generous and legions of his abandoned girl-friends would declare with their dying breath that he was the kindest man in the world was little short of a miracle.

'Of course my mother is over the moon,' she said. 'She didn't expect to get a second chance.'

Robert squeezed her hand sympathetically. 'If your mother wants you to be a bridesmaid, sweetheart, you might as well surrender gracefully.'

If? That was the understatement of the year. Her mother had an agenda all her own. With one daughter married and doing her duty in the grandchildren department, and with her son about to follow suit, Margaret Galbraith already had her sights firmly fixed on her difficult youngest child. Twenty-four and not an eligible suitor in sight.

Phase one of her mother's plan involved getting Daisy to change her image. She was thinking *feminine*, she was thinking *pretty*. She'd already spent weeks trying to involve her in a clothes-buying sortie to take advantage of a large and fancy wedding at which there would undoubtedly be a number of eligible males. Now one of the raven-haired bridesmaids had thoughtfully broken her leg, showing off on the *piste*, and with Daisy the only possible replacement, her mother was in seventh heaven. There was absolutely no chance of escape.

Phases two and three would undoubtedly involve a major make-up job and the services of a hairdresser with orders to get her fluffy yellow hair under control for once. Daisy sincerely pitied the poor soul who was confronted by that hopeless task.

She looked at Robert's hand, covering her own. He had beautiful hands, with long, slender fingers; a jagged scar along the knuckles only enhanced their strength. He'd got that scar saving her from a vicious dog when she was six years old; she'd loved him even then.

For a moment she allowed herself the simple pleasure of his touch. Just for a moment. Then she withdrew her hand, picked up her glass and swirled the remaining inch of wine about the bowl. 'Mother thinks I'm being silly, that I'm being ridiculously self-conscious,' she admitted. 'She thinks being centre-stage will be good for me.'

He was still smiling, but with sufficient sympathy to put him back in her good books. 'I'm truly sorry for you, Daisy, but I'm afraid you're just going to have to grin and bear it.'

'Would you?'

'Anything for a quiet life,' he assured her. 'But I'll wear a yellow waistcoat to demonstrate solidarity,' he offered, 'if that'll make you feel better.'

'A yellow velvet waistcoat?' she demanded.

'If that's what it takes.' Easy to say. They both knew that unless it was part of the plan, Ginny's mother would veto it. 'Or you could dye your hair black to match the other girls,' he offered. 'Although whether a black duckling would have quite the same appeal—'

'You're not taking this seriously.' But then, when did he ever take anything seriously? He might be a touch aggrieved because his latest girlfriend had worked out that he had a terminal aversion to commitment and cut her losses a full week before he'd made the decision for her, but since he would be beseiged by women eager to take her place, it wouldn't worry him for long.

Daisy sipped her wine in a silent toast to the woman; so few of Robert's conquests were that clever.

'Or you could wear a wig,' he suggested, after a moment.

She told him, in no uncertain terms, where he could stick his wig.

That made him laugh out loud. Well, she had intended it to. 'Don't get your feathers in a tangle, duckie,' he said, teasing her. 'You're getting the whole thing out of proportion. I mean, who'll notice? All eyes will be on the bride. Won't they?'

For a man reputedly capable of charming a girl out of her knickers without lifting more than an eyebrow, Daisy considered that was less than gallant. But then he had always treated her like a younger sister, and what man ever felt the need to be gallant to a sister? Her own brother never had, so why would his best friend be any different? Especially since she went out of her way to keep the relationship on that level. No flirting. No sharp suits or silk shirts when she was meeting him for lunch.

She might love him to the very depths of her soul, but that was a secret shared only with her diary. Robert Furneval wasn't a till-death-us-do-part kind of man, and when you really loved someone nothing less would do.

She downed her claret and stood up. Leaving him on the right note was always difficult; she had to take any chance that offered itself. 'Next time you need a shoulder to cry on, Robert Furneval,' she said, 'try the *Yellow Pages*. Since you're so fond of the colour.'

'Oh, come on, Daisy,' he said, picking up her boxy little beaded handbag from beneath the table and rising to his feet. 'You're the one female I know I can rely on to be sensible.' She might have been placated by that. But then he spoilt it by handing her the bag and saying, 'Except for a tendency to raid your grandmother's wardrobe for dressing up clothes.' She didn't bother to correct him. Her sister had bought her the little Lulu Guinness bag for her birthday, probably egged on by their mother to improve her image. Her image was clearly beyond redemption. 'Don't go all girly on me about some stupid bridesmaid's dress. It's not as if you'll have to show your legs.'

'What have you heard about my legs?' she demanded.

'Nothing. I just happen to remember that you have knobbly knees. I assume that's why you make such a point of keeping them covered up. Trousers, jeans, long skirts…' He smiled down at her with that little-boy smile. His smile did for her every time. Oh, not the knickers. She would never be that stupid. But it still melted every resolve she had ever made in the solitude of her room, still reduced to mush every heart-felt promise she'd made to herself that she would break herself of the Robert Furneval habit. 'You wouldn't want me to lie and say that you'll look fabulous in yellow? Would you?' It might be nice, she thought. Just once. But they had never lied to one another. 'We're friends. Friends don't have to pretend.'

Yes, they were friends. She clung to that thought. Robert might not woo her with roses, might not take her to expensive little restaurants and ply her with smoked salmon and truffles, but he didn't dump her after a couple of months either. They were true friends. Best friends. And she knew, she had always known, that if she wanted to be a permanent part of Robert's life, that was the way it would have to stay.

And she was part of his life. He told her everything. She knew things about Robert that she suspected even her brother didn't know. She had cultivated the habit of listening, and she was always there for him between lovers...to meet for lunch, or as a date to take to parties. Just so long as she never fooled herself into hoping that they would be leaving the party together.

Not that he ever abandoned her. He always made sure that someone reliable was detailed to take her home. Reliable and boring and dull. Then he teased her for weeks afterwards about her new 'boyfriend'.

'Do they?' he persisted.

'What?' She realised he was frowning. 'Oh, pretend? No,' she said quickly, with a reassuring smile. 'I wouldn't ever want you to do that.' She glanced at her watch. 'But now I have to go and submit to the indignity of having the dress taken in.'

'Taken in?'

'The dresses are empire line.' She spread her hands wide and tucked them beneath her inadequate bosom. 'You know, straight out of *Pride and Prejudice*. All the other girls have the appropriate cleavage to show them to advantage.'

'Wear one of those lift 'em up and push 'em together bras,' he suggested.

'You have to have something to lift and push.'

He didn't argue about that, but rubbed his hand absently down the sleeve of her jacket. 'Don't worry about it, Daisy. Everything will be fine. And the wedding will be fun, you'll see.'

She gave him the benefit of a wry smile. 'For you maybe. Best man gets the pick of the bridesmaids, doesn't he?'

He gazed down at her. 'I've never been able to fool you, have I?'

'Never,' she agreed.

'Better cut along to this fitting, then, so that you can give me the low-down on Saturday.'

'Saturday?'

'There's a party at Monty's. I'll pick you up at eight and we'll have dinner first.'

It never seemed to occur to him that she might have something else planned, and for just a moment it was on the tip of her tongue to tell him that she was busy on Saturday night. There was only one problem with that. In all her life, since she was old enough to toddle after her brother and his best friend, she had never been too busy for Robert. 'Make it nine-thirty,' she said, forcing herself to be a little difficult. Just to prove to herself that she could be.

'Nine-thirty?' His dark brows twitched together in gratifying surprise.

'Actually ten o'clock would be better,' she said. 'I'll have to give dinner a miss, I'm afraid.'

'Oh? Are you sure you can manage the party?' The edge in his voice gave Daisy rather more satisfaction than was quite kind. After all, she'd chosen the path she was treading. 'You haven't gone and got yourself a boyfriend, have you? You're my girl, you know.'

'No, I'm not,' she said, putting on her sweetest smile. 'I'm your friend. Big difference.' His girls lasted two, three months tops, before they started hearing wedding bells and he, with every appearance of reluctance, let them go. 'But I was going to Monty's bash anyway and I'll be glad of the lift.' Just occasionally he needed to be reminded that she wasn't simply there at his beck and call. Just occasionally she needed to remind herself, even if it did mean passing on dinner at some fashionable restaurant and dining alone on a sandwich.

Then, having made a stand, having started a tiny ripple in his smoothly ordered world, she held up her cheek to be kissed, punishing herself with the brief excitement of his lips brushing her cheek, the scrape of his midday beard against her skin that did things to her insides that would rate an X-certificate.

It would be so easy to prolong the hug, just as it would have been easy to indulge herself and stretch out lunch over coffee and dessert. But Daisy's little-sister act had its limitations; too much close contact and she'd be climbing the office walls all afternoon.

Besides, keeping him at a distance was probably the only reason he didn't get bored with her.

'Thanks for lunch, Robert. I'll see you on Saturday,' she said briskly, making for the restaurant door and not looking back once. It had been harder today. Much harder. Today he was unattached, momentarily vulnerable in a way she hadn't seen before. Maybe that was why she had made such a fuss about the bridesmaid dress. Not to amuse Robert, but to distract herself.

It would have been far too easy to forget all about

the fitting, to suggest he walk her across the park, linking her arm through his, inviting him up to her flat with the excuse that she wanted to show him her new computer, plying him with coffee and brandy.

The trouble was she knew Robert too well. All his little weaknesses. Today, dumped by a girl with the wit to see through him, with his self-esteem needing a stroke, he might have been tempted to see what Daisy Galbraith was really made of beneath the trousers, the long skirts, the carefully neutral, sexless clothes she wore whenever she met him.

The trouble with that inviting scenario was tomorrow. Or perhaps next week. Or maybe it would be a month or two before someone else, someone elegant and beautiful, someone more his style, caught his roving eye. And after that nothing. No more precious lunches. No more of those early Sunday mornings at home when he dropped by with his rods to suggest they might go fishing, or take the dogs for a run. No more anything but awkwardness when they met by chance.

Worse, she would have to pretend she didn't care, because her brother would never forgive his best friend for breaking his little sister's heart.

While a treacherous part of her mind sometimes suggested that an affair with Robert might be all it took to cure her of his fatal attraction, Daisy had no difficulty in ignoring it. She might be foolish, but she wasn't stupid. She'd been in love with him since she had gazed from her high chair at this seven-year-old god who had come home with her brother for tea. The very last thing on earth she wanted was to be cured.

*   *   *

'More coffee, sir?' Robert shook his head, retrieving his credit card from the plate and, on an impulse, heading quickly for the door, hoping to catch Daisy so that they could walk across the park together. She always walked, but then she always wore good sensible shoes, or, like today, well-fitted laced ankle-boots, even in London. She was so easy to be with. Always had been, even when she was a knobbly kneed kid trailing after him and Michael.

Then he frowned. Yellow? What was wrong with yellow? What was wrong with 'cute'? What was wrong with ducklings, come to that?

From the pavement outside the restaurant he could see her bright froth of hair bobbing along in the distance as she strode across the park, and he realised that he'd left it too late to catch her. Oh, well. He'd see her on Saturday. And as he hailed a cruising cab, he frowned. Ten o'clock? What on earth could she be doing until ten o'clock?

Being stripped to her underwear, with her reflection coming back at her from a terrifying array of mirrors, was doing nothing for Daisy's self-confidence, and she was almost grateful for the covering of yellow velvet despite the fact that it emphasised her own lack of curves.

The seamstress attacked the spare material with a mouthful of pins, tucking it back to fit Daisy's less generous curves. Once satisfied, she nodded. 'All done. Can you come back early next week?'

'I couldn't bribe you to spill something indelible on it, could I? A pot of coffee? A squirt of ink?'

'What's the matter? Don't you like it?' The woman seemed surprised.

'With my colouring? Yellow would not be my first choice.'

'Well, there's a first time for everything.'

'Yes. And a last.'

'It's just different, that's all. With the right make-up you'll make a really pretty bridesmaid.'

Oh, Lord, that, if anything, was worse. Prettiness was her mother's fantasy; she had known better than to attempt it. She certainly didn't want to look as if she were competing with the other bridesmaids.

'Daisy!' Ginny burst through the door with the rest of her adult attendants in tow. Dark, glossy and gorgeous to a girl. Robert was going to have a ball, she thought with that detached part of her brain that dealt with everything Robert did when he was not with her. It was just so much easier when she wasn't part of the show. 'You're early!'

'No, darling, you're late.'

'Are we? Oh, Lord, so we are. We've been having facials,' she giggled. 'You should have come.'

There was more than one way to take that remark, Daisy decided, but was sure that Ginny hadn't meant it unkindly. Ginny didn't have an unkind bone in her body and, while her figure might leave something to be desired, Daisy knew there was nothing wrong with her skin. There was, unfortunately, precious little that a facial could do about an over-large nose or mouth.

She arrived back at her office, breathless and feeling just a bit low. 'Ah, Daisy, there you are.'

Yes, here she was. And here she'd probably be for

the rest of her days; Robert's best friend and stand-by date. She pulled herself together; feeling sorry for herself wasn't going to help. 'I'm sorry, George, I did warn you I might be late.'

'Did you?' George Latimer was nearing seventy, and while few could challenge his knowledge of oriental artefacts, his short-term memory was not quite what it might be.

'I had to be pinned into the bridesmaid dress,' she reminded him.

'Ah, yes. And you had lunch with Robert Furneval,' he added thoughtfully. In the act of hanging up her jacket, Daisy turned. She'd said she was lunching with a friend; she hadn't mentioned Robert. 'Your clothes give you away, my dear.'

'Do they?'

'You're covered from neck to ankle in the most unattractive brown tailoring. Tell me, are you afraid that he'll get carried away and seduce you in the restaurant if you wear something even moderately appealing when you meet him? I only ask because I get the impression that most young women would enjoy the experience.'

Her feigned surprise had not fooled him for a minute. His short-term memory might be a touch unreliable, but there was nothing wrong with his eyesight. And noticing things was what made him so good at what he did.

'I didn't realise you knew Robert,' she said, avoiding his question.

'We've met in passing. I know his mother. Charming woman. She's something of an authority on netsuke, as I'm sure you know. When she heard

I was looking for an assistant she called me and suggested I take you on.'

Daisy sat down rather quickly. 'I had no idea.' Jennifer Furneval had always been kind to her, taking pity on the skinny teenager who had hung around hoping to be noticed by her son. Not that she'd so much as hinted that she knew the reason why Daisy had developed such a fervent interest in her collection of oriental treasures. On the contrary, she had loaned her books that had been a blissful excuse to return to the house, to hang around, ask questions. And she had eventually pointed her in the direction of a Fine Arts degree.

Of course, she'd stopped hanging around for a glimpse of Robert long before then. She stopped doing that the day she'd seen him kissing Lorraine Summers.

She'd been sixteen, all knees and elbows, an awkward teenager whose curves had refused to develop and with an unruly mop of hair that had repulsed every attempt to straighten it—assaults with her mother's curling tongs leaving her with nothing but frizz and the scent of singed hair to show for her efforts.

Her friends had all been developing into embryonic beauties, young swans while she'd seemed to have got stuck in the cygnet phase. The archetypal ugly duckling. But she hadn't minded too much, because while the swans had made eyes at Robert they'd been far too young to win more than an indulgent smile. Daisy, on the other hand, had kept her eyes to herself, and had never asked for more than to sit and watch him fishing.

Her reward, one blissful summer when Michael had been away on a foreign exchange visit, had been to have Robert give her an old rod and teach her how to use it.

That, and the Christmas kiss he'd given her beneath the mistletoe. It was the best present she'd had that year. The glow of it had lasted until June, when she'd seen him kissing Lorraine Summers and realised there was a lot more to kissing than she'd imagined.

Lorraine had definitely been a swan. Elegant curves, smooth fair hair and with all the poise that a year being 'finished' in France could bestow on a girl. Robert had just come up from Oxford, a first-class honours degree in his pocket, and she had gone racing around there to just say hello. Congratulations. Will you be going fishing on Sunday? But Lorraine, with her designer jeans and painted nails and lipstick, had got there first.

After that she had only gone to see Jennifer Furneval when she'd been sure that Robert was not there.

He had still dropped by, though, when he'd been home. Her brother had been in the States, doing a business course, but Robert had still called in early on a Sunday morning with his mother's dog, or with his rods. Well, he'd always been able to rely upon Daisy to put up some decent sandwiches and bring a flask of fresh coffee, and maybe Lorraine, and the succession of girls who had followed her through the years, hadn't cared to rise at dawn on a Sunday morning for the doubtful honour of getting their feet wet.

'She worries about him, I think,' George Latimer continued, after a moment's reflection.

Daisy dragged herself back from the simple plea-sure of a mist-trailed early-morning riverbank to the exotic *Chinoiserie* of the Latimer Gallery. 'About Robert? Why? He's successful by any standards.'

'I suppose he is. Financially. But, like any mother, she'd like to see him settle down, get married, raise a family.'

'Then she's in for a long wait. Robert has the per-fect bachelor existence. A flat in London, an Aston Martin in the garage and any girl he cares to raise an eyebrow at to keep him warm at night. He isn't about to relinquish that for a house in the suburbs, a station wagon and sleepness nights.' Not sleepless nights caused by a colicky baby, anyway.

He didn't argue. 'So that's why you dress down when you have lunch with him?'

Yes, well, she knew George Latimer was sharp. 'We're friends, George. Good friends, and that's the way I plan to keep it. I don't want him to confuse me with one of his girls.'

'I see.'

Daisy wasn't entirely comfortable with the thoughtful manner in which George Latimer was re-garding her, so she made a move in the direction of her office, signalling an end to the conversation. 'Shall I organise some tea? Then we can go through that catalogue,' she said, indicating the glossy cata-logue for a large country house sale that he was hold-ing, hoping to divert him. 'I imagine that was why you were looking for me?'

He glanced down at it as if he couldn't quite remember where it had come from. 'Oh, yes! There's a fine collection of ceramics up for auction. I'd like you to go to the viewing on Tuesday and check them out.' She felt a rush of pleasure at this token of his trust. 'You know what to look out for. But, since you'll be representing the gallery, I'd be grateful if you'd avoid Robert Furneval while you're there.' He peered over his half-moon spectacles at her. 'Wear that dark red suit, the one with the short skirt,' he elaborated, in case she was in any doubt which one he meant. 'I like that.'

'I didn't realise you took such an interest in what I wear, George.'

'I'm a man. And I like beautiful things. Have you got any very high-heeled shoes to go with it?' he continued before she could do more than retrieve her jaw from the Chinese rug that lay in front of her desk. 'They'd do a fine job of distracting the opposition.'

'I'm shocked, George,' she said. 'That's the most sexist thing I've ever heard.' Then, 'Actually, I've seen a pair of Jimmy Choo's that I would kill for. Can I charge them to expenses?'

The lenses gleamed back at her. 'Only if you promise to wear them next time Robert Furneval asks you to lunch.'

'Oh, well. It'll just have to be the plain low-heeled courts I bought for comfort, then. Pity.'

CHAPTER TWO

SATURDAY 25 March. I've bought the shoes. Wickedly sexy, wickedly expensive, but I used the money Dad sent me for my birthday. Oh, the temptation to wear them to Monty's party tonight! I would if Robert wasn't going to be there. I wonder if anyone else notices that I dress differently around him? Michael, probably. But then I'm sure that Michael knows the truth and, since he's made no attempt to matchmake, understands why. I'll probably still be filling the 'girlfriend gap' when Robert's heading for his pension. And still be going home alone.

Daisy had plenty of time in which to contemplate her wardrobe and worry about what she should wear to the party. Plenty of time to call herself every kind of idiot, too.

She could have been dining in some exquisite little restaurant with Robert when, for pride's sake, she had chosen a lonely cottage cheese sandwich and the inanity of a Saturday-night game show on the television. The fact that it was the sensible option did not make it any more palatable.

This was no way to run a life. She switched off the television, abandoned the half-eaten sandwich and confronted her wardrobe. Just because she knew better than to join in the queue for Robert's attention, it didn't mean she shouldn't make the effort to get into some sort of relationship, if only to allay her mother's for once unspoken but nevertheless obvious fears that her interests lay in another direction entirely.

She might not be able to compete with Robert's glamorous 'girls', but her lack of curves didn't appear to totally discourage the opposite sex. Most of the young gallants that Robert had deputised to escort her home from other parties had at least made a token pass at her. One or two had tried a great deal harder. Asking her out, phoning her until she'd had to be quite firm…

Oh, no! He couldn't! He wouldn't! Would he? She flushed with mortification to think that Robert might have encouraged them to be, well, *nice* to her.

Could it be that his only motive in taking her along to parties was to try and match her up with some eligible young male? Was it possible that her mother had asked him to? With a sinking feeling she acknowledged that it was exactly the sort of thing that her mother would do. She could just hear her saying, *Robert, there must be dozens of young men working at your bank. For goodness' sake try and fix Daisy up with someone before she's left on the shelf…*

She knew she should be grateful that her mother had never harboured ambitions for her in Robert's direction. Clearly he was far too glamorous, good-looking, too everything for the plainest member of the family.

She pulled out a pair of wide-legged grey silk trousers. She'd intended to match them with a simple black sweater which was elegant in a rather dull, don't-notice-me sort of way. If she could have been sure that Robert wouldn't be at the party, she would have worn something rather more exciting.

Maybe she should anyway?

After all, if Robert thought she was so unattractive that he pushed his reluctant juniors in her direction, what she wore wasn't going to make a blind bit of difference, was it?

Damn, damn, damn. Why did it have to be so complicated? She just wanted to be his friend. That was all. But you don't patronise friends…

She blinked at eyes that were suddenly stinging, but nothing could stop the tear from spilling down her face. She had tried so hard to be sensible, but she loved him so much. Not like the constant parade of the lovely women who moved through his life. She wasn't in the least bit impressed by the glamorous job in the City, his money, the fast cars, his good looks. She'd love him without any of the fancy trappings because she cared about *him*. She always had. Not because she wanted to. Because she couldn't help it.

She'd hoped that going away to university would have stopped all that. Really hoped that she would meet someone who would make her forget all about Robert. Maybe she hadn't looked hard enough. Maybe, deep down, she hadn't wanted to. But maybe it was time to put a stop to this stupid game she'd been playing. Walk away, before she did something really stupid.

After the wedding, she promised herself, drying her cheek with the heel of her hand.

She'd stop being available. Make herself busier. Take up knitting.

Oh, for heaven's sake! Now she was being pathetic. Well, she could put a stop to that right now. This minute. Tonight she wouldn't hang around waiting for Robert to remember to dance with her. Tonight she'd pick her own escort home, or at least leave with some dignity on her own.

She looked her reflection straight in the eye and promised herself that if she could sort herself out a date for the wedding, she'd do that, too. It would please her mother, if nothing else. She palmed her eyes, trying to cool them.

Then she blew her nose, stood up and headed for the shower, determined that there would be no dressing down tonight. None of that barely there make-up.

She painted her nails bright red, she sprayed on her scent with reckless abandon, and instead of squeezing her hair into a French plait in order to keep it under control she left it fluffy. It wasn't chic. It wasn't that sleek, glossy stuff that swung and caught the light and looked like a million dollars in the shampoo adverts. In fact all that could be said in its favour was that she did have a heck of a lot of it.

She'd tried cutting it short once, but it hadn't helped. She'd simply looked like a poodle after a less than successful encounter with the clippers. The only thing that had stopped her cutting it to within an inch of her scalp had been the sure and certain knowledge that what remained would curl even tighter, and shaving her head would just have been a temporary solution. Maybe that was the answer now, she thought, grinning as she flattened her curls against her skull with her hands. Not even dear, sweet, kind Ginny would put up with a skinhead as a bridesmaid. Would she?

A brisk ring at the doorbell put a stop to such nonsense. She checked her watch; it was still a quarter of an hour until ten o'clock. He was early, impatient with her delaying tactics, and that was unusual enough to make her smile as she pressed down the intercom.

'You're early.'

'Then I'll have a drink while I wait,' Robert's disembodied voice informed her.

She let him into the building and then opened her flat door before retreating to her bedroom to paint her lips as red as her nails. 'There's wine in the fridge,' she called from the bedroom, staring nervously at her reflection now that he had arrived, wondering if she'd gone a bit too far.

'Shall I pour a glass for you?'

'Mmm,' she said. She definitely needed a drink. Oh, well. In for a penny... She fitted a pair of exotic dangly silver earrings to her lobes and then stepped into the new shoes. They would be wasted, she decided. No one would see them. She stepped out of them again and, like the coward she was, put on a pair of low-heeled pumps.

Robert, tall, square-shouldered, with the fine, muscular elegance of a fencer and utterly gorgeous in pale suit and a dark green shirt, paused in the kitchen doorway as he saw her. Paused for a moment, taking in the wide silk pants, the tiny black and silver top that crossed low over her small breasts like a ballet dancer's practice sweater and tied behind her waist... and said nothing.

He thought she looked like a little girl who'd been caught playing with her mother's make-up, but was too polite to say so; Daisy could see it in his face and wanted to run howling back to the bathroom to scrub her face.

'Have you been somewhere special?' he asked finally, handing her a glass. For a moment she couldn't think what he meant. 'You couldn't make dinner,' he reminded her, eyes narrowed.

'Oh. Um…' She floundered for a moment. 'It was just a gallery thing.' Work. That was it, she decided, clutching at straws. Anything rather than have him think she'd done this to impress him.

'A viewing? I'd have come if I'd known. I'm looking for something for my mother's birthday.'

'Are you? What?' she asked, hoping to divert him further.

'When I see it, I'll know. So? Was it a viewing?' he persisted, refusing to be sidetracked.

'Um… No. Not exactly.' He raised one of his dark, beautifully expressive eyebrows and took a sip of wine without commenting, leaving Daisy with the uncomfortable feeling that he didn't quite believe her. But what else could she say? She refused to own up to staying in and watching television rather than have dinner with him. He wouldn't understand why and she certainly couldn't explain.

'You shouldn't let George Latimer work you so hard,' he said, after a silence that seemed unusually awkward.

'He doesn't,' she snapped back. 'I love my job.' Perhaps it was guilt at lying to him that made her so sharp. She certainly didn't feel capable of the usual easy banter that sustained their conversation. 'Shall we go?'

Robert Furneval reached the pavement and without thinking hailed a passing taxi. 'We could easily have walked,' Daisy said.

'If you've been working, you deserve to ride.' If? What on earth had made him say that? The feeling that she hadn't been quite honest with him? Daisy had looked so guilty when she'd told him that she'd been working late. Guilty and unusually glamorous. If George Latimer had been forty, thirty years younger even, he might have suspected there was something going on.

Ridiculous of course. But being busy until nine-thirty smacked of the kind of affair where the man needed to be home with his wife and children at a respectable time. He glanced across at her, and even in the dim light of the cab he could see that her eyes were very bright. And she'd flushed so guiltily. But Daisy would never have that kind of affair. Would she?

He thought he knew her, yet it occurred to him that he had no idea what she might do if tempted. What exactly did she do in the evenings when the shutters came down at the gallery?

She never talked about herself much. Or was it that he never asked? No, that wasn't right. He was good at relationships, knew how to talk to women… But he knew Daisy so well. Or thought he did. The girl sitting beside him in the taxi seemed more like a stranger.

He'd always thought of her as Michael's kid sister,

always there. Good natured, fun, a girl who didn't make a fuss about getting a bit muddy. But tonight her eyes were shining and her cheeks looked a touch hectic. It was a look that he knew and understood. On Daisy, it made him feel distinctly uncomfortable. Almost as if he had lifted aside a veil and seen something secret.

She turned and caught him looking at her, and for a moment he had a glimpse of something much deeper. Then she cocked a quirky eyebrow at him and grinned. 'What's up, Robert? Still missing the gorgeous Janine?' she teased.

He relaxed. She hadn't changed. He was the one who was tense. 'Hurt pride, nothing worse,' he admitted.

'You're getting slow. If you're not very careful one of these days you'll find yourself walking down the aisle and you won't be the one behind, flirting with the bridesmaid, you'll be the one in front, with the ring through your nose.'

'That's it, kick a man when he's down.'

'I'll give you half an hour before you're bouncing right back. Tell me, which terribly nice young man are you planning to send me home with tonight?'

'Who said I was planning to send you home with anyone?' he demanded.

'Because you always do. I sometimes think that you must keep a supply of clones handy, to be activated in emergencies.'

'Emergencies?'

She clutched her hands to her heart. 'You know... Fabulous redhead... Let's go on to a club... Duh!

What'll I do with Daisy…?' She grinned. 'That kind of emergency.'

'Oh, cruel! For that, miss, I shall take you home myself and—'

'And?'

And what? He might have teased her about boyfriends, but as far as he knew she'd never taken things further than goodnight-and-thank-you with any of the guys he'd deputised to take her home, some of whom had begged him for the privilege. Not that he was going to tell her that. She didn't deserve to be flattered. 'You won't get away with a polite handshake and goodnight with me. I'll expect coffee and a doorstep-sized bacon sandwich for my trouble.'

'How do you know they just get a polite handshake?' she asked archly. 'Do they report back to you?'

'Of course,' he lied. He didn't need to be told, their disappointment was self-evident. 'I want to know that you arrived home safely.'

She grinned. 'And it never occurred to you that they might not be telling the truth?'

'They wouldn't dare lie.'

'Is that right?' She was laughing at him. So that was all right. Wasn't it? 'One day, Robert, you'll come seriously unstuck. But if you can tear yourself away from the first gorgeous redhead who smiles at you, or the first blonde, or brunette, you can have all the coffee and bacon sarnies you can eat. But don't expect me to be holding my breath.'

'Actually, I'm saving myself for the lovely bridesmaids,' he said, mock seriously. 'You did say they were lovely, didn't you?'

'Stunning. I'll give you a run-down over supper. If you remember.'

'Cat,' he murmured, as the taxi slowed. He climbed out first, and by the time he had paid the driver Daisy was inside, the welcoming crowd parting to swallow her up in its warm embrace. She was, he knew, one of those girls everyone was glad to see. He was always glad to see her, too. He didn't see her often enough.

Someone put a drink in his hand, then he was grabbed by an acquaintance who wanted some free advice about an investment, and he had just been buttonholed by a girl who seemed to know him, but whose name he couldn't remember, when he saw Daisy chatting to a tall, fair-haired man he didn't know. A man who was looking at her in a way that suggested he had only one thing on his mind.

It was a look that aroused all kinds of ridiculous protective male urges in him. 'Excuse me,' he murmured to the blonde, abandoning her and the mental struggle for her name without a second thought.

The man was Australian, lean and suntanned and revoltingly good-looking, and Daisy was laughing at something he'd said. In fact she looked as if she was having a very good time. That irritated him. She was his date. 'Can I get you a drink, sweetheart?' he said, slipping his arm about her waist.

'No, thanks,' she replied, turning to look at him with some surprise. Justifiable surprise, since he rarely worried about her once they were at a party. After all she knew everyone. Almost everyone. 'Nick's looking after me. Have you met?' she asked.

'Nick, this is Robert Furneval. Robert, Nick Gregson.'

Robert gave the Australian the kind of look that suggested it was time to find someone else to talk to. For a moment he looked right back, then, getting no encouragement to stay from Daisy, he shrugged and disappeared into the crowd.

'What's the matter?' Daisy asked, turning to him. 'Didn't the blonde go for your usual chat-up line?' She raised her voice as someone turned up the music.

He got the impression Daisy wasn't very pleased with him. 'What chat-up line?' he demanded.

'I've no idea, but you must have one. You can't possibly think up something new to say to every girl you meet.'

'You're very touchy tonight, sweetheart. Is this my payoff for agreeing that you'll look like a duck at Michael and Ginny's wedding?'

'What?'

'For saying that you'll look like a duck...' Unhappily, "...you'll look like a duck..." coincided with one of those sudden drops in noise level that occasionally happens in a crowded room, and everyone turned to stare.

Daisy flushed. 'Well, thanks, Robert,' she said. 'I really needed that.' And she placed her glass in his hand and walked away.

Daisy was furious. She couldn't ever remember being angry with Robert before, and the sensation was rather like taking a deep breath over the bottle of smelling salts that her mother used as a reviver on particularly strenuous jaunts around stately homes. A dizzy blast that was a lot more intoxicating than the wine she had been drinking.

Maybe that was why, when her natural circulation of Monty's flat brought her back to the Australian with the sun-bed tan, she was rather more encouraging than she might have been. Especially since Robert was glowering at him rather than giving his full attention to a luscious brunette who quite evidently hadn't learned a thing from her predecessors' mistakes. But then maybe she didn't care about commitment. Robert was *very* good looking.

Nick jerked his head in Robert's direction. 'Are you and he…' He shrugged, leaving her to mentally fill in the gap with whatever relationship she thought appropriate.

She dragged her gaze back from Robert and gave Nick her full attention. 'Robert and me?' She managed a laugh. 'Heavens, no, we're just good friends. I've known him since I was in my cradle. He's more like a brother.'

'Is that right?' He grinned. Well, he did have an exceptional set of teeth, dazzlingly white against the tan. 'It must be brotherly concern, then. But since your good friend looks as if he'd like to put a knife in my back, maybe we should move on. Try a club, maybe?'

Why not? The brunette was clearly intent on getting her wicked way with Robert. Another five minutes and he'd have totally forgotten the bacon sandwich deal, if he hadn't already. Forgotten about her, in all probability until the next time he needed someone to stick a maggot on a hook, or fill in as a date at a dinner party. Well, that was the way she'd chosen to play it, and he did always come back to her for tea and sympathy. If she was careful, he always would.

In the meantime it was rather pleasurable having a good-looking man showing a more than passing interest.

As she looked up at him, it occurred to Daisy that Nick would impress the heck out of her mother. Well, why not? 'Do you have anything planned for two weeks today?' she asked.

Nick opened his mouth, closed it again, then said, 'Not that I can think of.' He flashed his teeth at her again, using them in much the same way as the brunette was using her eyelashes. It could get boring, she decided. 'What do you have in mind?'

'Nothing exciting. I wondered if you'd like to come to my brother's wedding, that's all.'

'Brother as in brother?' He glanced across at Robert. 'Or brother as in "good friend"?'

'My brother Michael is the one getting married. Robert is just the best man.'

'Then I'm sorry, because I'd love to have come. There's nothing I enjoy more than a good wedding. Unfortunately, I'll be in Perth.'

She considered the logistics of getting him from Scotland... Then the penny dropped. 'You mean Perth, Australia, don't you?'

He was grinning again. She was beginning to suspect he advertised toothpaste for a living. 'I'm afraid I do. But we could still have that date. Give your brother's wedding a miss and come with me. We could have a wedding of our own.' On the other hand there was nothing boring about a man who issued that kind of invitation. Eccentric, perhaps. Over-endowed with imagination, maybe. Drunk, even. Although he didn't sound drunk.

'Well, that's different. But I'm afraid I'll have to say no. I'm fourth bridesmaid, you see.' Although the fact that her mother would never speak to her again if she jetted off to the other side of the world with a complete stranger simply to avoid being fourth bridesmaid might be considered a positive reason for accepting his invitation.

Of course, if she ran away to get married she might just be forgiven. It would certainly put her out of reach of temptation where Robert was concerned. No comfortable backsliding into gap-filling if she was in Australia. Unfortunately, Nick and his teeth were part of the package.

'They won't miss one bridesmaid, will they?' he pressed, when she didn't immediately answer.

'I'm afraid they would. Three would look so un-tidy on the photographs. Besides, I make it a rule never to accept proposals of marriage from men I've only just met.'

He wasn't deterred. 'We've got three days before I leave. Plenty of time to get to know one another. Why don't we start with a dance?'

'Three whole days?' she repeated as he relieved her of her glass in a masterful manner and, taking her firmly about the waist, pulled her close. He was more heavily muscled than Robert. Undoubtedly the consequence of hours spent on a surfboard getting that improbable tan. 'You don't waste much time, do you?'

'Life's for living, not wasting.'

he had a point, but she laughed anyway. 'You're crazy.'

He looked hurt. 'Why? Because I want to get to know you really well? Suppose we were made for each other and you went to this wedding and I went back to Oz and we never found out?'

'That's a risk I'll just have to take,' she said, although she didn't think it was that big a risk. She had the strongest suspicion that he meant getting to 'know' her in the physical sense, rather than intellectually. In fact she suspected that the frank, open, big-hearted act was just that. An act. He was just looking for a girl to fill the gap between now and catching his plane, and he wasn't particularly fussy about which girl.

Okay, so she didn't object to filling Robert's little gaps. But she loved Robert. Well. Maybe not right at this moment. At this moment she felt like telling him that he was crazy, too. That life was a two-way street and that if he wasn't careful he'd end up old and lonely. Of course she'd just be wasting her breath. And who was she to tell him that he'd end up old and lonely, when it was far more likely that she'd be the one who was everyone's universal great-aunt rather than anyone's grandmother?

He'd probably still be pulling all the best-looking nurses when he was in his dotage, and she'd probably be the sap pushing his Bath chair.

'Wouldn't you like to find out?' Nick asked, as he came to halt in a corner.

She hadn't been paying too much attention to what he was saying, but this seemed to require an answer. She looked up. 'Find out what?'

Stupid question. The lights were dim, they were in one of those little out of the way corners, and he needed no further invitation to lower his mouth to hers and kiss her.

It was pleasant as kisses went. Nothing heavy. Just a testing-the-water kind of kiss, and Daisy pulled back before it got too serious, looking up at the big, bronzed hunk with just a touch of regret. Her mother would have really loved Nick.

'I'm sorry,' she said. 'I think I'd rather just leave it like this. With you wondering.' She already knew. Had known since her cradle that there was only one man in the world for her.

For a moment Nick looked puzzled. Then he laughed. 'I think I like you.'

'You see? Right decision. Will you excuse me?' She eased herself out of his arms, turned, only to be confronted by Robert.

'You haven't forgotten our deal, have you?' he said, glaring past her at Nick.

Deal? He was still planning on taking her home? 'Oh, for goodness' sake, Robert, go away and flirt with someone your own age,' she said crossly.

'Later. Let's dance.' He didn't wait for an answer, but slipped his arm about her waist. Not like Nick. There had been nothing subtle about the way Nick had held her. He'd held her close, leaving her in no doubt what he was thinking. Robert, of course, didn't see her that way. Usually by this time he'd forgotten all about her. Was he really so upset about Janine's desertion, or was the party lacking in the kind of girls that caught his fancy? 'I'd ask if you were having a good time, but the question would appear to be redundant.'

'It's been interesting,' she said, as they moved together in time to the music. Her cheek was against the peachy twill of his shirt and she could feel the slow thudding of his heartbeat. He didn't dance with her often enough for her to get used to it. Each time was special. The chance to touch him, hold him, feel the hard muscle and bone of his shoulder beneath her hand, breathe in the scent of him, warm and faintly musky. His arm tightened about her possessively and for a long blissful moment she allowed herself to drown in the pleasure of their closeness. Then, because breaking away was so very hard, she added, 'I've already had one proposal of marriage.'

It had the desired effect. He stopped, pulled back a little, his forehead creased in a frown. 'No, I mean really. You seem a bit edgy. Not quite your usual self. You would tell me…'

'What?'

There was a long pause before he said, 'Well, if things weren't…all right.'

'All right?' Of course things weren't all right. He wasn't supposed to take it for granted that she was joking about the proposal, for a start. Okay, so she was, but, really, he might try and play along. 'Well, I may have broken his heart,' she said, 'but I'm sure he'll recover.'

'What?' He frowned. 'What on earth are you talking about?'

'He lives in Australia, you see. If I went to Australia I couldn't be Ginny's bridesmaid. Could I?'

'Er, no, I suppose not.' He seemed bemused and

Daisy sighed. 'I'm fine, Robert.' She gave him a little push. 'Go. You've done your duty. I'm going to see if Monty needs a hand with the food.' She headed for the kitchen. Robert followed her, stopping in the doorway as their host greeted her with delight.

'Daisy, my darling! Just the girl,' he said, handing her an apron. 'The caterer left boxes and boxes of stuff but I haven't got a clue what to do with it.'

'Stuff that lot in the oven to heat up and put those on plates. Of course it would save time, effort and washing up if you just lined the boxes up on the table. I don't suppose anyone would notice.'

She saw Robert and Monty exchange a startled look, and without another word she tied the apron around her waist, but it occurred to her that she would be better occupied getting to know Nick Gregson, trying to forget about Robert, than acting as unpaid kitchen hand. Probably.

She shrugged and gave her attention to the task in hand, arranging a pile of little savoury tarts on one plate, heaping chicken goujons around a bowl of sauce on another. When she turned to put them on the table, Robert was still standing in the doorway.

It was disconcerting to be the focus of his attention. He didn't usually take so much notice of her, and she couldn't believe that the silver and black top she was wearing was so spectacular that he was unable to take his eyes off her.

'There's another apron if you want to help,' she said.

It had the desired effect. Robert helped himself to a pastry and deserted without another word.

A couple of hours later she'd had enough. She'd

passed around food, caught up with the gossip, danced rather more than usual. It was a lovely party, except that every time she turned around Robert seemed to be there, watching her. It was unsettling. She didn't want him looking at her. Not with that little crease that might just be concern dividing his brows. She'd thought she knew everything there was to know about the way his mind worked, but this was different.

Not that things had changed that much. He was still the focus of attention for every unattached girl at the party, and quite a few who weren't, and she had no expectation that, come the witching hour, he would still be looking for a cup of coffee and a bacon sandwich. But there was no way she was going to allow him to delegate the task of seeing her home to anyone else.

Taking advantage of a distraction caused by the still hopeful brunette, she retrieved her coat and considered looking for Monty, but decided instead to phone him later in the week. Nick cut her off before she reached the door.

'Hey! You weren't thinking of leaving without me, were you? We're almost engaged.'

Torn between irritation and a certain satisfaction that someone was capable of seeing more to her than a girl who could fill the gaps, or pass around the canapés, she found herself laughing. 'No, we're not.'

'You're playing very hard to get.' He made it sound as if she was the one being unreasonable.

'I'd hoped you realised I was playing impossible.'

'Nothing is impossible. Once, in Las Vegas, I married a woman I'd only just met.'

'Really?' Why didn't that surprise her? 'Only once?'

'Well—'

'And are you still married to her?'

'Of course not.' He looked hurt at the suggestion. 'I'm not a bigamist. That's the great thing about Las Vegas. Married today…' he clicked his fingers '…divorced tomorrow.'

'Just like that?'

'Well, very nearly.' She wasn't sure whether to believe him or not. On balance she was rather afraid he was telling the truth. 'Where would you like to get married? We could stop over somewhere exotic and have one of those beach ceremonies. I've always rather fancied one of those. What about Bali?'

It was a tough choice. Right now Bali sounded a lot more fun than yellow velvet, but it wasn't really any contest. The dress, after all, was just for a few hours whereas, unlike Nick, she viewed marriage as a lifetime commitment. 'I'm allergic to sand,' she said. 'And I'm scared of flying.'

'Are you?' That seemed to throw him momentarily. 'A shipboard wedding, then? The ship's captain doing the honours?'

'It's a myth that you can be legally married by the captain of a ship,' she told him. The joke was beginning to wear very thin. 'And right now all I'm interested in is going home. Alone.' She turned and walked out into the street.

He wasn't that easy to shake off. 'The streets aren't safe for a woman on her own,' he said, following her.

'Maybe not, but how safe are they with you?'

And this time when he smiled she fancied it was less a sexual display of teeth than genuine good humour. 'As safe as you want them to be. Scout's honour,' he promised.

Before she could tell him that she didn't believe he had ever been a Scout, he had hailed a passing black cab.

'Daisy!' *Robert.* 'There you are, sweetheart. I was looking for you. I'm just about ready for the coffee and sandwich you promised,' he said, taking her arm and smiling cordially at Nick as he opened the taxi door and held it for her while she stepped inside. 'Thanks for the taxi, Gregson. Black cabs are as rare as hen's teeth at this time of night.'

And with that he stepped in after her and closed the door, leaving Nick Gregson standing alone on the pavement as they drove away.

CHAPTER THREE

SUNDAY 26 March. Church with family for final reading of the Banns for Michael and Ginny's wedding and everyone home for lunch afterwards. Mother will be in her element.

Robert offered me a lift. I said I'd rather walk. I do hope he didn't take me seriously.

'Daisy?'

She knew it was him as soon as the doorbell rang. Even at the crack of dawn her heart gave one of those painful leaps that betrayed her every time.

She glanced at her watch, yawned, tightened the belt of her dressing gown about her waist. Why was it so much harder to get up in London than in the country? 'Go away, Robert. It's the middle of the night.'

'It's seven-thirty. Halfway through the day.'

'Is it?' She blinked at her watch. 'Oh, Lord, so it is. I thought it said twenty-five to six.'

'Perhaps you'd better get some spectacles.'

'I don't need spectacles; I need more sleep. Did you have to come this early?'

'No, but I was rather hoping you'd make me some breakfast. Since I didn't get the supper you promised.'

'You didn't deserve supper.'

'Maybe not. But then I never said I was perfect.'

No. He'd never said that. 'Pretty damn near, though.'
She could hear the smile in his voice and she rested
her forehead against the door. Yes. Pretty damn near.

'You don't deserve breakfast, either.'

'No? Who else would get up at the crack of dawn
to give an ungrateful brat a lift home?'

'You were going home anyway.' She released the
door catch. 'But I suppose you'd better come up,'
she said, and retreated to the kitchen to make coffee.
She heard him come in, knew the very moment he
came to a halt in the doorway behind her.

'You're not really angry with me.' It wasn't a
question. He said it with the confidence of a man who
knew he was irresistible. She didn't turn around, she
knew he would be smiling and of course his smile
would be totally irresistible.

It wasn't fair. But then who said life had to be
fair? If it was fair she'd have the same sleek hair as
her sister, the same lovely figure, or, failing that, at
least Michael's height. But her siblings had inherited
all the most attractive genes from both parents and
there hadn't been any left over for her.

'Of course I'm angry with you,' she replied, keeping her back firmly to him. 'Just because you've been
abandoned by man's best reason to stay in bed on a
Sunday morning, there's no need to wake me up at
the crack of dawn.'

'I meant about last night.'

'Last night?' She pretended to think. 'Oh, you
mean about Nick? Thanks for reminding me. For
once in my life I managed to bag the best-looking
man at the party...' he snorted derisively '...and you

chased him off in case you missed out on your supper.'

'I missed out anyway,' he pointed out.

She spun around. 'You didn't think I was going to feed you after that?'

'I was simply taking care of you. Did you know he's divorced? Gregson,' he added, in case she wasn't sure. 'Twice. Monty told me.'

'Monty's an old gossip.'

'He's the diary editor of a national newspaper. Gossip is what he does.'

Daisy shrugged. Twice? It figured. A man that quick with his proposals was bound to get caught out once in a while. 'You didn't think I'd be tempted to become wife number three, did you?'

'Well—'

The wretch sounded doubtful. 'Do you imagine I'd contemplate marrying a complete stranger on the spur of the moment? On a whim?' She poured the near boiling water on the coffee.

'It happens. He's got two alimony payments to prove it. And you said it; he is good-looking…if you go for the muscle-bound type.' Robert was leaning against the doorjamb, arms folded, legs crossed, and the casual arrogance of the man suddenly infuriated her.

'It may interest you to know, Robert, that some of us require a little more substance before we fall into bed…' She knew as soon as the words left her tongue that she'd said the wrong thing. His head came up sharply, and although his posture hadn't changed significantly, it was no longer relaxed. 'I realise that he wasn't on your approved list of escorts, that he couldn't be relied upon to report back.' Robert said nothing. She ploughed on nervously. 'Heavens, I might even have been tempted to try him out—on approval, as it were…'

'I imagine that he was the one with that in mind,' he said abruptly.

'What's the matter, Robert? You can play the field but I have to be tucked up safely in my virginal little bed by midnight? Is that it? Sauce for the goose, my friend…'

'I thought we had decided that you were a duck—' She glared at him. He held up his hands in mock surrender. 'You know Michael would have done exactly the same if he'd been there.'

'Michael is my brother. What's your excuse?'

'Good grief, Daisy, I'm beginning to think you were seriously taken in by the man.'

He sounded positively affronted, and Daisy, concentrating on stirring the coffee, allowed a tiny smile of satisfaction to soften her mouth. She might not have welcomed the manner in which he'd taken charge last night, but she was human enough to take some pleasure from the fact that he'd cared enough to abandon the lovely brunette in order to charge to her rescue. 'Quite the contrary. It was the fact that you'd think I might have been taken in by him that made me mad.'

'What? Oh, I see. Well, for that I do apologise.' She kept her back to him while she struggled to bring a wild urge to grin firmly under control. She simply allowed her shoulders to lift an inch or two in an unimpressed shrug. 'Sincerely,' he added. She picked a couple of mugs off the stand. 'Am I forgiven?'

'This time,' she conceded, with every appearance of reluctance. Duck, indeed.

'I am sorry, you know. About last night. I'm afraid I take you for granted.'

She finally turned, solemnly meeting his honey-brown gaze. 'Yes, Robert, you do. But only because I allow you to.' And the room seethed with silence as Robert digested her remark. 'So, what did you have in mind for breakfast?' she asked brightly, to break the sudden tension.

For a moment he remained quite still, a frown marking the space between his eyes. Then he turned away and opened the fridge door. 'It would be a pity to let that bacon go to waste,' he said, scanning the contents. 'Except that you don't appear to have any bacon.'

'No.'

'You never intended to feed me last night, did you?'

'I never imagined I would have to. Scrambled eggs?' she offered, reaching past him and taking a box of eggs from the fridge without waiting for an answer.

'Daisy…'

She cracked the eggs carefully into a basin. 'Get some plates out of that cupboard, will you?' she asked, as she began to beat them.

He found the plates, set a couple of places at her kitchen table. 'Daisy, can I ask you something?'

'Will you put some bread in the toaster?' she countered. She had the feeling he was going to ask her what she was doing when he wasn't monopolising her time, taking her for granted. What could she say?

That she was busy improving her knowledge of oriental pottery? That she read a lot? Spent far too much time watching stupid television programmes? All true. Not that she didn't have a social life. Far from it. But not the kind of social life that Robert had suddenly developed an interest in. It was a conversation she had always sought to avoid, but, suddenly ambushed, she had every intention of fighting a spirited rearguard action. 'It's over there,' she prompted, when he didn't move. 'In the breadbin.'

'Right.' He finally took the hint and did as she asked. She glanced up from the eggs, suspicious of such an easy victory.

Daisy left Robert to deal with the dishes, while she showered, battened down her still damp hair in a French plait and dressed in an undemanding grey skirt that wouldn't crumple in the car. She stuffed a pair of jeans and a sweatshirt in a small bag, along with a pair of boots so that she could take the dog for a walk after lunch, and some calming bathtime treats she'd bought for her mother. The role of groom's mother might not be quite as stressful as that of mother of the bride, but she had a feeling they would still be needed. Maybe she should lay in a stock for her own use.

'Ready?'

Robert had made fresh coffee and helped himself to her newspaper. 'I've been ready for half an hour,' he said, folding the paper and getting to his feet.

'And it's still not nine o'clock.' She tutted, shaking her head. 'You'd better get yourself another girl and quick, or Sundays are going to seem very long.'

'I do have other interests, you know.' She gave him the kind of look that suggested she wasn't fooled for a minute. He grinned. 'It's true. I like to fish.'

'And when was the last time you went fishing?'

'I don't know.' He thought about it as they walked down the stairs. 'A couple of weeks ago?' he offered. 'You were with me.'

'Then it was before Christmas. You met Janine at a Christmas party and I haven't been fishing since...'

'Ouch.'

'So, do you want to hear about the three little maids?'

He frowned. 'Who?'

'The luscious bridesmaids,' she reminded him, as he held the car door for her, saw her settled into the thick leather upholstery and then climbed behind the wheel. 'They were going to draw lots for you, you know.'

'Lots? Do you mean with me as prize?' He sounded shocked. Daisy was not totally convinced by that shock. Any man would be flattered by such attention. 'They wouldn't.'

'Well, no, they didn't.' She allowed a pause for an expression of relief then, when he'd obliged, she continued. 'In the end they decided there was no point.'

'Oh?' Daisy had been a sister all her life and she knew there wasn't a man born who could resist that little querying, 'Oh?'

She smiled demurely. 'It was obvious that none of them trusted the others to play fair.'

He threw her a startled glance. 'You're making this up.'

'I think Diana will be the most…' she searched for the right word '…inventive.'

'You're just having a little fun at my expense—'

As if she would… 'Then there's Maud.'

'Maud? What a sweet, old-fashioned name.' His voice had changed very subtly. She recognised every nuance, knew that he had caught on to the game and was now playing along with her.

'For a sweet old-fashioned girl.' The kind that believes in marriage. 'She's pretty, Robert. Very pretty. And quietly confident. She knows the hotel where the reception is being held and I fancy she's already worked out where she's going to ambush you. There's a huge, rather gothic conservatory, apparently.'

'That would be the place. I just love gothic conservatories, don't you?' Chance would be a fine thing, Daisy thought. 'And very appropriate for a girl called Maud. And?' She raised a brow in silent query. 'There are three of them. What does number three have in mind?'

Playing the game and already one step ahead. 'If you come through rounds one and two unscathed, Robert, I think I can guarantee that Fiona will ensure that you don't get bored.'

'It's going to be an interesting day. Thanks for the warning. I'll treat you to lunch somewhere quiet on the Sunday after the wedding and tell you how they performed, shall I?'

Quite without warning, the joke turned sour in her mouth. Daisy might have been making up stories to tease him with, but they wouldn't be that far off the mark. She could cope with Robert's 'girls' in theory.

At a distance. She didn't want to hear about them. 'Lunch will be lovely, but you can keep the macho stuff for the men's room. I'm far too young for such tales.'

'Probably.' Then he glanced at her. 'Although Nick Gregson didn't seem to think so.'

'Nick Gregson is just an overgrown adolescent. What would he know?'

Robert dropped Daisy at her parents' home, on the opposite side of the village from the house where his mother had lived since she'd divorced his father.

She opened the door quickly, not waiting for him to do it for her and slid out of the seat. 'Thanks, for the lift. See you in church.'

He watched her walk quickly away down the path, then, as she disappeared round side of the house, he eased the big car slowly around the village green, deep in thought.

Just how old was Daisy? He'd known her since she was a baby. She'd always been there, toddling after Michael, toddling after both of them. A real nuisance. Then a real pain of a tomboy. Then a gawky teenager. The braces had long disappeared from her teeth, but she still wore her hair in a plait, or tied back in a band. She still wore jeans and a baggy sweatshirt most of the time. He'd have said she still looked like a teenager, except teenagers made a lot more effort to look twenty. And last night—

'Robert!' His mother met him at the gate. She'd been walking her elderly Labrador and the dog waddled up as fast as middle-aged spread would allow, his entire body wagging from side to side as he swung his heavy tail to show his excitement.

'Hey, steady, Major!' He rubbed the dog's ear, kissed his mother's cheek and walked with her round to the back of the house and into the mud room.

'I didn't expect you so early,' she said, putting some bare larch twigs into the old stone sink before bending to wipe the dog's paws with a piece of towelling.

'I gave Daisy a lift.'

'Did you?' She paused for a moment, then said, 'Well, it's nice to have company. Pass me that jug, will you, darling, and give Major some water?' Robert handed her a big stone jug, then filled the dog's bowl while she arranged the larch. 'I haven't seen Daisy for weeks. How is she?'

'Getting into a bit of a stew about the wedding. You know she's had to stand in for one of the bridesmaids at the last minute?'

'Her mother told me. Margaret's delighted, of course.'

'Margaret might give Daisy's feelings a little consideration. She hates the very idea.'

'Does she? How odd. Most girls would love to dress up and be the centre of attention.'

'Oh, come on. You know Daisy better than that. She never dresses up.' Well, hardly ever. She'd looked pretty special for Monty's party. Or for whoever she'd seen before Monty's party. The idea that there had been someone had lodged in his brain and refused to go away. She might have flirted with Gregson at the party, but she hadn't really been bothered when he'd been left behind on the pavement.

No matter how much she'd pretended. He frowned. It wasn't like her to make such a fuss.

'Doesn't she?' His mother turned with the jug and stood it in the windowsill to catch the sun. 'I didn't realise you saw her that often.'

'We have lunch sometimes.' What did she do the rest of the time? She never talked much. She listened brilliantly, though. Maybe he should take a leaf from her book; he might learn something. 'And I took her to Monty Sheringham's party last night.' He shrugged as his mother glanced at him. 'She was going anyway.'

'I assume that means Janine is history?'

'Her decision. She was looking for a husband, a family. The whole "till death us do part" bit.'

'In other words, all the things you think you're incapable of offering.'

'Happy is the man who knows his limitations.'

'Maybe.' She patted his arm absently. 'Although I sometimes think that whoever said "ignorance is bliss" had a point. I often wish that I'd never found out about your father's amorous adventures. I'd probably still be happily married to him.'

'Living a lie?'

'We all live lies to a greater or lesser degree, darling. You allow the young women who fall in love with you to hope that you might be persuaded to change your mind about marriage.'

'I always make my feelings on the subject absolutely clear.'

'But they don't believe you. And you know they don't believe you.' She shrugged. 'They simply pretend they aren't interested in marriage while they set about convincing you it is the one thing in the world you need.'

'That's very cynical.'

'But nevertheless true. Why don't you make some coffee while I take a shower?'

'Can I ask you something?' His mother paused at the foot of the stairs. 'You never stopped loving him, did you?'

'Your father? You've seen him recently?' The way her face lit up from the inside was all the answer he needed.

'He called me, wanted to talk, so we had dinner. He asked about you. He always asks about you.'

'He's getting old, and girls aren't quite so thick on the ground these days. How is he?' Robert shrugged and his mother laid an understanding hand upon on his shoulder. 'You're not like him, you know.'

'On the contrary. Seeing him is like looking into a mirror thirty years from now.'

'Looks mean nothing. It's what you are inside that matters. But you're right, of course. I never stopped loving him.'

'So why didn't you just look the other way? Nothing had changed, after all.'

'Now who's being cynical?' Then she shook her head. 'If I could have ignored the facts, darling, I would have. For you as well as for me. But once you're faced with reality, nothing can ever be the same.'

'You've really got to take more of an interest in yourself, Daisy.' Her mother was shaking her head.

'Don't you care what kind of impression you make? You should take a leaf out of your sister's book—'

Sarah and her husband were sitting in state in the living room, ensuring that their exquisitely dressed children didn't get dirty before church.

'We're going to church, Mum, not a fashion parade. Can I give you a hand in the kitchen?'

'Mrs Banks has got everything under control. Come upstairs and I'll see what I can do with your hair.'

Daisy threw a mute, impassioned plea towards her father. David Galbraith shuffled his feet, cleared his throat, glanced at his watch. 'I think I'll, er, go and talk to Andrew.' His wife waved him away impatiently as she ushered Daisy upstairs and then circled her like a hungry shark.

Twenty minutes later Margaret Galbraith admitted defeat and allowed Daisy to weave her hair back into a French plait. 'It's all your father's fault, of course.'

'What is?'

'All his family have impossible hair,' her mother replied obliquely. 'Michael and Sarah take after me, thankfully, but you…' She sighed. 'You're going to have to do something about it before the wedding.'

'Yes, Mother,' she said meekly. Her mother gave her a sharp look. 'I am,' she protested. 'Ginny gave me the number of her hairdresser. He's coming down to do everyone's hair on the day, but he wants to see me first so that he'll know what he's faced with. I've an appointment at the crack of dawn on Monday.'

'Oh, well, that's something, I suppose.' Margaret Galbraith didn't sound entirely convinced. Flicking a dissatisfied eye over her daughter and the simple grey skirt she was wearing, she said, 'It's not too late to change, you know. That skirt is so dull and so long. Now, I've got a gorgeous little pink two-piece which would be absolutely perfect—'

Pink! Yellow! All it would take was a scoop of nuts and a dollop of chocolate sauce and she'd turn into an ice cream sundae. 'You've got me into a bridesmaid's frock, Mother. Can we leave it at that for now? Please?'

Her mother struggled to hold her tongue for a moment before giving a little couldn't-care-less shrug. 'What are they like? The bridesmaids' dresses?'

'They are so-o-o pretty.' Daisy gushed with enthusiasm. Anything to change the subject. And they were pretty. If you were a buxom brunette. Maybe she should get a lift 'em up and push 'em together bra as recommended by Robert. Presumably he knew what he was talking about. It might help, and she wouldn't, after all, be competing with the other girls. She didn't have their natural advantages, for one thing. But she would be able to look her mother in the eye and say she'd tried, without having to cross her fingers behind her back.

Her mother was temporarily distracted by her description of the dresses, then Michael arrived and she hurried downstairs, forgetting all about Daisy.

'Hi, sis.' Michael gave her a hug and a slightly sardonic smile, once he'd extricated himself from his mother. 'Thanks for stepping into the breach.' She could see by his face that he knew what an effort it must be.

'Hey. No problem. Where's Ginny?'

'I dropped her off at home. She's walking over to

church with her parents.' He grinned. 'All very proper. What about you? All alone?'

'Well, I did pick up this really gorgeous man at a party last night. A big suntanned Australian. Mum would have loved him, but unfortunately Robert disapproved and saw him off.' Michael's brows lifted in surprise. 'Apparently he'd been married a couple of times already.'

'Oh, I see. Well, Robert's always been very protective where you're concerned.'

'Has he?' Daisy's cheeks heated up. That wouldn't do. She had the feeling that Michael was the one person in the entire world who suspected how she felt about Robert. 'Yes, well, he doesn't have a little sister to boss about, does he?' she said, just a touch sharply. 'And you've always shared everything with him.'

Michael's grin widened. 'Not quite everything. If he wants a wife he's going to have to find one of his own.'

'He doesn't. Want a wife.'

'He just says that. He hasn't met the right woman, that's all.'

'I *see*. That's his excuse for going through so many of them.' Michael laughed and Daisy made a pretty good fist of joining in. It was only the cast-iron belief that Robert was in deadly earnest about not getting married that made his romantic entanglements bearable. The knowledge that he would always be there.

But suddenly a moment of doubt assailed her, catching at her breath. What if Michael was right? What if, one day, Robert turned up with a wife on his arm? Because that was how it would happen. He wouldn't submit to all this performance. He'd simply disappear to the Caribbean, or the Pacific, or somewhere...

'It's time we were leaving,' Margaret Galbraith said, emerging from the kitchen, smoothing on her gloves. 'Daisy? Are you wearing a hat?'

'What? Oh, no.'

'That's a pity. There's nothing like a hat for disguising problem hair. I'll find you something—'

Daisy snapped out of her distraction, caught Michael's eye and, dredging up a big smile from somewhere, linked her arm through his and headed for the front gate before her mother had a chance to dig out some awful felt monstrosity and insist she wear it. 'Come on, Michael Galbraith, bachelor of this parish. This is it, for the last time of asking. Time's running out.'

'It can't run out fast enough for me. Just wait, you'll see.'

'Me? No way. I'm with Robert on this one...'

'Daisy!' She turned at the sound of Jennifer Furneval's voice and, surrendering Michael's arm as he joined Robert, she walked across the green towards the older woman, who kissed her cheek and fell in beside her as they walked towards the church. 'I'm so glad to see you.'

'How are you, Jennifer?'

'Well enough. Robert said he gave you a lift down this morning. You don't have a car of your own?'

'I don't see the point in London. Although if I'm going to be travelling to auctions I'll have to think about it.'

'George has surrendered that chore to you, has he?'

'Well, maybe. I'm going to a country house sale in the Wye Valley next week.' She mentioned the location. 'There's an interesting collection of oriental pieces being auctioned. Maybe you're going?'

'Unfortunately I can't. There is a piece of Imari ware I particularly like the look of, but it's too risky putting in a phone bid for something on the evidence of a photograph.'

'I could check it out and phone you. If you trust my judgement. And I'll be happy to bid for you, too. I understand I owe you a big thank-you for my job.'

Jennifer laughed. 'Nonsense. I was doing George the favour. How is he?'

'Another one bites the dust, eh, Rob? Although rumour has it that this time the lady jumped before she was pushed.'

'Janine?' Robert shrugged, hiding his increasing irritation that no one seemed surprised by the break-up, just vaguely amused that this time he was the one who'd been dumped. 'It was inevitable. She's a peach, but getting to that time of life when the biological clock is demanding a mortgage and babies with increasing persistence.'

Michael grinned. 'So?'

'So, my biological clock is on a go-slow. Or maybe it never got wound up. Michael, I'm a bit concerned about Daisy,' he said, changing the subject. He had more on his mind than a girl who was already history.

'Daisy? Why? What's she been doing?'

'I'm not sure. She never talks much about herself, did you notice that? Most girls are bubbling over with who they're seeing, where they've been.' He glanced ahead. She was chatting away to his mother easily enough, but that would be about their shared passion for porcelain. 'Has she always been secretive, or is it a new thing?'

'You see as much of her as I do.' They had fallen behind the others and Michael came to halt. 'But, yes, she is very...private. So what's bothering you?'

If he knew that, he wouldn't be bothered; he'd be dealing with it. 'Nothing I can put my finger on exactly. But last night I took her to Monty Sheringham's party. I thought we'd have dinner first, but she said she was busy until ten. She said she was working.'

'But you didn't believe her?'

'She didn't look as if she'd been working. She looked...fired up, different. I just got this feeling that there was a man involved. Mike, do you think she could be having an affair?'

'An affair? What a wonderfully old-fashioned word.' Then, as he caught on, 'With a married man, you mean? Daisy?' And he laughed. 'Are you crazy?'

'I know it seems unlikely, but what else could it be? If it was straightforward she'd have brought him to the party, or gone somewhere else with him—'

'Rob...' Michael interrupted him as if he knew something, was about to tell him something.

'What?' But Daisy's brother simply shook his head and walked on. 'You know something, don't you?' Robert wanted to grab him by the throat and throttle it out of him. 'Tell me...' He realised that Michael was staring at him and he turned away, stuffed his hands hard into his pockets and resumed walking towards the church. 'I'm sorry. But she's always been there for me, Mike. I don't want to see her making the kind of mistake that will ruin her life.'

'I don't think she has much of a choice about that,' Michael said, falling in beside him. 'You're right, of course. There's a man she's been in love with for a very long time, but marriage appears to be out of the question.'

'In love?' He hadn't taken his eyes off her, and now she was standing at the lych gate of the church in a little knot of people, laughing at something his mother had said to her. The early spring sunshine was lighting up the tiny wisps of hair that had escaped from her plait like a halo, and as the sound of her laughter reached him he felt a sharp stab of envy for the man who could capture her heart and hold it. 'Who is he?'

'I really don't think she'd want me to tell you that.'

'Why? What's the big secret?' He turned back to Michael. 'I was right. He's married, isn't he?'

'Look, forget it, will you? I shouldn't have said anything.' Mike was plainly uncomfortable about something. 'Daisy is old enough to make her own decisions.' Then he shrugged. 'Whether they're the right ones…'

'He's married but he can't possibly leave his wife.' Robert knew the type. He'd be the kind of man who would invent some tale about his wife being chronically ill, or hooked on tranquillisers, or alcohol, or anything that meant it was impossible for him to leave the children. He'd manage to appear vulnerable and hurting and at the same time incredibly noble: a lethal combination, particularly when the girl was young and vulnerable herself. And, of course, any woman who got involved with him would understand from the outset that divorce was utterly impossible. 'I knew there was someone on Saturday night—'

Michael grasped the opportunity to change the subject. 'A big Australian, so Daisy told me,' he said, laughing. 'She was hoping to bring him along to the wedding to distract Mum. You are not in her good books.'

He couldn't believe Michael could be so blasé about this, and he refused to be distracted by a twice-married Australian. 'I can't believe you're taking this so lightly! She's your sister, for heaven's sake. You've got to do something…'

'She doesn't need me to wet nurse her. Daisy knows what she's doing.' Michael glanced at him. 'She always has.'

'How can you say that? She's a child and she's going to get hurt.'

'Actually, Rob, she's a grown woman. She's twenty-four,' he added, just to make his point.

'Twenty-four?' But she was just a baby—'

'When you were seven years old. You'll be thirty next birthday. We both will.'

'Twenty-four?' He stopped. 'Good lord. I always think of her as your kid sister.' Or he had, until Saturday. *Twenty-four? Where had the years gone?* He turned to Michael. 'She is *still* your kid sister, Mike, even if she is twenty-four. Have you talked to her about this?'

'No. We've never talked about it. And she'd be devastated if she knew I'd mentioned it to you.'

'Would she? Why?'

'Trust me, Robert. I know what I'm talking about.' Michael gave him a sideways look. 'You won't say anything to her? It's your duty as best man to get me to the altar in one piece,' Mike prompted in the face of his hesitation.

'I won't say a word.' And he wouldn't, although he was oddly hurt that she hadn't confided in him. He told her everything. 'I'm not promising I won't do something, though.'

'Oh? What have you got in mind?'

'Find out who he is and tell him to take a hike. Any objections?'

Michael shook his head and Robert could have sworn he was doing his best not to smile. 'None whatever, Galahad. In fact I'd be most interested to know how you get on.'

'It isn't funny, Mike.' Daisy was his friend, the one person who was always there when he needed her, quick with a kind word, quicker still with a sharp one when he was in danger of pomposity. More than that, she was a girl who was not afraid of silence.

He always felt *renewed* by her company, and he was damned if he was going to stand by and let some selfish lout break her heart.

CHAPTER FOUR

SUNDAY 26 March. I've never seen Michael so happy. He arrived at church with such a ridiculous I-know-something-nobody-else-knows smirk on his face that really it almost made me want to slap him. Anyone would think he was the first man in the world to fall in love. If just reading the last of the Banns makes him feel that good, heaven knows what the wedding will do to him. Ginny is so lucky.

Robert, on the other hand, is acting very oddly. Almost as if he can't bear to let me out of his sight. Weird.

'What time do you want to leave?' Daisy asked.

Michael and Ginny had made a move soon after lunch and everyone else had quickly followed. But Robert appeared to be in no hurry to get back to London. His mother had been invited to lunch, but had other plans, and now he was stretched out languidly in front of the fire, chatting to her father. 'There's no rush.' Then his look became more intent. 'Is there?'

'No. I just wondered if I had time to take Flossie for a run, get a blow of fresh air before we drive back.' Her mother's spaniel lifted her head at the sound of her name and Daisy, who had changed into the comfort of jeans the minute they had returned

67

from church, slapped her thigh encouragingly. 'I'll make some tea when I get back.'

'Wait. I'll come with you.'

'You don't have to—' she began, ignoring the sudden charge of her heart at the prospect. She tried not to appear too eager for his company. It wasn't always easy.

'On the contrary,' he interrupted, before she could finish making her point that he wasn't exactly dressed for a muddy lane. It was hard, wanting something with all your heart that you knew you could never have. Walks with Robert were bliss, and she craved them, but she knew she would pay for self-indulgence with long hours when the loneliness would seem all the more intense. 'I definitely need to walk off the effects of your mother's cooking.' Daisy raised her eyebrows in disbelief as he got to his feet. Square at the shoulders, slender at the hips and with not an ounce of spare fat anywhere in between, the idea of Robert needing exercise to keep in trim was laughable. He caught her look and shrugged. 'You don't think I keep this way overdoing it on the apple pie, do you? Pastry like that has to paid for with pain.'

'Oh, well, just as long as walking with me is a penance for gluttony, you're very welcome. You can borrow a pair of Dad's wellingtons,' she said, with all the carelessness she could muster. It was getting harder. Maybe it was the wedding, Ginny and Michael's obvious happiness, the knowledge that she wouldn't ever have that, because marriage to anyone else would be settling for second best. Never an option.

Margaret Galbraith put her head around the door. 'Is anyone ready for tea? Oh, are you leaving already?'

'No, Mum. Just taking Flossie for a run. Put your feet up and I'll see to the tea when we get back. Robert will help me.'

'Will I?' he asked, surprised.

'You've got to burn off those calories, remember?'

'Well, I must say that would be pleasant,' Margaret Galbraith said, subsiding onto the sofa. 'You won't go far, will you? It looks as if it might rain any minute.'

'I'll look after her, Margaret.' Robert's hand on her shoulder was unexpected and she jumped. 'Come on, Flossie,' he said. 'Walkies.' Flossie needed no second bidding. Some things could be relied upon never to change.

They walked in silence for a while, following the lane down to the river, Flossie bounding ahead of them, starting up a pheasant. 'Are you still mad at me for cutting out Nick Gregson?' he asked, after a while.

'Don't be silly.'

'Am I? Being silly? You've avoided me all day.'

'I've been busy all day. And, if you must know, I only flirted with Nick because I hoped he might come to the wedding. As my date. Unfortunately he's going back to Oz on Tuesday.'

'Three days is a long time in a relationship.'

'It didn't take three hours to work out that Nick wasn't exactly my cup of tea, but that's the trouble with asking men out. They think you fancy them.'

'Equality has downs as well as ups.' He stopped

on the path and she turned, sure he was laughing at her, but when she looked up his face, shadowed in the gathering gloom of the threatening rain, was still, intense. 'Would I do? As a date?'

Her heart leapt, her pulse quickened and all those other stupid things that could get a girl into all kinds of trouble. 'No, Robert. You wouldn't do at all. My mother wouldn't take you seriously.'

'Your mother!' He laughed. Then he wasn't laughing. 'Oh, I see. Your mother.'

'Exactly. I could never convince her that you were likely husband material, could I?'

He didn't answer and they walked on for a while, the silence more oppressive, full of the unspoken, the unspeakable.

'I was thinking,' Robert said finally. 'There's no reason why we couldn't stay overnight and drive back first thing in the morning. We could take a stroll down to the pub later.'

A stroll down to the village pub, the chance to spend an hour beside the fire, just the two of them. She'd had Robert's undivided attention all day and now this. It was too much. It was perhaps just as well that she was unable to succumb to temptation. 'I'm sorry, Robert, but I do have to be back tonight.'

'Oh, well. Just a thought. Are you going somewhere later?'

Daisy glanced at him. He wasn't usually that interested in what she was doing. But he was looking straight ahead and she couldn't see what he was thinking. 'No, I've got a particularly early start in the morning, that's all.'

'I wouldn't have put George Latimer down as a

slave-driver, but first he has you working on Saturday evening and now he wants you in at the crack of dawn on Monday. Perhaps I should have a word with him on the subject of employment law.'

'No,' she said, quickly. 'It isn't work.' The last thing she wanted was Robert quizzing George about Saturday. 'I'm going to see the wedding hairdresser. Eight o'clock tomorrow morning was the only time we could both manage this week. I've got the final fitting for the bridesmaid dress, too. No lunch for me, either.'

'I see.' He glanced down at her, smiling a little. 'You're going to have your feathers clipped, are you?'

'Lord knows. He's going to try and sort out some way to make my hair and the headdress compatible. Poor man, no one should be put through that first thing on a Monday morning.'

'Your hair looked very pretty on Saturday night. You should wear it loose more often.'

Daisy managed to retrieve her mouth before it hit the ground, and since Flossie chose that precise moment to chase a duck into a thicket, she used the excuse to dive after them both, thus avoiding the need to say anything.

By the time she had caught the dog, extricated her from the thicket and made sure that the duck was unharmed, her hair had been largely wrenched from its plait and was anything but pretty. But at least the need to comment upon the unexpected compliment had passed.

She was always doing that, Robert realised, as she fidgeted with escaping wisps of hair. Mocking her appearance before someone else could do it for her. A habit she had slipped into, he had no doubt, to protect herself from her mother's incessant comparison with her older sister. He'd never been able to see it. Sarah might be attractive in a conventional, exquisitely groomed sort of way, but she talked too much and, unlike Daisy, she rarely listened.

But maybe it was like a dripping tap; if someone constantly undermined your self-confidence you might, eventually, begin to believe them.

Was that what was behind her secret affair? He had always thought of Daisy as a strong person, but everyone had their weaknesses. If some man without morals or principles had latched onto that insecurity, she might have been vulnerable.

'You don't mind going back this evening, do you?' she asked, after a while.

'No. Not at all.' Did she really have an early start, he wondered, or was she hoping to snatch an hour with the mysterious lover? 'It was just that today reminded me what we've been missing.' He came to halt when they reached the towpath. 'It seems to me that all my best days were spent on this riverbank. Do you remember that time Mike poked a stick in a wasps' nest and they flew into your hair?'

'Oh, yes, that was a *lot* of fun. Especially the bit where you threw me into the river so I wouldn't get stung.'

'I pulled you out.'

'Yes, Robert, you pulled me out. And you picked the soggy wasps out of my hair and you were the one who got stung.' She lifted his hand and held it between her own. 'Your fingers were so swollen and red.' She turned it over, rubbed her thumb over the scar along his knuckles. 'And you got this when you dragged Billy Pemberton's dog off me.' She looked up. 'I was a bit of nuisance, wasn't I?'

'A total pain,' he agreed. 'We only put up with you because you always had the sense to bring food.'

'I knew you wouldn't send me home if I brought sandwiches.'

Six years old and she'd already known the way to a man's heart, he thought. 'Maybe we should come down next weekend. If you bring the food, I'll bring the maggots.' She didn't leap at the idea. 'If you're not working late again.'

'I'm not sure. It's going to be a bit hectic this week. I'm going away for a couple of days on a buying trip. Can I let you know?'

'Do that. I'll give you my mobile number, just in case I'm not in the office.' They walked on for a while. 'Where are you going? On this buying trip?'

'It's a country house sale,' she said, apparently glad to change the subject. 'In the Wye Valley. I may be bidding for something for your mother, too. There's an Imari bowl she'd like, but she can't get to the sale herself.'

'Really?' He'd never given much thought to what she did at the gallery. His mother had told him that Latimer needed a dogsbody and she'd thought Daisy would enjoy working for him. And, from the way Daisy talked about her job, he had assumed she spent her days answering the telephone, making the tea and dusting the treasures. Apparently it was not just her mother who underestimated her. 'That sounds like fun.'

'I'm a bit nervous to tell you truth. It's the first time George has allowed me out with the chequebook on my own.'

She gave a little shiver. Nerves, he thought, rather than the temperature, but he stuck his hands in his pockets and poked out his elbow, offering her his arm. 'Here, tuck in, keep warm.' After the slightest hesitation she did as he said, looping her arm through his. How long had that hesitation been there? Since she'd had this mysterious lover? The thought of her lying in the arms of some unknown man made his guts twist uncomfortably, and he tucked her arm hard against his side, wanting to hold her, keep her safe.

She shivered again. 'I think it's time we went back,' she said. 'Flossie! Here, girl!' And before he could stop her she had extricated her arm from his. 'Race you!' she said, and set off back down the path. 'Last one back cleans the dog.' From behind, she still looked like the lean-limbed girl he remembered. But his mother was right. Once you'd seen the reality, you recognised the deception. Daisy Galbraith might wear her hair in a plait, but, whatever else she was, she certainly wasn't Michael's kid sister any more.

It was nearly eight by the time they arrived back at Daisy's apartment. 'Thanks for the lift today, Robert. I really appreciated it,' she said, not waiting for him to open the car door for her but bounding out, as if she couldn't wait to get rid of him.

He ignored the unspoken suggestion that she didn't want company. Every time he'd edged the conver-

sation in her direction on the way home, attempting
to discover what she'd been doing, who she'd been
seeing, she'd diverted his interest by regaling him
with the wonders of her new computer. Well, two
could play at that game. 'Grateful enough to let me
have a look at this fabulous PC of yours?'

She looked at him as if he were crazy. 'Don't you
see enough of them at the bank?'

'It's not the same. My mother was talking about
getting one, hooking up to the internet, getting into
e-mail; with her worldwide contacts, it makes sense.
Since you're so enthusiastic about yours, I thought
maybe it would suit her. Is it easy to use?'

'Piece of cake. I'll send you the details.'

'Show me.' He locked the car door, ignoring all
the ''go away'' signals. 'Of course, I wouldn't say
no to a cup of cocoa,' he added. 'If you're making
one.' Well, it was exactly the sort of thing she would
expect him to say. 'In fact I wouldn't say no to a
piece of cake, either. Real, rather than virtual.'

'I don't do cake.'

'Toast will do.'

'All right,' she said, relenting. 'You can come up
for half an hour. Not a minute longer. I'm planning
on an early night. I need all the beauty sleep I can
get.'

'Whatever you say,' he replied, because that was
what he always said.

'My hero,' she said wryly, and then laughed. She
was a lot more comfortable with his casual insults
than with his earlier comment about her hair, he noticed. She didn't want his compliments. Well, she

wasn't exactly used to getting them. Why? Compliments were second nature to him.

'I make it a rule never to disagree with a lady,' he said easily, but it occurred to him that her skin was flawless and her hair might be unruly but it shone with health. She didn't need beauty sleep. No amount of sleep would give her a more voluptuous figure or a smaller nose. Although, now that he was taking notice of her appearance, it occurred to him that her nose complemented her face, and her character, perfectly.

Her sister's face had even, well-proportioned features, but Daisy's face was a lot more interesting. As for her figure, well, since that was usually well disguised by loose-fitting clothes, he would just have to take her word on that.

Once inside, she switched on the PC, and while it was booting up she went into the kitchen. 'What's your password?' he called, after a minute or two.

'What?'

'Your password. It won't go any further without it.'

She appeared in the doorway looking slightly flushed. 'I'll do it.' She crossed to the desk, edged him away from the keyboard. 'Turn away, then. It's supposed to be secret.'

'I'm not planning to come back at dead of night and steal all your secrets,' he protested.

'That's not the point.'

'I'll tell you mine if you tell me yours,' he offered. She waited for him to move and after a moment he shrugged and turned away, not fooled for a minute. It would be her lover's name, that was why she wouldn't let him see. He listened. Six keystrokes, then a return. Six letters. First name? Surname? First name. 'Okay, you can look now. It's pretty straight-forward. You click on this to get e-mail, this to get on to the internet—'

'What about records? Does it store addresses, that sort of thing?'

'Of course it does. Here.' She clicked on an icon and got a list of files. 'Look, this is how you get the address book.' She clicked the mouse. 'See? It's all very simple—'

'Daisy, did you leave some milk on the stove?'

She stared at him for a moment. Then his words seemed to filter through and she turned and raced into the kitchen. By the time she'd returned, with two mugs on a tray and a pile of toast, he had helped himself to a blank disk from a box beside the com-puter, copied her address book and was apparently engrossed in surfing the net. 'I just saved it,' she said, putting the tray down on a small table.

'What?'

'The milk.' Then she grinned. 'I knew it. Men can never resist a new toy.'

'It's a good machine.' He logged off, closed it down, turned and saw the pile of buttery toast, spread thinly with Marmite. A nursery treat. 'Did anyone ever tell you that you're destined for sainthood?' She didn't look impressed. Well, he hadn't expected her to. That was one of the things he enjoyed about Daisy; she didn't take herself, or him, at all seriously. 'I think I'd better wash my hands.'

'Help yourself.'

Her bathroom was painted dark matt green, with

an ornate gilded frame around the huge old mirror over the basin. There were fat little white and gold candles everywhere and the faint exotic scent of bergamot filled the small space. For just a moment Robert had a vision of Daisy lying back in the milky water of the bath, her fair skin translucent in the light of a dozen candles, her hair in soft damp curls about her face and shoulders. It was an image at once disturbingly sensual and faintly shocking and he took an involuntary step backwards. He'd never thought of Daisy in those terms before. As a woman.

Except why else was he there? His sole purpose for visiting her bathroom had been to look for evidence of a man in her life. But a quick search reassured him. There was nothing. Surely even the most careful man would leave some trace of his presence? A razor, a toothbrush? And wouldn't a woman in love cling to any small proofs that he belonged to her? His relief, though, was considerably soured by the discovery that spying on a friend did not make a man feel very good about himself.

He punished himself with the possibility that Daisy's lover was too discreet to come to her flat. What had Michael said? Not much. Just that marriage appeared to be out of the question.

What the devil did that mean? Separated, maybe, and unable to divorce because of scandal? Someone well known? Was that what Michael had been hinting at. Whatever it meant, he'd already decided that while Michael might be too preoccupied with his wedding to do anything about the situation, he wasn't going to rest until he got to the bottom of it.

But he didn't linger. The disk in his jacket pocket

was burning him like a brand and he was certain that
guilt was written all over his face. 'I'll call you later
in the week,' he said, making his excuses as soon as
he could. 'Maybe we could have dinner.'

She seemed unusually reluctant to take him up on
his offer. 'Can we leave it for now, Robert? I'm going to be rather busy this week.'

'That's the second time you've turned me down in
as many days. I'm beginning to think there's something my best friend isn't telling me.'

'Oh, sure. Mr Insecure.' She gave him one of those
grins that made her look about ten years old. 'It's just
I've got the sale this week, and the wedding...'

And fitting in a clandestine relationship, he
thought. That must take a lot of time. Hanging about,
hoping for a call. Always being available, just in
case. She deserved better than that. 'You've got to
eat,' he pointed out. 'And I was rather hoping you'd
have some ideas for Michael's stag night.'

'Does a stag night require ideas? I thought all that
was needed was buckets of alcohol, a sexy stripper-
gram and a nearby lamp post for the ritual handcuff-
ing of the bridegroom.'

'That's what you'd recommend, is it?'

'Far be it from me to defy convention.' She
grinned. 'Ginny's having a hen night next week, and
I promise you, we'll be doing it by the book. Frozen
margaritas, TexMex food, and I have it on good authority that Zorro, or at least a reasonable facsimile,
will be putting in an appearance.'

'Well, I'm shocked.' He made a good stab at looking shocked, but he could tell she wasn't convinced.
'You will tell me all about it afterwards, won't you?'

'You've got to be kidding. Unless you're prepared to tell me what you get up to at Michael's party?'

'Ah.'

She laughed. 'Perhaps some things are best left to the imagination.' She crossed to the door. 'Time to go, Robert. You've had more than half an hour.'

'Times flies when you're having fun.' He bent to kiss her cheek and then, on an impulse, left the lightest of kisses on her mouth, sweetly bare of lipstick, instead.

She didn't speak, just looked at him, and her eyes were like the memory of a dream tugging at his consciousness but always just beyond his reach, a waking memory in which he was falling into huge, dark pupils, drowning in wide, silver fox eyes. Without warning he was fighting a desperate need to take her into his arms and kiss her the way she was made to be kissed, not in some hole in the wall hideaway by a mendacious man, but with a whole heart and total commitment. And for the second time that evening he found himself taking a step back.

Daisy closed the door and leaned against it. She was shivering, shaking so much that she clung to the doorknob with both hands. 'It didn't mean anything. It didn't mean anything.' She whispered it over and over. He was just being Robert. Kissing a woman meant about as much to him as shaking hands. It hadn't even been a real kiss. Just one of those tokens between friends. Meaningless. He'd kissed her once before, just like that, and she'd been fooled into thinking he meant it. Well, she'd been little more than a child then. She wouldn't be fooled again.

She tore herself away from the door and went to gather the plates and mugs, put them on a tray. But her hands were still shaking too much. Everything was shaking too much. Maybe she should turn up the heating. Maybe she should take a hot bath.

It wasn't until she slid beneath the warm, lavender-scented water that she stopped shivering for long enough to gather her wits and promise herself that no matter what enticements Robert held out to her, from now on he would have to fill his own gaps. She had no intention of seeing him again until the wedding. None.

But it would be so much easier to believe herself if her lips weren't still burning from that meaningless kiss, if her body wasn't in danger of instant conflagration. Hot bath. Cold shower. Nothing helped.

Robert slammed the disk into his PC and keyed in the instructions for his computer to print out a hard copy. Then he shut himself in the bathroom and tried to shower away the grubby feeling that he'd been left with after digging about in Daisy's personal life. It didn't work.

He wrapped a towel about his waist, gripped the basin and stared at his reflection in the mirror. He was doing it for *her*, he reminded himself. In the long run she would thank him, he knew she would. His reflection did not look convinced, so he covered his face with shaving foam and picked up a razor. Then he put it down again. He'd shave in the morning, when his hand was steadier.

His flat seemed very quiet. Janine had always had music playing when she was there, had always been on the telephone. He would have welcomed the peace, except that this time it simply meant the printer had stopped. That it was time to get on with the distasteful business of dissecting Daisy's private life.

First he poured himself a drink—he would need a drink to see him through the next hour or so—then gathered the sheets of paper spewed out by his printer before folding himself onto the sofa, glass in hand, and spreading them out across the low table.

She knew a lot of people, but quite a few could be ruled out straight away, he realised. The women, for a start. He paused, his pen above the first name. Women? A woman? For a moment everything suddenly seemed crystal-clear.

Then, with a very un-PC feeling of relief, he realised that couldn't be right. Michael had definitely said it was a man…a man she had been in love with for a very long time. How long was long? Where did they meet? How could he not have noticed? It was obvious that Michael knew who the man was, so why didn't he?

What had Michael seen that he had failed to notice? Whatever it was, Mike had made it quite clear that he wasn't going to tell, that he was on his own. Well, how hard could it be? He'd work on the process of elimination and whoever was left, no matter how improbable, had to be the answer. So he went through the list, crossing out all the women, then members of her family. Some of the men he knew and could rule out, too. His own name was there and he struck through that.

Of the remainder, three had names with six letters and, since he had to start somewhere, he circled them.

Samuel Jacobs had the distinction of offering a double six. The name suggested that he was Jewish, and if the family were Orthodox that might pose a bar to marriage, he supposed.

Conrad Peterson. The name sounded familiar, but the man lived in New Zealand and seemed an unlikely prospect.

The third name was Xavier O'Connell. Father Xavier O'Connell. And Robert's heart sank like a stone as he realised that the man was a priest. The ultimate impediment. He picked up his glass and then put it down again. That was not the answer.

He checked his watch. It was still short of eleven o'clock. Not too late to call a priest. And he picked up the telephone and dialled the number beside the name.

'St Catherine's. Can I help you?'

Robert hadn't expected a woman's voice, and it threw him for a moment. 'Er, may I speak with Father O'Connell, please?'

'It's rather late. Father O'Connell may have retired for the night. Can he call you back in the morning?'

Late? Retired for the night? Tough. 'I'm afraid not. I need to speak to him urgently.'

'Then I'll go and see if he can come to the phone,' the voice replied, rather less eager to please now.

There was a pause, then a softly lilting Irish voice said, 'This is Father O'Connell. How can I help you?'

Robert gripped the receiver so hard that his knuckles whitened to the bone. 'Father O'Connell, my

name is Robert Furneval. I'm a friend of Daisy
Galbraith.'

'Robert Furneval?' The voice repeated his name
thoughtfully. 'You'd be Jennifer's boy, I expect?'

He'd been expecting bluster, or stunned silence.
Anything but this. 'You know my mother?'

'That I do. We met in Hong Kong twenty years or
more ago, and a fine old time we had treasure-
hunting for her bits and pieces, I can tell you. How
is the dear woman?'

'Er… She's very well.'

'And Daisy? How is she? There's no problem, is
there?' he added, a touch anxiously. 'She's not ill?'

'No. She's not ill.'

'Then maybe it's the translating you've called
about? I'm doing it as fast as I can, but I'm afraid
I'm not as young as I was. I was just fine until I
reached eighty, but since then, well, my eyes aren't
quite what they were and things seem to take longer
than I expected.'

Robert swallowed. 'I'm sure she's happy to wait,'
he said. And for once in his life he could think of
nothing to say.

'And you, my son?' Father O'Connell prompted,
quite gently. 'You have a problem?'

'Yes, Father, I do. But it seems that it isn't one
that you can help me with after all. I'm very sorry to
have troubled you so late.'

'Any time, dear boy. And tell Daisy to drop by for
a glass of something warming very soon. Come yourself. This place is comfortable enough, but absolutely
stuffed full with boring old men. I should know, I'm

one of them.' And he chuckled. 'I'm always glad of some youthful company.'

St Catherine's, Robert realised, as he replaced the receiver, was not a church, but a home for retired priests. It was with a far lighter heart that he struck Xavier O'Connell's name from the list.

CHAPTER FIVE

MONDAY 27 March. Why on earth did Mike and Ginny decide to get married? No one gets married these days. Why didn't I think of going skiing? I could surely have managed to break something that wasn't totally immobilising…my nose would have been sufficient. Who'd want a bridesmaid with her nose in a splint? Painful, though…but not as painful as going to the hairdresser. And why did Robert kiss me?

'Well, this is going to be easy.'

Sitting in a Mayfair salon draped in vast swathes of pink and trying to avoid a reflection that was a particularly unhappy combination of darkly shadowed eyes and rather more damp little yellow curls than was quite decent, Daisy blinked.

'Easy?' No one had ever suggested that her hair might be easy.

The stylist smiled at her reflection. 'The secret is not to fight the curls, but to use them,' he said.

'But I don't like curls. I want to have sleek, smooth, swishy hair like that girl on the shampoo ad on the television.'

His smile widened. 'Yeah, and I'd like to be six foot two and look like Robert Redford. We just have to make the best of what we've got, chick, and what you've got is thick, healthy hair.'

'And curls.'

'And curls,' he admitted. 'Learn to love them.'

Love them? That was an idea she hadn't encountered before. She'd been told since she was old enough to care that her hair was a disaster. She'd tried straighteners, a machine that was supposed to flatten the wildest curls, used every kind of conditioner on the market...

Love them? 'I think I'll need time to get used to that idea. In the meantime, I'll leave you to worry about them.'

'You do that. It's what I'm here for.' The stylist snipped as he chatted. 'I'll just tidy you up a bit.' Most hairdressers spoke to her soothingly, presumably hoping to avoid an explosion when they failed to provide the sleek locks demanded by her mother and for which she'd yearned throughout her teenage years. This man's confidence was like a breath of fresh air, and she began to relax as he trimmed the length a couple of inches, thinned out the sides a little, before, with a final ruffle of fingers through her hair, declared himself satisfied.

'That's it?' Actually it didn't look that much different, except that the mop of curls looked as if they had been planned that way, rather than lived with under sufferance. 'Aren't you going to do something excruciating with rosebuds?'

'Not today. A strand or two of ivy, a couple of well-placed white rosebuds on the day and that will be it. You'll look stunning.'

Stunning? That was kind of him, but she wasn't convinced. Her only hope was that she wouldn't look ridiculous next to the gorgeous brunettes. 'I wish I had your confidence.'

'You don't need it, you have my reputation. The photographs will be in the society magazines, and I promise, I'm not about to let you walk up the aisle behind the bride looking less than perfect.' He smiled at her as he whipped away the pink enfolding wrap. 'In the meantime, stop using those nasty rubber bands to tie back your hair. And it would be a big help if you'd get some sleep the night before the wedding, or, failing that, use some concealer to disguise those dark rings, or nobody will be looking at your hair.'

'Well, that's one solution.'

'But not the correct one.' He wasn't particularly amused by her flippancy. Maybe she was supposed to fling her arms about his neck and thank him for transforming her. Before she could make up her mind, he dismissed her with, 'Ask my receptionist and she'll give you some.'

The concealer might have dealt with the dark shadows, but it wasn't much help with the lack of sleep. Daisy's lids drifted heavily over her eyes as she sat at her desk, working her way through the sale catalogue in a determined act of concentration that allowed no room for her imagination to wander off to relive Robert's gentle kiss as it had done all through the long night. She woke with a start as her head hit the desk.

For a moment she wasn't quite sure what had happened, where she was. Then she rubbed her hand over her face and glanced at her watch. Lunchtime. Or rather time for her fitting. Maybe a walk across the park and a little fresh air would help.

Robert hadn't been able to get an answer from Samuel Jacobs on Sunday night and now he knew why. Mr Jacobs had apparently founded an import company in the nineteenth century to indulge the fashion for oriental artefacts, perishing without an heir when his ship had foundered in the South China sea. The company that bore his name survived, and was still importing works of art from the Far East, he discovered. However, he rather doubted that Daisy was in love with an import company, even one dealing in oriental antiques. Having crossed Samuel Jacobs from the list, he was at something of a loss.

He'd already eliminated the third possibility. Conrad Peterson had never seemed a likely candidate as Daisy's secret lover, but since the name had seemed so familiar he'd used the Internet to check him out. He was apparently a well-known collector, which was undoubtedly why Daisy had his name in her database, but his claim to fame was less esoteric. It was the size of the divorce settlement his wife had wrung from him when she'd found him in the marital bed with a man.

Damn Michael for being so coy. How did he expect him to help if he didn't give him something to go on? Except, of course, he hadn't asked him to help; that had been his own idea. He wondered if Ginny knew. He couldn't just call and ask her outright…he needed some excuse to talk to her. Better still, some reason for them to meet.

And he smiled as he remembered the promise he'd made Daisy.

'Ginny? Robert. I wonder if you could do something for me? I need about a metre of the yellow velvet your bridesmaids will be wearing.'

'How do you know about the yellow velvet? It's supposed to be a state secret.'

'I won't tell anyone. But only if I can have a metre.'

'That's blackmail. What do you want it for?'

'It's a surprise for Daisy.'

'It's a pleasant one, I hope.'

'Scout's honour. Can you drop it round to the office this afternoon? I'll give you a cup of Earl Grey and a chocolate biscuit and tell you all about it then.'

'I'll do what I can, but it had better be good.'

It was. Michael had no secrets from Ginny, but luring her to his office in order to pump her for information was just part of his plan.

He needed to see as much of Daisy as he could, and listen to her for a change, but she had been quite definite about being too busy to see him this week, what with hairdressers and fittings and hen nights. If he phoned her, he'd just get a polite brush-off. Somehow he had to get her to ring him.

He reached for a sheet of his personal notepaper, wrote a brief note, folded it and tucked it into an envelope, then addressed it to Daisy at the Latimer Gallery and headed for the door.

'Mary, I'm going out for a few minutes,' he informed his secretary.

'You've got a video conference with Delhi in half an hour,' she reminded him. 'And the Partners' lunch after that.'

'Would I miss the highlight of my week?'

'What's this?' Daisy regarded the white waxed box from a seriously expensive delicatessen that was sitting on her desk when she returned with the black and gold box that contained the altered bridesmaid dress.

George shrugged. 'It arrived in a taxi about ten minutes ago. There's a note,' he added, quite unnecessarily; she had already picked up the thick square envelope that was sitting on top of the box.

Daisy recognised the writing at once and tried to remind herself that there was absolutely no reason for her heart to be fluttering in quite such a silly way. She had long ago stopped fluttering for Robert. Until last night. Since last night the fluttering had assumed volcanic proportions. She was fluttering right down to her fingertips.

She pushed a shaky thumbtip beneath the flap and flipped open the envelope, pulled out the single sheet of paper and unfolded it.

Dearest Daisy,
Since I am reliably informed that it is the best man's duty to take care of all the bridesmaids—not just the pretty ones—I have taken it upon myself to ensure that you don't miss lunch because of your dress fitting.
    Robert.
PS Thanks for supper.

'The rat!' she exclaimed. 'Not just the pretty ones, indeed.' She dropped the note and opened the box. 'Oh!' The box contained the most exquisite arrangement of delicate little treats and she was forced to blink very hard.

'Supper?' George queried, picking up the note and scanning it as he helped himself to a tiny pastry stuffed with fresh salmon.

'Just Marmite soldiers and cocoa.'

'Really?' He licked his fingers. 'I should think the last woman who offered him that particular combination was his mother.' Then, 'I'd say you've definitely come out on top.'

'Have I?' She looked at the expensive array of delicacies. 'Yes, I suppose I have.' But if that was the case why did she suddenly have this weird sinking feeling? A hollow somewhere around her middle that her carefully ordered life was under attack. That Robert was up to something.

Damn Janine for getting clever a whole two weeks before the wedding and leaving Robert with a bigger gap than usual in his busy social life.

There was a time when she would have welcomed it, hugging the brief pleasure of his company close, storing up the memories as a squirrel stored nuts against the winter. But right now she didn't think she could take two whole weeks of such close attention without betraying herself. Not after that kiss.

She pushed the box nearer to George, so he could help himself more easily. She didn't feel in the least little bit like eating.

'Well? Aren't you going to phone him and say thank you nicely, the way your mother taught you?' His fingers hovered indecisively between another pastry and a piece of chicken. 'I'm sure he's sitting by his phone just waiting for your call.'

Her fingers were twitching, desperate for George to leave so that she could make that call, so that she could hear the sound of Robert's voice, perhaps discover the answer to the question that was plaguing her.

She was weakening, she realised with a shock. One kiss was all it had taken to jar loose the restraints she had placed around their relationship. One kiss. And with that realisation came the answer to her question. Robert was simply at a loose end and flirting came to him as naturally as breathing. She'd turned down his invitations twice in the same week and suddenly she was a challenge.

That was why he had kissed her, she realised angrily, and, having worked out what he was up to, not phoning him became very easy indeed.

She wasn't ever going to be one of his adoring girls, doing the predictable thing and falling at his feet. No way. Let him wait for her call. She directed her fingers in the safer direction of the chicken.

'Do you want that little asparagus tart, George, or are you going to finish the salmon?' she enquired, ignoring his question.

He gave her a thoughtful look and then shrugged. 'It's your lunch; you choose.'

'Just so long as we're both sure about that.' She ate the chicken and, discovering that she was hungrier than she had thought, she picked up a cherry tomato and firmly changed the subject. 'Now, I've had a final look at the sale catalogue and marked what I'd like to bid for with guide prices. Perhaps you'd better double check it.'

'Let's see.' He ran his eye over the list. 'You could go a little higher on a couple of items.' He marked them. 'What's this?'

'Oh, that's something Jennifer Furneval asked me to look at for her. You don't mind, do you?'

'Of course not, but I'll bet you anything you like that it's not Japanese. You know what to look out for?' He made a note beside the lot number without waiting for her answer. 'Of course you do. But no matter what Jennifer tells you, don't pay more than that.' He glanced up, his smile rueful. 'Unlike you, she's inclined to get carried away when she wants something very badly.'

'Five years from now it could seem like a bargain,' she pointed out.

'Yes, well, that's the risk. No one ever won the world by playing safe, my dear.' She had the feeling that he was saying a lot more than the words implied. Then he shrugged. 'But no one ever got burned, either. Maybe that's why we're dealers rather than collectors. Pragmatists, in it for a percentage rather than a lifetime commitment.'

Daisy glanced up. 'Are we still talking about porcelain?'

'What else?' His smile was so innocent that she almost believed him.

'Maybe, if it's a copy, I'll see something else she'd like. Robert has been looking for a birthday present for her.'

'So long as you get the pieces I want, you can do what you like. Maybe even treat yourself. Did you manage to get a room at the Warbury Arms?'

'Any messages?' The Partners' lunch had seemed interminable, and while everyone around him had been full of the proposed merger, all he had been able to think about was Daisy and whether she had enjoyed her lunch.

Mary handed him a list of his calls along with a smart little black and gold carrier. 'A young lady called in with this.' She glanced at her notebook. 'Miss Ginny Layton. *Very* pretty—'

'And very early,' he said, checking his watch. 'No, I'm late. I wanted to speak to her, damn it.'

'She said she was sorry to miss out on the tea, but she's had a catering crisis that couldn't wait and she'd phone you later.'

'Ah, well, the best-laid plans…I wanted to pick her brains,' he added, when he saw Mary's cynical expression. 'She may be pretty, but since you'll undoubtedly have noticed the large diamond she's wearing on her left hand you'll have worked out for yourself that she's *very* engaged. In fact she's about to be married to my oldest friend.' He looked up from the list of messages she had given him. 'This is all? No one else called?'

'No one,' Mary confirmed. 'Maybe you're losing your touch, Robert. What's her name?'

'Daisy Galbraith…' He stopped. 'Oh, very funny. It's not like that; she's just an old friend.' Mary gave him an old-fashioned look. 'It's true. I've known her since she was in her highchair. If she calls you can ask her. But I'd rather you put her straight through. And in the meantime see if you can get hold of my mother.'

'It's *that* serious?'

'Serious?' Of course it was serious. Almost too late he realised that his secretary was still having a little fun at his expense and, recovering himself, he chided her softly. 'My dear Mary, when is it ever *that* serious?' Then he realised he was still holding the package. 'Have this sent over to my tailor, will you? He's expecting it.'

'Yellow velvet?'

'You peeked.'

'You didn't expect me not to, did you?' She waited expectantly for an explanation.

'It's material for a waistcoat. For the lovely Ginny Layton's wedding. I'm best man, and I thought it might be rather fun to match the bridesmaids' frocks.'

Mary chuckled at that. 'I'll bet you did. I'll bet the bridesmaids will think so, too. Velvet is so wonderfully touchy-feely—'

'My mother?' he reminded her, with just a touch of irritation. 'When you've quite finished being wittery-drooly.'

His mother wasn't at home, which on reflection, he decided, was probably just as well. If Mary assumed that his interest in Daisy was rather more than friendly, presumably anybody else he approached about her would take much the same view, but with rather less indulgence. And he wasn't in a position to defend himself against accusations of cradle-snatching.

Not that Daisy was in her cradle any more. Mike had rather forcefully made the point that she was twenty-four years old and a fully grown woman. Well, maybe she was, but he was light years older in experience, which was why he was eminently suited to the task of extricating her from whatever mess she was in. As her friend, it was his duty to extricate her from that mess.

Besides, the information he wanted was easily enough obtained by calling Monty Sheringham. There wasn't much point in having a contact on a national newspaper if you couldn't use him. He hadn't even needed to check with the Fine Arts correspondent; the sale Daisy was attending had to be the one at Warbury Manor; the family had provided Monty with many column inches in the past.

Since Daisy was going to be staying overnight, there seemed every likelihood that her lover would put in an appearance under the guise of visiting the sale on his own behalf.

Well, he would stay too. There was only one hostelry of any note in the village of Warbury, the Warbury Arms, and it had only one single room without bathroom available.

'It's the sale at the Manor,' the receptionist informed him apologetically.

'If it's all you have, I've no choice but to take it.'

He spent the rest of the afternoon, and quite a large part of the evening, clearing his diary and organising his office for his absence. It wasn't easy, and it was only when he reached home that he realised Daisy still hadn't called to thank him for her lunch. She must be very preoccupied to forget her manners, or very determined not to speak to him. But why?

He loosened his tie, switched on his answering machine and poured himself a drink. 'Robert?' Janine's voice floated teasingly across the room. 'Darling, I'm sorry to bother you, but have you found a scarf? Grey silk? I need it rather desperately. Call me if you have.'

He hadn't, but then he hadn't looked. Janine had waited longer than most to call, to give him a taste of missing her before offering a graceful opportunity to resume the relationship. But he had no capacity for commitment. Like father, like son. Nearly. His father was selfish; he'd wanted it all and his mother had paid the price. He wasn't about to do that to any woman. He'd look for the scarf and send it back by messenger.

The machine clicked. 'Robert, it's Ginny. I'm sorry I missed you today because I wanted to ask you do something for me. Something Mike said about Daisy make me think of it. I feel so guilty about pressuring her into standing in as bridesmaid, I know she hates the very idea, so I was wondering, would you look after her at the wedding for me? Make sure she has a good time? You're such an old friend and I can't think of anyone else who could do it half as well as you.'

'Flatterer,' Robert murmured wryly. 'Mike's a lucky man.' But what had Mike said to her? That was what he really wanted to hear.

'Robert.' At last. He checked the time of the message. Midafternoon, when she could easily have got him at the office. She was definitely avoiding him. Yet a warmth seeped into his veins at the sound of Daisy's voice. 'Thanks for lunch. It was a lovely thought and exactly what I needed after seeing myself in the finished dress. I'll see you at the wedding. You can't miss me, I'll be the ugly duckling on the left. Bye.'

He smiled, as no doubt she'd meant him to. 'I'll be looking out for you,' he promised. Then, more thoughtfully. 'In every sense.'

'Robert, would you do me a favour?' His mother's crisp voice brought him firmly back to earth as the next message clicked in. 'I asked Daisy to bid on a piece of porcelain for me at a sale this week, but never thought to organise some method of payment, and since it could be rather a lot of money I'd be grateful if you can ensure she won't be embarrassed for funds if she's successful? Bless you.'

He raised his glass in a salute to the machine. He'd been wondering how he was going to explain his presence at Warbury to a sceptical Daisy, especially since that 'I'll see you at the wedding...' had sounded suspiciously like a reprise of the 'don't call me...I'll call you' message he'd been getting from her.

'No, Mother, bless *you*, for giving me exactly the excuse I needed.'

CHAPTER SIX

Tuesday 28 March. The train journey was hell, the viewing was mobbed and as for the rain!

George was right, of course. The Imari bowl isn't Japanese. There's something else, though, something I'd like to buy for Jennifer. Fat chance. I can't be the only person to have poked around in the kitchen boxes hoping to find something that might have been overlooked in the sheer quantity of crockery. Maybe I should have said something to one of the porters. It might get broken... Oh, hell!

Daisy kicked off her wet boots, shook out her raincoat and hung it, along with her umbrella, in the bathroom, before stripping down to her underwear. She'd never seen such rain!

She draped her trousers and sweater over the towel rail to dry out, and because the hotel wasn't one of those big chains that supplied all the trimmings, certainly not expensive accessories such as bathrobes, she slipped into the Chinese silk wrap she'd brought with her. Then, taking a hand towel, she curled up into an elderly chintz-covered armchair while she dried the drips from her hair.

She'd felt guilty about the cost of a double room when she'd booked, but it had been the only decent room they'd had left, and after a day poking about the treasures, and the junk, collected by generations of the Warbury family, a day when the rain had come down like stair rods without ceasing, she knew she deserved it.

The first day of a Harrods sale would never seem like hard work again, she decided as she wiggled her aching toes and tried to summon up the energy to make herself a cup of tea. But her energy was on go-slow and her gaze shifted to the mini-bar. Would there be a brandy?

She thought about how blissfully warm it would feel sliding down her throat and decided to check it out. In a minute. Right now she just wanted to close her eyes. Just for a moment or two. Then she'd look.

The Warbury Arms was a mellow old country inn, all oak-panelling, open fires and copper warming pans, the very image of Olde Englande so beloved of tourists, and in this case, Robert could see, it was the genuine article.

The rain was genuine, too, and he had to push his way through a steaming crowd of dealers and collectors gathered for the sale just to get to the reception desk.

'Has Miss Galbraith checked in?' he asked, raising his voice against the babble as he signed the register.

'Miss Galbraith?'

Robert had assumed she would be staying close to the Manor, but, looking around at the heaving crowd, it occurred to him that she might have chosen somewhere quieter. Somewhere more discreet. 'She's with the Latimer Gallery.'

'Oh, yes, of course. She came in a few minutes

ago. Will you be dining together? I'd advise booking a table; we're very full.'

'I'll see what she wants to do and let you know.' It was entirely possible that she had other plans and would not be at all pleased to see him. The thought was so depressing that for just a moment he considered turning around and going home. But only for a moment. Michael might choose to look the other way, but he couldn't. 'What's her room number?'

It took him less than ten minutes to dump his bag in his room and freshen up and then he went in search of Daisy. Her room was at the front of the hotel and he paused for a moment before he knocked. He had his excuse all ready, but he still hesitated, feeling just a little like some cheap private eye in an old movie hoping to catch the guilty husband *in flagrante*.

He bunched his fist and laid it against the door. Confronting Daisy like this wasn't what he would have chosen. The desk clerk hadn't mentioned anyone else, but that didn't mean she was alone and he had no wish to embarrass her, or catch her out. He just wanted to help. Before he could do that, though, he needed information.

Maybe he should go downstairs and wait for her to come down. That would be kinder. Except maybe she wouldn't come down. Maybe it would be room service and champagne. Maybe he was just a coward.

He hadn't thought much about what he would do if she was with someone; he was certain that she would be embarrassed and he didn't want that. They were friends, the best of friends, and his concern for her was very real. Then he remembered the way her eyes had looked in that moment after he had kissed her. The way he had wanted to do a lot more than kiss her. And suddenly he didn't feel like being kind. He had to know.

He rapped on the door. There was no answer.

Maybe, he told himself, she was in the bath. Maybe she was, right now, deep in concentration in some reference book, swotting up for the sale and refusing to be disturbed. A week ago he would have expected nothing else, but it had been a long week and maybe, he thought, maybe she was lying in the embrace of her secret lover...

He brought his knuckles down hard against the old panelled door.

Daisy woke with a start. For a moment she wasn't sure where she was or what had woken her. Then she lifted her head, pushed her hair out of her eyes and checked her watch, wondering if she'd slept all night in the chair. It felt like it, but she'd been there for less than half an hour. She shivered a little and yawned.

Then was a knock at the door, loud enough to suggest that it wasn't the first. She sighed, hauled herself out of the chair and, assuming that it was the maid coming to turn down the sheets, she opened the door.

'Hello, Daisy.'

'Robert!' Usually she had time to gather herself, prepare herself, but caught unawares she took an involuntary step back, overwhelmed by his unexpected appearance. Taking it as an invitation, he followed her into the room.

Robert hadn't known what to expect, but Daisy, tousled, sleepy-eyed and wearing a thigh-length silk wrap, knocked him for six. His mouth dried, and any pretence that this was anything but personal flew out of the window. His only thought was to take her in his arms and carry on where he had left off on Sunday night.

Or was even that only half the story? Wasn't the whole truth that he hadn't been able to get Daisy out of his head since Monty's party? Hadn't the little green-eyed monster leapt on his shoulder the moment he saw her with Nick Gregson? Even now his eyes were everywhere.

'This is comfortable. Big for one, though.'

'There wasn't much choice,' she said defensively. 'It was this or an attic without a bathroom. Robert, what on earth are you doing here?'

'I'm on a mission.' He crossed to the tray, where there was a kettle for making hot drinks. The kettle was cold and empty and he glanced around, looking for the bathroom. Looking for any sign of dual occupancy. A man's jacket lying over the chair, the telltale shoes. Nothing. Relief was short-lived. After all it was early. Maybe it wasn't shock he had seen in her face, but disappointment. 'Any chance of some tea?' he asked.

'I was just trying to decide between tea or brandy when I fell asleep,' she confessed, dragging her fingers through her hair and stifling a yawn. 'What kind of mission?'

'It's too early for brandy.'

'Probably, but it's been a hell of a day. Here, give that to me before I weaken,' she said, taking the kettle into the bathroom to fill from the tap. 'What kind of mission?' she repeated, calling out to him.

'Maybe "mission" is putting it too strong. More an errand of mercy. I'm here to keep you company, buy you dinner...' She appeared in the bathroom doorway looking sweetly dishevelled, her short robe displaying a pair of remarkably long, slender legs. And he remembered the long-limbed child racing after Mike, racing after him when he was a boy and desperate to escape her hero-worship. Her legs had always been long and slender; that was why her knees had seemed so large. The memory made him smile.

'What's so funny?'

'What? Oh, nothing.' And the smile faded as quickly as it had come. The legs had shape now, and her knees were just fine. 'You've done something to your hair,' he said, simply to distract himself.

'I told you I was seeing the wedding stylist. He didn't do much, just snipped a bit off. Clearly he decided I wasn't worth the effort. Why are you here, Robert?'

'You didn't believe me about dinner?'

'Er, let me see. No,' she said, without even hesitating. Then she carried the kettle across to the tray. 'No one in their right mind would come out in this weather unless they had to.'

'That's true.'

'Are you saying you had to come?'

'Direct orders. I had a message on my answering machine asking me get down here with my cheque-book.' He took the kettle from her, plugged it in and switched it on before turning to face her. 'You're buying something for my mother?' he prompted. 'She thought you might need some money.'

'Oh.' Then, 'Oh, dear. I'm sorry, Robert, but you've had a wasted journey. The bowl your mother was interested in is just a copy.'

It was the excuse that had interested him, not the bowl. But she seemed disappointed. 'It was a fake?'

'No, a copy. The designs were copied by everyone. Some porcelain was even imported unfinished from Japan and then decorated in Europe. The bowl in the sale is listed simply as "Imari-style porcelain"; I guess the maker's mark was removed at some time by someone hoping to pass it off as Japanese. It might fool an amateur, but Jennifer wouldn't be interested.'

'Damn. I'd hoped to give it to her as a birthday present.'

'I was going to suggest it, if it had been what she wanted.'

'Well, maybe there's something else?'

'Maybe.'

Robert's eyes narrowed. Daisy was tired. She had dark smudges beneath her eyes that he'd never seen before, but there was nevertheless a sparkle about her, an edge of excitement that he doubted had anything to do with the sale. It made him feel quite sick, and he turned away, dropped a couple of teabags in the cups provided.

'I'll see what I can find. How much are you prepared to spend?' she asked.

He shrugged. 'Whatever it takes. I'll know when I see it.'

'See it?'

'Of course. Now I'm here, I might as well stay for the sale.'

'Oh.' For a moment Daisy had been tempted to tell him about the Kakiemon dish she'd spotted in a box of assorted kitchen china. She'd hoped to buy it for Jennifer herself, but it would make a wonderful birthday present for Robert to give her. If she could get it at a reasonable price. But you could never tell how even the most level-headed person would react at a sale, and she didn't want to take the risk of his excitement giving away her find. If she *was* right about it. 'Where are you staying?'

'In the attic without the bath that you turned down, I imagine,' Robert replied.

'Don't be silly. Haven't you seen the crowds downstairs? There won't be a room available within ten miles of this place.'

Robert realised she had misunderstood him, but he didn't enlighten her. If he *had* jumped the gun, and her lover was arriving later, it might be better if she thought him safely out of the way. Still it wouldn't hurt to tease her a little. In fact, she would expect it. 'Well, you've got a spare bed,' he said, indicating the twin beds with a night table separating them. Not his first choice for a night of passion. 'You wouldn't send me out into the rain, would you?'

'You won't dissolve.'

'Maybe not, but if I don't get out of these wet socks very soon I'll probably catch cold.'

'Pneumonia. You need a virus to catch cold.'

'Pneumonia? Do you think so? With a cold I might just make it as best man. I'd give it to all the guests, of course, but with pneumonia...' He left her to fill in the gap.

'And of course without you Michael and Ginny

would definitely have to cancel the wedding,' she said, then grinned. 'Not.'

The exchange was the usual jokey banter between friends, but he detected an edge to her voice. A nervousness. So, the spare bed was already spoken for and three would be a crowd. It was only what he had expected and yet a kind of impotent rage seemed to grip him. He had to *know*. 'I suppose I could drive back to Ross and find a room there, but there's no reason we couldn't have dinner first,' he said, pushing her the way he'd worry a sore tooth.

'Actually, Robert, I'd planned to have a sandwich up here and get an early night.' And she curled up in the big armchair as if to convince him.

'On your own?' The words just slipped out.

'Go back to London, Robert. I'll find something for Jennifer's birthday; you can pay me when you see me.'

He shrugged. She hadn't appeared to notice the implication behind his words. Or she was very good at hiding her feelings.

Private. That was what Michael had said. She was very private.

'You wouldn't begrudge me a cup of tea before you throw me out, would you?' He didn't wait for an answer, but poured the boiling water onto the teabags. 'There, just like Mother makes,' he said, adding the milk and passing her a cup. Then, looking down at her, curled up into the big armchair, her thick mane of curls tumbled loose about her face, he said, 'You know, you shouldn't worry about your knees. They're not in the least bit knobbly.'

She tugged self-consciously at the short wrap she

was wearing, trying to cover them, and something inside him boiled up and was in danger of bubbling over. Why on earth was she so coy around him? Her legs weren't exactly a mystery to him. He'd seen her more times than he could remember in a skimpy swimsuit when they'd all swum in the river. He and Michael and Daisy. It had been something they had done every summer until he'd gone away to university. No, later than that. Until he'd graduated and moved to London.

'What time does the fun start?' he asked sharply.

'Fun?'

She looked startled. Guilt? 'Tomorrow. The sale,' he said

'Oh, I see. I wouldn't have described it as fun, exactly, but there's an hour for viewing in the morning and then the sale starts at ten. 'With luck and a kind train schedule, I should be home by five.'

'Won't someone offer you a lift?'

'I never accept lifts from strangers,' she said.

'Maybe you'll see someone you know.' He finished his tea, put down his cup and crossed to the door. 'If I stayed I could take you myself,' he said, offering a lure.

She wasn't to be hooked. 'You'd get bored,' she said. 'It won't be like those dramatic sales you see on the news, with paintings going for millions.'

'I have been to a sale before. Sure you won't change your mind about dinner?'

She got up, followed him to the door. 'Quite sure. Thank you.'

Robert looked down at her, saw something very like desperation darkening her eyes, and because he cared so much about her he reached out, touched her cheek, forced his mouth into the kind of smile she would be expecting. 'You know, I'm beginning to think you're trying to get rid of me, duckling. You haven't got a secret lover hiding in the bathroom, have you?'

'Damn, you've found me out,' she said, and suddenly laughed, neat white teeth in bright contrast to warm lips, lips that were sweeter and more inviting than he could ever have imagined. But then, as she looked at him, her eyes misted over. 'Please drive carefully,' she said quickly. And, putting her hand on his shoulder to steady herself, she lifted herself onto her toes and kissed his cheek. Her hand on his shoulder, her soft breath against his skin left his immovable centre spinning out of control.

A week ago he would have laughed the thought of Daisy with a secret lover to scorn. Now he couldn't get the idea out of his head, and he glanced at the bathroom door, shut carefully after she had filled the kettle, and wondered if he had inadvertently stumbled on the truth.

For a moment Daisy leaned back against the door and groaned. Damn George for being so knowing. Damn Jennifer for being so thoughtful. Damn Robert for making her love him and for being so far out of reach... She groaned again.

Damn him, but she couldn't do it. She couldn't send him out into a black, wet night. She wouldn't do it to a dog, much less a man she loved, just to save herself from pain. Because sharing a room platonically with him was her idea of a nightmare. It wasn't as if he would even think of making a move on her. She'd be quite safe.

Lucky her.

She wrenched open the door, ready to call him back, but the corridor was empty. 'Damn!' She pushed her feet into her still damp boots and without stopping to tie the laces grabbed her key and, banging the door shut behind her, raced to the stairs before she quite lost her nerve.

'Robert!' He was halfway down the stairs when he turned and saw her, and for a moment stood quite still.

'What is it, duckling?'

'I, er, I changed my mind about dinner,' she said, suddenly aware that she was attracting rather a lot of attention from the bustle of men and women who had spilled out of the overcrowded bar and were filling the reception area, glasses in their hands.

Robert's quick smile distracted her. 'Just dinner?'

She flushed. 'Jennifer would never forgive me for sending you out on a night like this when there's a spare bed going begging.'

She waited, expecting him to say something silly to put her at her ease. Instead he came back up the stairs, took her hand and held it for a moment. Then he said, 'Why don't you go and put some clothes on while I book a table?'

Clothes? For a moment Daisy wasn't quite with him, then she realised that she was standing above a room full of people wearing nothing but a thigh-length wrap. A thigh-length wrap and a pair of brown ankle-high laced boots. Oh, wow. Great. Without waiting to answer him, she grabbed the edges of her wrap tightly about her and walked carefully back up the stairs. She would have liked to run, but this was not the moment to risk tripping over her trailing laces.

Behind her she heard a sudden bubble of laughter and she groaned. The dealers' world was such a small one. Today she had been able to poke about the trivia of the sale without anyone taking much notice of her. With one impulsive gesture she had made herself the centre of attention, and thirty years from now people would still be saying, 'Daisy Galbraith? I know her. I was at Warbury when she chased some man through the bar half-naked…' Antique dealers were like fishermen—they never spoiled a good story by sticking strictly to the truth.

She banged the door shut behind her. Why on earth couldn't she have just done the sensible thing? she asked herself. She was good at sensible. She'd been doing sensible very successfully since she was sixteen years old, when she'd realised that she had two choices. Let Robert Furneval break her young heart, or keep it firmly under lock and key.

Why did she have to lose her head now?

Before she could offer a sensible answer, she caught sight of herself in the cheval mirror and instead she shuddered. Too much leg, too much everything, and most of it flushed a revolting shade of embarrassment pink that clashed horribly with her yellow hair.

The very thought of going back down to the bar filled her with deep embarrassment. Maybe they could have room service? But that would be even worse. That would mean spending the whole evening alone with Robert in a bedroom. What would they do? What would they talk about? And then there would be the awkwardness of changing for bed…she'd bet pounds against pretzels that he didn't wear pyjamas.

If they were downstairs, she could make some excuse to come up first and be safely tucked beneath the covers with her eyes tightly closed before he climbed into bed. If she was quick, she could be properly dressed before he returned.

She eased her feet out of her damp boots and opened the wardrobe. There wasn't much choice. She wasn't a 'pack-for-every-occasion' girl. She had never seen the point of carrying more than she needed. She'd worn a pair of old, but serviceable trousers for rooting around the Manor, the kind of garment that wouldn't crease and wouldn't show the dust and at a pinch, with a silk blouse, would take her through to dinner. Or would have, if she hadn't dashed through a rainstorm and stepped in a puddle that had seemed to reach her knees.

So that only left the sharp little suit that, bearing George's instructions not to let the gallery down, she had decided to wear to the sale. And the shoes with five-inch heels that she had bought to go with it. She had rather relished the idea of distracting a rival bidder by crossing her legs at just the right moment.

Well, she'd distracted them, all of them, and she hadn't even needed the heels. It was just her timing that was off.

What she wouldn't have given for a long, anonymously grey skirt right now, and the sensible low-heeled shoes she'd taunted George with.

But something warned her that as far as this buying trip went she might as well strike the word 'anonymous' from her dictionary, and with that uncomfortable thought for company, she went to take a shower.

Robert wasn't sure how he was feeling. A little numb. In a minor state of clinical shock, perhaps.

He'd left Daisy's room in a mood that had bordered on misery. That alone should have been sufficient to alert him that he was heading for trouble. But then he'd turned at the sound of her voice calling his name, seen her a few feet above him wrapped in thin red silk that barely covered her thighs, her cheeks picked out in a pale pink flush... Well, most of the occupants of the Warbury Arms were probably in a state of shock, too. But it hadn't been the wrap, or the legs that had done it for him. He'd seen them just moments before, without the ardour-dampening effect of the boots.

It had been the heart-leaping sense of joy at what her change of heart meant. And then the equally rapid descent into somewhere very like hell as Michael's words had echoed in his mind. *There's a man she's been in love with for a very long time...* She might be alone tonight. Maybe he couldn't get away tonight. But there *was* someone.

Well, maybe it was for the best. The very idea of Robert Furneval falling in love was so ridiculous, so dangerous that he should be laughing. Instead, for the first time in his life, he felt more like crying at the cruel lack of something precious in his character, something that made falling in love with Daisy an impossibility. And the urge to protect her from heartbreak, seen for the selfishness at its heart, was suddenly grotesque.

He'd confess to the attic, stay over and give her a lift home. She deserved no less from him. Then he'd do what she wanted and stay away from her until the wedding. Hopefully Fiona, or Maud or Diana would provide sufficient distraction after that. It shouldn't take long to get over her if his usual attention span was anything to go by, he thought bitterly.

'I'd like to book a table for dinner,' he said to the reception clerk. 'For two.'

'Seven or nine o'clock, sir? We're having to double-stack the tables, tonight.'

'Seven—' he began, then turned as a middle-aged woman beside him raised a desperate voice.

'But you must have a room! I'll take anything. My car has broken down and there's absolutely no chance of getting it fixed until tomorrow.' She was soaking wet, exhausted and clearly at her wits' end.

'You can have my room,' Robert said. 'Twenty-three,' he added as the room clerk raised his eyebrows. 'I can double up with a friend.' The woman turned to thank him, but he cut her short. 'It's not a problem. I'll go and move my bag and bring the key.'

Not a problem. Not much. At least his good deed had wiped out the lie he'd told Daisy. Now all he had to do was live with the consequences.

She'd left the door on the latch for him; he could hear the shower running in the bathroom and he tapped on the door to let her know that he was there. 'Can I pour you a drink?'

The shower stopped. 'Er, yes. Thanks. I'll be out in a minute.'

'No rush.' He could do with a few minutes to gather himself.

He examined the mini-bar, found a brandy for Daisy and Scotch for himself and split a bottle of ginger ale between the two, and was very carefully watching the rain splashing onto the porch below when she opened the door.

'Is this mine?'

'Brandy and ginger. It'll warm you up.' And he half turned. His discretion was unnecessary. She had a towel around her hair, a bath sheet covering her from armpit to ankle and her wrap worn loosely over that. What remained visible was rather pink, and it occurred to Robert that the last thing Daisy needed was warming up.

'I'll take this through to the bathroom with me,' he said, picking up his glass. 'We haven't got long; I said we'd eat at seven. I thought you'd want an early night.' And suddenly his own face felt a touch on the warm side. 'After such a long day.'

'Seven o'clock is just fine.'

He closed the bathroom door behind him and allowed himself a momentary image of Daisy dashing about the bedroom, getting into her clothes and make-up in record time so that she'd be ready when he emerged. The thought provoked a welcome smile and he sipped at his drink, listening for the telltale sounds.

What he heard was the quiet ting of the telephone as she lifted the receiver to make a call.

CHAPTER SEVEN

TUESDAY night or Wednesday morning. It doesn't matter. All that matters is that I've been stupid. Thoroughly stupid. Robert's a grown man with the kind of car that would laugh in the face of bad weather, but I had to come over all melodramatic and conscience-ridden and now he's lying three feet away from me. Almost near enough to touch, and it's so quiet that I can hear him breathing. I can't bear it!

And as if that's not bad enough, everyone is going to know we spent the night together.

Daisy heard the bathroom door close. In a minute she'd hear the shower and then there would be nothing in her head but Robert. Robert standing naked beneath the spray, water glistening on his skin, dripping from his hair, running down his thighs... She snatched up the telephone, desperate for a distraction, any distraction.

'Hello, Daisy.' George Latimer had picked up the telephone so quickly that she suspected he'd been waiting for her to call. 'What kind of day have you had?'

'Long, cold and wet, but that's par for the course.'

'No problems, then?'

Problems? Ha! 'Not a problem, exactly.' The British talent for understatement was safe in her hands.

117

'Oh? Well, if it's not a problem, perhaps you'd better tell me what, "exactly", it is.'

How about Robert Furneval turned up this evening and right now he's in my bathroom—naked—and later on, we're going to be sleeping together? Well, not together, but in the same room, which is near enough to be a serious problem. That's what 'exactly' is... 'Well, the thing is, George, I think I might have spotted something rather special...'

'I don't suppose for a moment it's what you think it is, Daisy,' he said, when she'd explained at length about the dish she'd found amongst the kitchen china. 'It's so easy to get carried away.' Carried away? She was the least likely person to get 'carried away' that she knew. Suppression could be her middle name. Which was why she wasn't in the shower and naked herself right now. 'Finds like that are rarer than hen's teeth, you know.' George's voice wrenched her back to reality.

'But not unknown?' she persisted. Priceless bowls had been discovered being used to feed some pampered pooch.

'Not unknown,' he agreed, but she could almost *hear* his shrug. 'But don't let desire for glory run away with your common sense.'

'You think I should forget it, then?'

'Unless you want a box of banqueting size kitchen china. You're a professional, not a bargain hunter.'

'But if I'm right?'

'Why are you calling me, Daisy? I can't authenticate a piece of porcelain over the telephone. Use your best judgement.'

She hadn't been asking for his opinion on its authenticity. That wasn't her dilemma. She knew what she'd seen. 'That wasn't why I rang. I just wondered if I should mention it to the auctioneers.'

She had half expected him to question her sanity. Instead he considered her question and then said, 'Well, I suppose you could.' He sounded doubtful.

'But you don't advise it.'

'I'm thinking of you, my dear. If you're right, they'll look stupid, and they won't enjoy the experience and they won't forget it, either. And neither will anyone else. You'll be followed round sales for evermore by reporters, dealers, just about anyone looking for a bargain or a story. Of course, if you're wrong, you'll be the one with egg on your face and they'll have a good laugh at your—and Latimer's—expense.'

'But what about the seller?'

'You're a dealer, Daisy. If the auctioneers haven't spotted something interesting, it's not your concern.'

'I know, but—'

'The present Baronet has inherited all his family's talent for wasting money, in his case gambling, drink and expensive women. Anything left after the sale will undoubtedly go the same way.' Having dealt with the Warburys, he changed the subject. 'Are the lots we discussed up to scratch?'

After they'd discussed the items she was to bid for and she'd hung up, she realised that she'd got what she wanted. George had distracted her with a vengeance. In fact his dismissal of her opinion had seriously irritated her.

She pulled the towel from her hair and fluffed it with her fingers. She'd buy the box of china and jolly well show him, and if she'd made a mistake, well, she knew a caterer who would be more than happy to take good dishes off her hands. And if the dish was genuine, well…she wouldn't be rubbing any-one's nose in her find, so that wouldn't be a problem.

She was in her lacy black teddy, sitting at the dressing table painting on her lipstick, when the bath-room door clicked open. 'Are you decent?'

Not particularly. She'd planned to be dressed, but-toned up to the neck and waiting at the door to bolt the moment he emerged from the bathroom. But he'd think her modesty funny, and after George's casual dismissal of her ability, she wasn't in the mood to be laughed at.

'Compared with my recent appearance in Reception wearing next to nothing and a pair of boots, I'd say I was probably overdressed.' He didn't answer and she turned her head. He was leaning against the bathroom door, wearing a bathsheet tucked around his waist and nothing else. Not even a smile. Well, that was all right, then.

Except that his dark hair was slicked back from the shower and a tiny spot of shaving foam clung to his jaw, lending an almost unbearable intimacy to his presence in her room.

It was a long time since she'd seen Robert without a shirt and time had only improved him. His chest had broadened and was now spattered with a shadow of dark hair that arrowed towards his waist. His shoulders were wider and his arms strong and sin-ewy. This was the body hinted at by the golden youth she had fallen in love with, and her mouth momen-tarily dried at the sight of him. Then, when he still said nothing, she swallowed and found her voice. 'What is it?'

'I never quite saw you as the kind of girl who would wear black underwear.'

'Really?' From some unexpected reserve of strength she managed sarcasm. 'So you've thought about it?' Actually, she didn't want to know that, and before he could answer, she added. 'Strange, I've never given your underwear a moment's thought.'

Liar, liar, pants on fire. You've thought about it, Daisy Galbraith. Black cotton boxers. Black close-fitting briefs. Or those soft clinging shorts that left nothing to the imagination. In black. She could never quite make up her mind.

She forced herself to turn away, blot her lipstick, then stand and walk across to the wardrobe. She was conscious of his gaze following her every movement as she took down her suit, stepped into the skirt and fastened it at the waist.

It was too short. Far too short. She felt naked in it. She slipped into the neat little jacket and fastened the buttons. It didn't help much. She turned and picked up the drink he had poured for her and which she had barely touched.

It was both hot and cold, the sharpness of the ginger cooling the back of her throat, the brandy warming her from the inside out as it spread through her system. It made her feel a little light-headed. Something was making her feel light-headed.

Robert finally moved, opened his bag and shook out a dark red shirt, a tie. She held her breath. His shorts were the soft clinging kind. But white.

Surprises all round, then. He retreated to the bathroom and shut the door.

In the safety of the bathroom, Robert finally let out
a long-held breath. He had doubted Mike when he'd
said his little sister was a grown woman. Mike must
have thought he was out of his mind. Or blind. Or
both.

Dear God, what had he been doing while Daisy
was growing up? Why hadn't he noticed how much
she had changed? Because he'd never seen her looking like that before? Or maybe he just hadn't been
looking.

Or maybe she hadn't wanted him to see.

No. That was ridiculous. Yet there was no denying
the fact that she was like some Jekyll and Hyde character. One side of her the casual, friendly Daisy that
he'd always known and had come racing to Warbury
like some latter-day Galahad to protect. The girl
who'd come to lunch whenever he was at a loose
end, the girl who'd sit quietly all day on a riverbank,
dangling her toes in the river, and who never took
herself too seriously. But apparently there was another side.

Elegant, slightly distant and sexy as sin. The
woman who had sat at her dressing table in black silk
underwear, blotting her lipstick, knew exactly what
she was doing. She was a woman with creamy shoulders and a long, sensuous waist and small, high
breasts that for once were not hidden beneath layers
of clothing but clearly etched by a trimming of fine
black lace.

She was a woman with a secret lover, and one who clearly didn't need anyone to protect her.

His fingers shook slightly as he fitted cufflinks into his shirt. He shouldn't have done this. He shouldn't be here. But he'd burned his boats roomwise and, unless he was prepared to drive home through torrential rain, here he'd have to stay. Maybe the rain was safer.

The lightning flash that lit up the small frosted window pane swiftly followed by a threatening rumble of thunder suggested otherwise, and he wasn't a fool. Not much.

Yet still he lingered in the bathroom. Until today he'd never had to think about what he might say to Daisy. Conversation had been easy, unforced. Now he didn't even begin to know what to say to her. What would they talk about? How would they spend an evening in trivial conversation, teasing one another in the way they always had, when his mind had a completely different agenda.

The wedding, he thought, clutching at straws. They could talk about the wedding. No. Oh, God no. Anything but white-lace-and-promise talk. That would remind him too painfully of what he could never have. What he had never, until this moment, wanted.

Neutral. He needed something neutral to talk about. And, taking a deep breath, he opened the bathroom door. 'Right,' he said, as he pulled on his jacket. 'If I'm going to this sale tomorrow you're going to have to educate me. I don't want to walk out of there tomorrow with a stuffed parrot under my arm.'

Daisy laughed on cue as he opened the bedroom door and ushered her through it, determined to get them both into the safety of the public area as quickly as he could. 'I thought you said you'd been to one of these things before.'

'I have. I was rising seven and my father made me sit on my hands through the entire day.'

'Your father?' She glanced at him in surprise. 'Is he a collector, too? Jennifer never mentioned it.'

'That's because he wasn't. Isn't. He's a historian. His area is social history and his interest was purely intellectual. Poking about in the lives of families who'd lived in the same place for generations. He met my mother at a sale.'

'Did he?' He rarely mentioned his father and Daisy seemed lost for words. 'You must have been bored to death,' she said finally.

'No.' To have his father to himself for a whole day had been worth the agony of sitting still, keeping quiet. 'He took me out to lunch, gave me a glass of watered-down wine and let me eat what I liked.' And he'd flirted with one of the pretty waitresses. With the twenty-twenty vision of hindsight, and an adult's knowledge of human behaviour, it seemed probable that his father's sole purpose in visiting the restaurant had been to meet with the waitress, the freedom of the menu and the glass of wine the simplest way to distract his son.

'Do you ever see him?'

'My father? Occasionally. When he's between affairs he's deluded into thinking my mother is the only woman he's ever truly loved, so he invites me to dinner and tries to persuade me to intervene with her, on his behalf.'

'And do you?'

'There's no point. He has an attention span where women are concerned roughly similar to that of a goldfish. If he cared enough he'd make the effort himself.' He turned as they reached the stairs. Was it his imagination or did she seem taller? He glanced down and realised that it was no illusion. Daisy was wearing seriously high heels.

Janine had worn shoes like that. They'd cost a fortune, but she'd taken the view that for jaw-dropping sex appeal there was nothing to beat them and he'd agreed with her. But that was Janine and this was Daisy. Daisy, who wore sensible shoes and jeans or long skirts over boots. Daisy, who tied her hair back in elastic bands. At least she did when she was with him.

He stopped. 'What happened to the boots?'

'They're stuffed with newspaper and drying out,' she said, and, realising that he was staring at the exquisite black peep-toe shoes that she was wearing, she put her feet neatly together and looked down at them too. It must have been to disguise the sudden rise of colour to her cheeks, because she presumably knew what they looked like. 'George recommended these,' she said, before moving off with that hip-lifting swing that very high heels demanded. 'He expects me to use them to distract the opposition.'

'It works for me.'

'Oh, this is nothing.' She giggled, as if she'd remembered something slightly wicked. 'Just wait until I cross my legs. I've been practising in the mirror.'

That he refused to believe, but he forced himself to smile back. Keep it light. 'Are you *determined* to cause a riot here tonight?'

'Now that's a thought. If all these hard-nosed dealers think I'm just a blonde airhead, they won't take me very seriously tomorrow, will they?'

'Don't you want them to take you seriously?'

'Not tomorrow.'

Daisy saw the doubt in Robert's eyes. Well, she'd have to try harder. If she could convince him that this Daisy was the pretend one, she might have salvaged something from the mess.

'With luck,' she added, 'I might get away with it for quite some time. Will you help?'

He looked somewhat startled. 'If I can. What do you have in mind?'

Think…think… 'Well, you've known lots of girls—'

'Are you suggesting I'm a serial airhead fancier?'

'Would I do that?' Daisy widened her eyes in a terrific impression of the fluffiest of girls and she laid her fingertips lightly against her breast to emphasise her point. 'I think Janine was really quite clever.'

'Only *quite* clever?'

'Well, she was clever enough to jump before she was pushed. But if she had been really smart she'd have been planning her own wedding right now.' Her smile invited him to laugh at himself. 'Wouldn't she?'

Robert chuckled obligingly, but Daisy had the feeling his heart wasn't in it. 'You know, for a duckling, you're really quite bright.'

'Shh. That's a state secret.' Then, because she'd seen airheads in action, she giggled again.

'Don't overdo it, sweetheart,' he warned.

'Is that possible?'

'Cat.' That was better. They were back to trading casual insults, and her spirits lifted a little as they paused in the entrance to the dining room. 'I'm afraid we didn't get as much head-turning attention crossing Reception as you deserve.' His voice had just the right amount of edge, Daisy was glad to note. The words might have been right, but he hadn't been paying her a compliment.

He was right, though; the crowds had thinned, mercifully, with guests either retiring to their rooms or to the dining room. But she wasn't about to let him get away with that jibe. 'There's only one solution to that. Champagne. The pop of a champagne cork always attracts attention.' She snapped her fingers to prove a point and a number of heads swivelled obligingly.

'You're tired and you're hungry. It'll go straight to your head.'

She sparkled her eyes at him. 'Promise?'

Was that what she was like with her lover? Silly? Flirtatious? Robert felt sickened by the way his mind was running, but he couldn't help it. Was that who she'd telephoned the minute he was out of the way in the bathroom? Had she called him to warn him not to come? Or just because she couldn't bear not to speak to him even for one evening?

Daisy flinched as something very like anger seethed back at her, heating the depths of Robert's dark eyes, but before he could say what was on his mind they were shown to a table in a secluded corner of the restaurant.

'Would you like to see the wine list, sir?'

Robert shook his head. 'Just bring a bottle of Bollinger.' He glanced briefly at the menu. 'And we'll have the wild mushroom pancakes followed by...' he paused momentarily, flicked a glance in her direction and smiled a little grimly '...roast duck-ling.'

'Excuse me!' Daisy declared the minute the waiter was out of earshot. 'I prefer to choose what I eat for myself.'

'You're an airhead, remember? Airheads like to be told what to do, what to eat. Believe me.'

'Oh, I do,' she retaliated. Then blushed.

'And they don't have the sensibility to blush.' And the wretch glowered at her as her colour deepened even further. 'But then, it's something of a lost art.'

Robert, despite everything that had happened, was beginning to enjoy himself. Their usual bantering conversational style had taken on an edge. A touch of danger. They were pushing one another in a way that had never happened before and it was oddly exhilarating. And the champagne would only add to the tension.

The waiter opened the bottle without making a fuss, and the cork breathed politely from the neck as a well-handled cork should. But nevertheless a number of people did turn and smile indulgently as they imagined some special celebration.

'So, you have your champagne,' he said, as they held their glasses. 'Now there has to be a toast.'

'Why?'

'It's traditional. It's what champagne was created for.'

'To the sale tomorrow, then. Successful bidding.'

He shook his head. 'Give it up, Daisy. It'll take more than a couple of giggles, a short skirt and a pair of high heels to turn you into the candyfloss kid.'

'Really? Oh, well, I'll try again.' She lifted the glass. 'Let me see, now, how about…to an undiscovered treasure at a knock-down price?'

'Not bad. Not quite silly enough, but not bad. Let's go for broke and make it a whole box full of treasures and no other bidders.'

She laughed out loud, attracting more attention. 'That's *very* silly.' Then she shrugged. 'But then so's the lottery. It doesn't stop George and I having a line between us every Saturday. To a box full of treasures and no other bidders, then.' And she touched her glass against his and sipped the champagne.

'What would you do if you won?'

'The lottery? Easy. I'd take a slow boat to China and another one to Japan. Then I'd hop on the *QE2* to the States and visit all the great museums there.'

'You're not in a great hurry to get there?'

'Well, yes, but I'm scared of flying.'

'I don't believe it. I don't believe you're scared of anything.'

'Flying and earwigs.' And being in love with Robert Furneval. 'I'd buy something very rare and beautiful and give it to the Victoria and Albert Museum,' she rushed on. 'That way I wouldn't ever have to worry about it, but could go and look at it whenever I liked.' She paused. Then, because he was still looking at her as if he didn't believe her, she added, 'Buy you a new fishing rod. It's so long since you've fished, your old one must be broken. What about you?'

'I don't buy lottery tickets.'

'It doesn't matter. I'm never going to win; it's just a fantasy. So fantasise.'

Robert tried. He must want something, something so far out of reach that it would need lottery millions to buy it. But there was only one thing he longed for, yearned for. He hadn't known it, or particularly missed the lack of it, until this evening. But the ability to love one woman with all his heart and soul for the rest of his life…well, that wasn't something that money could buy.

'A tropical island,' he began a little desperately as Daisy's gaze seemed to burn into him, seeking out his secrets. 'A yacht.' Pathetic. He tried to laugh. 'A football club…' He saw the disappointment in Daisy's eyes. She thought him shallow. Well, she probably thought that anyway. He certainly couldn't tell her the truth. 'This isn't fair. You've had time to think about it.'

Robert was lying. For an instant, Daisy had seen something in his face, in his eyes, something he wanted so desperately that he couldn't put it into words. Or was afraid to.

She would have asked him what it was, but she knew that depth of hidden longing, knew he would pretend he didn't know what she was talking about. In his place, she would have done exactly the same. Instead she reached out and briefly touched his hand. 'Tell me another time,' she said, before turning to smile up at the waiter who had arrived with their pancakes. He served them, topped up their glasses and departed.

Usually their silences were restful things. Now the small sounds of silver against china seemed only to emphasise the quiet tension. He wasn't accustomed to awkward silences, not with Daisy.

What made it worse was that it wasn't a lack of something to say that constrained him. He had a heart full of words, all of them desperate to spill out and declare themselves. And if they did? She knew him better than anyone. She wouldn't take him seriously. Worse, because she knew him so well, she would be offended. And she had loved someone else for a long time.

Yet the touch of her fingertips burned against his skin and he wanted her to know that he cared.

'How about this?' he said. 'If I won the lottery I'd buy the fishing rights to a stretch of salmon river in Scotland and a comfortable cottage alongside it. And a pair of rods. One for you and one for me.'

Daisy had been pushing a mushroom around her plate, but now she raised her lashes and looked at him. 'You can't fool me, Robert Furneval. You just want me along to make the sandwiches.'

She thought she could see right through him. Well, maybe it was better if she continued to think that. 'You make great sandwiches. I love the baguettes you do with brie and stuffed olives. And the egg and bacon ones. And that thing you do where you wrap buttered bread around hot sausages…' His hand momentarily covered hers. 'Would you come?'

Her smile deepened and she twisted her hand beneath his and held it for a moment. 'Win the lottery and then ask me. But hurry. If I win first I'll be off on the first boat…'

'Well, isn't this sweet? Daisy and Robert holding hands. And champagne, too. Is there something you haven't been telling good old Monty?'

Daisy snatched back her hand. 'Monty! What on earth are you doing here?'

'Covering the sale, sweetheart,' he said, as he bent to kiss her cheek. 'I thought I'd see you here.' He glanced pointedly at Robert. 'I hoped I would. I never thanked you for all your help at my little do last weekend.'

'No problem,' Daisy said too quickly, too anxious to change the subject. Robert could almost see the gossip columnist's antennae homing in on a story. 'It was a lovely party.'

'Nick didn't think so. The poor boy had the girl of his dreams snatched from right under his nose.' He turned. 'You're a sly one, Robert.'

He was too experienced at fishing himself to rise to the bait. 'I was just looking out for a friend.'

'Such devotion. Or maybe you've inherited your mother's eye for lovely things?'

Monty was so clever with words. However he replied it could be misconstrued, quoted out of context and given whatever spin the man fancied. 'I'm simply here in a cheque-signing capacity. My mother asked Daisy to look at some porcelain for her and possibly put in a bid for it.'

'Did she? It's nice work if you can get it.' He grinned at his own wit. 'Well, my trout is getting cold so I'll leave you young things to your hand-holding, but do join me in the bar later for a brandy. You can tell me all about it.'

Robert watched him return to his table. 'Oaf,' he muttered, when he was out of earshot.

'Monty's all right,' Daisy said. 'Just a bit silly. But what on earth is he doing here? He's not an arts columnist; he writes the gossip column.'

'Yes, well, this sale is the last gasp of a venerable dynasty with a whole wardrobe full of skeletons. Let's hope he'll be too busy rattling them to waste column inches on us.'

'Oh, but…' She began to laugh. 'He wouldn't!'

'He's a professional gossip, sweetheart. I wouldn't count on it.'

Robert was waiting for Monty when he entered the bar and he signalled the waiter to bring the brandy he'd ordered.

'On your own, dear boy?'

'Daisy's had a long day. I'm sure you'll have a chance to speak to her tomorrow if the dismantling of a dynasty doesn't keep you fully occupied.'

'No. The story's well documented and already written. I'm just looking for a few touches of bathos: the hordes picking over the bones. You know the kind of stuff.'

'You should find plenty here to fill your column.'

Monty picked up the brandy balloon and swirled the pool of spirit at its base. 'If that's a hint that you'd prefer not to read about yourself, Robert—'

'I don't care about myself. I'm hoping you care enough about Daisy not to embarrass her.'

'I've already checked with the desk clerk, you know.'

'Then you'll know I booked a single room.'

'I also know that in an act of chivalry you offered it to a lady in distress. The young woman in Reception was very moved, but then there's nothing unusual about that. A smile from you would move mountains.' He sipped the brandy, then he sighed. 'I may be wrong, but I don't imagine you're sleeping in your car. Such a nasty night.' Robert didn't answer. Single beds wouldn't convince Monty. 'No. I didn't think so. You don't know a decent accountant who would do my taxes for me, do you? Someone who wouldn't charge the earth.'

Robert felt the tension ease from his shoulders. 'I'm sure I could find someone. For a friend.'

Monty nodded, apparently oblivious to any hint of sarcasm. 'Thanks. Shall we have another of these?' He summoned the waiter. 'Actually, you know, I'm not really surprised.'

'Not surprised about what?'

'About you and Daisy. Oh, two more brandies; he's paying.' He turned back to Robert. 'No, I was thinking about it over dinner. Well, you always go back to her, don't you? You have a little fling with some gorgeous girl but it never lasts. And then you're at a party or the theatre or somewhere and the girl at your side is Daisy. Again.'

'I'm not sure I'm following you.'

'Then you're not as smart as I thought you were.' And he lifted the glass the waiter put in front of him. 'Cheers.'

*   *   *

'Daisy?'

There was no answer, and in the small pool of light thrown by the table lamp across the space between the beds, Robert could see that she was asleep. She was lying on her side, her face pressed into the pillow, her hair a soft fuzz of curls, her body a gentle curve beneath the bedclothes.

He'd wanted to reassure her about Monty but there was no point in waking her. The morning would do. And he lowered himself onto the side of the bed, loosening his tie, unfastening his cuffs as he watched the gentle rise and fall of her breathing.

Monty was wrong. They were friends; that was all. They had always been friends. Even when she was a skinny kid and Mike had got so irritated when she'd tagged along he hadn't been able to resist that way she'd looked at him to back her up…

She still looked like a kid. Her soft pink lips were parted over the whitest of teeth and her skin had the peachy bloom of a baby. He reached out, wanting to touch it, stroke it, and for a moment his hand lingered a breath from her cheek. She looked untouched, brand-new, and he felt something deep inside him twist with pain. He didn't want anything bad to happen to her, knew that he would do anything in his power to prevent it.

His fingers curled back into his fist and he stood up, took himself to the bathroom to undress, horrified by the fact that while his mind was contemplating the lofty ideals of friendship, the rest of him appeared to be working on an altogether earthier agenda.

CHAPTER EIGHT

WEDNESDAY 29 March. I didn't sleep. Not one wink. I might have eventually drifted off—I was doing a pretty good job of pretending when Robert finally came to bed—but then he said my name and I nearly gave myself away. And he brushed my cheek. So gently. If he hadn't moved right then…

Robert was sleeping when Daisy finally crawled out of bed. No pretence about it.

He was lying on his back, one arm flung wide so that it hung over the bed, the sheets tangled around his waist. He looked so young, as if all the years since he had kissed Lorraine Summers had fallen away, and she longed to reach out, as he had in the night, and touch his face.

For a moment the tips of her fingers lingered over the hard line of his cheek, then she drew back. It would be better to let him sleep, dress without embarrassment, without him seeing her early-morning face. Not that he hadn't seen it before. But there was a whole world of difference between an early-morning kitchen and an early-morning bedroom, no matter how platonically shared.

She took her clothes into the bathroom, showered as quickly and quietly as she could. Then she made a single cup of tea and placed it on the night table beside him.

For a while she stood there, indulging herself in the pleasure of this unexpected intimacy. It seemed unlikely that she would ever have the chance again. He was laid bare for her. Shoulders, finely muscled arms, sculptured chest...all usually concealed by the civilising cloth of shirts made by hand in Jermyn Street.

'Goodbye...' The word whispered from her, then, as a tear squeezed beneath her lids, she bent and kissed his cheek. 'Goodbye.' Still he didn't stir. Well, there was no reason to wake him. And she turned and let herself quietly out of the room.

The phone woke Robert. He groped for the unfamiliar instrument, knocked over a cup, sending a cascade of cold tea over the night table, swore briefly before muttering an irritable, 'Furneval,' into the receiver.

In the dining room there was the quiet buzz of expectation, excitement as dealers and collectors gathered for breakfast. The thought of food almost choked her, but she needed juice, coffee, or she would never survive until lunchtime. She was beaten to the jug by Monty.

'Here, let me do that. Robert still sleeping it off?' he asked. Despite every attempt to appear cool, she blushed. 'Don't worry, I won't blab.'

'There's nothing to blab about, Monty.'

'No? Robert said that, too.' He smiled so sweetly that she was almost deceived into thinking that he believed him. 'But he was still prepared to buy me off.'

Buy? How much was a reputation worth these

days? And was it her reputation or his own that he
was concerned about? After all, the suggestion that
he'd spent a night with Daisy Galbraith wasn't going
to do much for his image. Hers, on the other hand,
might take on some serious gloss. George would be
delighted. Her mother would… 'You don't expect me
to fall for that one, do you? You know perfectly well
that Robert and I are just good friends—'

'Really?' He filled her glass with orange juice. 'I
didn't know it was as serious as *that*—'

'—and no one would have sent a dog out into last
night's rain.' She put down the glass quickly as her
hand began to shake, and began to sift through the
yoghurts so that she wouldn't have to look at him.
'Not even you, Monty.' She picked a strawberry yo-
ghurt, and because she knew deep down that running
away was not the way to handle this, that if he
thought she was trying to hide anything he'd never
stop digging until he discovered the truth, she turned
and looked him firmly in the eye. 'You can try to
convince me that you're a black-hearted villain, but
I know it's not true.'

'Oh, damn.' And he grinned like a naughty school-
boy. 'You won't tell Robert, will you? He's promised
to have someone sort out my tax return.'

Well, that answered her question. A reputation in
exchange for the services of an accountant. It was a
good job she didn't have an inflated image of her
own self-worth. She laughed and shook her head.
'Your secret is safe with me. I won't tell if you
don't.'

He'd been dreaming. Before the telephone rang. He'd
been dreaming about Daisy. After the crashing awak-

ening, when he'd remembered, far too late, where he was and who he was with, he'd turned, expecting to see her snuggled down beneath the bedclothes like a little dormouse, unwilling to face a wet and chilly day. But the rain had stopped some time in the night and the sun was streaming in through a chink in the the curtains…

And her bed was empty.

Something made him touch his fingers to his cheek. It was damp, and when he looked at them there was the faintest smear of red. He recognised the colour. It was the same colour as the lipstick that Daisy had been wearing last night. And the colour broke his dream, so that he remembered that it had been of Daisy's lips against his cheek as she'd kissed him goodbye. No dream, then.

'Daisy?' The bathroom door stood ajar, her bag was zipped up and waiting by the door and her coat had gone. 'Damn!' He tossed back the covers and checked the bathroom anyway. Only then did it occur to him check his watch. It was nearly nine o'clock.

It had been hours before he'd dropped off to sleep, hours in which he'd lain listening to her soft breathing, hours during which he'd racked his brain in an attempt to get to the bottom of the mystery…

And the dear girl had left him to sleep. He rubbed his hand over his face. He'd needed it. He could still do with a solid eight hours. He stared at his reflection in the shaving mirror, the faint smear of red on his cheek. But his cheek had been wet. He touched his fingers to his tongue and tasted the unmistakable salt of tears…

*   *   *

Despite a buzz of nerves around her stomach, and a sickening certainty that she was about to make a complete and utter fool of herself, Daisy could at least be certain that she wouldn't let the gallery down by looking dowdy. Haggard, maybe. But not dowdy. At least it had stopped raining. The sun was shining and, since Monty had offered her a lift across the road to the Manor, she hadn't had to sully her expensive new shoes on the pot-holed drive.

Monty disappeared to look at the glories and the waste of the Warburys while she registered to bid, picked up her number and took one last look at the pieces she hoped to buy, including a casual walk past the bench with the boxed lots of kitchenware, barely glancing at the one she was interested in. When she went to take a seat in the marquee, Robert was standing just inside the entrance, waiting for her. He didn't look happy.

Robert saw her the moment she entered the huge temporary sales marquee that had been erected in front of the house. There were dozens of people arriving to stake their claim to the best seats, but among the men and women dressed for just another working day in clothes rubbed to a shine by countless salesroom benches she was impossible to miss.

Until a week ago, he'd have said he knew everything there was to know about Daisy Galbraith. He'd have been wrong. It was now quite obvious that he knew nothing about her. This woman, this totally stunning vision, was a stranger, a stranger who, under any other circumstances, he would have been breaking his neck to get to know.

It wasn't just the way her ridiculous duckling-yellow curls ruffled about her face. It was everything about her. The beautifully cut dark red suit, its thigh-skimming skirt demonstrating to anyone who cared to look that there was nothing wrong with her knees. Or her legs. What really confused him was the fact that he hadn't noticed that she was all grown up.

And it hurt, really hurt, that someone else had.

'You should have woken me,' he said, without pre-amble.

Daisy barely glanced at him, too busy surveying the marquee, rapidly filling with eager collectors. Or was it one collector that she was looking for? 'You looked so peaceful I didn't have the heart to disturb you. What's the problem? Did you miss breakfast?' she asked.

Her pertness irritated Robert, as did the sharp, sexy image which seemed so much more blatant in daylight. He didn't like it. He much preferred that soft, sweet girl he had watched over last night. A girl who would never have worn that shade of lipstick.

Yet the lipstick did it for him too. The thought of her leaning over him to kiss his cheek while he slept provoked a flood of heat that swept away the irritation. 'Breakfast was the least of my worries. Your sister rang you.'

'Sarah?' Her forehead crinkled into a little frown. He wanted to smooth it away with the pad of his thumb, with his mouth... 'Why?'

He blinked. 'I haven't the faintest idea. She was in too much of a hurry to get off the phone and start spreading the news that I'd spent the night with you to leave a message.'

'Did you tell her that you did?' she said, a little catch of her breath doing ridiculous things to his heart-rate. 'Spend the night with me?'

Lord, but she was cool. When had she got this cool? 'No.' He hadn't. Not *with* her. 'She leapt to that conclusion when I answered the telephone. I was asleep when it rang, or I wouldn't have been so dim. That's why you should have woken me.'

That catch again, somewhere between a little shudder and a sigh. 'Oh, dear.' Or was she just finding it difficult not to laugh? 'I'm really sorry.'

'Why are you apologising?'

'Well, you seem upset, and I can see why. That kind of gossip won't do anything for your image.'

'*My* image?' What image? What the devil was she talking about? 'What about yours?'

'Ah, but I don't have an image, Robert. Well, not that sort of image, anyway.' She appeared to give the matter some consideration. 'I suppose that kind of gossip might give me one, though. Look, can we find a seat before they're all taken? Over there, I think.'

For just the briefest moment Daisy had felt something akin to flying. The world would think Robert Furneval was her lover. It was the kind of dream she'd confided to her teenage diary...

It had never been pop stars for her. There had just been Robert, and one day he would look at her as if he saw the whole world in her eyes and everyone would understand that she was the only one for him. For a moment, a precious moment, she had thought it would happen.

But teenage diaries and real life had about as much in common as chalk and china. And because it wasn't ever going to be like that she had turned that little gasp into something more like laughter, made a joke of it and let it go.

Well, she was good at that; she'd been doing it all her life. Monty had believed her. So would everyone else. Robert, though, looked confused. Did he think she'd throw a vast wobbly and say she'd never be able to show her face in public again?

'Don't worry about it,' she said, and looped her arm through his. 'I'll call Sarah as soon as I get home. Explain what happened.'

'You expect her to believe you?'

'Why not? She'd do the same for a friend caught out in bad weather without a bed for the night.' A few minutes of clear thought and even Sarah would have to admit that the very idea of her little sister and Robert Furneval as a hot item *was* laughable. 'There wouldn't be any reason for me to lie.'

But what about her lover? How would he take it? In his shoes, Robert thought, he wouldn't be so sanguine. 'If the choice had been between sharing a room with Sarah and the deluge, I'd have taken the deluge.'

'She does talk rather a lot.'

'Well, I can promise you that she quite lost the power of speech this morning.'

They took the two remaining seats on the centre aisle, with Daisy on the outside so that she could see around a couple of hefty dealers, and the sale began.

'Is that it?' Robert asked, a couple of hours later, when she'd outbid the opposition and taken the final item marked on her catalogue. 'Can we go and get some coffee?'

'Not quite.'

'But I thought that was all you wanted.'

'I'm hoping to get a box of kitchen china.' His disbelief must have been easily read in his face because she added, 'It's for a friend.'

What friend? 'I see. And how were you planning to get it home on the train?'

She looked nonplussed. 'You're giving me a lift, aren't you?'

'And if I hadn't turned up?'

'Oh. Well, I'd have managed somehow.'

Which answered any question about who she'd phoned last night. He'd hoped to find out when he paid the hotel bill, but Daisy had got there before him. Clearly whoever she was seeing had been warned to stay away. 'Yes, I'm sure you would.'

'Look, why don't you go and get some coffee? I won't be long.'

'No, I'll wait.'

'Then for goodness' sake stop twirling your bidding number about, or you'll end up with a box of old saucepans. Give it to me.'

He handed it over without demur and watched while she bid in a desultory manner for lot after lot of all kinds of kitchen junk without success.

'What on earth are you doing? Do you want this stuff or don't you?'

'At the right price.' She was tapping her bidding number against her knee as a number of small bids were made for yet another box of mouldy old china. She bid once, then again. Her rival, sitting a few rows back on the opposite side of the aisle, upped it again. Daisy appeared to lose interest, but then, just as the auctioneer was going to knock it down, she flipped up her number and at the same time slowly crossed her legs. By the time her opponent had got over the shock, the lot was hers.

'Come on. That's it,' she said abruptly. 'Let's go and sort out the paperwork.'

'I'm shocked.' Daisy turned to him. 'That was the most appalling exhibition of feminine mischief I've seen in my entire life.'

'I don't believe you. Besides, he'd been leering at me all morning.'

'What do you expect in a skirt up to your knickers and black stockings—?'

'They're tights. Stockings *would* have been tacky.'

'I'm glad you realise that.' He caught her arm as she moved away from him. 'What are you up to?'

'Me? Dozy Daisy?' She handed him back his number. 'Pay your bill, Robert. That last lot was knocked down to you.'

Robert, about to argue, realised that he was missing something, and instead got out his chequebook and paid for a carton of filthy old kitchen china. 'Now what?'

'Go and fetch your car and then put that box on the back seat. Very carefully. I've just solved your birthday present problem.'

'What is it?' Robert had carried the box up to Daisy's flat and was now looking at the rather grubby and not particularly exciting piece of china that she was holding.

'A seventeenth-century Kakiemon dish. It's from Japan.'

'You're kidding.'

'No.' She gave little sigh and finally placed it carefully on the cloth with which she had covered the kitchen table. 'I couldn't be one hundred per cent sure until I'd held it,' she said, looking up at him. 'But that's definitely what it is.'

'Won't George Latimer want it?'

'George had his chance but he assumed that I was hallucinating. Besides, there's no question of George having it. You bid for it, it's there in black and white on the receipt. You bid for it; you paid for it.'

'I thought that was an accident.' She didn't answer. 'You could have told me.'

'I might have been wrong, in which case I would have reimbursed you and sold on the china to a friend who runs a stall in a fleamarket.'

Every aspect covered. 'While we're on the subject of paying for things, I have to split the hotel bill with you.' He would have settled it himself if she hadn't beaten him to it, but somehow he didn't think Daisy would respond very positively to any suggestion that he paid for the bed she'd slept in.'

'No need. Latimer's will pay. And they didn't charge any extra for you. I don't know why. The woman in Reception said that under the circumstances there was no charge.' She frowned. 'What circumstances?'

Robert placed the tip of his thumb against the space between her eyes. 'Don't frown.' Well, he had to distract her somehow. And then because the world seemed to shrink to that square inch of warm, vibrant skin, and because he'd been thinking about it all morning, he moved his thumb and kissed away the faint, puzzled crease. Her silky grey eyes widened and darkened, and for a heartbeat he had this feeling, deep down, that all it would take to change the world would be to say the three most precious words in the world. Unfortunately, there was no way on earth she would believe him. So instead he made his face smile. 'The wind might change.'

'Heavens.' Daisy's laugh was shaky and so was her hand as her fingers touched her forehead. He wanted to take that hand and put his arms around her and hold her. It would be the most shocking self-indulgence. 'Ginny's mother would kill me if I wasn't smiling on the wedding photos.' Her voice was shaking too. But she'd forgotten all about the hotel bill.

'I have to go.' He picked up the dish. 'Can you wrap this in something for me?'

'Um. Yes. No, leave it with me and I'll clean it, box it up for you. Men are hopeless at gift-wrapping.'

'That's why department stores offer the service. Are you sure you don't you want to keep it for yourself?'

'No. I love this stuff but I have no yearning to possess it. I was planning on giving it to Jennifer anyway, as a thank-you present. I just discovered she suggested George take me on.'

'Then it must be from both of us. Her birthday's on Sunday; will you come home with me? Unless of course you're busy?' She gave him a long look. 'What?'

She shook her head. 'Nothing. Only that's the first time you've ever asked me if I'm busy. You usually just assume I'll be available.'

Was he really that insensitive? Well, not any more. He'd taken Daisy Galbraith for granted for the very last time. He didn't understand why she'd let him get away with it for so long. 'I'm not assuming anything. I'm asking you because I want you to come with me. Will you?'

There was just a moment of hesitation before she said, 'I must admit I'd love to be there when Jennifer opens her gift.' Which put him in his place. 'But don't come knocking for me at seven-thirty. It's Ginny's hen night on Saturday and I'm anticipating a certain amount of remorse on Sunday morning.'

'We're hitting the town on Friday.'

'Well, don't get arrested. Ginny would murder you. Both of you.'

'Don't worry, I've never lost a bridegroom yet. And you—well, have a good time.' He paused in the doorway, remembering the last time they had stood on that threshold, the tender kiss that they'd shared. But that had been unpremeditated. This time it would be different, and as he hesitated, she brushed her cheek against his and closed the door.

This was getting to be a habit. Saying goodbye to Robert and feeling so weak that she couldn't let go of the doorknob. Her fingers shakily brushed against her forehead, where he had kissed away her frown.

She had been so sure just then, at the door, that he was remembering the way he had kissed her before. Ridiculous, of course. Why would he remember?

She closed her eyes and a deep moan escaped her. How would she ever forget?

The phone began to ring. She didn't want to speak

to anyone, but she forced herself away from the door and picked it up, noticing that there were half a dozen messages waiting for her on her answering machine. No prizes for guessing who three of them were. Her sister, her mother, George… 'Daisy Galbraith.'

'Daisy, I've been ringing and ringing.'

'Sorry, Mum. I've only just got back from the Warbury sale.'

'Good trip, was it?'

'I got everything I went for. Is there something special, or is this just a chat? Only I'm desperate for a shower.'

'No, nothing special. Sarah was trying to get hold of you and I gave her the hotel number. I wonder if she found you?'

Her mother's attempt at being subtle could teach a sledgehammer a thing or two. 'I had a message that she'd rung. What does she want? Do you know?'

'A babysitter for Friday night.'

'She rang me at Warbury for that?'

'It's desperate, apparently. The success of her charity dinner depends on it. I've got a committee meeting or I'd have driven up.'

'Oh, well, then.' She laughed, suddenly back in control. 'It's clearly a crisis. Don't worry, I won't let her down.'

'How was the visit to the hairdresser?'

'Surprisingly easy. He doesn't seem to think I'll spoil the photographs.'

'Good, good.'

'If that's it, then?' It was cruel. Her mother was breaking her neck to know what had happened at Warbury but she was clearly having problems about asking the question outright. What was so difficult? Did you spend the night with Robert Furneval? Easy. And the answer. Not quite so clear cut. Yes and no. Mostly no. 'Mum?'

'Are you coming down at the weekend?'

'Well, Robert and I are going to see Jennifer on Sunday—'

'Oh?' It was a couldn't-quite-believe-her-ears kind of oh. 'Any particular reason?'

Anyone with a cruel streak would be enjoying this. Daisy was beginning to find it tiresome. 'It's her birthday. I found something rather special at the sale for her and Robert wants me to be there when he gives it to her.'

'I'll take her some flowers, then.'

'I'm sure she'll be delighted to see you. And I'll drop in and see you some time on Sunday. I'll bring the bridesmaid dress down with me…' how was that for a quick-thinking distraction? '…but I can't say what time.'

'Lovely.'

She pressed the playback button on the answering machine. 'Daisy, it's Sarah. I was so surprised by Robert answering the phone this morning that I completely forgot why I rang. I hope you know what you're doing. He's not exactly husband material and I always thought that you were a one-man sort of girl. Anyway, can you babysit on Friday night? Andy's going out on this bachelor thrash with Mike, I'm running a charity fundraiser for the local hospice and my regular girl has flu'. I'm desperate.'

That was it? Her mother had been so restrained she had nearly choked herself, and Sarah was being unbelievably restrained by her standards. She went on to the next message.

'Daisy, did you get it?' George asked. 'Was it Kakiemon?'

Oops.

The rest of the calls were hang-ups. Sarah or her mother, or even George, trying again, maybe. Or double glazing salesmen.

Robert flung his jacket over the nearest chair and headed for the phone. He was going crazy. He couldn't get Daisy out of his head. 'Mike? You've got to tell me who it is—'

'Hey, steady on. Calm down. What's the problem?'

'Daisy. She's the problem. She's wearing five-inch heels, skirts up to her thighs and black underwear. She's driving me crazy.'

'Black underwear?'

'Who is she seeing, Mike?'

'You're the one telling me what colour skimpies she's wearing. Besides, I don't remember saying that she was seeing anyone.'

'But you said—'

'I said she was *in love* with someone. Of course the difference may be too subtle for a man who thinks "love" is a four-letter word—'

'It is.'

'But there *is* a difference.'

'I see. You mean I've been running around like an idiot for nothing? She's not having an affair?' Robert tried to get his head around this unexpected turn of events while his system did a quick tour on a white-knuckle ride. There was no lover. Up. But she was in love. Down. 'Who?' he demanded. 'Who is she in love with? Do I know him?'

There was a long pause, and he could almost see the resigned shrug before Mike said, 'Yes.'

'Then for pity's sake put me out of my misery.'

'I can't. But I'll give you a clue. Elinor James.' And he chuckled. The wretch thought it was funny, did he? 'I'll see you on Friday.'

Robert dropped the receiver on the cradle and sank into a chair, rubbing his hands over his face. Daisy loved some unknown man so much that even though it was unrequited, unconsummated, she couldn't handle any other relationships. He wasn't sure whether that was better, or worse. A lover who was little more than a fantasy was unfair competition for any real flesh and blood man.

A fantasy couldn't forget birthdays or anniversaries because he wasn't ever expected to remember them. He couldn't say the wrong thing, or behave badly. There were no expectations for him to live up to. He moved through life being loved, but with no responsibility for that love. How did he know? Elinor James.

She'd been his fantasy once. Hell, she'd set the hormones jangling of every male in the school. Sixteen years old, silk blonde hair a yard long and with skin that looked as if it had been drenched in sunlight.

CHAPTER NINE

SUNDAY 2 April. Some time between remorse and lunchtime.

Ginny's sister certainly knows how to throw a party. And no one mentioned Robert. Not even Sarah. The words 'discretion' and 'valour' linked with her name seem an unlikely combination, but she managed not to bring the subject up at the party. Maybe she was afraid that if she did I might do something dreadful to her with Zorro's sword.

Daisy dressed for comfort rather than style. Comfortable trousers, a soft shirt, a favourite angora sweater.

'You look…'

'Comfortable?' Daisy offered, when words seemed to fail Robert.

'I was going to say cuddly, but it occurred to me that you might not appreciate that as a compliment.'

He was worried about offending her? 'You mean like a teddy bear?' she offered kindly.

'Do I?'

'It's the angora sweater,' she assured him. 'It's a bit like fur.'

'Can I check that out?' Before she could stop him, Robert wrapped his arms around her in a bear hug that trapped her arms and held her so close that she was instantly swamped in an emotive cocktail that overloaded her senses.

The cold touch of his chin, the slight rasp of it against her temple. The mingled scents of shaving soap and shampoo and toothpaste that suggested he was not long from bed and that while she had been standing beneath a cool shower, hoping the water would pummel some life into her limbs, a mile or so away he had been doing much the same thing. Her eyes, in the brief moment before she slammed them shut, had a widescreen close-up of his throat, the smooth skin beneath his ear and the thud, thud, thud of his heartbeat came as a deep counterpoint to her own. And she swallowed, hard.

'Mmm. Maybe you're right.' For a moment, as his arms loosened their grip, his hands spread wide across her back, and for a moment they stroked against the soft fluffy wool. And Daisy knew why cats purred. Then he stepped back, holding her for a moment at arm's length, his face creased in a frown of the most determined concentration. 'But I'll have to try that again without the sweater to be sure.' He smiled. 'It's entirely possible that you're cuddly without it. Are you ready?'

Not in a million years. In a heartbeat. Take your pick. 'For another hug?'

'Ready to go,' he said, and grinned. Inside her everything groaned. Groaned that she had fallen for such a cheap trick, groaned that she had wanted to fall for it. That was how he did it. A hug and a little teasing and that grin. That was how he swept girls off their feet. Well, she refused to be swept. 'We can try the hug again later, if you like,' he offered.

'No, thanks.' She handed him the box with the bridesmaid's dress. 'Here, put this in the car. I'll bring your mother's present.'

'How was the party last night?' Robert glanced at her as they sped through the Sunday quiet of Knightsbridge.

'We had a ball. And Zorro was a big success.' She realised she could have put that more delicately and yawned to cover her gaffe. 'Mike's party?'

'No complaints. Did Sarah mention Warbury?'

'I had the most dire warning on the answering machine. Nothing since. I think the combination of frozen margaritas and chilli must have numbed her tongue.'

'That'll do it every time. What did the warning consist of? Or shouldn't I ask?'

'I'd rather you forgot the whole incident.' And she yawned again. 'I'm sorry, Robert, but I can hardly keep my eyes open.'

'Put the seat back. Have a little snooze, if you like,' he suggested. 'You don't want to fall asleep over the birthday cake.'

She adjusted the seat, lay back and closed her eyes, glad of an excuse to avoid talking about the night they had spent at the Warbury Arms. She'd been trying very hard not to think about it ever since it had happened, with precious little success. She had this weird feeling that everyone knew but no one was saying anything, just holding their breath, waiting. For what, she hadn't the faintest idea. For someone to say April fool? But April Fool's Day had been yesterday...

She sighed, thinking about the way she had kissed

him and said goodbye the morning of the sale. The
tear had taken her by surprise, and she hadn't understood it at the time, but in the days since then the
feeling had grown in her that the word had been more
than a simple whisper into the dark. She had meant
it. After the wedding she would go away. Leave
London, leave Latimer's. Leave Robert.

It was time to turn her fantasies into reality. At
least the ones that were in her power. China,
America, Japan...

Robert parked the Aston in front of his mother's
house, hooked his arm around the back of Daisy's
seat and watched her sleeping. For a while back
there, when she had so swiftly taken the chance to
close her eyes and shut him out, he had suspected
that she simply didn't want to talk to him, that she
was hiding away from him rather than face what troubled her.

But beneath lids faintly dusted with a colour so
vague that he would have been hard pressed to put a
name to it, her eyes were moving as she dreamed.
He wondered about Daisy's dreams. Were they
happy?

As if to answer him, a tear welled up from beneath
her lashes and then seeped over onto her cheek. It
almost broke his heart.

'Oh, my darling,' he murmured, closing his hand,
stroking her cheek with the back of his fingers in an
attempt to comfort her. Another tear followed the first
and, unable to bear it, he whispered her name. Her
lids flickered over pupils dilated black and for a moment she blinked, uncomprehending. 'Come on,

Sleeping Beauty,' he said, and he smiled to reassure her. He wished he could reassure himself. 'We're home.'

'What?'

'We've arrived.'

'Have we?' She shivered a little. 'I must have been dreaming. I thought I was in Japan.' As she struggled to sit up, Robert straightened the seat-back. 'I'm sorry,' she said, knuckling away the dampness around her eyes. 'I just meant to have forty winks.'

'Don't be. Sorry.' He tried to see in her face what had caused the tears, but awake she was far less vulnerable. 'If you can't sleep with a friend, who can you sleep with?'

'Oh, very funny,' she snapped. 'You should go on the stage.' She turned as Jennifer appeared at the front door, opened the door and without waiting for Robert swung her long legs from the car and swooped up the path. 'Happy birthday, Jennifer,' she said. And she hugged her.

There had been a time when she'd hugged him like that. A long time ago. When she was a girl and she hadn't seen him for ages, she would fling herself into his arms and hug him. When had those hugs turned into polite kisses to the cheek?

'I hate to break up the party, but I promised Mother I'd drop in with ''The Dress''. She's desperate to see it.'

'Do you want a hand with the box?'

'No, I can manage. Stay and help your mother with the washing up. But if I'm not back in half an hour please come and rescue me. Bring Major and suggest a walk. Flossie'll do the rest.'

'She's a lovely girl, Robert.' His mother joined him at the window as he watched her cross the green. 'And very bright. She should have kept the dish for herself, you know. Or sold it. She wants to go to Japan and China to study, and that costs money.'

Japan. She'd been dreaming about Japan. 'She wouldn't hear of it. She was going to give it to you anyway.' He turned to look down at his mother. 'Tell me about her.'

'You've known her most of your life. Longer than me.'

'I know, and I thought I knew her as well as anyone, but this last week or so… Well, it's as if I've met a complete stranger.'

'I see.' His mother's lips twitched into something close to a smile.

'You see? What?' He felt utterly frustrated. What was it that everyone else could see that he couldn't? 'What do you see?'

'Daisy hasn't changed, Robert. You have.'

'That's not true. You just see this girl.' He waved towards the window. 'This girl who wears shapeless trousers and old baggy jeans and no make-up—'

'I thought she looked very sweet in that sweater.'

'She looks utterly adorable in that sweater.' Sweet and sexy, and all he could think about was taking the damn thing off and doing the hug thing again and never stopping… He dragged himself back to the point. 'But you should see her when she's working. Skirts up to here,' he said, with a gesture that demonstrated exactly where the offending skirt had ended, 'dark red lipstick and black stockings—'

'Tights, surely? If the skirt is up to, um, there?' He glowered at his mother. It might be her birthday, but that was no excuse for not taking him seriously. 'I'm sorry, Robert, but I don't understand what your problem is. You don't expect her to work in a West End art gallery dressed in jeans, do you?'

'No.' But he remembered the neck-to-toe clothes she'd been wearing when they'd last had lunch—about as alluring as a horse blanket. Nothing like that red suit. 'She never wears clothes like that when she sees me, whether she's working or not.' The little beaded handbag had been something of a giveaway, though, if he'd had the wit to see. With the horse blanket it had looked like something from a child's dressing up box. With the red suit it had been sharp and witty and sexy as hell.

'You'd like her to?'

'What? No!' Then he shrugged. 'Well, maybe.' He raked his fingers through his hair. 'I don't know what I want.'

'I think you probably do. You're just not ready to admit it.'

'There wouldn't be any point, would there? It's Daisy we're talking about. I wouldn't, couldn't, ever do anything to hurt her.'

'I know that.'

'Then you can see how impossible it is.'

'Because you think you're like your father? Incapable of commitment?' He shrugged helplessly. 'Why do you put so much store by the way he behaves? I left him when you were seven years old. I raised you. I have loved the same man all my life, although heaven alone knows he doesn't deserve it. You are my son, too.'

'Nature versus nurture? I'm nearly thirty-one years old and I've never yet met a woman who could hold my attention for more than a few weeks.'

'Except Daisy.'

He didn't deny it. 'Except Daisy.' Was that what Monty had meant about him always going back? 'Why didn't I realise the truth until it was too late?' Major bumped up against his leg and, glad of the distraction, he bent to rub his silky ears.

'It's never too late. Sometimes, though, it's too soon. Daisy was too young for a long time, Robert. When she was sixteen I was rather afraid she might do something very silly.' She was very still. 'I was afraid that *you* might do something very silly.' He looked up, but he didn't speak and she lifted her head a little. 'Do you remember that Christmas when you kissed her underneath the mistletoe?'

'The mistletoe.' His breath seemed to freeze in him as the elusive dream flooded his conscious mind and formed a solid image and he remembered. That was where he'd seen that look before, the sweet, sad yearning for something only to be guessed at, the look that turned a man's will to putty. 'I didn't realise anyone had seen.'

'I'd have said you were in another world...' She paused. 'Maybe I was wrong?'

'No.' He shook his head. 'What did you do?' His mother didn't answer. 'You did do something, I can see it in your face. What was it?'

'I called your father and asked him to take you

skiing. And then, because she looked so miserable and I felt so guilty, I took Daisy to London for a few days to visit the British Museum, the V&A.' She looked up at him. 'Do you remember how she used to come flying round to the back door when she heard you were home from university?' He nodded. 'The year you graduated she'd been like a cat on a hot brick waiting for you to come home. She must have been out when you finally turned up, because Lorraine Summers beat her to it.'

'Lorraine?'

'She'd just come back from a year in Paris and she looked like a princess. She married a solicitor in Maybridge. She's got three children now.'

'I know who Lorraine Summers married,' he said. 'I was simply wondering what she had to do with this.'

'I imagine Daisy saw you kissing her. Or her kissing you.' She turned to look straight at him. 'She never came to the house again when she thought you might be home.'

'But that's ridiculous. I saw her all the time. I still see her all the time.'

'No, darling. You see her by appointment. You ask her to lunch, or to a party, or whatever it is you do in London. You don't see her by chance. Do you?'

'Well, no. But London is just a bit bigger than the village. When I'm home I see her all the time—'

'At home she has nothing to hide.'

'Hide?'

'At home she's the girl you've always known. You see her, darling, but only in the way she wants you to see her. Was she expecting you to turn up at Warbury?'

'No.' He felt hot with embarrassment at the way he had gone spying on her to Warbury.

'I thought not. I assumed you would simply telephone her and make the necessary arrangements. I never thought you'd go haring after her…' She smiled. 'If I'd thought about it, I would have arranged things rather better.'

'You couldn't have arranged things better if you'd thought about it for a month,' he assured her. 'It's a pity I didn't make better use of my opportunities. But I didn't go to Warbury because of the money. That was just an excuse.'

'Oh?' She began to stack cups onto a tray. 'Why *did* you go?'

'I was worried about her. Mike told me she was in love with someone. He made it sound very mysterious. I thought she might be having an affair with a married man.'

'Daisy?' She laughed. 'You mean you went racing off to Warbury in order to snatch her from the clutches of some self-serving man? Oh, darling, that's so sweet.'

'Not really. On closer inspection my case of the galloping Galahads was the result of pure jealousy. I was so angry that someone else had taken something I treasured…something I had always thought was mine.'

'Daisy.'

'Yes, dammit, Daisy. Mike was giving me a prod; I can see that now. Making me think about her.' He raked his fingers through his hair. 'By heaven, he succeeded. I haven't been able to think about anything else for days.'

'Even though she's back in her cuddly sweater and her comfortable trousers?'

'Will you please stop talking about that sweater?'

'What is it about men and angora? No, don't answer that.' She laughed as she stood up and picked up the tray. Robert took it from her, carrying it into the kitchen. 'I always assumed, once she'd grown up at little, nature would take its course with the pair of you. But I hadn't bargained on Daisy. She's a girl with a mind of her own and she wasn't prepared to play. Wasn't prepared to be just one of Furneval's Funcies '

'For heaven's sake!'

'Isn't that what they're called?' He didn't answer. 'She's a till-death-do-us-part sort of girl, Rob.' She touched his arm. 'You're going to have to convince her that you're worthy of that kind of commitment.'

'Like Elinor James.'

'What, dear?'

'Nothing. Just something Mike said.' Elinor James could have had any boy in the school at her feet. He had been no different, but he hadn't been prepared to put up his hand and say, Me too. He'd kept his distance and his pride. For a while his friends had kept a book on how long he could hold out. Then, one day, they'd begun to bet on how long it would be before she asked him out.

How many of his friends were watching him now? Waiting to see how long it would take him to realise that Daisy was there...

Monty, certainly. He'd said as much. Monty spent

his life watching people make fools of themselves; he saw relationships form and disintegrate even before the people involved knew what was going on.

Mike, of course. But Mike had never said anything; he understood him too well. He would probably never have said anything except, giddy with a happiness that he wanted everyone to share, he hadn't been able to resist throwing out a hint. Or had it been a veiled challenge? Had Mike realised all it would take would be a little plain old-fashioned jealousy?

He dragged his hand over his face, saw his mother was looking at him, waiting… His mother knew. Maybe even Sarah knew. Suddenly it was all so clear, so obvious, that he wondered if he was the only person in the world who hadn't been able to see the truth.

Or maybe he had shut it out, buried the memory of a young girl who had spirited away his heart and kept it. 'You were right, you know. About Daisy. But wrong, too. I knew that she was too young. Lorraine was simply a distraction. I've been distracting myself for years, waiting for her to grow up. And when she did, I was—'

'Distracted?'

'How on earth am I ever going to convince her to trust me? To take me seriously?'

'Do you want her to?'

'Oh, yes.'

She patted his arm. 'Maybe a walk will clear your head. Take Daisy through the orchard and perhaps you'll recapture some of that mistletoe magic.'

'You've brought the dress!' Margaret Galbraith took the box from her and carried it upstairs. 'Oh, Daisy, it's lovely,' she said, lifting it from the tissue. 'Put it on. I want to see what it looks like.'

'It won't look right without the shoes and the hair,' she warned.

'I can imagine those. Oh, my goodness, look at this.' She picked up the lacy bra that provided some special effects in the cleavage department.

'Yes, well, I needed a little help. It's that sort of dress.'

She'd known how it would be, but anything that distracted her mother from what happened at Warbury was to be welcomed. She pulled off her sweater and blouse and stepped out of her trousers, but she wasn't stripping off in front of her mother. It was going to be bad enough without that. 'I can manage. I'll give you a call when I'm ready.'

'No, come down. Dad will want to see too.'

As she eased herself into the exquisite lace underwear, Daisy felt about six years old, trying on a pretty new frock and going downstairs to show her daddy. The more things changed, the more they stayed the same.

She stepped into the dress, fastened it, fluffed up her hair. But it wasn't modelling the dress that bothered her, it was the inevitable look of discontent on her mother's face. The fact that she would never wear it as well as her sister could have done.

'Daisy?' Her mother was getting impatient.

'I'm just coming. You've shut Flossie in the kitchen, haven't you?' Reassurance was swift, and there was nothing for it but to lift the softly draped

white voile skirt and go downstairs. For a moment
neither her mother nor father said anything. 'Well?'

'You look lovely, Daisy. Doesn't she, Margaret?'
her father said, encouragingly.

'Well. I thought the yellow would be a disaster,
but, no… The bodice is very small, very neat, and
the white skirt is very light and pretty. The idea is
charming. Of course on the other girls, with their
dark hair, it will be much more striking, but even so,
with the right make-up… Turn around.'

Daisy obediently turned. Robert was standing in
the doorway. He was looking at her in a way that she
couldn't fathom. No teasing smile, no silly grin, just
the kind of look she'd always dreamed of. Intense,
deep, soul-searching. It seemed like for ever before
he broke the silence.

'Ducklings, it seems, are getting more swan-like
every day.' Then, realising that everyone was staring
him, 'The back door was open. I've left Major in the
mud room.' Then he slapped his hand to his forehead.
'Oh, no, don't tell me it's unlucky for the best man
to see the bridesmaid before the wedding.'

Her father began to laugh, her mother spun around
and glared at him and he immediately stopped.

'I'd better go and change,' Daisy said.

She had to wait for Robert to move aside. He took
his time. 'You needn't have worried about the colour,
you know.' His face was smiling now, the way it
always did when he was teasing, but his eyes were
still dark and intense and full of secrets. 'It matches
your hair perfectly.' And he flipped a curl. Teasing.
But it was teasing for the benefit of their audience,
not for her.

'Swans, indeed.' Her mother, affronted, bustled her out of the room and followed her up the stairs, as if afraid that Robert might take it into his head to offer to help with the hooks and eyes. 'Don't let him turn your head with that silver tongue of his, my girl.'

Daisy tugged at the hooks. 'He never has before.'

'He's never tried before,' she said, her voice heavy with meaning. 'He's just like his father.'

'I didn't know you'd ever met Robert's father.'

'I haven't, but I've seen a picture of him.' She put the dress on a padded hanger. 'Divorced for more than twenty years and poor Jennifer's still got a photograph of him by the side of her bed. She's a good-looking woman, but I've never even seen her with another man. Of course, that combination of good looks and charm is absolutely fatal. There ought to be a law against it.' She hung the dress in the wardrobe, busied herself draping it with the tissue paper. 'Robert looks just like him, you know.'

'You said.'

'Behaves like him, too. I suppose it's a case of like father, like son.'

'Mum...' She was going to explain, reassure her mother that nothing had happened at Warbury. Instead she heard herself saying, 'I'm twenty-four. And I've known Robert for ever. I trust him. He wouldn't do anything to hurt me.'

For a moment her mother looked startled. 'I know that.' Then she sighed. 'I know that. I'm sorry. I'm lecturing you as if you were still a child. But then, to me, you always will be. All of you. Sarah says I treat her like an infant, too...telling her how to bring up the children as if she isn't the most capable mother. But once the nest is empty what do you do?'

'Live the rest of your life. Enjoy yourself. Take a holiday.' Daisy put her arms about her mother and held her. 'Next week the wedding will be over and you'll be feeling horribly flat. It's April, Mum. Ask Dad to take you to Paris. Or book the tickets yourself and take him. You don't have to be young, or newly married, to take a honeymoon.'

Flossie was whining with excitement in the kitchen, and when Daisy opened the door she practically threw herself on Major before bounding out of the door, heading towards the river. Robert whistled to her and turned the other way. 'It'll be muddy,' he said.

'It usually is. Where are we going?'

'This way.'

Daisy glanced at him, about to respond with something sarcastic, but he seemed so deep in thought that she left it and they walked on in silence for a while.

'Flossie!' The spaniel, pushing her way through the hedge, finally caught his attention. 'For goodness' sake, that dog is the worst behaved animal—'

'Hey, don't be so tense.'

Robert glanced at her. 'No. I'm sorry.' He stopped by the kissing gate into the old orchard next to the church and swung it open for her.

'It's too early for blossom,' she said, when he stopped to look up into the branches of one of the old trees.

'I'm not looking for blossom; I'm looking for mistletoe. It grows on apple trees. Well, on this apple tree, anyway.'

'Not in April.'

'It's always there. It's just that when you can't see it, it's easy to forget.' She lowered her gaze from the branches. Robert's face was shadowy, his eyes unreadable, but she could read his thoughts as clearly as if they were her own.

'I think we'd better go. Where are the dogs?' As she began to turn, he reached out for her, turned her gently to face him. 'Do you remember the Christmas you were sixteen, Daisy?' She remembered. 'When I kissed you underneath the mistletoe?'

She swallowed. 'Yes.' Her first kiss. So sweet, so special. She'd had the most vivid reminder only a few days ago.

'I cut it from this tree.' He looked up. 'I'm sure it was this tree.' She didn't know what to say, except that without him mistletoe was a pointless custom. And she couldn't say that.

'They're going to fell the orchard this year.'

He wasn't to be diverted. 'Do you remember what I said?'

A little spark of something like anger seemed to ignite inside her. How would she ever forget what he said to her that night?

'Do you?' she demanded.

'I'd forgotten.' His hand moved against her shoulder in a tender caress. Gentling her, soothing her, as if he understood how much his admission would hurt. 'I knew there was something. I think I must have blocked it out, but I knew there was something precious, something special, just out of reach. You know how it is when you wake and you know you've been dreaming and that, more than anything, you want to be dreaming again, but you don't know why.' She knew. Oh, yes, she knew. 'The memory of it is like a will-o'-the-wisp, always there, but always slipping away down the side alleys of the mind before you can catch hold of it.' His hand moved to tilt her chin so that she had no choice but to look at him, or close her eyes. She closed her eyes. 'I said… ''I'll wait for you.'''

She felt his breath close to her cheek, the merest touch against her lids, and like the sun opening a flower his touch loosened the traitorous words from her tongue. 'I didn't want to wait,' she said, and because hiding was no longer an option, either from him or from herself, she opened her eyes.

'No.' It was shadowy beneath the tree; the sun was low and everything was tinged with a luminous pink so that the leaves above them looked like blossom. 'Neither did I. But you were too young. If I'd been sixteen too, well, that might have been forgivable…'

This was unforgivable. Making her remember. It had taken months, years to forget the heartache, to pretend to herself that it had been nothing more than an unaccustomed glass of wine that had gone to her silly girlish head and made them both say things that in the cold light of day they'd hoped would be forgotten. He had forgotten. She never could. This was like tearing her heart in two all over again.

He looked up again, then smiled. 'Will you kiss me beneath the mistletoe one last time, Daisy?' *One last time? That sounded so very final.* 'Before they cut down the tree.'

'I…' Can't. Mustn't. Shouldn't. The words wouldn't come and he took her silence for assent.

It took a while. His lips hovered tantalisingly close and she tilted her head a little to one side and waited, as eager as her sixteen-year-old self had been all those years ago. He drew back a little, one corner of his mouth lifted in a self-conscious little smile. He tried again, and again, an inch from her lips, he paused. It was sweet and silly and she began to giggle.

'Shh. This is serious. We're kissing each other for the very last time beneath this apple tree.' His arm slid about her, his hand spread across her waist, keeping her still. Keeping her close. 'Laughing is not allowed.'

'No.' She tried to straighten her face, but it wouldn't co-operate. Being kissed by Robert was never going to be serious. Never.

And without warning all desire to laugh evaporated. Like father, like son. This wasn't funny It was almost certainly the stupidest thing she had ever done. Bar none.

'Robert, no—' But her protest came too late. He brushed the words from her lips, erased them with a touch that was like a feather against her mouth, once, twice, three times in a tender evocation of that long-ago kiss.

Then he drew back a little, the teasing smile back in place. 'It's all coming back to me now.'

'Robert—' She grasped helplessly at the chance to escape before she betrayed herself beyond all recall. Maybe he would have let her go. Maybe not. She was no longer too young, he was at a loose end and maybe, just maybe, she would have been foolish enough to believe his silver words… But Flossie, excitable and silly and covered in mud, came hurtling through the trees, flinging herself at them.

And somehow, in the confusion, the sponging down of their clothes, a cup of her mother's tea, normality gradually reasserted itself.

CHAPTER TEN

SATURDAY 8 April. Ginny and Michael's wedding day. Very early. Robert came over a while ago and I heard him and Mike take the dogs out. He usually tosses a little gravel up to my window to see if I want to tag along, but not this morning. Maybe it was a 'man' thing.

Not that I would have gone with them. I don't have time for a walk. After that kiss in the orchard nothing is ever going to be the same. But I won't…I will not… Even if it does mean I have to leave the country to avoid temptation.

All I have to do is get through today. With any luck Robert will have forgotten that he asked me to have lunch with him and won't discover I've bolted back to London until it's too late.

The church looked glorious, the lych-gate garlanded with yellow and white flowers entwined with evergreens, every pew-end decorated with matching ribbons and glossy green ivy. And Ginny so beautiful…

Daisy knew that crying at weddings was acceptable, but this lump in her throat, the solid ache that was like a stone in her heart, surely that was more than convention demanded?

If only Robert hadn't worn that silly yellow waistcoat. She had prepared herself for everything but that. He'd done it for her, and as he half turned, half smiled, she knew she was expected to indicate in some small way that she appreciated the effort.

She tried. She really tried. She made every effort to put out a quirky smile, all eyebrows and mouth so that he would know that she'd duly noted the trouble he'd taken to amuse her.

But the lump in her throat was doing something to her mouth, and if she quirked her brows, the tears would spill over and spoil the careful make-up which had been applied by a woman brought all the way from London for the purpose. That would be the most dreadful waste.

So instead she looked at the neat little posy she was carrying and pretended not to see.

Japan. She hung on to the promise of Japan. Her bag was packed, her ticket booked. Dear George. He'd done far more than simply let her go without a murmur about the inconvenience. He'd contacted friends, organised somewhere for her to stay until she could decide what she was going to do. Maybe he was glad to let her go; he hadn't been entirely happy about the dish incident. She didn't have the instincts to be a dealer, he'd said; she should stick to scholarship. Maybe he was right.

All Sunday night Robert's kiss had kept her awake. She'd tossed and turned but all she'd been able to think of was her mother saying *'like father, like son'* and *'poor Jennifer'* and imagining herself, thirty years from now, having people say *'Poor Daisy. She was in love with Robert Furneval, but he was just like his father…'*

Then on Monday morning she'd walked into the gallery and George had told her that they'd had a little win on the lottery. Ten pounds. Five pounds each. And she'd thought about the 'this year, next year, some time, never' fantasy that she and Robert had played over dinner at Warbury. It had seemed like fate. She'd had a win on the lottery. The amount didn't really matter; she had some money that her grandfather had left her—Mother always referred to it as her 'dowry'. Well, she wouldn't be needing a dowry, and it was time to choose between the dreams.

She glossed over the following hour. She wasn't proud of that. But George had offered her his handkerchief and listened as it had all poured out of her, all the pain, all the dammed-up passion, all the love. Then he'd made her green tea from his special caddy, and while she'd sipped it through the hiccups he'd made some calls to friends. Then he had sent her home to organise herself.

And so tomorrow she would be on her way to Tokyo, to a new life discovering the mystery and beauty of another culture. It was dream-come-true time.

Then Robert had to go and wear a yellow velvet waistcoat and destroy the illusion.

Wrong dream.

Through the swimmy veil of tears she saw Michael kiss Ginny, and then, somehow, Robert was holding her arm and they were following the newly-weds into the vestry to sign the register. Robert witnessed the entry and the pen was passed to her to do the same.

She sniffed. 'My hand's all shaky.'

Robert produced a handkerchief, tilted her chin and then gently dabbed at her eyes so that the make-

up wouldn't smudge. Then, for just a moment, he
held her, and she closed her eyes and let the comfort
flow over her. 'There now, big breath.' That was
shaky, too, but it did the trick and Robert handed her
the pen, his eyes not teasing but sympathetic, as if
he knew exactly how she was feeling.

Ridiculous.

But when the deed was done, the formalities concluded, he retrieved her fingers and kept them com-
fortingly tight in his as they lined up behind the bride
to leave the vestry and follow the newly married pair
out of the church and into a new life.

Confused, Daisy glanced back at the other bridesmaids, her look apologetic; this wasn't how it was
meant to be. Robert, however, appeared oblivious to
the three exquisite brunettes who lined up behind
them.

Once at the reception, they tried, they really tried
to catch his attention, to lure him into quiet corners,
but even the wonderful Victorian conservatory
proved no temptation. Robert was polite and charming, to be sure, but no more than that to the dozens
of aunts, cousins, grandmothers and every other va-
riety of female relation to whom he was introduced.

For once in his life he wasn't flirting. It made her
nervous.

The speeches were done, the bride and groom were
changing and Robert had disappeared. She took the
opportunity to slip out onto the terrace, get away
from the noise and the laughter. A few more minutes.
Once Ginny and Mike had left, she too could escape.

'Cast not a clout till May is out...' Not yet. Not

quite yet. Robert crossed the terrace, taking off his morning coat. 'And I'll bet any amount of money you're not wearing any clouts beneath that dress. Whatever they are. Here.' He slipped the coat about her shoulders.

It was warm from his body and she pulled it around her. 'Thanks. It's a bit noisy in there.'

'It's very noisy,' he said, leaning his arms against the balustrade. 'In fact it's a great wedding. If you like that kind of thing.'

'Mmm.'

'Well, that was…noncommittal. I expected to be read the riot act for speaking heresy at the nuptial feast.'

'I'm sorry to disappoint you, but weddings don't do a lot for me. Call me unromantic, but I take the view that it would be a lot less trouble just tearing up fifty-pound notes in a force nine gale.'

'You could be right. What will you do?'

'Me?'

'When you marry.'

She turned and looked at him for a moment and then looked away again. 'I'm not going to get married. I'm going to be a distinguished oriental scholar and travel the world.'

'Starting with Japan.' For a moment, for just a heartbeat, she thought he had discovered her secret. It had to be a secret. He had to think he had time. She knew Robert. Had seen him at work. Warbury had given him ideas, reminded him of unfinished business, and the scene in the orchard had been the opening salvo in a campaign to get her into his bed. But for Flossie… 'Humour me,' he said, when she didn't answer. 'If you did decide to marry, who would you want to be there?'

Relief made her garrulous. 'Oh, I think two people somewhere very quiet, very peaceful, very beautiful would be all the company that was necessary.'

'No bridesmaids, then.' He looked down at the waistcoat. 'No yellow velvet.'

'Not even a best man,' she assured him. Especially not a best man.

'I'm sold. Will you marry me?'

She made a noise that might have been a laugh. Just. 'Haven't you got something very best-mannish to do, Robert? Like tying balloons and old shoes to the getaway car?'

'It's done.'

'Well, what about seducing a bridesmaid, or something?'

He glanced back at her. 'Are you volunteering?'

'Robert…'

'Robert! Daisy! There you are.' Sarah emerged from the ballroom looking slightly dishevelled from the dancing and with a silly grin plastered over her pretty face. Then she looked from her sister to Robert and she stilled, seeming to sense that she had interrupted something important. 'I'm sorry, but Ginny and Mike are just leaving.'

'We'll be right there.' Daisy slipped off Robert's coat and gave it back to him. Then she shivered and walked quickly inside to join the crowd gathering at the foot of the ornate staircase. Ginny was standing at the top, bouquet in hand, and as she saw Daisy she grinned and turned her back before tossing her flowers over her head into the waiting guests.

Someone behind her caught them, and as heads turned there was an expectant hush. Robert. He'd come in behind her and the flowers Ginny had aimed in her direction had instead been caught by him.

It was the moment for wit, the sharp, telling remark that would make everyone laugh. But wit was beyond her, and when Robert offered them to her with the slightest of bows she could do nothing but take them and submit, in silent misery, to the gentle, 'Ah!' that swept through the room.

It could only have lasted a few seconds, but it seemed like for ever before everyone surged after Ginny and Mike, and with a last flurry of flashes from half a dozen cameras, waved them away down the drive.

'I don't understand. How can there be a problem?' As if flying wasn't harrowing enough. 'My ticket was confirmed last week.'

The woman behind the check-in smiled. She was clearly used to irate passengers and had done the course about keeping her voice low, her expression positive. 'We tried to contact you yesterday, but there was no reply from your number. And there isn't a problem, as such. We've found you a seat on another flight leaving within half an hour.' Another flight going via Delhi, with a twenty-four-hour stop-over. Daisy was not happy. She'd booked a direct flight to avoid unnecessary take-offs and landings. 'We have upgraded you to first class,' the woman continued swiftly, 'and there will be a complimentary sight-seeing excursion...'

There was no point in getting angry. It wasn't this

woman's fault that some computer had messed up. She phoned her mother to tell her the change of plan. 'Tell George, will you, Mum? He'll have to let people know at the other end.'

'Of course. Send me a postcard of the Taj Mahal.'

'The what?'

'And, darling…be happy.'

Before she could answer, her mother had rung off. She'd been unusually emotional when they'd said goodbye. Daisy had put it down to the wedding, to the champagne, but even now she'd sounded on the edge of tears…

The Taj Mahal?

She hadn't realised that her mother knew India that well. Had she even mentioned that she was stopping over in Delhi. She'd just said, Oh, well… It was probably just one of those things you said to someone visiting India. Send me a postcard of the Taj Mahal.

She brightened a little. If that was the complimentary excursion on offer, she'd definitely be taking it.

She settled herself in her seat at the front of the first-class section and took out her book. She hated this. The minutes before take-off, the slow taxiing to the end of the runway, the winding up of the engines…

'Will you please ensure that your seats are in the upright position and your seatbelt is securely fastened…?'

She knew it was silly. She knew the statistics. More people died falling out of bed… But still she clutched at the armrests and closed her eyes.

Someone took the seat next to her. She heard the click of the seatbelt. She knew she must look like an idiot, but nothing could make her open her eyes until they were safely off the ground.

Nothing but a cool hand covering her own. Robert's voice saying, 'It's true, then.' Her disbelief was more powerful than her fear and she swung round.

'Robert?' She could see it was him, he was holding her hand, but she still didn't believe it.

'I thought you were going to take a boat?'

'I couldn't afford it.'

'But I heard you'd won the lottery.'

'Ten pounds. Well, five pounds, actually, George and I share...' She stopped. It wasn't important. 'What are you doing here?'

'Holding your hand. Going to India for the bank. Asking you to marry me. Not necessarily in that order. I have a week before I need to start work.'

The plane began to move but Daisy didn't even notice. The surge of longing for it to be true was choking her. 'You're going to India? What an amazing coincidence.'

'I think putting this down to coincidence would be stretching the boundaries of common sense beyond any natural limit. Will you marry me, Daisy?'

This couldn't be true. 'I'm going to Japan.'

'India's on the way.'

'Only if you take the slow plane. How long will you be there?'

'As long as it takes. You're running away, Daisy. Hiding from me again.' The plane stopped, turned. 'We've both been hiding, but it's time to stop. Will you marry me?'

The noise of the engine built up. 'You're not the marrying kind, Robert.'

'You've been listening to gossip. But then, so have I.'

'You've been living it. I understand where you're coming from, Robert. You're thinking, Hell, this is *Daisy*. Now I've seen her legs I want to add her to my collection. But I can't just have a little fun with Daisy because…well, *because*…'

'Because Mike would never speak to me again? Or my mother would disown me? Or even, heaven help us, your mother would use her rolling pin for something other than pastry…' She said nothing. 'You see? I know where you've been coming from, too. It took a while, and I needed some help.'

'Help?' Who from? How much worse could this get?

'Mike gave me a prod. He said you'd been in love with someone—well, for ever. I spent days trying to find out who was giving you a hard time… I was going to deal with him…'

'Oh.'

'What *is* the password for your computer?'

The conversation was surreal. 'Rabbit.'

'Rabbit?'

'I call my computer Peter…' He shook his head as if he couldn't believe it. 'Is it important?'

'Apparently not.' His grip on her hand intensified. 'Did I mention that Monty knew? He pointed out how you were the one girl I never tired of, always went back to.'

'Monty said that?'

'It surprised me too. But it's what he does, my

love. Watches people make fools of themselves as they fall in and out of love.'

'This gets worse.'

'I haven't finished.' She groaned. 'My mother told me that you saw me kissing Lorraine Summers, and that's when you began avoiding me. You were far too young for a proper relationship, Daisy. And I was far too young to know how to wait. Please marry me, Daisy.'

It was getting harder to ignore his question. But she would try. Just a little longer. 'Does your mother know? That you're here?'

'They all know. Come on, Daisy. You know you want to—'

'Stop it!' She put her free hand to her head. 'Stop it!' The plane was shaking. 'I need to think.'

'No, you don't. You're on this plane because you're running away again. I'm telling you that I won't let it happen.' He took her other hand. 'You've always had the best of me, Daisy. I've never lied to you. I'm not lying to you now. I love you. I've always loved you. I'll wait if I have to prove it, but I think we've both waited long enough.' He released her hand, captured her face and held it so that she couldn't look anywhere but at him, couldn't avoid eyes that promised her his heart on a plate. 'Will you, please, please, marry me?'

They were rocketing along the runway; her heart was pounding with the explosive beat of the engines. Risk. Life was a risk. But she knew Robert. He never lied; he never cheated. He might be like his father, but he was like Jennifer too. His heart, once given, would never belong to anyone else. And the truth was as bright as the sunlight above the clouds. They were flying; her heart was flying.

'Champagne, sir, madam?'

He was looking at her. 'Champagne, Daisy?'

One long shuddering breath and then she was lost. 'Yes. Oh, yes, please.' But, as he handed her a glass, 'No. Wait. I don't understand. How did you know I'd be on this plane? I should have been flying direct…' Robert touched his glass to hers. 'To computers, bless them, for always being there to take the blame. And a travel agent with a soul that was pure romance.'

'Are you telling me that you *fixed* this?'

'With a little help from some friends. After George had fixed everything up for you he began to wonder if he'd done the right thing, so he called my mother for advice. And because she knew how I felt, she called me.'

'Robert, people are expecting me—'

'People have been warned that you might be delayed,' he said gently. 'It's your choice. Marry me, go on to Tokyo next week and I'll join you as soon as I can. Or stay with me and we'll go on together. I'll take a sabbatical to study the way the Japanese do things while you do whatever it is you want to do.'

'You've got it all figured out, haven't you?'

'I'm a banker. Figuring is my job. But I have to tell you that it's been a tough week.'

'So why didn't you say something before I left?'

'Because there was too much going on. Too many distractions.' He lifted her hand, kissed the palm. 'And because I thought I was going to need every minute of eight and a half hours without muddy dogs, or sisters with terminally bad timing—eight and a half hours with you securely fastened into a seat beside me and no escape—to talk you round. I overestimated by about eight hours and twenty-five minutes.'

'You just caught me at a weak moment.' Then she grinned. 'It was a terrific cure for fear of flying, though.' She turned her hand to clasp his, touching it to her cheek. 'I guess that does it for me. I'll have to stay with you, Robert, if only to have you there to hold my hand on take-off.'

Daisy wore a red and gold wedding sari, Robert a cream tropical suit. The paperwork had been dealt with. The officials. The legal stuff. Now they sat together, looking at the world's most beautiful monument to love and its perfect reflection in the still water, holding hands and considering the future.

Then, as a huge white moon rose into the blackness of the sky, Robert turned to Daisy. 'I love you,' he said. 'I will always love you.'

And Daisy said, 'I love you. I have always loved you.'

He touched the exquisitely worked gold and diamond wedding ring she wore for him before lifting her hand to his lips. 'The waiting, my love, is over.' And then he took her in his arms and kissed her.

Susan Fox is an American writer living in Des Moines, Iowa, where she was born. As well as being a popular author, she is the mother of two sons. Her enjoyment in reading romances led to writing them and they reflect an early interest in westerns and cowboys. She has won two Romance Writers of America Golden Heart Awards.

Tender Romance™ brings you a wonderfully, emotionally intense story from bestselling author Susan Fox.

CONTRACT BRIDE
Out this month!

THE COWBOY WANTS A WIFE!

by
Susan Fox

CHAPTER ONE

JOHN Dalton Hayes reined in his sorrel gelding at the edge of the pecan trees that formed the east boundary of the two acre lawn surrounding the main house on the Hayes Ranch. His ranch, passed down to him through five generations of Hayes fathers and sons, his home. He knew every rock of it, every blade of Texas grass. He'd ruled over its thirty thousand acres with the considerable force of his strong will like a benevolent despot; benevolent when he could afford to be, despot the other ninety-five percent of the time. He'd poured his sweat and blood into his ranch like the hard, uncompromising men before him, and wrested a living and a life-style from the obstinate ground just as they had. No threat, either man-made or of nature, had ever been able to shake a Hayes man's iron grip of possession. Until now.

Anger at himself and the world in general churned in his gut. The shameful knowledge that the threat to the Hayes Ranch in his generation had been a blonde cocktail waitress with movie star aspirations crawled around his insides every waking moment and haunted many a sleepless night.

He'd lost his head to Raylene Shannon on one of his few trips to Dallas for a rare bit of hell-raising. And raised hell they had, for three nights in his motel room until his guilty conscience prodded him into showing her the respect of a marriage proposal. After the quickie wedding, the hell-raising continued, but this time, it was the hell-raising year of being leg-shackled to a woman who hated his home and hated him because he couldn't understand her aspirations for stardom. His reluctance to invest mega bucks to ensure her rise to fame sent the flames higher, burning off any promise of real love, leaving them both with the cold ashes of regret.

Then came the most tortuous kind of hell-raising. The hell of losing a chunk of capital and a third of his ranch in the divorce. Money could be replenished by sweat and know-how. Getting Raylene to let him pay market price to buy back that third of his ranch had been impossible— her revenge for delaying by a year her star billing on the silver screen.

And now she'd sold that one-third interest to some Hollywood loonie. He'd refused to attend the meeting of his lawyer with his new co-owner and her lawyer. Refused to extend the courtesy of meeting the woman, but sending with his lawyer an offer to buy her out at a brow-raising profit. Which she'd turned down.

And now it was the first of June and his new co-owner was due to arrive any moment to take up residence. His lawyer had glossed over personal information about the mystery woman, but he'd been annoyingly specific when he warned J.D. about her rights and his obligations. All he had to go on was that she was a glamorous blue-eyed blonde, and that she'd signed every legal document with a godawful name that he took as both a portent of doom and a sure indication of ditzy character: Zoe Yahzoo.

As he rounded the front corner of the lawn, a movement drew his attention toward the ranch drive. A slim woman strolled along the whitewashed fence toward a small cluster of cows and calves. A deep-crowned Stetson shaded her profile and he glimpsed a pair of large-lensed sunglasses. Dressed cowboy chic in black lizardskin boots, tight designer jeans and a bright blue silk blouse, the woman was like an electric flash on his vision. The huge silver buckle at her waist winked at him when she turned to stroll back. The woman was petite, her small size and feminine aura multiplied several times over in contrast to the cattle on the other side of the fence.

John Dalton Hayes was a man who knew few fears, and was as stunned as he was ashamed of the faint twist of fear in his gut. A strange uncertainty gripped him as he watched the woman stop and reach between the rails of the fence to coax a calf closer. The urge to ride off to the harsh comfort of open spaces battled with the more familiar urge to ride straight to the problem and stare it down. In the end, the big man was aware of a sort of compromise as he nudged the sorrel along the front edge of the yard. When he reached the ranch drive opposite her, he drew his horse to a halt and watched.

A brash red convertible, which the house had blocked from his view, was parked under the trees that shaded part of the driveway. The California license plates cinched it, more grim reminders that his domain was being invaded by a Hollywood socialite.

Grateful for the sunglasses, which would conceal the intensity of his observation of his new "partner," J.D. focused his attention on the woman. He needed to gauge how much of an unfriendly welcome he could get by with without overstepping the legal constrictions of the joint tenancy. His lawyer's description of her as a glamorous blonde suggested a type of fragility that might make her easy to intimidate.

His hope was for her to find an association with him intolerable, but he didn't want to come off a bully. Since

she was from Hollywood, he figured any romance toward
the west that might have inspired her to come here would
get choked out by the day-to-day isolation and reality of
ranch living. Hollywood was a dreamworld, and the people who lived that life probably didn't have enough encounters with reality to believe in it the first few times.
He planned to discourage any delusional ideas on her part,
hoped for her to detest living on a Texas ranch. Once that
was accomplished, she'd sell out to him and hightail it
back to fairyland ASAP. Then, challenge overcome, he'd
have every acre of his heritage back, including his pride.

The musical sound of her voice drifted across the drive
as he looked on. To his surprise, the calf she'd been coax-
ing ventured her way like an overgrown puppy starved for
attention. Which she practically slathered on as she
reached through the fence with both hands and rubbed the
youngster around the ears and face, all the while cooing
in baby talk.

"Oooo, you sweet baby calfie," she was saying as the
calf pressed close.

Just that quickly, every other cow and calf was at the
fence, pushing in for their share. Her delighted, "Hi,
y'all," grated only slightly on J.D.'s nerves. He didn't
know whether to swear or get a camera. His cattle weren't
pets, weren't treated like pets, and on their best days never
behaved in any way that could remotely be considered
petlike. Yet, there they were, crowding around Zoe
Yahzoo like a litter of pups for a scratch behind the ears
or a silly word.

Her strange power over the stock made him uneasy.
Particularly since his insides were humming in response
to the sweet lilt of all that baby talk. Compelled to put a
stop to it, he started the sorrel in her direction.

*   *   *

Zoe heard the sorrel's approach and glanced briefly over her shoulder. Realizing she might be overheard, she turned back to the cattle, bid them a whispered goodbye, then gave several hurried pats of farewell.

She wasn't as relieved as she should have been to finally have someone notice her arrival. Largely because she was certain the unfriendly looking cowboy on the sorrel was John Dalton Hayes. That J.D. Hayes was antagonistic toward a partnership with her had been made clear by her lawyer, so she guessed this first meeting with him would be difficult.

But then, she acknowledged with a wry inward smile, she'd faced difficult situations more times in her twenty-three years than most people imagined. Perhaps she'd reach her quota this time and be spared the most potentially devastating opportunity just ahead, the one she was forced to confront before she was ready.

And all because Zoe Yahzoo's time was running out.

She took a scant moment to start a smile, then turned toward the big man astride the sorrel who'd stopped just behind her. She came eye-level with a muscular thigh encased in batwing chaps. Her shaded eyes slipped to the cut-out front of the chaps, which were the unintentional frame of the man's masculinity, then up his green plaid shirt, which had no doubt been custom-made to accommodate such wide shoulders. She had to tip her face up so far to see his expression that it made her dizzy.

Dark sunglasses met dark sunglasses. Zoe flashed him an engaging smile, then turned up the dazzle when his jaw hardened and he glared forbiddingly down at her.

For a fractured moment out of time, she was cast back to her childhood. She must have looked up just as far at her adoptive father when she was small; she was certain she'd got this same response, tried the same hopeful dazzle in her smile to garner the tiniest bit of softening, and met with the same devastating failure.

But she'd learned something from all those heartbreaks, learned to give the appearance that she was either impervious to rejection, or oblivious. She'd watched her adoptive parents, probably the most talented actors of stage and screen, and had picked up enough acting ability to project any illusion she chose. And the illusion she'd chosen to project was the playfully flamboyant, tin-foil shallow, Zoe Yahzoo.

"Can I help you with something, miss?" The gravelly drawl was distinctly unfriendly.

Zoe turned up the wattage on her smile when his expression remained formidable and he refused to show her the courtesy of dismounting for a proper introduction.

"I was waiting for someone to come along. There didn't seem to be anyone home when I knocked." She put up her hand to offer him a handshake. "I'm Zoe Yahzoo. I think you must be J.D. Hayes." Zoe felt the rebuff when J.D. made no move to shake her hand.

"Sorry," he said, instead touching a finger to his hat brim in a way that communicated how thin the polite gesture was meant to be. "I've been working. My hands are dirty."

Zoe withdrew her hand, careful not to give any hint she'd noticed the insult. "Well, as far as that goes, I'm not sure how clean my hands are." She gave him an impish grin. "Your cattle are a bit dusty, Mr. Hayes. Perhaps we should postpone the proprieties until we've both had time to freshen up."

J.D. glanced away. It was a signal of irritation. Zoe automatically followed the shift of his attention and spied three ranch hands nearby who had evidently come out of hiding.

"If you could spare someone to help me with my luggage, I'll get settled in," she offered.

J.D. shook his head and raised his voice enough to be heard by his ranch hands. "I can't spare anyone to help you right now." J.D.'s words caused every man there to suddenly vanish, as if they were duty-bound to make true every word that came from his lips.

The absolute rule J.D. would have to have, to accomplish what she'd just witnessed, was impressive. It was also hurtful. But then, she'd expected to take some painful hits. And J.D.'s efforts were nothing compared to what she expected to receive from the people she'd come here to meet if they refused to accept her. This hostile partnership with J.D. was merely a means to an end, something she would endure to achieve her real purpose.

His full attention returned to her and his mouth quirked in faint mockery. "We don't have bellhops on Hayes, Miss…Yahzoo. My housekeeper keeps my house and cooks meals I like at times I set. She doesn't carry luggage, won't wait on you hand and foot, and God help you if you mess up her kitchen, sleep till noon or bitch about her cooking."

J.D. was as subtle as a freight train. Zoe gave him a cheeky smile. "I appreciate knowing where I stand, Mr. Hayes. Where do you suppose your housekeeper would like me to put my things?"

J.D. didn't hesitate. "In California."

Zoe made herself give a light laugh. "You have a sense of humor, Mr. Hayes. I appreciate that in a man." She punctuated the words with a flirtatious pat on the knee of his chaps and stepped around the sorrel.

The air fairly cracked with surprise as she strode to her car for the first of her things. She hefted out two suitcases and lugged them to the huge porch that wrapped around the Victorian ranch house before she turned back toward the car and dared a peek to see where J.D. had gone.

J.D. hadn't gone anywhere. He'd pivoted his sorrel and watched from where she'd left him at the fence, stunned at the idea that she'd not turned a hair at his rudeness, then gave him a brazen smack on the knee before she'd waltzed off. Volcanic wasn't a strong enough description for the sensation that had stormed through his system and short-circuited his nerve endings.

It must also have short-circuited his brain, he realized grimly, because his conscience was making a ruckus. He'd been too rough on her. Letting her move that small mountain of luggage into the house by herself might be overdoing it. Particularly if she dragged it in and unloaded it in the wrong bedroom. He was the one with the beef against her. It wouldn't be fair to set her up on Carmelita's bad side. Besides, Ms. Hollywood was probably spoiled enough to accomplish that on her own.

J.D. urged his sorrel across the drive to the grass and dismounted, leaving the reins dragging. Zoe was hefting another bag from the back seat and he took it from her smoothly with a gruff, "You get the small stuff." She said nothing, but rewarded him with a toothpaste-commercial smile.

Zoe sensed the difference in J.D. At best, it was only a minimal softening, but it soothed the sting of his antagonism. The small mountain was moved efficiently to the porch, then carried inside.

Zoe removed her sunglasses and took a brief glance around while J.D. went back after the last box. The two-story house was decorated with a hodgepodge of heavy masculine furniture that must have spanned every generation of Hayes ownership. Only a few pieces showed feminine influence, but each one, from the curved glass china closet she spied through the wide dining room door, to the delicate rocking chair in front of the hearth, took obvious pride of place.

Zoe wondered if the Hayes women had influenced their husbands and occupied their lives in those same proportions. If so, it wasn't surprising that J.D.'s ex-wife bore him such enmity. Zoe knew what it was like to be relegated to a trivial corner of someone's life; she was intimately acquainted with the pain and resentment that caused.

Her speculations vanished the moment J.D. entered the house and, because his path to the stairs was blocked by her things, sat the box down near the door. She watched with interest as he pulled off his sunglasses and stashed them in a shirt pocket. There was nothing now to conceal or soften his hard expression.

Eyes as dark and brown as she'd ever seen took her measure from the crown of her head to her boots. Wide, well-defined brows formed a nearly straight slash across his strong forehead. His face was ruggedly male, tough, his cheekbones high. Unsmiling, there was clear evidence of deep, cheek-climbing creases beside his firm mouth. It struck Zoe that J.D. was a younger version of actor Tommy Lee Jones. She was instantly attracted.

J.D. wasn't happy. He didn't want to analyze the depth of that unhappiness, but as he stared over in secret dismay at his new partner, he sure as hell knew its source. From her perky wedge of platinum curls to her neon blue eyes and delicate features, Zoe Yahzoo was more perfect and more female than any woman he'd ever laid eyes on. And as his vision was again seduced downward to the petite body below her remarkable face, his libido took extreme note of each delectable curve, all the way down the length of her thighs, knees and ankles until it reached the toes of boots so small she must have got them off a children's rack.

The flowery musk of light perfume that had already driven him nuts wafted his way on a fresh cloud and made his mouth water. Suddenly famished, the small plump curves of her breasts drew his gaze upward, but it was the happy dance of all those platinum curls when she tugged off her Stetson and tossed it to a table that helped him tear his attention from places it shouldn't have wandered in the first place.

The compulsion to put more than his attention on all those places was unlike any male urge he'd had in all his thirty-four years. A thundering heartbeat later, he realized that any trouble a woman had ever given him—including Raylene—was minimal compared to the potential for trouble this one presented.

J.D. breathed a silent curse and consigned his lusty thoughts to hell. He would never again allow his libido to overrule his good sense. The next woman he let himself be attracted to had to have dark hair, a mousy disposition, and no ambitions beyond a half dozen babies and entering pies at the county fair.

Zoe felt chastened by J.D.'s severe expression. She'd been scorched by the bold stroke of that blatant male gaze and felt a decided weakness in her knees. Her breath caught when he suddenly started her way, easily negotiating the obstacle course of her belongings with those long powerful legs. She couldn't get a full breath until his harsh gaze released hers to focus on the luggage nearest the steps.

Still a bit giddy from being on the receiving end of J.D.'s sensual scrutiny, Zoe picked up two small cases and trailed after him as he led the way up the stairs. He'd managed to somehow take most of her luggage at once by stuffing a piece under each arm and carrying the handles to three suitcases in each of his big hands. Zoe had never been particularly attracted to large muscular men, but the difference in J.D.—that he'd come by his physique via a combination of genetics and hard work—impressed her enormously. A man like J.D. wouldn't need to pump iron under the watchful eye of a trainer.

Oh, no, she thought with a burst of merriment. J.D. had likely gotten his by bull-dogging steers all day and wrestling bulls on weekends.

Zoe didn't realize she was grinning until J.D. stopped and turned to glance back at her as he stepped sideways through a door with his load. Zoe quailed inwardly at the mighty frown he sent her. She made a valiant effort to sober her expression, but nervousness defeated her. Luckily, J.D. was through the door and was no longer looking.

Zoe followed him into the room, then almost collided with his big body. She lurched to a halt, her nose a scant two inches from his wide chest. Her first impression was that the green plaid wall in front of her smelled of sweat, leather and sunshine, and that it was as solid as oak. That it also radiated heat like a furnace didn't escape her notice. Her hopes that the heat wasn't a barometer of his temper died quickly.

"Miss Yahzoo." J.D. hesitated enough before he growled "Yahzoo" to give the definite signal that he found the name irksome. "In Texas, most *ladies* avoid following strange men around with that kind of look on their faces."

Zoe quickly set her suitcases down and traced the row of green buttons to his face. Brutal was somehow the only way she could describe his frown this time. She hoped she could make her expression serious enough to appease him.

"My apologies, Mr. Hayes. I meant no offense." The moment the words were out of her mouth, an explosion of nervous hilarity burst up. The best she could do to stop it was to bite the insides of both cheeks and make as dignified an escape as she could. Thank heavens there was still some luggage to bring up.

Zoe's amusement wound down by the time the last of her things was carried upstairs. In spite of those moments when J.D. had cast a lustful look at her, he was clearly not favorably impressed with anything else about her. Evidence of that was the way he'd simply exited the room once he'd unloaded the last box. He'd not spared her another word, much less a glance, and Zoe was stunned at how much his dislike unsettled her.

Zoe unpacked in record time, considering the number of things she'd brought with her. The room and its private bath were done in yellow rosebud wallpaper, the heavy woodwork painted a glossy white to match the high-gloss white paint on the restored triple dresser, night tables and armoire. The bed was a queen-size brass bed with elaborately curved metalwork and was, along with the rosebud lamps, the only new piece in the room. White pricilla curtains at the windows completed the cheery effect. It was all a nice contrast to what she'd seen so far.

She hurried downstairs, then discovered J.D. had left the house. A quick glance outside told her the sorrel was gone. A bit disappointed that he had abandoned her after their less than cordial beginning, Zoe went back upstairs to change into work clothes.

When she stepped out of her room later and started downstairs, she sensed by the silence of the big house that she was still alone. For all she knew, J.D. wouldn't be back anytime soon. She guessed he wouldn't appreciate her initiating her own tour of the ranch, but at least she was dressed for it.

She'd expected resistance when she'd bought into the ranch. Her lawyer hadn't needed to fill her in on any of that since she'd heard the circumstances from the California Realtor she'd hired to find her a rural house to rent here in Texas. She'd hoped to find something close by. When she'd discovered she could actually buy into the very ranch her young brother and sister lived on, she'd initially rejected the notion. But once the Realtor had told her that a group of environmentalists had raised funds to buy into Hayes, she'd reconsidered. Because of her, the people on Hayes were going to be drawn into enough trouble and scandal. Since she'd had the financial means to spare them further upset, she'd used it.

Zoe gave a grim sigh. She'd used her small fortune to manipulate people and circumstances, something she normally despised since it was a tactic her adoptive parents used as regularly as credit cards. That she'd done it for a good purpose made it only marginally better in her mind, though she imagined if J.D. knew what she'd done his reception to her that day would have been a good deal more congenial.

Zoe hadn't anticipated the impact he'd made on her.

Aside from his close resemblance to one of her favorite actors, J.D. wasn't the socially polished, civilized type of man she'd been attracted to in the past. He was a huge man, wide-shouldered, narrow-hipped, with a hard strength that was evidence of his outdoor life-style. He was no gentleman rancher, content to sit on the porch while hirelings did the chores. He was too rough for that, too elemental.

And yet, in spite of his harsh manners, it was his in-ability to let her carry things into the house by herself that made a favorable impression on Zoe. However hostile he might be toward her, he'd not been able to bring himself to be a total cad. He'd been rude and aloof when she'd introduced herself, but she was suddenly glad he hadn't faked a welcome he didn't mean.

Something inside Zoe relaxed at that. All her life she'd had to be wary of anyone who paid her notice. Her adop-tive parents were celebrities, and though she'd existed on the periphery of their charmed lives, the number of people who'd tried to get close to her to find favor with them had been legion. She sensed J.D. didn't give a rip about social climbing, wouldn't give a damn for hobnobbing with the rich and famous. His career was in land, cattle and oil, so there would be no value to linking his name with Jason and Angela Sedgewick.

On the other hand, he would be relating to Zoe Yahzoo as a person. Zoe saw no point in tipping the odds in her favor by revealing the fact that she'd been the better of his two buyers, not yet. If possible, she wanted a chance to be accepted for herself, though even she at times wasn't completely certain who that was. Zoe Yahzoo wasn't a total illusion, she knew that. She sensed her natural personality was lighthearted and sparkling, but pain and pride had intensified it so much that Zoe often felt like a fake.

Which was part of the reason she'd come here as she had, intending to get to know the people she was so obsessively curious about before her secrets were revealed to the world.

Of course, she acknowledged to herself, there was also the very real possibility they'd want nothing to do with her. Particularly considering the magnitude of the notoriety that would soon shadow her every move. Zoe tried not to give in to the anxiety that accompanied the reminder.

Zoe wandered through the living room, not comfortable familiarizing herself with the rest of the big house without a guide. She did find the kitchen, however. It was a large room, remodeled from what it once must have been, boasting custom-made wood cabinets and enough counter space to land a small plane. It was also immaculately kept, without a shred of clutter beyond a colorful assortment of cookbooks that crowded two long shelves. Zoe set her Stetson on a counter and got out a glass for water.

As she turned on the tap, she considered again the wisdom of keeping her identity a secret for a few more days. Memories of the show of affection her parents made when cameras rolled or others looked on gripped her for several moments. Sadness permeated the images, reaffirming her decision. Whatever the response of her birth family, acceptance or rejection, she had to know. She could no longer bear for anyone to feign affection for her because it made them look good or because it might gain them an advantage. It would be just as bad if they felt they had to manufacture feelings because of blood ties.

Resolved, she turned off the tap and had a long drink

of water, grimacing a bit at the different taste. The door
to the back porch opened, and she started guiltily. The
impression J.D. had given her of his housekeeper made
her leery of getting on the woman's bad side, but she
collected herself and turned. Surely the woman wouldn't
begrudge her a glass of water.

Only it wasn't the housekeeper who stepped inside. J.D.
stood just inside the door, his six-foot-plus height dominating the kitchen she'd thought so large just moments
ago. The welcoming smile Zoe sent him nearly faltered.

His dark eyes pinned hers. "You gonna leave that convertible out there like that?" His question came out more
belligerently than he'd intended, but there was no sign in
those remarkable blue eyes that he'd either riled her or
hurt her feelings.

Zoe shrugged. "Is it in the way?"

J.D. reached up and yanked off his hat, then tossed it
toward a counter. The slant that came to his mouth hinted
at amusement. "Not unless you count birds and pigeons."
He crossed the kitchen and Zoe stepped aside as he got
out a glass. He moved to the refrigerator, opened the
freezer door to scoop out some ice cubes, then stepped to
the sink to fill the glass.

That she didn't fall all over herself to rescue her car
from bird droppings intrigued J.D. He turned to lean
against the counter and sample the water while he waited
for a reaction. When she remained less than two feet
away, leaning against the counter that was at right angles
to the one he was backed up to, he decided Hollywood
socialites didn't know too much about the big outdoors.
And that meant any nasty little surprises that dropped on
or in that red speed buggy would diminish her notions
about ranch life. That, he was all for.

Zoe took note of J.D.'s speculation and the dark glint in his eyes that passed for humor. Though she guessed his amusement was at her expense, it was evidence of a sense of humor, however bent. Her nerve endings were sizzling from standing in his close proximity. And when those dark eyes made another bold head-to-toe sweep, she was reminded he wasn't entirely antagonistic toward her.

What she needed to know was how much of that antagonism he'd passed to others on Hayes. If J.D. had cast her too deeply in the role of wicked witch, it might prove difficult, if not impossible, to win over the very people she'd come here to find. She smiled at him to cover her anxiety.

"What have you told your people about me, Mr. Hayes?"

Her question hardened his expression. "No more than I had to," was his rough reply.

"Can you tell me...specifically?"

There was little more than a flicker of vulnerability in that tiny pause, but something in J.D. was alert to it. Every question he'd had about the reasons a Hollywood socialite would buy into a Texas ranch, then show up to live there, flashed through his mind, stirring his suspicions afresh. All at once he saw that her toothpaste-commercial smile was fake. Just as swiftly, he got a clear sense of the vulnerability it covered.

"Look, Ms—" J.D. hesitated irritably, as if he couldn't quite bring himself to say "Yahzoo." "Raylene made sure folks knew she turned my pockets out and got a third of Hayes in the divorce. The local paper printed the story of her selling it to someone from Hollywood. My foreman knows you were arriving today, my men have been wondering what the hell a Zoe Yahzoo is, and my housekeeper threatened to quit if you claim to have been abducted by aliens.''

Zoe giggled at J.D.'s grumpy humor. All was well. Pride had kept him from making too many negative remarks about his new partner. If the circumstances about what he'd lost in his divorce were that well known, the only face-saving thing left for him to do was to keep his objections—and disparaging comments about her—to himself.

''And what about you, Mr. Hayes? What were you expecting?''

He pressed his lips together in a disgruntled line and didn't answer.

Zoe studied him before she said quietly, ''I'd like to hear it.''

Silence dominated those next moments. Zoe waited, willing herself not to fidget. J.D. looked as if he wanted to let her have it with both barrels, and it might take everything she had to maintain her smiling facade. ''Mr. Hayes?''

J.D. set his water glass on the counter, then brought his gaze back to hers. His look was level and hard, but his gravel-edged voice was surprisingly soft. ''I was expecting a pain in the ass.''

His statement, blunt as it was, didn't hurt her feelings. Mainly because she sensed it was not meant to. It occurred to her that he saw himself as the main target for his anger, since his own actions were responsible for the situation he was now faced with. There was something fair-minded about that and Zoe's attraction to him deepened.

''I'll try not to be a pain, Mr. Hayes,'' she said, though she knew because of the revelations that were coming, it was inevitable.

"Then sell out to me." There was steel in his tone and the look in his dark eyes was utterly determined.

Zoe was flustered into the slip, "Not yet," then recovered herself and started to step away from the counter.

J.D. noticed and seized her wrist to halt her retreat. "Not yet? Explain that."

Zoe turned fully toward him, unable to evade that penetrating glare. And the feel of those hard fingers wrapped so firmly around her wrist was nothing if not electrifying. Somehow, she regained her composure.

"I mean, when I'm ready to move on, I'll sell only to you, fair market value."

The light in his eyes blazed higher. "Why not now?"

"I want to be here now."

A frown line divided the space between his dark brows. "I want my ranch back. All of it."

"Enough to let me stay on peacefully?"

"Why the hell should I?" he demanded, clearly tantalized by the hint she didn't plan to stay forever, but frustrated because he had an indefinite wait to endure.

"Because I'm asking, Mr. Hayes," she said softly.

His voice went low, to an almost intimate growl. "And why should I do you any favors?"

Sensuality was so thick between them suddenly that the air was hard to breathe. J.D.'s fingers had somehow become a warm caress on the tender flesh of her inner wrist.

Her voice was barely above a whisper as she acknowledged, "I guess from your point of view, there's no reason."

J.D. gave her a sarcastic, "You're my partner."

"Not your adversary," she countered. "I don't want to take over, I don't want anything more than for you to honor the fact that we have a legal paper that gives me the right to live here. I'd like for you to allow me to do that in peace. You'd still be the boss.''

J.D. gave a snort. ''You're damned straight.''

Zoe's smile was genuine and delighted, breaking the tension of those last moments. She gave him a sideways look. ''Are you a tyrant, Mr. Hayes?''

Surprise flickered across his hard features, but he responded instantly with, ''I'm a despot, Miss…Yahzoo.''

''Can we get along peacefully?'' she pressed.

''That remains to be seen.''

Zoe considered a moment. ''Fair enough.''

He released her wrist slowly. There was no mistaking the heat that lingered in J.D.'s eyes, or the shivery tingle that zoomed through her in response. Zoe turned away and reached for her hat in a way that she hoped was a frivolous dismissal of the sensual undercurrent between them.

''Do you have time to show me around?'' She settled her hat on her head and glanced back at him.

Unable to keep from tracking her every move, J.D. yanked his gaze from his avid contemplation of her backside to meet hers. His defensive, ''Looks like you're dressed for it,'' amused her and she gave him a smile that let him know it before she let herself out the back door.

J.D. expelled a harsh breath that ended in a snort of self-directed disgust. As lustful as his relationship with Raylene had been in the beginning, it was little more than mild indigestion compared with the conflagration that had roared to life the moment he'd touched Zoe Yahzoo.

And if his instincts were right, he'd just got his first taste of the hell he'd have to suffer to honor her request to stay on peacefully.

CHAPTER TWO

J.D. FOLLOWED her out of the house, taking what he hoped was clinical note of her changed attire. Gone was the western chic outfit she'd arrived in. That black Stetson she had on now showed the unmistakable marks of long use, as did the brown work shirt, well-washed Levi's and the pair of scuffed brown boots. Even with her short wedge of curls and peaches-and-cream complexion, she looked as at home in work clothes as she had in her dude outfit. He resisted the urge to ask where she'd got the secondhand duds. Instead, he fell into step beside her on their way to the barns, resolving to keep her as far out of his line of sight as possible.

Zoe listened as J.D. gave her a brief overview of acreage, head of cattle and number of active oil wells and output. She looked on with interest as he walked her through the barns, stables and outbuildings. Every structure was in good repair, every horse still at the stables or in corrals in top condition. What cattle she could see, she recognized as Santa Gertrudis, and listened with only half an ear to the breed's advantages. Though J.D. wasn't boastful, there was an undercurrent of pride in his voice she suspected he was completely unaware of. She, on the other hand, loved his low-pitched drawl, content to stroll at his side and let the lazy sound of it flow over her.

She glanced his way, then had to look up quite a distance to see his profile. Her attraction to J.D. was a pleasant distraction. Never in her most grandiose dreams about finding her family had she imagined anyone else would so capture her attention. All her life she'd lived among some of the most charismatic people in the world, beautiful people who were so glamorous they weren't quite real.

J.D. was as rugged as a granite avalanche. There was none of the beefcake handsomeness of a Hollywood leading man, but J.D. was one of the most visually compelling men she'd ever met. His stern personality only enhanced his appeal. After dealing with shallow personalities and celebrity facades, people like John Dalton were nearly as overwhelming as they were a relief, and Zoe cautiously appraised him.

Money, fame and celebrity wouldn't impress him. Those were transient things, more fluke of nature than the norm. To a man with both boots set squarely in the stark reality of ranch living, hard work and good character would be the yardsticks he measured others by.

Zoe felt adrift suddenly, uncertain there was anything about her that a man like J.D. would respect or value. And if she couldn't earn his respect and regard, would she be able to earn those things with her birth family?

A lifetime of insecurity burst up and settled like lead in her chest. Money, fame and celebrity—but more particularly, the Sedgewick name—had gained her whatever acceptance she'd enjoyed. The Sedgewicks themselves had denied her admission to their hearts, but the rarified life they'd bestowed on her had guaranteed her entry nearly everywhere else. Zoe was abysmally aware that on her own, without the Sedgewick name and fortune, she might never have attracted the notice of most of the people she'd ever known.

Even her name change when she was eighteen and determined to get back at her parents had only hyped her celebrity with everyone else. Whatever fascination she'd attracted as the only daughter of the Sedgewicks soared to near star status once she renamed herself. Every talk show that had ever done a program on the children of celebrities pestered her, gossip columnists tracked her every move, and Zoe Yahzoo was on the A-list of every celebrity bash in the country. She charmed, she entertained, a pseudo-star at the edge of her parents' universe.

But none of that would mean anything on the Hayes Ranch. Not yet. She was merely the new co-owner, a rich Hollywood oddball with a crackpot name. And when Zoe Yahzoo's secrets were revealed to the world, the Hayes Ranch would share ground-zero status with the scandal that would rock Hollywood. Zoe felt a fresh sting of despair and forced those dismal thoughts to stop.

J.D. was saying something and it was suddenly vital to listen to his every word. She looked his way, then was snared by what she read in his dark eyes. Solid, stable, hard to win. Character traits Zoe found absolutely irresistible. The sudden knowledge that J.D. was somehow both a signpost and a turning point in her life stunned her. That she hadn't the vaguest clue as to what to do with the knowledge was terrifying.

"We need to get you started on riding lessons right away," he was saying, his statement startling her, particularly when he added the dig, "Unless you'd planned to lay around the house in the air-conditioning the whole time."

Zoe shook her head and proclaimed, "Oh, no, Mr. Hayes. I mean to live here and participate fully."

J.D. ignored the "participate fully" part. That was out of the question. It was reasonable though, for her to learn to ride. Carmelita might not take to having Ms. Hollywood underfoot the whole time.

"Then you'll need lessons," he insisted.

Zoe shook her head again. "I'm a fair rider, J.D."

He gave her a narrow glance and a skeptical twist of lips. "A fair rider, huh?"

Zoe grinned up at him. "You can judge for yourself." She headed for the stable, leaving J.D. to follow. When they stepped inside and started down the aisle, Zoe asked, "Can I choose my own mount?"

When she turned to him suddenly, J.D. abruptly stopped. He gave her a stern look from his superior height. "Depends on which one you choose," he said gruffly. Zoe smiled at him, then paced down the aisle, peering into the stalls on her way past, then turning to come back to one of the first ones.

Inside, a muscular bay gelding with a wide blaze looked out at her with interest. Zoe glanced J.D.'s way. "How about this one for now?"

J.D. seemed to consider a moment, then gave a faint nod. "Go ahead and choose your tack. You'll have to saddle him yourself, then make sure he's properly put up later. My men are cowboys, not maids." He leveled her a meaningful look. "Or nannies."

Zoe ignored the gibe and was off toward the tack room returning moments later with a saddle and bridle. J.D. had taken himself off somewhere, so Zoe unlatched the stall gate and stepped inside. She took a few moments to get acquainted with the bay, then slipped the bridle on smoothly and led him from the stall.

After a quick grooming, she reached for the saddle blanket and closely inspected it before she tossed it on the horse's back. J.D. had returned by then, leading his sorrel.

J.D. watched critically as Zoe hefted the saddle atop the bay, impressed in spite of himself at her quick, competent work. He could find no fault with her skill so far, which added favorably to his private observation that she'd made a good choice with the bay.

Brute was a spirited horse, young, but with enough cow savvy and heart to satisfy J.D. That he often used the horse himself was testament to his regard for the animal. It was interesting that Zoe had chosen him, particularly when he suspected she was a weekend rider at best.

Zoe finished with the saddle. J.D. looked on as she took a moment to adjust the length of the stirrups, then turned toward him. "All set."

Her thousand-watt smile was back, he thought sourly, then was struck by the idea that there was something about Zoe that was familiar to him. The impression became stronger as they left the stable, leading their horses down an alley that bisected the network of corrals. He glanced her way more than once, looking for something specific to recognize, some special image that would confirm the notion. Though he was no avid fan of movies or TV, he'd watched his share during slow times of the year. She was starlet material in his book with those platinum curls and that movie star face. Looking at her didn't spark any particular memory, but the sense that he remembered her from somewhere was growing stronger by the moment.

They didn't mount until they were through the last gate and the vast expanse of range that surrounded the ranch headquarters stretched before them. J.D. turned to his horse. He'd no more than got his foot in the stirrup when

Zoe was in her saddle, leaning forward to whisper something that sounded like nonsense in Brute's ear.

She gave the bay a pat, then straightened and glanced his way. "Ready?"

He couldn't have missed the eagerness on her face. J.D. nodded grimly and they set off at a slow pace.

Uncertain of her ability on the lively bay, he monitored her closely. He was determined for her to tire of ranch life and sell out to him at the earliest possible moment, but he didn't want her to get hurt.

And because he had no desire to see her hurt, it didn't bother his conscience in the slightest to use this opportunity to chafe a bit of the rosy glow off Ms. Hollywood's romantic notions about playing cowgirl. If she was the once-around-the-park weekend rider he figured she was, keeping her in the saddle for the entire four hours between now and supper might serve his purpose nicely.

Feeling charitable suddenly, J.D. glanced Zoe's way and gave her a rare smile. Zoe's thousand-watt response was blinding, giving him fresh hope that this perky little daffodil would wilt quickly and spare them both a long, hot afternoon in the Texas sun.

Zoe Yahzoo was a hell of a rider, J.D. concluded unhappily much later. He was hot and tired, bathed in sweat and gritty with dust as they headed to the cook house for supper. Zoe, he noted irritably, didn't sweat. Hell, no, he groused to himself, she got *dewy*. And the Texas dust that dared to land on that dew-kissed complexion managed to do so in such a way that could only be described as cute, with a streak here, a smudge there. It had surprised the hell out of him when she'd pulled out a hankie at the last stock tank and hadn't been squeamish at all about "fresh-ening up'' using the same water his cattle and horses drank from every day. It didn't fit his notion of how pernickety socialites behaved, even when they were playing cowgirl.

Worse, instead of being tired and whiny and sore from a hot afternoon on horseback, Zoe fairly bounced at his side, chattering in glowing terms about Brute and the ranch, as loose-limbed and invigorated as if it were a crisp fall morning following a long vacation.

He looked away from her high-energy exuberance, determined to keep from getting discouraged. She'd get tired of riding his horses. She'd be bored with Hayes in a week and get homesick for clean, lazy indoor afternoons in air-conditioning with house servants to cater to her life of ease. The social whirl of Hollywood would draw her back. Particularly since there was nothing on Hayes or in the vicinity that remotely resembled a celebrity party circuit.

J.D. comforted himself with that thought and the reminder that it was Carmelita's day off. They'd have to eat supper at the cook house. While Zoe had taken to him well enough, he was her co-owner, the boss, more in keeping with her station. She'd probably consider his ranch hands commoners. It would be interesting to see how this California glamor girl fancied sitting down to a table with that bunch, exposed to their rough manners while she faced a meal of red meat and potatoes.

They washed up at an outdoor spigot before they reached the cook house. J.D. got a step ahead of her as they walked up on the porch. He pulled open the screen door for her, then pushed open the inner door. Zoe flashed him a quick smile, then preceded him into the large dining room.

Ten of the ranch hands who lived on Hayes were already sitting around the long plank table. At the sight of Zoe, they jumped up almost in unison, causing an awful squall of the heavy backless bench seats as they were shoved back.

J.D. pulled off his Stetson and hung it on a nearby peg before he introduced Zoe. ''Boys, I'd like you to meet Zoe Yahzoo. Miss Zoe will be sitting down to supper with us.'' He flicked Zoe a glance to see how she was taking his men, but Zoe had disposed of her Stetson and was stepping forward to shake the nearest man's hand.

She didn't give him a chance to introduce her to them separately, but asked for each name herself. She took her time working her way around the table, placing that small elegant hand in each blunt-nailed callused one as if she couldn't wait to make their acquaintance. That she was in no hurry was evident when she asked each man what they did on Hayes or if they had family nearby.

J.D. followed along until he reached the head of the table, where he waited to sit down until Zoe finished. Zoe appeared oblivious to the fact that the cook was about to sit the meat platters on the table, until she happened to see him, and turned to treat him to a smile.

''You must be the cook,'' she said brightly, then waited until Coley set the platters down before offering her hand and getting his name. ''You set quite a table, Mr. Coley,'' she commented as she glanced over the table crowded with meat, potatoes, gravy, biscuits, four kinds of green vegetables and big bowls of canned peaches. ''Is that apple pie I smell?''

The normally cantankerous Coley blushed, then blustered, ''Ain't no Mr. Coley to you, Miss Zoe. Just Coley. And that's Dutch apple. I gotta couple gallons of homemade vanilla ice cream for the top, if'n ya ain't feared of spoilin' yer figure.''

Zoe laughed. "If I put both gallons on my piece of pie, I probably would." She gave him a curious look. "Do you keep a lot of homemade vanilla ice cream around?"

"Sure do," Coley said, his chest puffed out a bit. "Make some nearly every day."

"Uh-oh, that was the wrong answer," she said with a groan and rueful shake of her head that indicated a weakness for homemade ice cream.

J.D. laughed along with the others, then waited until she made her way to the spot to his right that the men had left open for her on the bench. He was surprised at her reaction to his men, and couldn't help warming to her a bit despite the idea that meeting the ranch hands and sharing a meal with them didn't appear to dim her enthusiasm.

Zoe Yahzoo, despite her Hollywood background and starlet looks, was no snob. That his men were instantly taken with her was hardly a surprise, not when she looked like she did and had seemed so interested in getting acquainted with each one.

He looked on in silence as she bantered cheerfully at the table while she helped herself to generous portions and passed bowls and platters his way. She managed to mention enough names in her exchanges with his men to convince him that she remembered them all.

The men grew silent to eat and Zoe did, too. J.D. expected her to pick at her meal, but she packed away an astonishing amount of food for a woman whose slim figure suggested a careful diet. And when Coley brought in the pies and ice cream, Zoe helped herself again, not slowing until she'd finished every bite. She pushed her dessert plate away with a sigh and dragged her cup of coffee closer.

By the time they left the dining room to head back to the ranch house, Zoe's energy seemed to have wound down to an air of quiet contentment. J.D.'s mood darkened. Zoe was a hit with his men and his attraction to her was growing.

It aggravated him to realize that he was suddenly not as hot as he had been for her to sell to him and clear out. She was a bright curiosity to him, something new and decidedly foreign in his environment, yet she managed to fit in. No, he realized, she didn't fit in. It was more like she made a place for herself. He didn't have time to ponder that impression, because he glanced her way and saw her brow furrow thoughtfully.

"Didn't you mention having a foreman?"

They'd reached the back porch and he automatically opened the door to let her go ahead of him before he answered. "My foreman lives in the house by the highway. His son and daughter live with him, so they take their meals at home. He'll be around in the morning, if you're up."

Zoe managed to mask the tingle of anxiety and anticipation that went through her at J.D.'s first official mention of his foreman and his children. She'd been in suspense all afternoon and during the meal at the cook house for someone to mention Jess Everdine's name or his son's or daughter's. Since no one had, she'd finally had to ask something outright. Now she could force herself to get by the wait of one more night.

She couldn't, however, let J.D. get by with that "if you're up" wisecrack.

"Mr. Hayes." She hung her Stetson next to his on the

wall pegs inside the kitchen, then turned to him with a chiding smile. "You seem to have a few unflattering ideas about me." She held up a hand to start ticking them off. "Unless I want to lay around the house in air-conditioning, your men aren't maids, bellhops or nannies, *if* I'm up in the morning…"

He gave her a look from his height that seemed to emphasize his big stature.

She pointed up at him. "Ah, yes—that reminds me. There it is again, that superior look, that 'I'm the biggest gorilla in the jungle' pose."

J.D. gave her a bland twist of lips. "I thought you Hollywood types called them 'rain forests.'"

Zoe cringed and pressed a slim finger to her lips. "Ooops—don't tell."

"And what's wrong with acting like you're the biggest gorilla if you are?" he went on, the arrogant smile on his lips deploying the engaging creases that slashed upward to his cheekbones.

Zoe was staggered by the appeal of that smile and those deep-cut creases. J.D., gruff arrogance and all, would be an easy man to fall in love with. She laughed and couldn't resist flirting a bit.

"You've certainly made your point, Mr. Kong," she said as she leaned his way and nudged him with her elbow before she turned and started across the kitchen.

J.D.'s blood pressure shot roof high at that playful nudge. The fact that she'd immediately flitted away caused an instant frustration that made his breath catch. The woman was like the hot end of a downed high-voltage line, dancing and snapping, capable of frying a man alive the moment he came into contact with her.

He couldn't tear his eyes away, so it was a fresh shock

to his system when she stopped at the door to the hall and looked back at him.

"I'm going to have an early night. Do you mind?"

He shook his head. "Not at all."

She gave him a smile that was not dazzling or commercial fake. "And thanks for letting your men meet me and form their own opinions. You could have so easily made having a good time with them tonight impossible."

J.D. couldn't respond to that. The utter sincerity and vague trace of wistfulness in those incredible eyes caught him as much off guard as her playful nudge had. He suddenly had the sense that this wistful, somber side of Zoe was the real thing. It contrasted sharply with all her bright smiles and good cheer, emphasizing the idea that there was much about the Zoe Yahzoo he'd seen so far that was somehow fake.

Words like glamor, image and pretense came to him. Words that suddenly didn't fit this strong impression of vulnerability. Even her soft, "Good night, John Dalton," touched him in that same peculiar way. He managed his own good night to her before she turned and disappeared through the doorway.

That night, J.D. dragged back the bedspread and top sheet, then fell into his big bed, worn out. Zoe's arrival and an afternoon in the heat had left him bone-weary, but he was too restless to fall asleep instantly. Instead, he stretched out and stared up at the darkened ceiling.

For the first time in what felt like years, he actually looked forward to the next day. He was anticipating it. Keenly.

He frowned, regarding that emotion with suspicion. From the day Raylene had walked out on him, he'd driven himself mercilessly, taken no time off, allowed himself few diversions. He was aware that his grueling routine was the means to both work off his anger at himself and do penance for his mistakes with Raylene, but he'd thrived on it. He'd found a measure of satisfaction in pushing his limits, denying his emotional needs and testing his mental and physical stamina until he'd proven himself equal to the task. He hadn't needed wimpy emotions like eagerness and anticipation to be the engine for the way he'd lived his life.

He sure as hell didn't need them now, he assured himself. But a quick flash of sunshine curls and laughing blue eyes burst on his thoughts and made a lie of his secret declaration.

From his first glimpse of her, Zoe had captured his attention and given his austere emotions a banquet of strong sensation to feast upon. She had a way of absorbing his focus that wasn't limited to or dependent on her looks, though they were a hell of a draw. Her bright personality, bouncing energy and cheerful humor were enormously entertaining, but his insight into a more somber Zoe was a contrast that fascinated him. She was a shining oasis in the dry sand of his existence, and J.D. was suddenly profoundly aware that he'd been slowly dying of thirst.

He cursed and flopped over to pummel his pillow. For a man not given to whimsy, he was practically infested with it tonight. He was no navel-gazer, so he couldn't account for this impulse to take stock of himself and the way he lived his life.

That could only mean the blame for his mental and emotional turbulence rested squarely on Zoe Yahzoo. He'd expected her unwelcome presence to throw things out of whack until he could get her to sell out and leave. He hadn't expected her to throw him out of whack.

And the fact that she was completely responsible for this gut-jumping anticipation for morning when he would surely see her again made him give his pillow another surly punch.

At last, he got settled and expelled a deep, tired breath. Tomorrow he'd set himself—and her—to rights. He was boss of Hayes and boss of himself. There would be no more emotional disruptions, no more letting himself be distracted from his determination to have her clear out of his life. He'd make himself scarce for most of the day. By the time Ms. Hollywood got out of bed, he'd have eaten breakfast and would be a good three miles away.

Comfortable with that, J.D. closed his eyes.

CHAPTER THREE

Z[OE] didn't meet J.D.'s housekeeper, Carmelita Delgado, until breakfast that next morning. Though Zoe hadn't heard the woman come home the night before from her day off, she was on duty in her immaculate kitchen that morning, shoving a coffee cake into the oven at 5:05 a.m.

Zoe halted in the doorway, not wanting to startle the woman. She called out a soft, "*Buenos días, Señora Delgado,*" then smiled when the woman turned from the oven, her dark brows raised in faint surprise. "My apologies, *señora*. I didn't mean to startle you."

"Do you know what time it is?" The question was almost a demand.

Zoe's brow crinkled slightly. She scanned the kitchen for the clock and checked her watch to compare the time. "It's 5:05. Am I late?" Her smile faded slightly at the intent way Carmelita was regarding her. Anxiety made a sharp pass through her middle. "Am I too early?" Zoe cast a belated glance around. "I see Mr. Hayes isn't here yet."

"Are *you* this Zoe Ya-hoo?" the woman asked in richly accented English, her dark eyes showing the tiniest bit of welcome with the surprise.

Zoe sat her saddlebags next to the table, then crossed the kitchen to shake Carmelita's hand. "That's Yah-*zoo*, but please call me Zoe. It's nice to meet you, *señora*."

Carmelita absently gave her hand a shake, seemed to see something she was looking for in Zoe, then pumped her slim hand vigorously. "Are you a movie star?" There was genuine interest in the woman's voice.

Zoe shook her head. "Not unless you count a one line part in a teen horror film when I was nineteen, and a few public service commercials."

Zoe hoped that would be enough to satisfy Carmelita's curiosity. She didn't want to deal with questions that demanded answers which would bring up the Sedgewicks, not yet. She knew she would have to mention them sometime, and soon, so that the people on Hayes would have some preparation for what was coming. But selfishly, if only for a little while, she wanted people to meet her and have a chance to get to know Zoe Yahzoo without the magic of the Sedgewick name to win them over.

Her resolve wavered when Carmelita suddenly asked, "Is your family named Yahzoo, or is your name made up?"

Zoe smiled and tried to evade the question by saying, "It's made up," but Carmelita was surprisingly persistent.

"What name is your family name, *señorita*?"

Zoe's breath seemed to lodge in her throat a moment before she could say, "Sedgewick. My parents named me Spenser Trevyn." She hoped the sheer snobbery of her first and middle names would distract Carmelita from the name Sedgewick. It was a futile hope.

Carmelita threw up her hands and let out a whoop before she grabbed Zoe's hands again. "Jason and Angela Sedgewick—" Whatever she'd been about to say ebbed into swift Spanish that Zoe couldn't follow too closely with her limited command of the language. She didn't need a translation to know the woman was making glowing comments, and Zoe couldn't help the disappointment she felt.

Carmelita switched back to English and fixed her with a puzzled look. "But why would you not keep your family name?"

Zoe gave her a wry smile. "Because when I was eighteen and in a very silly, rebellious frame of mind, I changed it."

The housekeeper drew back and placed her hand on her chest in surprise. She shook her head and gave Zoe a disapproving look. "This is not good, this dishonor to your parents."

Zoe's smile drifted away and she said quietly, "Perhaps not, *señora*. As I said, I was in a very silly, rebellious frame of mind." Zoe tried to redeem the confession Carmelita so clearly objected to. "And I can assure you, they greatly appreciate that the name Yahzoo is in the credits of that teen horror film, instead of theirs."

Before either of them could say more, a big voice sounded from the doorway. "So how come you didn't change your name back when you got over your rebellion?"

Startled, Zoe turned to see J.D. enter the room, his dark eyes making a brisk pass over her before he crossed to the coffeemaker to help himself to coffee.

"Maybe I never got over it," she answered swiftly, then went to take the steaming cup he held out to her. "Besides, I think even you have to admit that the name Spenser Trevyn Sedgewick stinks of elitist snobbery, not to mention raising questions of gender." Zoe laughed at the look that suddenly blunted his expression.

"But what the hell kind of name is Zoe Yahzoo?" he demanded, his big voice a deep growl.

"It's a fun-sounding name, Mr. Hayes. It's a name that reminds me not to take myself too seriously, particularly

since I used to have a lot of problems doing just that.''
She grinned at him as if she wasn't making the somber
revelation she really was.

But J.D.'s stare was intense and she had the unsettling
feeling that he could see straight through her. She turned
instantly to Carmelita.

''I can cook, *señora*. Would you like help with breakfast?''

Her offer seemed to break the loaded silence. Carmelita
smiled and waved her off. ''The boss will probably have
you working hard enough today. Best you rest where it's
quiet and cool while you can.'' With that, she went on
with her meal preparations.

Zoe looked over at J.D. as they sat down across the
table from each other. She raised her light brows and
leaned forward conspiratorially. ''Oooo, that sounds ominous, J.D. Do you have visions of sending me back to
the house saddle-sore and whining by noon?''

''I won't be sending you back from anywhere, because
you won't be working,'' he groused, then shot Carmelita
a surly look for saying so. Carmelita wagged a fork at
him and turned away.

Zoe took confidence from Carmelita's insubordination.
''But I want to work, J.D. That's what I meant when I
said I wanted to participate fully.''

''I know what you meant,'' he said darkly as he reached
for the newspaper and unfolded it. ''But ranch work is
hard and dirty and dangerous.''

Zoe made a face of mock horror. ''Oh, John Dalton—
you aren't one of those Neanderthals who thinks women
are too weak for men's work, are you?''

''I sure as hell am. Damned proud of it,'' he said with

exaggerated boredom as he opened the paper and began to scan an inside page.

Carmelita gave an unladylike snort that drew Zoe's attention, but the housekeeper appeared to be absorbed with turning two breakfast steaks in the skillet.

She looked back at J.D. "What do you suggest I do all day?"

"Ride Brute, use the pool, run up the phone bill, do your nails—whatever you like as long as you don't get in anyone's way." His instant answer belied his concentration on the newspaper.

Zoe stared over at J.D.'s aloof expression as he scanned the paper, not certain if she was offended or amused. She decided not to protest just yet. She sensed there was a way around his refusal to let her do ranch work. Besides, proving she was not only experienced with ranch work, but reasonably competent wasn't uppermost in her mind just now. Getting a first glimpse of Jess Everdine and his children was.

Her blithe, "Okay," as she reached for a section of newspaper drew a suspicious glance from J.D. that she pretended not to notice as she opened the section and began to scan the print.

Breakfast was served shortly, and Zoe dug in, intending to fortify herself for the day ahead. She intercepted several dark looks from J.D., and responded with an airy smile to a few of them. By the time they finished eating, his expression was as black as a storm cloud. Zoe drank the last of her coffee and raised her light brows as she looked over at him.

"Something bothering you, J.D.?"

His answer was instant. "You."

"Me?"

His low growl was apparently a confirmation. "What are you going to do all day?"

She couldn't resist. "Ride Brute, use the pool, run up the phone bill, do my nails—mainly, I'll try not to be a pain in your backside, John Dalton." She gave him a bright smile. "Go on about your business, and don't give me another thought."

She stood and glanced over at Carmelita, who was assembling ingredients for what looked to be chocolate cake. "Thank you for breakfast, *señora*. You're a wonderful cook."

Carmelita smiled her thanks and went back to work. J.D. was getting to his feet when he took note of Zoe reaching for the saddlebags she'd set aside earlier.

"What have you got in those?"

Zoe gave him a chastening frown for his grouchy tone, then lifted them to the table. She tugged a thong, then flipped one side open to show him. "A compass, a map of Hayes, a snakebite kit, sunblock, a collapsible drinking glass, gloves." She paused to open the other side. "A steel thermos, sandwich box, granola bars…" She looked up and smiled. "Everything but a horse and a saddle to tie them to. All right?"

By the look on his face, it wasn't, but he nodded. "Just stay close to the house. It's too damned much trouble to organize a search party. Stay away from the cattle. If you open a gate, close it. Don't get in anyone's way, and don't stay out too long."

Zoe rolled her eyes and swung the saddlebags onto her shoulder, leaving the thermos out. "I don't suppose you'd care to have me tag along with you this morning," she said hopefully.

"We're moving cattle to another pasture first thing,"

he muttered. "It's hot, rough work on that part of the range and no place for a greenhorn."

She gave him a teasing smile, then took her thermos to the sink to fill it with water. "Perhaps you ought to see for yourself how much a greenhorn I am. I could wander off someplace with my map and compass…" She let her voice trail off meaningfully.

"Not if I restrict you," he said darkly.

Zoe flashed him a look. "Good luck with that notion."

J.D. frowned at her, then the saddlebags, and expelled a harsh breath. "Come along, then. But if you get in the way, I'll send you back to the house."

"Fair enough." She turned on the tap and filled the thermos before she twisted the cap on and secured it in the saddlebag. She hurried over to grab her hat from the peg, then followed J.D. outside, rushing to get ahead of him to retrieve a couple things from her car's trunk on the way past.

J.D. didn't remark when she got out a set of blunt-roweled spurs and a pair of batwing chaps as he passed by, but the coil of rope she'd slung over her shoulder by the time she caught up and fell into step beside him got an immediate response.

"Where the hell did you get that rope?"

"I bought it." Zoe ignored the dark look he sent her.

"You can leave it in the barn," he declared.

Zoe didn't argue, and when they reached the barn where four of the ranch hands were saddling up, she had no problem keeping the rope out of J.D.'s sight. She swiftly groomed and saddled Brute, fastened the rope and saddlebags to the saddle, then buckled on her spurs and got on her chaps.

That J.D. was accustomed to having his every edict

obeyed to the letter was evident when he didn't bother to check to see whether she'd left her rope behind or not. By the time they left the barn, Zoe had forgotten about the rope herself. J.D. had said she'd meet his foreman if she was up early enough. She assumed this was early enough, since it was just past six o'clock. Her nerves were taut with suspense, but the only men she saw were the ones she'd met at supper the night before. It was on the tip of her tongue to ask J.D. about the foreman, but she decided such a question might attract attention.

The six of them were well away from the ranch headquarters before J.D. looked her way.

"I thought I told you about that rope," he groused.

Zoe looked over at him and shrugged. "I figured you didn't realize that I use it for more than a prop. You said we were going to move cattle."

"When I said 'we', I didn't include you. What the hell would you know about moving cattle?" he challenged, then smirked. "Hayes isn't some gigantic petting zoo, Hollywood. You leave that damned rope tied on your saddle, or I'll take it away."

Zoe's smile was forced as she felt the heat of embarrassment climb her cheeks. The four men riding with them had heard every word.

They reached the pasture J.D. designated some time later. It was on a hilly section of the ranch. Stands of mesquite that provided shade punctuated the hills, some of the scrubbier stands making Zoe glad she'd taken note of J.D.'s chaps and worn her own to protect her legs. The pasture was large, and because of the small valleys between hills, finding the cattle and moving them would be a greater challenge.

Zoe tugged her hat down more firmly, then glanced

over at J.D. The four cowhands with them fanned out in what must have been a prearranged pattern.

"Which direction are we moving them?" she asked.

J.D. gestured to the south. "That way." He gave her a stern look. "Ride with me, but stay out of the way."

Zoe did as he ordered, and they rode down a wide path that paralleled the distant fence that marked the west boundary of the section. They found eight head of cattle just past the shallow crest of the first hill. The small bunch started to mill when they noticed the riders' approach. Zoe held Brute back a reasonable distance from J.D.'s sorrel, leaving him to start the cattle in the direction he wanted. For now, she'd do as he said and stay out of the way.

She'd moved cattle before, so she was aware of how easily a stray or two could double back. Zoe had spent every summer since her ninth birthday on one ranch or another in Colorado, Texas, Wyoming or Montana. It had irked her parents that she'd been so in love with cowboy life that she'd wanted to live on ranches all summer. But the fact that they could ship her off anyplace that vaguely resembled the summer camp their friends sent their children to had made them tolerate her choice.

Zoe'd had the benefits of an outdoor life that was worlds different from the high-society pretense that had crushed her; her parents could turn her and a bucket of money over to someone else to bother with for the summer. They'd neither noticed nor cared that each year she'd requested to go to a new list of ranches, each one more of a working ranch than the ones before.

She'd known since she was small that her biological mother had grown up on a ranch somewhere. She'd overheard enough of Angela's disparaging comments about "Spenser's hayseed origins" to find that out. Ultra-refined

Angela had been appalled at her repeated requests to spend summers on a ranch, railing at her husband about the poor breeding of the child he'd insisted they adopt. In the end, she'd given in, mainly because Jason had been feeling a rare occasion of pity for Zoe's emotional neglect. He'd finally decreed it as a kind of bribe.

And so had begun in earnest Spenser Sedgewick's childish search for her mother. Summer after summer, she'd lived on one ranch after another, getting to know everyone on the ranch and as many people in the area as she could. She'd searched every face, a naive child certain she'd know her mother on sight. Year by year, she'd watched for the woman who might be her mother, trying to find her in the only way a lonely child could. Hoping, wishing…

"Dammit, Zoe! Get out of the way!" J.D.'s shout yanked her from her thoughts in time to see one of the range bulls bearing down on her and Brute. Brute lunged to the side and Zoe kept her seat, pivoting the bay and automatically riding after the bull. Instinct rushed to the fore, both Brute's and hers as they raced fearlessly after the animal and came alongside. Almost without conscious thought, Zoe's rope was in her hand and she whacked the young bull on the neck, startling him into a turn. In moments they were chasing him back to J.D.'s gather. Zoe pulled back on the reins to let the bull slow and rejoin the bunch.

A scant moment later two cows broke to the right and Zoe angled Brute up the side of a hill to cut them off and start them back in the right direction. She took a position to the right rear of the gather and slapped her rope on the leg of her chaps as both a reminder to the cattle that she was there, and to make a sound that would keep them moving straight ahead.

The only note she took of J.D. was where he was riding in relation to the small herd. He had breakaways of his own to chase back, so he'd have little time to chastise her. Over the next hill, Zoe saw three more cows off to her right, closer to the boundary fence. After taking a quick glance at the cattle ahead to be sure they were moving along peacefully, she started Brute in their direction. While she was still a distance away, the three cows bolted the wrong way.

Zoe touched a spur to Brute, delighting in his quick reaction and impressive burst of speed. They rode to block the cows, and Zoe got a taste of Brute's cow savvy and agility as she gave him his head to work the cows, lunging and feinting, until all three cows turned tail. With no more than a bawl of protest, they moved off to join the gather.

Zoe grinned to herself, pleased. The trick of moving cattle was to do it with a minimum of fuss to avoid overtiring her horse and running weight off the cattle. By the time the three cows reached the others, Zoe had again taken up her right rear position.

J.D. was too surprised to be angry about Zoe's rope. She rode Brute like a pro and handled his cows as if she knew what she was doing. She hadn't been trying to defy him about the rope, and it was certainly no prop. His curiosity about her rose several more notches as he both watched for cattle to add to the gather and kept track of Zoe as she did the same.

By the time they reached the south gate, they had accumulated thirty head of cattle. His ranch hands hadn't arrived yet, so as soon as their cattle were through the gate, J.D. closed it and they rode back to join the others.

They had a busy morning, searching every valley and mesquite stand until the number of cattle they moved matched the tally of cattle that were supposed to be in this pasture. When the gate was finally closed and they started back, J.D. spoke.

"So, how many head of cattle do you Hollywood socialites run on those big fancy lawns out in Beverly Hills nowadays?"

Zoe laughed at J.D.'s question, delighted that his attitude toward her had brightened considerably, and that the four men who'd heard his warning about the rope now rode close enough to hear this, too. She got the strong impression J.D. was trying to make up for what he'd said earlier. It was also a wonderful acknowledgment that he credited her with at least a bit of skill.

"Not many," she answered, realizing with some surprise that she wanted J.D. to know something about her life. At least the better parts. He'd find out about the not-so-nice parts soon enough. "This socialite spent all her summers on working ranches that let wannabe cowgirls pay big money for the privilege of working as a hired hand."

One of the men with them swore in surprise, then blushed a deep red. "Beg pardon, Miss Zoe. You did a fine job this morning."

Zoe gave him a happy smile. "Thanks for saying so, Gus. That's a nice compliment from someone who does the work all the time." She faced forward, feeling a rare surge of contentment. She'd earned a bit of something with J.D. and these men this morning and it felt good.

But that feeling lasted only long enough for the headquarters to come into view. The people she'd come here to see were there somewhere. The foreman who may or may not be her natural father was the last of J.D.'s employees remaining for her to meet. The sharp needle of anxiety she'd managed to set aside while they'd moved the cattle was suddenly driving through her like a spear.

Once everyone knew who she was and realized the magnitude of trouble she'd brought to Hayes, she'd be lucky if any of them would have a good word to say to or about Zoe Yahzoo.

J.D. was alert to the mood shift in Zoe. Those megawatt smiles were coming more frequently, and her lighthearted facade seemed a touch more forced once they arrived back at the barn. Because he was watching more closely, he took grim note of the tremor in her hands as she unsaddled Brute. Something wasn't right, but he was distracted from further speculation.

"Mr. Hayes?" A boy's voice called from the open doors at the far end of the stable.

The sound of that voice struck something in Zoe's chest with the force of a blow. A soul-deep certainty that she'd never felt the like of, had her turning in wonder. A boy of about ten started down the aisle that bisected the stable, eagerness hurrying his steps until he reached J.D. Zoe turned Brute into the stall, then stepped into the shadows with him to peer out the rails.

"Mr. Hayes? You said you'd think about letting me build a tree house over in that one tree behind the east pecan grove." He dug in his back pocket and pulled out a paper that he quickly unfolded and held out to J.D. "I drew up the plan like you wanted." J.D. took the paper and examined it closely while the boy looked up into his hard features with a mixture of eagerness and hope.

Zoe stared. The boy was sturdy, of average height and

build for his age. His shirt and jeans were already dusty and smudged with dirt from a morning of doing what boys did on ranches. His Stetson was tipped back on his head, and a few lanky strands of dark blond hair angled from a side part to lay in charming disarray across his forehead.

She didn't need to hear J.D. say the boy's name; she needed nothing more than hearing his voice and looking upon that young, handsome face to know who he was. For the first time in her twenty-three years, she was setting eyes on her own flesh and blood.

Zoe swayed with the force of the revelation, sagging dizzily against the rails of the stall. The search of a lifetime was suddenly centered on the boy with J.D., the years of brutal disappointment soothed away by this first glance. The pain of never meeting her mother face-to-face, the knowledge that now she never would, finally didn't feel so terrible. Something that was both tender and fierce twisted her heart, assailing her so spontaneously that it stole her breath.

Somehow, she kept from crumpling to the straw-strewn floor as she fought to get a grip on the emotions that were choking her. Somehow, she collected herself, and through sheer force of will, she wrestled Zoe Yahzoo's sparkling facade back into place and stepped out of the stall.

And without a moment to spare as J.D. gestured in her direction, prompting the boy to notice her. The sudden shyness that made Bobby Everdine snap his mouth shut and blush was endearing.

Zoe closed the stall gate and picked up her saddlebags before she walked over, struggling to behave with some semblance of normalcy. J.D.'s dark eyes would catch anything unusual, particularly since she noted his attention was suddenly sharp on her flushed face. It wasn't time for anyone to figure things out. Not before she met Jess Everdine and found some way to talk to him first.

"Hello, there. W-who might you be?" she asked with a smile, secretly dismayed at her slight stammer.

J.D. took over the introduction. "This is Bobby Everdine, my foreman's boy." He placed a big hand on Bobby's shoulder. "And this is Miss Zoe Yahzoo."

Zoe put out her hand, unaware of its tremor as she gave Bobby a handshake. The contact was brief and she managed to release his hand at the appropriate time.

"Pleased to meet you, ma'am," he said awkwardly, his blush climbing a bit higher.

Zoe's heart was given an added twist. "Did I hear you say you're building a tree house?"

"*Might* be," he corrected, then shyly looked up at J.D. "But I gotta get permission."

Zoe turned to J.D., instantly taking the boy's side. "Every boy ought to have a tree house, John Dalton."

J.D.'s expression gave no clue to his decision as he looked from her to the boy. "What's your daddy say about this?" he questioned sternly.

"He said it was up to you, sir, since you own the tree." As if he sensed permission was coming, the eagerness in his eyes made their blue color sparkle with excitement.

"Where're you gonna get the wood and nails?" he questioned next.

"From the scrap wood they're gonna throw away from that new bowling alley. And I've been saving my allowance for the nails."

J.D. shook his head to that and Zoe's temper flared in indignation until he said, "There's plenty of scrap wood left over from the new stud barn. It's in the loft, in the way, so you'll have to get it down." He passed the boy's drawing of the tree house back to him. "There're weeds around the machine shed that need clearing. If you'll clean them out and rake the ground, the wood's yours and you can use as many of my nails as you need. You can borrow a hammer and hand saws, as long as you take care of them and put them back where they belong."

Bobby let out a whoop, his bright face lit by a wide smile. "Thanks, Mr. Hayes." He latched onto J.D.'s big hand and gave it a shake. "I'll get those weeds outta there right now." As if he couldn't wait to get started, he let go of J.D.'s hand and whirled around to run down the stable aisle. He got only a few strides before he skidded to a halt and turned back to look at Zoe. "Nice to meet you, ma'am," he called back, then spun around and tore out of the barn.

Zoe watched him go, her eyes smarting with unshed tears. She blinked them back and looked at J.D. "You're a nice man, John Dalton Hayes." She gave him a soft smile, then reached over to briefly touch his arm in a way that hinted at friendly affection. "So how about taking me to lunch? I'm so hungry even Brute was starting to look good."

J.D. wasn't fooled by that smile. His blood pressure was soaring as a result of another of Zoe's hit-and-run touches, but he wasn't about to be distracted from what he'd just witnessed. For all her playfulness and starlet looks, there was something melancholy and tenderhearted about Zoe Yahzoo.

Unfortunately for him, sensing that there was more to Zoe than megawatt smiles and disarming charm only made her that much more appealing. And as a man whose life-style had been disparaged and scorned by one woman, the idea that another had some fondness for it was one hell of a temptation.

CHAPTER FOUR

"You can park your car in the garage," J.D. told her as he quickly finished with his sorrel and turned the horse into his stall. "There's a spot for it on the east end."

Zoe looked on, still recovering from her brief meeting with her young brother. Her anxiety about meeting her sister and the man who might be her natural father was soaring. It was all she could do to keep from fidgeting with nerves, but she gave J.D. a grin.

"Thanks. I appreciate that, J.D. But you were wrong about the birds."

He gave a gruff chuckle and closed the stall gate. "You must lead a charmed life, Hollywood."

Zoe abruptly broke contact with the unexpected glimmer of humor in his dark eyes, saddened by the remark. That Zoe Yahzoo lived a charmed life was a lie. The worst sort of pretense and an overabundance of money had created that image. The world would be finding out the particulars very soon. Zoe was not only terrified of having that glittering veil yanked away, she wasn't certain how she would fare without it.

"That bother you?" J.D.'s low voice startled her from her thoughts, and she lifted her head to meet his close study of her.

Some instinct about J.D. urged her to dare a bit of candor, but the habits of a lifetime—not to mention cowardice—made her give him a bright smile to cover her offhand hint. "Charmed lives aren't all they're cracked up to be, John Dalton.'' She started down the aisle toward the far door and he fell into step beside her. ''And because they aren't, I'll move my car to the garage—*before* lunch.''

Zoe had dug her car keys from her pocket by the time they stepped out into the sunshine. She automatically glanced toward where her car was parked under the tree and faltered.

A girl of about seventeen—the same age as her sister—was standing beside her red convertible, looking it over. Wearing a white T-shirt and jeans, her western hat hanging down her back by a thong, the girl had the almost exact shade of blond hair that was also Zoe's natural color before she'd lightened it.

The same overwhelming certainty she'd experienced with Bobby—that she was looking upon her own flesh and blood—assailed her, with the same poignant twist of her heart. Zoe's breath caught, struck by the revelation that her sister, Rebecca, bore a strong facial resemblance to the high school yearbook picture Zoe had of their dark-haired mother.

As if surviving her first contact with her family made it easier the second time, Zoe recovered, and moved with shaky confidence toward her car.

''How do you like it?'' she called out as she and J.D. came closer.

The girl glanced up, her pretty face alight. ''It's a really neat car. It's yours?''

Zoe nodded and stopped next to the girl as J.D. made the introductions. ''Becky Everdine, this is Miss Zoe.''

Zoe waved away the formality. ''It's just Zoe, and I'm pleased to meet you, too,'' she repeated back, nearly unable to keep from staring at the girl's face too long.

Instead, she gestured toward her car. "Mr. Hayes just invited me to move it into the garage. Would you like to drive it over?" She held up the keys.

Becky shot J.D. a shy look before her gaze fastened on the keys with instant longing. She shook her head with regret. "I probably shouldn't."

"Don't you have a driver's license?"

Becky glanced at the car. "Yeah, but I'd be afraid of scratching it or something."

Zoe smiled. "It's insured, the garage is close, and I'm not a fanatic about dings and scratches. It's just a car."

Becky turned back with a wry grin. "But *what* a car!"

They both laughed at that, and Zoe shoved the keys in her direction. "Go ahead and put it away. Just leave the keys in the ignition so I know where they are."

"Well…" She looked at Zoe, grinned the same impish grin Zoe had seen in the mirror on her own face, then took the keys. "Okay!"

Zoe managed to maintain her smile and watched, unable to keep from staring as if she were memorizing every move and expression her sister made. J.D. remained silent beside her as Becky hurried around the car then opened the door and got behind the wheel. She looked over the dashboard gages and switches, then took a moment to run her hand over the white leather seat before she slipped the key into the ignition.

The engine hummed to life and Becky put the car into gear. Hesitating only long enough to give Zoe a smile and a wave, she started the car cautiously forward.

Zoe was so engrossed, she didn't notice anyone approach.

"That girl's been moonin' over that red convertible since you drove by our house yesterday."

The deep drawl startled Zoe, and she turned toward it. A big man who rivaled J.D. for height stood no more than three feet away. A black Stetson didn't quite cover his telltale dark blond hair. The tanned, sun-lined face that looked over at her was smiling and friendly, the blue eyes that regarded Zoe only shades darker than her own. She knew instantly this was Bobby and Becky's father, Jess. The reminder that there was a chance that he might also be her father exploded on her consciousness.

Suddenly it was all too much. Weeks of dread and hope, a lifetime of hurt and longing, the relentless emotions that had both led her here and driven her, were overpowering. Everything she'd missed, everything she'd needed, was suddenly here at this moment in her life. The horror of being rejected by this man, the terror that he might forbid her contact with the only two people she was certain were related to her, combined with the emotional turbulence of that morning.

Zoe tried to smile, but the best she could manage made her lips tremble. Her knees went weak, and a new terror—that she was about to faint—overrode everything else. J.D.'s steady drawl as he introduced her to Jess Everdine, penetrated her dizziness and snatched her back from the edge.

"Pleased to meet you, Miss Zoe," Jess said as he offered his hand.

Zoe took it, gathered strength from his warm grip, and mumbled what she hoped was an appropriate response. Anything more was beyond her. She searched Jess's gaze, desperate for some spark of recognition, yet just as desperate for him to see nothing. She, on the other hand, was looking for any sign in his sun-weathered face, any clue that would tell her if he was her father. Though it was near certain he was, there was always the chance she was the product of her mother's intimacy with someone other than her high school sweetheart.

It was then that Zoe realized she'd gone about everything in the worst possible way. As she let go of Jess's hand, she couldn't immediately look away from the handsome face that bore both the squint lines of happiness and the grim etchings of hard times. Her impression of the man—that he was honest and straightforward—made the way she'd manipulated her way into his life suddenly seem a monstrous deception. The self-delusion that had fogged her judgment and urged her on began to evaporate and Zoe felt the shock to her toes.

She'd come here under false pretenses as J.D.'s new partner, determined to fully indulge her own selfish need for acceptance from her birth family before she let any of them know who she was. It was only now, at this moment of terrible insight into her own weak character, that Zoe could see she'd never meant for either Jess or his children to have a truly fair opportunity to like her or not. Somewhere in a love-starved, greedy part of her heart, she'd become so obsessed to win them over, that she'd aimed to do whatever it took.

Zoe glanced toward J.D., struggling to recover from her stark insights, intending to summon her lighthearted facade to arrange an escape. But the instant her gaze connected with the alert glimmer in his, she faltered. It was on the tip of her tongue to say something to prompt him to get them into lunch and away from Jess, but the glib words failed to come. To be so abruptly stripped of her sparkling veneer was horrifying. And the fact that J.D. was watching her so intently elevated her panic to unbearable proportions.

"I'd better let the two of you get on in to your meal,"
Jess said, unknowingly rescuing Zoe. "After I see to the
kids, I'll be gettin' down the road. I'll give you a call
from Ft. Worth," he said to J.D., then added, "And if
those kids of mine cause any bother, you be sure to give
them what for. Melanie's comin' out to stay with them
nights, so let her know if there're any problems."

J.D. gave a brisk nod. "They'll be fine. Have a safe
trip."

"Will do."

With that, Jess glanced at Zoe and touched a finger to
his hat brim before he strode off in the direction of the
garage.

Zoe turned to hurry for the back porch, desperate to
find a few moments of privacy to compose herself. The
tender violence of her feelings for her family were whirling like a cyclone, but the black truths about herself
weighted her heart with despair.

How on earth could she face Jess Everdine now and
tell him who she really was? What had ever made her
think she could buy her way into his life, get his children
to like her, then drop her awful bombshell? Why hadn't
she simply written him a letter to introduce herself, then
followed it up with a phone call? She would have at least
demonstrated some regard for his wishes. Then she could
have confessed that her secret search for her birth family
had been found out, and the details—with names—would
soon be published in the Sedgewick's unauthorized biography. Jess would have been shocked and possibly angry, but he and his children wouldn't have suffered the
additional emotional complications Zoe would be perpe-
trating on them this way.

And all because of her twisted need to meet them first

and win them over. The pitiful search little Spenser Sedgewick had embarked upon all that time ago and doggedly pursued year after year to its fruitless conclusion had been devastating. It must have also damaged her judgment and her consideration for the feelings of others, she realized grimly.

The truth was, she'd never wanted to allow Jess a say in her determination to enter his children's lives. She'd simply vetoed his choice in the matter. Even buying into Hayes hadn't been quite the noble act she'd let herself think—not when becoming J.D.'s partner put Jess in a position that was subordinate to hers.

Suddenly the scope of her machinations seemed as breathtakingly vast as they were despicable.

Zoe entered the house and charged through the kitchen, headed for the refuge of the small bathroom down the hall. Once she shut herself in, she whipped off her Stetson, twisted on the cold water tap, then bent down. She repeatedly dashed her hot face with cool water, but was shaking so badly that water splattered everywhere. She was finally forced to stop and instead hold both wrists under the cascade as she waited for calm.

It was several minutes before she was able to return to the kitchen and sit down for lunch. By the time she did, the outward sparkle of Zoe Yahzoo was too blindingly bright to be anything but a poorly over-acted performance.

Zoe didn't know if she'd survive the afternoon. Particularly when J.D. seemed determined to run her from one end of the ranch to the other. She'd resented having no time alone to sort out the mess she'd made and find some solution to fix it all. But by day's end she was grateful for the fatigue that had taken the razor edge off her anxieties. By the time they'd had a quiet supper and she'd gone upstairs to shower, the glum knowledge that she'd made a horrendous mistake that couldn't be fixed settled over her.

She'd continue on with her plan to spend time with her brother and sister, perhaps get to know them a bit, but she wouldn't go out of her way to win them over. As soon as Jess returned from Ft. Worth, she'd talk to him, confess what she'd done and offer to help in any way she could to minimize the fallout from the biography on Bobby and Becky. Though she feared there was little chance of that, at least Jess would have time to prepare them for what was coming.

Too restless for bed, Zoe dressed and went downstairs, hoping for a distraction from her gloomy mood. She wound up in the hall outside J.D.'s office. The door was open, so she stopped and knocked softly on the door frame.

That J.D. was in bad humor was evident by the surly look he leveled on her. "No early bedtime, Hollywood?"

Zoe shook her head and slipped her fingers into her front jeans' pockets. "Nope. That shower and fresh change of clothes perked me right up, J.D."

His dark eyes made a head-to-toe pass over her that made her smile. For all his crankiness, J.D. liked her. It was a perception that made her dare an attempt at friendship, but she didn't want to push him. The upsetting insights into her character and motivations that day made her more cautious about going out of her way to win anyone over. Even someone she liked as much as she liked J.D.

She shrugged. "Just thought I'd stop by and get a look

at your office before I went in to watch TV or listen to some music." She hesitated. "If that's all right."

"Fine with me." He'd raised his hands to rest his fists on his hips and was simply watching her.

Zoe felt uneasy under his hard gaze. Her lighthearted "Thanks" and her quick turn to head down the hall was nothing less than a fast getaway. It was an enormous relief to escape the scrutiny of his dark gaze. Something in its intensity was a fresh reminder of the look he'd given her after she'd met Jess. J.D. was far too perceptive, and worse, he must have detected something then that had made him suspicious. She'd hoped their wearing afternoon together and the fact that she'd eventually recovered enough to behave with Zoe Yahzoo normalcy had made him forget. That he hadn't was plain.

Zoe took a quick detour upstairs for her CD case, then brought it back down to the living room. She set the case on a nearby table, then selected the first disc. Taking a moment to look over the stereo system, she put in the disc and wandered several steps away. In seconds, Led Zepplin's "Whole Lotta Love" erupted from the speakers.

Startled, Zoe raced back to the volume control and slid the lever to a much lower range. Her hope that J.D.—and Carmelita in her quarters on the east end of the house—hadn't been unduly alarmed faded the instant she turned and saw J.D. leaning against the side of the wide doorway, his arms crossed over his chest.

His "What the hell is that?" was so prickly, she smiled.

"Led Zepplin." Her answer made him cock his head as if he either couldn't hear her or hadn't understood. She reached over and popped out the disc. "I take it you're not a fan," she said, then put in another disc. The Garth

Brooks CD sent some lively country music through the speakers. "Better?"

His low, "Much," and the way he uncrossed his arms and came toward her made her smile widen. He paused at her CD case and glanced over the eclectic mix of music from Bach to the Eagles, and Zoe noted with relief that some of his surliness eased.

She dared a soft, "Do you slow dance, John Dalton?" as the song neared its end. The next tune would start soon and its slow pace would be suitable.

J.D.'s head came up suddenly, the surprise that flickered in his dark eyes the tiniest moment shunted aside by a wariness that was macho male. Her hint for him to dance with her had evidently usurped what he might consider his male prerogative.

On the other hand, perhaps he wasn't used to women asking him to dance. It made Zoe wonder how many idiot females lived in this part of Texas.

His voice was stern. "Are you flirting with me, Hollywood?"

Zoe appeared to consider it, then nodded and said somberly, "Yeah, John Dalton, I think I am."

The shockwave of her admission hit his chest like a soft punch. She smiled another high-watt smile, but the look in her neon eyes was a beguiling mix of sincerity and anxiety. The idea that Zoe, for all her brash playfulness, might be a tad worried about how he'd respond, was another confirmation of the emotional vulnerability he kept sensing. It was also a flattering indication that there was something serious about her flirting with him.

Which made him wary as hell. His eyes narrowed. "Why?"

Zoe shrugged. "I guess I like you."

He gave a skeptical shake of his head and Zoe laughed softly. She fixed him with a glittering look, then stepped in front of him. Just that quickly, she placed one small hand on his shoulder and caught hold of his hand.

Unable to resist, J.D. slipped his free hand around her, then flexed his arm to pull her flush against him. Her eyes widened at his sudden forcefulness. J.D. glared down at her as the song ended, then waited several beats into the ballad that followed before he started them in the slow steps.

Zoe's breath caught. Everything about the man was a thrill, and everything feminine in her went into an uproar. She could barely breathe as he moved against her, leading her in the simple steps that forced the softness of her body against the warm hard abrasion of his.

She couldn't look away from the earthy sensuality that gave his rugged features a fierce cast. She'd never before been the object of such concentrated intensity from a man who was so blatantly male. Moving against him was like pressing into flames and she felt herself melt. The instinct to somehow wrap herself around him and never let go compelled her to pull her hand from his and reach up to encircle his neck. As her arms tightened around him, his arms tightened around her, bringing her soft cheek against the hard angle of his jaw.

Zoe pulled herself higher until her lips hovered close to his ear. She'd meant to make a frivolous remark, but her voice was a little too breathless to carry it off. "If you're trying to give me a thrill, John Dalton, you're succeeding."

He gave a rough chuckle, his warm breath gusting into her ear. "Are you amusing yourself at my expense, Goldilocks?" The harsh edge of his growled words was an unintentional revelation, and Zoe's heart swelled with tenderness. The idea that big, gruff John Dalton might have an emotional vulnerability or two touched her.

She snuggled tighter against him, her cheek pressed firmly to his. "I don't think so."

His low, "When will you know for sure?" made her laugh softly.

"I know right now that I like you," she admitted recklessly. "That I think you might be the most appealing man in Texas—perhaps the most appealing man I've ever met. I know I'd like to get to know you, I'd like to see if the attraction I feel toward you is mutual. And…if anything could come from it—"

At his disbelieving snort, she drew back and grinned up at him. "But if I said all that to you now, either you might not believe me, or you'd be scared off, so…" She paused to tap a finger on his lean cheek. "I think I'll stick with 'I don't think so,' and let you wonder."

J.D. swore and gave her another of his hard looks. "You're a hell of a flirt."

She grinned. "I've been practicing a long time while I waited to meet you, John Dalton."

As if her outrageous confessions had finally won him over, the long creases on one side of his face curved to his cheekbones in a half smile that was as cynical as it was amused.

"You could get yourself in a lot of trouble with talk like that."

Zoe's whispered, "Is that your personal guarantee?" as she snuggled her cheek against his jaw, drew a growled, "Ah, hell," from him, but his arms tightened to hold her in a pleasant crush that felt so heavenly that Zoe sighed.

Only dimly did she realize when the song ended. Eyes

closed, she was so lost in the incredible security and sensual heat of him that she wasn't aware of much else.

Until the next song on the CD didn't start. Until the strange rigidity that swept J.D.'s body registered. The disappointment of being slowly released was indescribable. But it was nothing compared to being gently pushed away from all that male heat and opening dazed eyes to catch the harsh twist of J.D.'s mouth.

His low, "Song's over," was final. The way he turned to exit the room made it so.

Though Zoe slept well enough that night, she awoke the next morning edgy and bursting with nervous energy. Trying to eat breakfast while sitting across the table from a silent J.D. made her nervousness spike higher. Had he guessed that her flippant remarks about liking him were more serious than she'd made them sound?

As he worked steadily at clearing his plate, Zoe had the strong impression that he was sorting through his thoughts in much the same methodical, efficient way. That his thoughts were somehow centered on her was just as startling an impression. He was a rancher who should have had the workings of the vast Hayes Ranch on his mind, but there was something penetrating in his occasional glance, something personal that seemed to probe deeper into her with every stroke.

Unnerved, Zoe finally gave up on her meal. After a lifetime of successfully hiding her true feelings, the mere idea that J.D. might have x-ray vision into hers was disturbing.

She quickly got up and carried her dishes to the sink to rinse with water. Stepping out of his line of sight

helped. "What do you have planned for us today, J.D.?"
she asked.

He waited until she turned off the tap before he answered. "I'd planned for 'us' to go our separate ways."

The statement dealt a mild sting, but Zoe turned to give
him a smile to cover it. "Tired of me already, huh? I
thought you Texans were made of sterner stuff."

"We are," he answered, "but I was hoping to ask my
partner for a favor."

Zoe was instantly intrigued. There was something nice
about the way he'd said the words "my partner." And
that was no mean feat for a man opposed to sharing a
square inch of his birthright.

"A favor?" Her beaming smile was genuine. She
would bet her trust fund that John Dalton Hayes rarely
asked anyone for a favor. "A big favor, a small one—or
are you joking?"

"I'd have to have a sense of humor to make jokes,
Hollywood." He scraped his chair back and stood. "You
can decide for yourself how big the favor is."

The way he delayed by pushing his chair up to the table
and gathering his dishes to carry to the sink heightened
Zoe's suspense. "So what's the favor?"

J.D. turned on the tap to rinse his hands as he answered.
"Becky Everdine is trying to save money for college. I've
hired her to paint the wood fence from the highway. It's
a big job in the heat." As he dried his hands on a nearby
towel, the half smile he gave her bore traces of the sense
of humor he denied having. "Since you and I are co-
owners and we both benefit from ranch improvements,
you could give her a hand and our joint tenancy wouldn't
have to pay a nickel more."

Zoe struggled to keep her smile in place and reveal

nothing of the excitement that stormed over her at the prospect of working with her sister. The dread that followed was a reminder that she would be compounding her mistakes if she involved herself with Becky to that extent. Jess would be livid once he knew everything, but Zoe knew already that she'd risk it. "The two of you have already agreed on a price?"

"That's right."

Zoe's smile faded and she gave him a stern look. "You aren't paying her what would really amount to minimum wage, are you?"

J.D. shook his head to that. "I got a professional painter's bid before I offered the job to her. She's getting paid the going rate of the pros."

Zoe couldn't help the impulse to look out for the girl's interests. "Pros would do the job with a power sprayer."

A faint frown line deepened between J.D.'s brows. "No power sprayer. I don't want paint sprayed into pasture grass, so they'll have to be done by hand."

"She gets the same amount of money if I help?"

J.D. gave her a narrow look. "You're awfully worried about what she's getting paid."

Zoe shrugged. "Sometimes people take advantage of kids. They expect them to do adult work, but they don't want to pay adult wages."

His scowl was immediate. "I don't treat kids that way, Hollywood."

Zoe's smile and her, "I didn't think you would, but I had to ask," seemed to appease him.

He tilted his head back and looked down at her. "Have you ever painted anything besides your fingernails?" The gleam of amusement in his eyes was retaliation.

Zoe waved the question away and smiled. "How hard can it be?"

J.D.'s chuckle both delighted her and gave her the strong hint that there might be more to the job than she thought.

Zoe would ever be grateful for the case of sunblock she'd brought with her to Texas. Every square inch of skin not covered by her tank top, cut-off jeans and boots was liberally coated to thwart the harsh rays of the Texas sun. That she'd insisted Becky's young skin was also thickly coated amused Becky. When Zoe made them stop painting fence at almost eleven that morning so they could apply a fresh layer of sunblock, Becky groaned.

"We're going to run out of sunblock before we run out of paint," she teased, but dutifully uncapped the tube Zoe had given her earlier and squirted some into her palm. "It's a good thing we've got work gloves, or our hands would be too slippery with this gunk to hold the brushes."

Zoe sent her a mock glare. "Sermonette number four. Taking care of your skin is a high personal priority, young lady. You have a fabulous complexion, but if you don't protect it, everyone will be calling you saddle-face before you're twenty-five."

Becky laughed. "I'm not going to be a movie star or a model, Zoe."

Zoe shook her head. "Doesn't matter. Aside from health concerns, you have the looks and the brains to be anything you want. Why not take care of both and keep all your options?"

Becky shrugged to that, and Zoe was struck again by the familiarity of the gesture. Though Zoe privately admitted that she was vain enough to have spent significant time in front of mirrors checking her appearance, those times had acquainted her with a spectrum of her own natural expressions and gestures. That she'd witnessed several of them from Becky that morning was a bit staggering.

Were such things as biting the insides of your cheeks to keep from laughing, flipping a skein of hair behind an ear in a certain way, or setting your mouth just so when you worked at a detailed part of a task genetic? Were impish grins, wide-eyed, mock-horror faces and giggles engraved somewhere in DNA? Zoe had met her sister less than twenty-four hours before, but she'd seen enough that morning to convince her that it had to be.

Watching Becky as they worked facing each other from opposite sides of the board fence had been a lot like looking at herself in a mirror. Zoe was too fascinated by the whole idea to think of worrying about how strongly she and Becky resembled each other.

Until J.D. drove the pickup down the ranch drive to pick them up for lunch. He pulled over to their side of the drive and stopped the truck to call out, "Never underestimate the ability of females to get the job done."

Becky and Zoe automatically glanced down the fence line to the highway, noting that they'd painted almost half of the fence on that side of the drive. Their shared grin of accomplishment when they looked over the fence at each other was another mirror expression that jolted Zoe.

Nervousness had her looking away to bend down to tap the lid on her paint can and gather her rag and brushes. She took her time, giving Becky a chance to collect her own and slip through the unpainted section of fence next to them. She let Becky choose her own route through the shallow ditch, deliberately crossing it herself a few feet away.

Now that she was so acutely aware of the resemblance between her and her sister, she couldn't imagine how anyone else could see the two of them side by side and miss it. Eagle-eyed J.D. was sure to catch on, and she was suddenly terrified he'd figure out everything before she could talk to Jess. Without a word, she hefted her empty cans into the truck bed. As Becky did the same, Zoe was relieved that J.D. was staring out the windshield. Becky waited for her on the passenger side of the pickup, but Zoe waved at her to get into the truck first. She figured she didn't need the added flurry of nerves that would come from sitting next to J.D.

"Nice job, ladies," J.D. remarked, putting the pickup into gear to make a turn in the wide drive.

"Thanks," Becky said, "but you can drop me off at home. Bobby's already there."

"Do you kids want to eat at the main house?" he asked.

"I made lunch ahead and I've got to get the laundry done this afternoon before we start on the fences after four. Besides, I need to shower off all this sunblock." Becky turned her head to send Zoe a sparkling look that made Zoe smile. "Don't be surprised if we slide off the seats."

J.D. chuckled and started the pickup down the drive toward the foreman's house. They let Becky out moments later, and Zoe climbed back in the pickup, adjusting the air-conditioning vents to hit her flushed face. When she'd stepped out of the truck to let Becky out, she'd happened to catch the sharp look J.D. gave them as they stood together briefly. Though she now stared straight ahead, she could feel the touch of J.D.'s gaze whenever he glanced her way.

"You and Becky look enough alike to be cousins," he drawled.

The alarm that shot through Zoe nearly stopped her heart. Her shaky, "Is that right?" was so flimsy that she winced.

His casual, "That's a fact," bore a thread of purpose that Zoe was alert to. She resisted the urge to look over at him to confirm it. His much softer, "Or sisters," suddenly made her light-headed with distress.

She somehow got in enough air to give a light laugh. "My roommate one year at boarding school was a blonde. Given my father's reputation, there was constant speculation that we were half-sisters. She was shorter, thinner and wore glasses. We finally decided that because we were blue-eyed blondes, people didn't really look past our coloring to see the differences."

Zoe said no more, scooting forward on the bench seat to pull her tube of sunblock from her back pocket, hoping the casual movement would be a distraction.

That it didn't distract J.D. was evident in his faintly skeptical, "Uh-huh," before he eased the pickup to a stop under a shade tree near the house.

Several times in those next two days, Zoe was tempted to acknowledge the undercurrent of speculation in J.D. and try out her revelations on him. She chickened out every time. Meanwhile, she and Becky worked like fiends mornings and late afternoons until almost dark, finishing the fences two days later. It pleased Zoe that Becky had asked if she could come to the big house for makeup tips some evening. She'd even got to spend some time with Bobby when he'd invited her to see his progress on the tree house and took her to a nearby creek to look for frogs.

Zoe came to the not-so-surprising conclusion that her brother and sister were the two most lovable and fun kids on the planet. That they both seemed to like her was an enormous relief.

And that increased her sense of doom. Jess would return home in two more days, and what she'd have to tell him could get her banished from Bobby and Becky's lives. Once their names and their location on the Hayes Ranch was published, the media would all but parachute into their front yard for photos and interviews. Their mother's premarital indiscretion would become common knowledge, and their memories of her would be tarnished. That they might suffer the ridicule of their classmates was another torment for Zoe, a dark confirmation that her existence would bring no more joy to her biological family than it had to her adoptive one.

Zoe's mood swung low, but she kept it carefully hidden behind bright smiles and unflagging good humor. Once the painting was finished, she was J.D.'s shadow, teasing him, working at his side, fairly beaming with Zoe Yahzoo brilliance. J.D.'s men seemed to like her, and her twice-a-day raids on Coley's homemade ice cream were always attended by Becky and Bobby, with more of J.D.'s men joining in each time, until J.D. complained his cowhands were likely to put on more weight before fall than his cattle.

But no matter how lively and fun she was, none of it was enough to completely remove the speculation that shone in J.D.'s dark gaze from time to time. In spite of her worries about that, Zoe enjoyed playing a bright counterpart to his prickly moods and gray humor. That she was able to tease a real smile or a gravelly chuckle from him was fast becoming the highlight of her day.

What she'd sensed from the first—that she could easily fall in love with John Dalton Hayes—was rapidly becoming a real possibility. Not even the dismal knowledge that she possessed some mysterious flaw that kept others from loving her back was enough to thwart her increasing affection for him.

CHAPTER FIVE

"Is SOMETHING wrong, Carmelita?"

Zoe had just stepped into the kitchen from the back door to the loud sounds of Carmelita banging pots and pans together as she unloaded the dishwasher. Carmelita's angry scowl and her muttered words, which were probably as close to swearing as she ever came, surprised Zoe.

"*Señora?*" Zoe hung her hat on a wall peg as she waited for the woman to hear her over the din and notice she'd come in.

Carmelita swung toward her, the large skillet in her hand unintentionally threatening. Zoe's grin seemed to interrupt the Mexican woman's tirade long enough for her to realize she held the big skillet like a club. Flustered, she lowered it and bent to shove it in a low cupboard.

Zoe tried again. "Is something wrong, *señora?*"

The Mexican woman nodded, and a new flush of anger surged up her cheeks. The spate of rapid Spanish that followed was so swift that Zoe could only pick out and translate two words. But those two—heifer and Boss— combined with Carmelita's obvious outrage to hint that her upset had to do with J.D. and his ex-wife.

When Carmelita paused to take a breath, Zoe interjected, "Is J.D. upset?"

Which set off a whole new tirade, complete with dramatic arm waves and a new attack on the hapless pots and pans in the dishwasher. Zoe nodded seriously, as if she understood every word, then carefully stepped around Carmelita toward the refrigerator.

She quickly opened the door, snagged two bottles of J.D.'s beer, then turned toward Carmelita and held them up. Carmelita continued on with her rapid-fire Spanish, but nodded and jerked her head in the direction of J.D.'s den.

Zoe popped the lids off on the bottle opener, then started for the hall and made her way to J.D.'s private lair. The door was standing open, but Zoe hesitated to catch sight of J.D. and try to gage his reception to her intrusion.

He was slumped on the leather couch along one wall, his head back against the cushions, his eyes closed. Zoe stepped into the room and his lashes opened a slit, then squeezed closed in obvious irritation.

"You look like you might be in the mood for a beer and some sympathy, Pilgrim."

J.D. raised a wide hand and ran it down his face before he let it fall to his chest. "Don't you ever run low on energy and Pollyanna cheer?" he muttered darkly.

Unfazed by his surly manner, Zoe dropped down next to him on the sofa and passed him the sweating longneck when he opened his eyes. He took the bottle with clear reluctance, but put it to his mouth and swallowed nearly half the contents before he set it aside.

"What're you doin' in here? Did Coley run out of ice cream early?" he grumbled, then eased his head back on the cushion to glare at her. It was a look that never failed to intimidate anyone else.

The smile she gave him was so bright, he couldn't keep a corner of his mouth from quirking.

"It's not so early, J.D." Zoe took a quick sip of her

beer, then grimaced at the taste. "How do you stand this stuff?" She shoved it in his direction and he took it. Zoe turned more fully toward him and braced her elbow on the back of the sofa to give him a long, thoughtful look. The fact that she said nothing for several moments aggravated him.

"What is it you came in here for?" he groused.

"First, to find out what happened. Carmelita explained everything, but she was talking at warp speed and my Spanish is a little faulty." She gave him a wry smile. "Something about the Boss and a heifer. I guessed she wasn't talking about the cattle, so I figured she was talking about your ex-wife."

His eyes narrowed. "That's a sore subject."

Zoe nodded and said, "No doubt," before she went on. "The other reason I came in was to assess the damage and see if I could cheer you up and help you recapture the optimistic world view you're so well known for." She grinned when he snickered. "Partners ought to do that for each other, you know."

"Ah, hell," he growled on an outrush of bad temper, and closed his eyes. "Go find your wings, Tinkerbell, and fly on outta here."

"So you'd rather pine after Raylene in private, huh?" she persisted. When his eyes flew open and he fixed her with a sour look, she reached over and gave his arm a pat. "I get the message."

For J.D., that little hit-and-run touch was one too many. He reflexively caught her hand as she pulled it away. "What did you really come in here for?"

Zoe pulled her elbow from the back of the sofa and leaned her shoulder against it, her expression sobering as she looked down at the firm grip he had on her hand. An instant later she was looking him straight in the eye, her lips on the verge of another megawatt smile. "To flirt a little and see if I could take advantage of you. What else? I've heard all about men on the rebound."

"What did I tell you about talk like that?" he grumbled.

Zoe gave a shrug. "That I could get into a lot of trouble," she answered softly. "But so far, it looks like you Texans are all talk."

The gauntlet was down. The few inches between them fairly crackled with sensuality. Zoe couldn't breathe as she kept her gaze locked firmly with the sudden intensity in J.D.'s.

His gravelly drawl was deadly serious. "This is a bad idea, Hollywood."

Zoe's voice was just as serious. "I have lots of bad ideas, John Dalton." She leaned so close to his lips that he felt the soft gust of her breath as she added, "This is probably the only one I won't regret acting on." She let her mouth drift just close enough to touch his, then stopped, the sudden agony she felt when J.D. didn't respond tearing through her like razors.

His lips chafed against hers as he whispered roughly, "What's the matter, darlin'? Lose your nerve?"

In that incredible moment, Zoe knew she had. For all she'd sensed of the high-voltage sensuality between them, her strong belief in being ultimately rejected by anyone important to her was clamoring for her to retreat. Nothing less than the terror of adding J.D. to that list could have given her the will to back off.

In a flash, Zoe was off the sofa, the unexpected yank of her hand breaking J.D.'s light grip.

But if she'd thought to make a fast getaway, she was

mistaken. J.D.'s long arm whipped out and he seized her other wrist before she could take a step. Alarmed, Zoe looked down into eyes so dark with purpose that her knees went weak. Time seemed to slow as he towed her toward him. As if he had all the time in the world, J.D. controlled her descent, maneuvering her until she was flat on her back beneath him on the sofa. Keeping his dark eyes locked with the faint apprehension in hers, his head came down at the same relentless pace.

At the last second, Zoe's lashes drifted closed and his mouth covered hers, his tongue shoving past her lips to work with shattering expertise. Zoe could barely get enough air as she allowed J.D. access. His kiss was blatantly carnal, worthy of his overwhelming maleness. His heavy weight pressed down on her, satisfying a craving she'd been unaware she possessed.

Joy pulsed through her veins, a dizzying counterpart to the heavy beat of arousal that thundered through her body. She suddenly knew she loved this gruff, harsh man, and would to the end of her days. He was real and solid, a man of the land. He was settled and enduring, and the security she'd hungered for her whole life was such a natural by-product of who he was that he was irresistible.

I have so little to offer a man like him. The despairing thought made her clutch at him, as if she could forget her flaws and meld with his solid essence while there was still time. But she was a bit of fluff to a man like him, shallow, unprincipled and selfish. Soon, he'd know it all. In the light of his strongly defined character and down-to-earth life-style, she was a flighty fake, too given to impulse to have put down roots, too unsure of herself to be reliable.

The bleak despair she'd lived with all her life welled up. Loath to let it mix with the passion thudding through her, she turned her head and broke off the kiss. She clung to him tightly, both to get control of her pain and to hoard the wonderful feel of him.

J.D. was certain he'd lost his mind. He never should have caught her, never should have compelled her to make a payment on all her little flirtations. Hadn't he learned anything? The last fancy little blonde he'd fallen for had made a jackass of him. This fancy little blonde, Hollywood-bright and irrepressible, had the potential to leave him bare-assed in a cold wind.

J.D. slowly lifted his head. He looked down harshly into neon eyes shiny with emotion and suddenly knew he couldn't be cruel. It was a grim fact that he already liked Zoe too much.

So, he settled for silence. He was stunned that it was so hard to ease himself off her delectably curved little body, shocked that turning his back on her and leaving the room could give him such an ache.

Zoe felt the terrible impact of J.D.'s silence as it underscored and confirmed her innermost beliefs about herself. She didn't speak, either, could only watch as he pulled back and she let him go. A chill settled over her without the heat of him. The chill pierced her heart as he walked from the room and she heard his heavy step retreat down the hall and eventually go up the stairs. She lay a long time in the awful silence of the room before she got up and made her way to her own room.

The fact that Zoe sat across from him at breakfast that next morning, as cheery and playful as ever, knotted J.D.'s gut with guilt. He knew his abandonment the night before had hurt her; he'd seen it in those remarkable neon eyes.

That she was treating him to the full Zoe Yahzoo persona was a sure indication that the hurt lingered.

J.D. didn't understand why he knew that, or why he cared so much. He sure as hell hadn't been this perceptive with anyone else, Raylene included. But there was something about Zoe that got to him, something about her that sent out signals he could decode. A lot was going on beneath her sparkle and fun, and hurt over his abrupt withdrawal the night before was just part of it.

J.D.'s mood darkened at the reminder. Zoe's intrusion into his life was much more significant than the self-indulgent cowgirl whims of a rich socialite. He'd got an inkling of that when she'd met the Everdines. He'd found out later from movie buff Carmelita that Zoe was the *adopted* daughter of the Sedgewicks.

So, when he'd seen the uncanny resemblance between Zoe and Becky the day they started painting the fence, the truth had hit him like a lightning bolt. He'd been disappointed in Zoe when she'd rebuffed his remarks about the resemblance, but if his suspicions about why she was here were correct, that made Zoe Yahzoo one of the most dishonest and manipulative people he'd ever met.

So why couldn't he judge her as harshly as she deserved? Why did he care that he'd hurt her feelings the night before?

J.D.'s dark mood faltered. It was precisely because there was something about Zoe that got to him. There was something lost and a little broken underneath that Tinkerbell facade, something so melancholy and unsure that there was no way he could bring himself to crush it.

Jess Everdine might not feel the same way. Which landed J.D. squarely between a trusted and respected friend, and a deceitful little partner who'd brought sparkle to his life and had awakened a tenderness in him he hadn't known existed.

It took a surprising amount of energy to be Zoe Yahzoo that morning at the breakfast table. Nonchalance was the best choice, both for her and for J.D. There was no point in making the man feel bad because she wasn't his cup of tea. There was certainly no point in acting hurt and making him leery of spending time with her. Zoe knew herself well enough to know that she'd probably still flirt, still hope for J.D. to return some of her feelings for him. Anything long-term with him was doomed, of course, but Zoe realized that she would rather have a little with J.D. for a short time, than make herself do without entirely.

When this was over, she'd go someplace else, patch herself up and find something to do. She still had her little hideaway ranch in California and her house in the Hollywood Hills. There were plenty of charities and causes that might still want her patronage after the biography was published. Then again, she could write a new screenplay. The first two had sold, but had not yet been produced. She had several more ideas. Immersing herself in those—in anything—would likely once again rescue her emotionally.

It was in the midst of reviewing her options for a life after she left the Hayes Ranch, that Zoe fully realized how strongly she believed in her capacity to fail with the Everdines and to have any possibility with J.D. jinxed. Common sense told her no one could be so profoundly hopeless when it came to finding love. Experience had given her a much more dismal expectation on the subject.

So, Zoe smiled and bantered her way through breakfast

with J.D. She'd wait out the last two days before Jess's return, selfishly take as much as she was allowed with Bobby and Becky, grab whatever she could with J.D. After she talked to Jess, she'd weather what he dished out, then endure J.D.'s choler when she told him about the biography and the trouble she expected it to bring to the Hayes Ranch.

But the really tragic part of it all, was that none of the animosity she would endure could spare young Bobby and Becky a particle of the hurt and upset she was bringing into their lives. No level of immersion into a life after Hayes would ever lessen her guilt and regret on that score.

"Is Bobby doing what I think he is?" Zoe squinted toward the shaded end of the barn as she and Becky rode back to the ranch headquarters. The late morning heat beat down on them from a Texas sun that was now blindingly bright. They'd been checking fences all morning, and Zoe was relieved at the prospect of the noon break.

Bobby, however, was throwing some good-size rocks toward the apex of the stable roof. That could only mean that he'd spied the wasp nest up there and was engaged in the boy-child sport of stirring up trouble.

Becky's exasperated sigh was answer enough as she glanced in Bobby's direction. She abruptly neck-reined her horse and turned off. "I'm going to the other door. If he knocks that one down, I don't want to be anywhere near that side of the barn when it falls. You coming?"

Zoe glanced toward Bobby, then looked over at Becky and shook her head. "You aren't going to stop him?" She couldn't help but be surprised. She thought that occasionally pulling rank on a younger sibling was a big sister's prerogative.

Becky rolled her eyes. "What for? He wouldn't stop anyway, unless the wasps sting him. Or J.D. catches him at it." Becky grinned at that.

Zoe looked back to see Bobby getting ready to pitch another rock, not able to be as pragmatic. Everything she'd ever heard about bee sting allergies made her worry for Bobby. The Hayes Ranch was a long way from trauma level medical attention. "Has he ever been stung before?"

"Nah, and that's the problem. If he ever got stung good, he'd probably quit." Becky paused. "On the other hand, he's so ornery, he'd probably do it again anyway. Are you coming this way, or are you going to take your chances with the wasps?"

Zoe waved her away. "You go ahead. I think I'll see if I can warn him off."

Becky rode in the other direction, her light laugh letting Zoe know what she thought of Zoe's chances.

Zoe rode on a few more feet, then dismounted to go the rest of the short distance on foot. Bobby's back was toward her, and he seemed so absorbed in perfecting his aim that he didn't hear her approach.

Zoe stopped directly behind him, waited until he pitched another rock, then gave him a light tickle on the ribs. Her stern, "What are you doing, young man?" timed with the tickle, made the boy jump in guilty surprise.

The next moment the wasp nest hurtled downward, landing with a thump in the dust not two feet in front of them. Bobby reacted automatically, vaulting out of harm's way to successfully escape the outraged wasps.

Stunned, Zoe's gaze dropped in disbelief to home in on the downed nest. Before she could move, the wasps swarmed her, their mad buzzing as unnerving as the occasional tap when one flew against her hat or her clothes.

Zoe froze, hoping her lack of movement wouldn't further agitate the wasps and give them a target. But they were too riled to ignore her. Zoe gasped as she felt the first sting, then several others.

A second later J.D. came barreling out of the stable, a can of wasp repellant in hand. In one sweep, the fog from the repellant misted the air in front of her from her shoulders to her feet before it was aimed at the downed nest. Zoe bolted for the shade of the stable, not stopping until she came to a halt at the far end. She barely had time to assess the damage when she heard J.D.'s shout and the reassuring sound of him running after her.

"Did you get stung?" Suddenly he was in front of her, concern drawing his dark brows together as he looked her over.

"Yeah, I think I did," she answered, managing an offhand tone as she glanced down at the places that throbbed with an odd sensation of numbness and sharp pain. Because she still felt as if she were still being stung, it was a surprise to see there were no wasps attached to her shirt and jeans.

Bobby came tearing up and halted anxiously at her side. "You got stung? I'm sorry, Zoe." The remorse in the boy's voice got her instant attention. "I'm sorry."

Zoe gave him a crooked smile and reached over to nudge the brim of his hat. "No harm done, squirt," she said, then leaned down into his face to add with playful menace, "Outside of *agonizing* pain. No more bee-baiting from you—ever—okay?"

Bobby's face was pale. "No, ma'am, I swear. I'll never bother bees or wasps again."

Zoe gave him a narrow look. "Not hornets, either, right?"

"Never, Miss Zoe. Nothing that stings, cross my heart." The childish vow and the accompanying X he drew on his chest was charmingly earnest.

Zoe straightened stiffly and patted his shoulder. "Good enough. How about getting Brute and putting him up for me?"

Bobby looked at J.D., but whether for permission or because he was expecting some sort of punishment, Zoe couldn't tell. Nevertheless, she intervened with a look that warned J.D. not to add to her mild reproof.

J.D. responded to it with a gruff, "Go ahead, Bobby. And keep your promise."

Bobby nodded animatedly. "Yessir, Mr. Hayes. I will." With that, the boy ran down the stable aisle just as Becky led her horse through the door behind J.D.

Zoe was too miserable with the sharply smarting wasp stings to have any questions from Becky delay her from getting to the house. She stepped briskly around J.D. and called a cheery, "See you later, Becky," as she left the stable for the house. J.D. was beside her in an instant.

"What about those stings?"

"Can't see or do much until we get to the house, J.D.," she noted with forced lightness. "I think I'll need Carmelita's help."

"Carmelita leaves lunch in the oven on Thursdays so she can do the shopping for the week."

Zoe chuckled and sent him a look. "Watch out, John Dalton. This situation just became rife with possibilities." In case he didn't catch her meaning, she wiggled her eyebrows.

J.D. glared over at her and gingerly took her arm to hurry her to the back sidewalk. "Why the hell do you do that?"

"What?"

"That whole damned I'm-gonna-make-a-joke-out-of-
this-if-it-kills-me act?"

"So what would be better, bursting into tears and
screaming that getting stung by a half dozen wasps hurts
like a son of a b?" She grinned at his surprise over her
near profanity. "Not my style, John Dalton."

Zoe ignored his gruff, "Hell," to that as they reached
the porch steps. The wasp stings felt sharper with every
step and she was eager to get inside.

They'd no more than got into the kitchen before the
insistent pain had her tearing at her shirt buttons. The snap
and zipper on her jeans were next. She spared J.D. a brief
glance and quipped, "If you can't stand the heat, get out
of the kitchen." With no more warning than that, she
carefully plucked the front of her shirt away from her skin
and peeled it off. She lowered her jeans next, wincing as
the cloth chafed the stings on her thighs. She'd turned the
denim fabric out to prevent any remaining stingers from
nicking fresh skin, then stopped abruptly when she got
them down as far as her knees.

"Uh-oh, John Dalton." She glanced up and gave him
a pained smile. "Can you help me get my boots off?"

J.D. was too stunned by Zoe's sudden disrobing to react
fast enough to exit the kitchen. Now that he could see the
size of the welts across her middle and on her thighs, he
was glad he hadn't. The misery that gave her eyes a suspicious sheen made him act immediately.

"Did you get any stings on your backside?" At her
soft no, he cautiously reached for her. "Then I'll lift you
to the counter."

Zoe straightened stiffly, and he slid his big hands under
her arms to quickly lift her. He muttered over the snug fit

of her small boots, but he got them off. He realized with some surprise that his hands actually shook when he dispensed with her jeans.

"You got allergies?" he asked as he carefully inspected the welts for any stingers he could see. Zoe's skin was like warm satin, its texture so delicate that his hands felt like huge patches of sandpaper.

Zoe looked down at J.D.'s bent head and smiled to herself as she gently removed his Stetson and set it aside. For all her brashness with him, her cheeks were on fire with embarrassment. It was one thing to flirt, but Zoe always avoided real intimacy. To sit on a kitchen cupboard in nothing but her bra and panties with a man like J.D, giving her nearly naked body his undivided attention was disconcerting. It also ranked as the most physically and emotionally intimate event of her life.

J.D. finished examining the welts and looked up into her flushed face. "I asked if you've got allergies. Ever been stung before?"

"I've been stung before, but not by wasps and not this many times. I got red and sore around the sting, but no big allergic reaction."

"We'll go see the doctor anyway," he decreed.

To Zoe's astonishment, J.D. plucked her off the counter to settle her in his arms and carry her across the kitchen. She automatically wrapped her arms around his neck.

"I can walk, John Dalton." In spite of the smarting stings, she couldn't help grinning at him. "And I probably don't need to see a doctor."

"We'll let the doctor decide whether you need to see him or not," he answered as they reached the stairs and started up. "Find something loose to put on while I call ahead to make sure they're ready for you."

Zoe laughed. "Do you think that's possible?"

J.D. hesitated at her door to give her a glare. His stony facade was cracking the tiniest bit and Zoe loved to see it. "No. I doubt I *could* prepare them for the full effect of a Zoe Yahzoo." He stepped through the door and gently stood her on her feet. For a handful of pulse-pounding moments, J.D.'s dark eyes probed into hers with a tenderness that stole her breath. "No one prepared me, but I'm finding out the surprise is part of the fun."

A second later his head lowered and he delivered a swift, hard kiss. "Get some clothes on." Just that suddenly, he turned and exited the room.

Zoe swayed on her feet, so surprised she forgot for a moment that she was standing in her underwear with a scattering of painful stings down the front of her.

I'm finding out the surprise is part of the fun. The words made her heart flutter wildly and, despite the stings, she practically flew to the armoire and riffled through the hanging clothes to find something loose-fitting—and attractive—to wear to town. She grabbed fresh underwear from a drawer and dashed to the bathroom for a quick shower. Moments later, she emerged, the lukewarm water aggravating the sting sites enough that even the soft flowing cotton of the pink sundress bothered them.

She got her sandals on and switched some of the contents from her purse into a small handbag that matched the sandals before J.D. returned. He came purposely toward her, but she held up a hand to ward him off.

"I need to walk, J.D." She demonstrated why as she held the sundress fabric away from the front of her. J.D. took her handbag instead, then escorted her down the stairs and out to the front of the house to where his big car sat idling.

*   *   *

By the time they left the doctor's office after two o'clock, Zoe was feeling much better, thanks to a sample tube of topical cream the doctor had given her. They made a quick trip to the pharmacy down the street to pick up an over-the-counter antihistamine and fill a prescription for more of the cream.

On their way home, J.D. stopped at the diner along the highway to treat her to a late lunch. They returned to the ranch sometime after three. J.D. pulled his car to a stop behind the big station wagon Carmelita used, which was now parked at the end of the back walk.

Zoe remembered then that she'd not collected her discarded boots and clothes from where she'd taken them off in the kitchen. She glanced over at J.D.'s profile. "You didn't happen to pick up my clothes, did you?" Her question brought J.D.'s head around.

His soft, "Hell," combined with the faint chagrin that drew one corner of his mouth into a sheepish quirk, made Zoe laugh.

She reached for her door handle and levered it open to get out before J.D. could come around and chivalrously open it for her. She sent him a sparkling look over the top of the car.

J.D. caught the look and pointed at her as if he were leveling a gun. "Don't you dare."

Zoe grinned. "Why not?"

"Carmelita's awfully straight-laced."

Zoe burst out laughing. "And J.D. Hayes is the pin-up boy for the adage, 'All work and no play.' Believe me, J.D., Carmelita won't object to the idea that you've gone Texas bad."

J.D. gave an emphatic shake of his head. "Carmelita will beat me black and blue with a skillet if she thinks I ravaged you in her kitchen the first time she left the house on an errand.''

Zoe walked around the front of J.D.'s car, her bright smile wide and playful. ''Now how could you know how Carmelita will react, John Dalton? Was the kitchen a favorite ravaging place of yours when you were married?''

The question blunted J.D.'s expression. ''It sure as hell was *not*—''

Zoe held up her hand to interrupt. ''Let me guess—your wife was an aspiring actress, right? She was probably into moods and techniques, but with a particular fondness for artsy scenes in a *boudoir* with lacy costumes and scented candles. Nothing spur-of-the-moment or just-in-from-a-hard-day's-work for her, huh?''

J.D. glared down at her. ''You've got a hell of a nerve, Zoe Yahzoo.''

Zoe grinned up into his formidable countenance. ''I certainly do, John Dalton Hayes. And do you know what else?''

He muttered what had to be a swear word before he gave in to the inevitable. ''What?''

Zoe reached over and touched his arm. ''I'm glad she's not around anymore.''

Something softened the tiniest bit in J.D.'s hard expression. Zoe looked up somberly into his face. ''And do you know what else?''

J.D. softened a little more. His voice was a gravelly whisper as he looked down at her. ''What else?''

''I think I might like kitchens.''

Zoe flitted away almost before she finished the outrageous remark, leaving J.D. to follow her to the back porch door. Zoe didn't wait for him to open it for her, but

breezed in ahead of him, calling out a cheery hello to
Carmelita.

"Are you all right, *señorita*?" Carmelita's face was the
picture of concern as she looked Zoe over.

"I'm fine, *señora*. I forgot about leaving my clothes in
the way. My apologies."

Carmelita's dark eyes went round. "*Sí*, I had questions
when I found them." She looked past Zoe to J.D. to give
him a stern look. "*Many* questions." Her attention returned to Zoe. "But Bobby and Becky came to help me
carry things in and told me what happened."

Zoe nodded and grinned. "That's good. By the time
we realized we'd dashed off too quick to pick them up,
J.D. was pretty worried. He had visions of being whacked
with a skillet."

Carmelita chuckled at that. "*Sí*. You are a young, unmarried woman. He is an experienced man. There is much
between the two of you that needs a close watch."

"Ah, Carmelita." Zoe stepped over and gave the
woman as good a hug as she could considering the stings.
"Thank you for keeping watch over my virtue." She drew
back and said in a loud whisper, "But it's really J.D. you
need to protect."

J.D. finally spoke up. "That's no lie, Carmelita. This
woman is the most shameless flirt I've ever met."

Carmelita wagged a finger at him. "And that is good
for you, *señor*. You need a woman who flirts with you
and makes you laugh." She then gave J.D. as stern a look
as J.D. had ever seen. "And you need to marry such a
woman and have many *niños* by her."

Zoe's breath caught at Carmelita's blunt advice. Her
gaze streaked to J.D. in time to see his mildly amused
expression ebb.

"Tried that once, didn't work out."

Carmelita shook her head to that. "That woman was a fortune digger who wanted your money. She did not want a home and a good man and many children." She turned her head to smile at Zoe. "This one has more money than you, a good heart and love for you in her eyes." She punctuated that with an affectionate pat on Zoe's cheek.

Zoe was so stunned by Carmelita's candor and unqualified endorsement or her suitability for J.D. that she couldn't speak.

As if the housekeeper knew the magnitude of the shock she'd dealt them both, she gave J.D. an admonishing glare, then turned to exit the room and go in the direction of her quarters on the east end of the house.

The heavy silence of the ranch kitchen wrapped around them both. Zoe held her breath, terrified J.D. would say something to spurn Carmelita's advice. She could only stare over into his lethally grim expression with round eyes as she waited for him to speak.

"Well, hell, Zoe," he said at last. "Now you've added *my* housekeeper to the Texas chapter of the Yahzoo fan club."

It took Zoe a moment to decide whether J.D.'s surly remark was meant to be humorous or not. She gave him a hesitant smile and dared a cheeky, "I'm still looking for a club president, John Dalton. Interested?"

J.D. reached up and gave his hat brim an irritable yank. "You stay in out of the heat this afternoon," he ordered gruffly before he turned toward the door. He wrenched it open, paused, then glanced back at her. "And be sure to play some of that Lead Balloon rock music for Carmelita while you're at it."

He shut the door firmly behind him, leaving Zoe to sag against the nearest counter in profound relief.

CHAPTER SIX

ZOE went upstairs to change into a brief pair of cut-off jeans and a cotton shirt. The shorts ended above the stings and tying the tails of the shirt above her midriff would keep the other stings uncovered. Zoe decided to forego ice applications. The welts were less red and swollen already, giving her hope that she could return to normal activity the next day.

Drowsy from the antihistamine, she wandered down stairs and found the TV remote before she lounged on the sofa to scan the channels. She eventually settled on a national news channel, then tugged a nearby afghan over her for warmth against the air-conditioning, bending her knees to tent the fabric over the welts. She drifted into a nap soon after, and awakened later on her side, the afghan still over her

The entertainment segment of the news channel came on and Zoe focused sleepily on it as she moved into a sitting position. She was trying to locate the remote to adjust the sound when a film excerpt of Jason and Angela Sedgewick came on.

Zoe's heart clenched at the unexpected feature, the surprise jolting her fully awake. She watched tensely as a montage of selective clips crossed the screen, the half dozen showing the Sedgewicks in some of their most volatile roles—from their vituperative exchange in *The Thorn*, to their Oscar-winning roles as maliciously clever schemers in *Wicked Ways*.

The reporter's story was to the point. "According to the unauthorized biography by Dillon Casey, the off-screen performances of the Sedgewicks bear close resemblance to some of their darkest and most critically acclaimed roles. From alleged infidelities of both during their twenty-five year marriage, their purported make-or-destroy influence over more than one actor's film career, to their alleged emotional abandonment of the daughter they adopted, Dillon Casey's tell-all book promises to be one of the most shocking revelations of the private lives of Hollywood greats ever written."

The segment went to a commercial and Zoe frantically made a new search for the remote. She finally found it on the floor just under the edge of the sofa, then switched it off. She sank back against the cushions as a huge wave of dread swept her.

News coverage had started—a full two weeks before she'd anticipated. Other than local newscasts and the small area newspaper, she hadn't watched or read much news since she'd got to Hayes, so it was possible coverage had begun days ago. And that meant every weekly magazine from *Newsweek* to the rags might be running articles. If any of them mentioned Bobby and Becky by name or gave away their location on the Hayes Ranch…

The thought sent Zoe springing from the sofa and hurriedly refolding the afghan. They'd been in the local pharmacy that afternoon and it hadn't occurred to her to check the magazine rack. The idea that the small towns nearby might already be saturated with news of the Sedgewicks sent her charging upstairs to change her clothes.

Mindless of the stings, Zoe tore through the armoire, trying to decide what to wear for a fast trip to town. If the story had already been published, she might be able to buy up every magazine copy and prevent it from being circulated in the area.

A new thought brought her to a sickening halt. Jess Everdine was in Ft. Worth. Whatever he was doing there, it would be unreasonable to expect that he wouldn't catch a newscast, read a newspaper or happen to pass a magazine rack. Her anxiety shot higher. It hadn't occurred to her to worry overmuch that his trip had delayed her from talking to him. What she had to tell him—particularly after her colossal manipulations to secretly enter his children's lives—was bad enough. If he discovered it all on his own from a premature news release, which might mention the kids' names or the Hayes Ranch, his reaction would be far worse.

Zoe swayed a moment, then grabbed a pair of jeans to go with the chambray shirt she'd selected. She made it to the bed before her shaking knees gave out. She sat several moments on the edge of the mattress as she fought to calm herself.

It hurt to realize that Jason and Angela had probably known about the early news releases for days. It was certain they'd have every article already published on the subject, as well as news videos. The fact that they hadn't bothered to warn her was further evidence that the breach between them had widened to unforgivable proportions.

Glumly, Zoe stood up just long enough to slide off her cutoffs, fling them aside, and sit back down to put on the jeans. She couldn't help that several former household employees of the Sedgewicks had consented to be interviewed by Dillon Casey as he'd researched his book. That they'd chosen to tell him the unpleasant details about the famous actors' relationship with their daughter hadn't been Zoe's fault, either. Not even the fact that Zoe herself had repeatedly spurned Casey's attempts to interview her had pleased Jason and Angela—not when they expected her to debunk the negative reports.

Zoe worked her jeans up enough to stand and tug them past the stings. In the end, she'd finally arranged to meet with Casey, but only because she'd learned that he'd found out about Bobby and Becky.

The meeting had been a nightmare. Casey had been ruthless in his efforts to get her to confirm or deny the information he'd gleaned during his research. Because she'd declined to comply, her straightforward plea that he not publish the kids' names and their location had fallen on deaf ears.

Dillon Casey wasn't intimidated by threats of lawsuits, wasn't persuaded by bribes. Jason and Angela had learned that. Zoe had learned that Dillon Casey had a rotten little black cinder where his heart should be.

She finished dressing, then went to the dresser. She took her wallet from her purse, then slid it in her pocket. If she hurried, she might be able to get to town, raid every magazine rack she could find, and be back in time for ice cream at the cook house.

She rushed downstairs, breezed through the kitchen and delivered a swift, "I won't be back until after supper, *señora*. I can make a cold snack out of what's left," and was out the door before Carmelita could do more than send her a surprised glance.

Moments later she'd got her car out and was on her way down the drive to the highway. She made the trip to town in half the time J.D. had driven it earlier, too anxious to get there to worry about a speeding ticket.

*   *   *

Zoe turned off the highway and started up the ranch drive with a small avalanche of magazines in the trunk. Sick at heart, still embarrassed by the store clerks' reactions to her bizarre purchases, she was light-headed with dread. From the looks of the magazine racks, not many copies had sold to anyone else, but once the clerks started gossiping about the goofy blonde who'd come in and bought every issue, everyone in the area would make an effort to discover what all the fuss was about.

No one in town but the doctor, his staff, the pharmacist and the diner waitress had seen her before. If she kept her car hidden away in the garage for a few days and stayed at the ranch, perhaps no one else would connect her with Hayes for a while—at least long enough for Jess to get home. After she made her confession to him, it wouldn't matter. By that time, the whole world would know she was on Hayes.

Zoe drove carefully into her space in the big garage and shut off the engine. Anxious to get a closer look at the magazines, she popped the trunk release and got out. She sorted quickly through the piles, trying to select one of every issue. She ended up with six. Too impatient to wait, she left the trunk open and leaned against the car to scan the covers and flip to the articles.

Tears of shame and frustration stung her eyes. The national rags were the worst, their headlines hyping scandal, the pictures dreadful, and clearly chosen to depict the Sedgewicks as villains. The only positive thing about them, she realized grimly, were that the pictures of her must have been selected to cast her in a better light.

Zoe's eyes were so blurred, she actually had to run a finger back and forth down the lines of print as she searched for the words Everdine, Hayes Ranch or Texas.

When she didn't find them, she went through each one again, not quite ready to believe she'd been that lucky.

She was scanning for names a third time when she noted that one of the scandal magazines was promising a four-part series of excerpts from the biography. That they would devote space in the next issue to excerpts which would detail Spenser/Zoe's life made her feel ill. If any article promised to reveal information about the children or the Hayes Ranch, that would be the one.

Zoe couldn't keep back the ragged sob that jerked up from her chest. She squeezed her eyes closed and gripped the magazine, unable to keep from giving in to several moments of misery.

J.D. watched silently from where he stood outside the open garage door. The brokenness he'd glimpsed in Zoe before was so starkly evident on her delicate face now, that he actually felt his chest hurt. It stunned him to catch her in an unguarded moment of such emotional distress. Because he sensed how deeply she'd be shamed if he walked in on her like this, he quietly backed out of sight, then took several steps away to give her privacy and time to collect herself.

J.D. had already figured she was Jess Everdine's daughter. She'd put herself in a hell of a spot with Jess, coming here the way she had. He hadn't dreamed that she was in any other kind of trouble, but seeing her crying over a handful of gossip magazines was evidence of that.

He knew he'd never get a straight answer out of her. Maybe Hollywood types learned early to be slippery, particularly when anything they said or did might be fodder for a gossip column. Zoe Yahzoo was as slippery as they came with that good fairy facade. Hell, the woman had everything but the wings and the magic wand that went with the image. J.D. couldn't imagine leading that kind of life, but something inside him understood, even if he didn't approve.

Uncertain how much longer he should wait, he called out a blustery, "Zoe Yahzoo, where are you?" in a ham-handed rhyme he figured she might normally appreciate.

Several heartbeats of time pulsed by before she called back a shaky-sounding, "A poet and he don't know it—" punctuated by the sound of the trunk lid closing. She stepped to the doorway, pushed the button to lower the door, looked his way and added, "But we can tell 'cause his feet are Longfellows."

J.D. chuckled at her corny attempt at lightheartedness, but he felt a new twinge when he saw how much effort she'd put in it.

"What are you doing, haring off to town? You're supposed to be doctoring wasp stings," he reminded her. Zoe started his way. Because he knew she wouldn't answer the question, he moved straight on with, "Carmelita said you weren't eating any cold leftovers from her kitchen. Got some of everything warming for you. Threatened to whack me with a wood spoon if I ate more than my share."

Zoe's smile was a little less forced as she scolded, "Now, J.D., I'm starting to suspect that you're deliberately trying to cast Carmelita as a skillet-bashing, spoon-whacking maniac. How could you malign such a sweet woman? You ought to be ashamed."

"Oh, darlin'," he said as he placed a big hand over his heart and turned to walk with her, "You have no idea the misery that woman has visited upon me over the years."

Zoe's much more normal "Get outta town," as she

gave him a light jab with her elbow, gave J.D. an odd kind of thrill to have helped her regain some of her playfulness. But as he glanced her way, the trace of pain still visible in her eyes made him feel guilty for encouraging her masquerade.

His expression must have sobered, because Zoe's abruptly did so, too, and those remarkable neon eyes shot away from his like a ricocheted bullet. J.D. angled his next step, bringing him close enough to take her hand and settle it companionably in the crook of his arm.

"Ever confide in anybody?"

Zoe's heart jumped at the blunt question. She stiffened, and would have pulled her hand away, but J.D.'s free hand pressed firmly over it to keep it in place. The choking emotions that overwhelmed her made her unable to speak. Oh God, had he seen her blubbering over those magazines?

J.D. drawled on as if she'd answered him. "I'm not much for hanging my private things on the front porch, either." They walked on a few more steps, the leisurely pace he set heightening her suspense. His big Texas drawl went so low that it was almost a whisper. "But then, I never had a partner before."

J.D., once he'd landed his little bombshell on her tattered emotions, said nothing more. Zoe couldn't have come up with an evasive response to what he'd said if she'd had a week to do it. Not when he'd just delivered the most profoundly moving offer anyone had ever made her. An offer to confide. Made by a down-to-earth man too honorable to tell another soul.

At that moment Zoe realized she loved John Dalton Hayes more than she'd ever loved anyone, more than she could imagine loving anyone else.

It was at that same moment that she realized how wide the chasm between them stretched.

Zoe didn't have much of an appetite for supper, but she did her best. She'd had a rocky few moments when she learned that Coley had sent some homemade ice cream. Because he'd thought she might not feel well enough to come down to the cook house, he'd sent up a generous portion. Zoe managed to make it to her room before she broke down.

Everyone on the Hayes Ranch had been good to her. They liked *her*, not because they were impressed with the Sedgewicks, not because she was rich, and not just because she was J.D.'s partner. Coley and Carmelita rarely bothered to pamper J.D., but they did her, and that only increased her guilt.

She was about to turn their lives upside down. Just the fact that Spenser Trevyn Sedgewick had been born and Zoe Yahzoo made selfish plans to indulge herself had put everyone on Hayes at ground zero.

And it would all be so much worse for Bobby and Becky. They were both wonderful kids, great kids. Sweet, innocent, and so refreshingly normal Zoe could hardly believe they were blood relation to her. But the book's revelations would traumatize them, tarnish their memory of their mother, and bring them the kind of notoriety and shame they'd never have been exposed to if not for Zoe.

If there was ever a time in her life when she wondered what earthly good Zoe Yahzoo's existence served, it was now.

About two o'clock that next afternoon, a pickup horn sounded from the ranch drive. The anxiety that had made

Zoe half sick all day rose to such acute proportions she was certain her heart would beat out of her chest. She didn't need to hear Bobby's excited, ''Dad's back!'' to know who'd sounded the horn.

Bobby and Becky had come up to the house earlier that afternoon to use the pool, and had coaxed Zoe out to watch them swim. Now they toweled off madly and pulled on T-shirts and cutoffs over their swimsuits before they ran out to meet their father.

Zoe eased herself off the lounge chair she'd placed in the shade, but her knees were shaking so much it took her a moment to stand. She wished she was dressed in something more conservative than her cutoffs and a blouse with its tails tied up. Being barefoot didn't lend her any more confidence, but then, Zoe already knew she was a coward.

So much so that she nearly fainted when she heard the pickup engine rev. She listened to the sound of it turning in the wide drive to move toward the house near the highway. Being granted a bit more time before she approached Jess felt like a stay of execution to Zoe.

At the same time the reminder that she still had to face him made her anxious to get it over with. Zoe went into the house, then upstairs to sit a good long time in her room as she worked up the courage to do just that.

Much later, she heard Bobby and Becky return to the pool. J.D. had been gone to town on business for hours now, and Carmelita was in her kitchen working at preparations for supper. Jess might still be at his house, alone. With everyone nearby occupied and well out of earshot, there would be no better time to talk to him.

Zoe changed into regular work clothes. The stings were fading well enough to wear jeans comfortably, but Zoe wasn't focused on comfort. Time had run out for her—

for them all—and she had to speak to Jess. She slipped out the front door quietly, then elected to walk down to the Everdines. Her hope that a brisk walk in the heat of late afternoon would take the edge off her anxiety was a futile one. By the time she stepped onto the side porch of the house and dared to knock on the door, her knees were rubbery with fear.

She scrunched her eyes closed, breathed a desperate prayer, then tried with everything she had to present something close to Zoe Yahzoo normalcy. She opened her eyes in time for the inside door to swing wide. Suddenly she was looking up into Jess's stern expression.

Zoe knew instantly his attitude toward her had changed. Which startled her because nothing she'd read in the magazines or seen on the news connected Bobby and Becky with her yet. She sensed the baffling anger that simmered beneath his cool countenance and felt her heart drop. Somehow, she found her voice.

"I was wondering if you had some time, Mr. Everdine?" Her throat spasmed closed when his expression turned stony. "I'd like to speak with you, if I may?"

The few moments that passed felt like an eternity. She offered him a hopeful smile, felt her mouth tremble at the corners, then let the smile fade as Jess's icy gaze bore down into hers. When he finally spoke, his voice had a hardness to it that wounded her.

"Haven't got time."

The drawled words were heavy with meaning, and a dozen tormented questions ran through her mind. She clutched desperately at a soft Zoe smile and tried again.

"It's really very important that we talk, Mr. Everdine. When would be a better time?" Zoe put great effort into stretching her smile wider, then felt it freeze on her lips when impatience passed bluntly over his handsome features.

"Look, Zoe, or Spenser—whoever you feel like being today. A better time came and went about five years ago." The twist of lips he gave her was bitter and harsh. "You said everything then that there was to say, and you were damned final about it."

Zoe's brittle smile vanished. Her bewildered, "What did you say?" was ruthlessly overridden.

"Just because some stray whim took your fancy doesn't mean that anyone else takes the same notion. I'd appreciate it if you went back to California and found yourself another little hobby. In the meantime, keep your distance from my kids." The warning in his voice drove through her like a lance. Somehow, she found the courage to try again.

"Please, Mr. Everdine. It's because of Becky and Bobby that—"

The violent slam of the door made her jump as if she'd been shot. Shock left her staring stupidly at the door, the rest of what she'd meant to say stunned from her lips as if she'd been slapped.

Reflexively, she raised her hand and knocked a second time on the frame of the screen door. The complete silence from inside the house was daunting, but she pulled open the screen and pounded urgently on the inside door. She had to speak to Jess, had to warn him. His bitter attitude toward her—whatever his astonishing statements meant—couldn't put her off. Bobby and Becky had to be prepared, they had to be protected. Zoe would suffer anything from Jess to accomplish that.

When the door remained stubbornly closed, desperation sent a frightening hysteria over her. "Mr. Everdine?"

His utter refusal to open the door to her resonated eerily with the most damaging experiences of her life. Zoe sagged against the door frame, almost too weak to stand. My God.

The words were as much prayer as her wild thoughts could put together. In a fog of shock, she straightened and took a faltering step backward. The screen door closed with a soft thud that seemed to heighten the screaming whirlwind of pain in her chest.

My God. Zoe took another backward step. The tiny sliver of intuition that had quivered to life sometime during those traumatic moments when she'd stared up at Jess and heard his bitter words, now thrummed with certainty in her heart.

Jess Everdine was her natural father.

As Zoe turned dizzily and nearly stumbled down the porch steps, she saw that it all made horrifyingly perfect sense.

Look, Zoe, or Spenser—whoever you feel like being today... The words tore across every insecurity she had, condemning her, calling down shame on who she had been, shaming who she was now. A pronouncement of deficiency that struck at the core of her muddled identity and declared her forever unworthy.

As the Sedgewicks had. Though Jason and Angela were far more subtle about it, it made perfect sense to Zoe that Jess would agree. Perfect sense.

Zoe's blurred gaze sought and rivetted on J.D.'s big house as she walked toward it in a mental and emotional daze.

Ever confide in anybody? J.D.'s low drawl came back to her so clearly she thought for a moment he was walking beside her. *I'm not much for hanging my private things*

*on the front porch, either…but then, I never had a partner
before…*

If Zoe hadn't been walking up the ranch drive where
anyone could see her, she might have bent double with
the pain those gentle words suddenly caused her. There'd
been such a wealth of tenderness in them, such a bounty
of meaning for someone who found it difficult to confide.

It didn't surprise her to realize that the pain J.D.'s
words caused her now was because she knew they promised the impossible. For all the potential trust and real
friendship they hinted at, in the end, they would prove to
be no more than an emotional mirage.

Spenser Sedgewick and Zoe Yahzoo had chased
enough emotional mirages. There were no truly loving
and secure places for either of them. No place called
home, no people to love who returned that love unless
some mysterious standard was met.

The Hayes Ranch was no different. By the time she
told J.D. about her sneaky manipulations and warned him
about the trouble she was about to cause everyone—particularly the pain and shame her existence would cause
Bobby and Becky—she'd be lucky if he didn't grab her
and throw her bodily off Hayes ground.

Zoe finally made it to the house, letting herself in the
front door as quietly as she could before she made her
way to J.D.'s office, closed the door and picked up the
telephone.

J.D. turned his pickup off the highway onto the graveled
ranch drive, taking the curve too fast to keep the truck
from fishtailing briefly. Something had happened. The
growing certainty that it was something terrible stole the

last of his pleasure at being granted the opportunity to get Hayes back.

The call from Zoe's lawyer in California had come through like magic just as he was finishing up late business with his lawyer. An offer to sell. Which he'd snapped up immediately. The paperwork had already been started before the idea started to bother him. Hayes would soon be all his. Every acre, every oil well, every head of cattle. His heritage, his pride. The moment he and Zoe signed the final papers and the money transfer was made, he'd have everything back that was rightfully his.

But why now? The question nagged him. Zoe had been on Hayes only eight days. Clearly, she loved the ranch and, unless he'd read everything wrong, the Everdines were her birth family. Which made this sudden offer to sell so shocking.

In the end, J.D. had called a halt to the process. His directive to his lawyer to put it all on hold until he could talk to Zoe had made the man red-faced with ire.

"Hell, J.D., a few days ago you'd have killed to get that one-third back. If the woman is this impulsive, how can you be sure she won't decide to back out—or sell it to those crazy environmentalists who were raising money to buy into Hayes before."

The part about the environmentalists had distracted J.D. He'd found out then that Zoe hadn't been the only buyer interested in Hayes. Raylene had managed to get more than market value out of Zoe for that one-third interest because Zoe'd had to outbid a radical group of grasslands preservationists. J.D. had been shocked to his back teeth over that bit of information. A fight with that bunch could have cost him a fortune and likely consigned a third of Hayes to public domain. Zoe hadn't breathed a word to him.

Which was all the more reason not to take advantage of her offer before he could find out why she was suddenly so hot to sell.

J.D. brought the pickup to a sliding halt next to the house and bounded out. He was late for supper, but the receptionist had called Carmelita for him. He wasn't surprised when he walked into the kitchen and saw the table set for two, but with no one in sight. A quick check of the top oven told him the food had been left warming so Carmelita could go along to some wingding at her cousin's for the evening.

It was then that the utter silence of the big house fully registered. Was Zoe even here? The heaviness in his chest dragged lower as he again got the sense that something had happened.

That feeling only escalated as he called out a loud, ''Anybody home?'' and got no answer.

CHAPTER SEVEN

ZOE heard J.D.'s pickup roar in and poured herself another three fingers of Jim Beam. She was sitting in one of the wing chairs in his office with the drapes drawn against the evening sun as she nursed a glass of whiskey. The pain had driven her nearly wild after she'd come back from Jess's. Calling her lawyer to arrange the immediate sale of her third of Hayes to J.D. had helped.

She ran a trembling finger around the rim of the tumbler and smiled grimly. Selling Hayes back to J.D. was a shameless bribe. A coward's attempt to make him feel too beholden to her to get nasty. Zoe raised the glass and took another bracing swallow of the amber liquid, noting that it no longer burned and choked her. Some of the sick knot in her middle had unraveled. Enough so that she muzzily considered that the vices of adult beverages might be vastly exaggerated. She'd never used drugs or alcohol in her life, never taken anything to blunt her pain or to help her screw up her courage.

But Jim Beam was proving to be such a dandy medicinal for both afflictions that Zoe decided perhaps the time had come to forsake such strict teetotaling. Take a break now and then. Feel better. No doubt Dillon Casey's book forecast at least one trip to the Betty Ford Center for pitiful little Spenser/Zoe. The offspring of the rich and famous seemed to migrate there in droves anyway. Why should she be so superior?

J.D.'s loud "Anybody home?" gave her only a mild

start. The medicinal effects of Mr. Beam were making more of an impression by the moment, so Zoe gave herself a dose that finished off what was left in the tumbler. Then, with a doggedness she normally would have been appalled at, she reached for the nearby bottle.

She'd just poured and settled back when she heard J.D.'s booted tread in the hall. The smile of greeting she had for him when he stepped into the den was effortless.

"How come you've got the drapes drawn?" J.D. asked gruffly, then crossed to his desk and switched on the lamp. Zoe squinted against the soft light, then swung her gaze higher when he turned toward her.

"You gettin' snookered on my whiskey, Hollywood?" His short, surprised chuckle sounded more amused to Zoe than it was.

"Yep, John Dalton, I believe I am." She tried to focus on his face. "Did you get my message?" She grinned as if she'd made a joke, delighted when J.D. smiled back and slowly came her way.

"Seems like you're sending me more than one message, darlin'. What's going on?" J.D. dragged the other wing chair over and placed it in front of Zoe's before he sat down.

Zoe frowned. More than one message? The people in Texas talked in too many riddles. Jess Everdine was apparently a master at it. Even under the influence of Jim Beam, she still couldn't make sense of what he'd said. Now J.D. was doing it.

She leaned forward a bit to assert, "My *message*, J.D. Only one." She thrust herself back in the chair and had another sip as she waited for his answer.

"You mean about selling me your interest in Hayes? Yeah, I got that message, Zoe. I'm much obliged."

Zoe frowned. From the grim look on his face, J.D. looked anything but "much obliged." She tried a little smile. "It's a bribe, you know."

J.D. leaned forward and rested his forearms on his thighs. The smile he gave her deepened those wonderful creases on both sides of his mouth and curved them to his cheekbones. Zoe responded to the friendliness of that smile and leaned forward herself, resting her forearms on her knees, taking care to keep the stout tumbler balanced with both hands.

"What kind of bribe?" J.D. was still smiling at her.

Zoe's light brows crinkled. "How did you know it was a bribe?" she asked, then caught herself. "Ooops, I just told you, didn't I?"

J.D. nodded and gave another chuckle, but even quite mellowed out, Zoe saw the serious intensity in his dark eyes. His drawl was so low and slow when he spoke that Zoe thought it might be the sexiest voice she'd ever heard. "That was an awfully big bribe, honey."

He reached the few inches that separated them to wrap his hand gently around hers. That his long fingers also curved under the tumbler to give it extra support wasn't noticed by her. "What is it you're bribing me for?"

The soft question managed to find the well of pain not entirely numbed by the whiskey. Zoe didn't realize her grin went out like a bright light suddenly switched off. She was briefly too overcome with emotion to speak.

She finally got out a slightly slurred, "I've brought trouble to Hayes, John Dalton. Big, big, *big* trouble." It was a bit easier then to confess, "I won't be able to stand it if you hate me for it."

J.D.'s other hand came out to wrap around hers, his smile so tender and appealing that Zoe felt it reach into her heart and cradle it with the same warmth that his hands cradled hers.

"Well, now, Zoe, I can't imagine any trouble bad enough to make me hate you."

Zoe nodded emphatically. "Yeah, you could. About the time you find out what I've done and a zillion photographers and reporters show up to hound everybody." She was watching his face as closely as she could, but her little bombshell didn't appear to take away a speck of tenderness or appeal from it. Maybe he didn't understand. She tried harder. "Especially Bobby and Becky." An unexpected sob silenced her for a moment.

For several more, she fell prey to the number of things she'd meant to confess to him. They were whirling around in her head, mocking her attempt to organize them.

J.D.'s low, "What about Bobby and Becky?" seemed to help her focus. He covertly slipped the tumbler from her shaking fingers, then wrapped his big hands around hers and gripped tightly. The hard warmth and firmness of all those thick calluses was comforting. The tenderness in his dark eyes as he gazed over at her was wonderfully reassuring. She hoped it wasn't another mirage.

"Bobby and Becky's mother, Sarah, was my birth mother." Once she got that out, her thoughts seemed to get in a bit more order. "I don't know if Jess Everdine is my natural father or not, but I know he is." The contradiction escaped her.

J.D. gave her a gentle smile. "I figured that out, baby. The day you and Becky started the fence."

Zoe stared at him a moment, then released a sigh. "I knew it." She nodded. "But a big writer is doing a book on the Sedgewicks. He found out about Bobby and Becky and where they are. I couldn't get him to leave their names out—''

Zoe was overcome, resenting that Mr. Beam appeared to be letting her down. She got out a choked, ''The reporters will be after them. They'll find out that our mother had an affair and that she gave up the baby. It will hurt their memory of her.'' Zoe bit her lips ruthlessly as she tried to hold back tears. ''They'll be ashamed because of me. H-how will they get through it, John Dalton? What about their friends and the kids at school?''

She clutched his big hands urgently, her eyes searching his face as if to find an answer. J.D.'s grim expression registered, and the tender, easily hurt side of her nature quailed with distress.

''Now you understand why I had to bribe you.'' With that, she tried to pull her hands from his and stand, but he refused to release her.

''Whoa, there—sit still. Have you told Jess about this yet?''

Zoe's gaze fled his, too ashamed to tell him about her encounter with Jess that afternoon. She couldn't tell J.D., couldn't tell anyone she'd got what she'd deserved from Jess for sneaking into his childrens' lives. She hadn't been able to figure out most of the things he'd said to her, but the fact that he wanted nothing to do with her had been brutally easy to understand. Particularly his warning to keep her distance from his kids.

Look, Zoe or Spenser—whoever you feel like being today. She hadn't been able to down enough Jim Beam to numb the devastation those words had caused. It was certain she'd never repeat them to anyone.

''Zoe?'' J.D.'s brusque tone demanded an answer. Her

soft "No" made him give a grim sigh. "Then you've got to tell him. Tonight, if we can get you sober enough."

Zoe's alarmed gaze shot up to his, the haze of alcohol lifting to fill her mind with horror. She shook her head. "No—I can't."

J.D. was stern. "He's got to know, Zoe. You've got to tell him."

"I can't, John Dalton." Zoe shook her head emphatically.

His dark brow furrowed. "That's what you came here for, wasn't it? To find your family and warn them?"

Her, "Not entirely," slipped out. It took her a moment to realize her mistake.

"What do you mean, not entirely?"

J.D. was more persistent than she could handle at the moment. Zoe realized she was either too drunk or not drunk enough to evade him. His dark eyes probed relentlessly into hers and it struck her that she had to tell him the truth or he'd know that she hadn't.

But the truth was humiliating. And selfish, self-serving and pitiful. This really was the end, she thought dismally. If she told him the whole truth about why she'd come here as she had, it would be the last flaw. Hysterical giggles burst up and filled her eyes with tears.

"If I tell you, it will be the last flaw," she said, then paused because she'd said it aloud. "You've heard of the straw that broke the camel's back? Well, this will be the flaw that broke the—the—the what?"

J.D. shook his head. "Now you're making no sense at all, Hollywood. Think."

"I'm making perfect sense," she declared, sobering a bit. "I made perfect sense to me—my whole plan made perfect sense."

"What plan?"

"My plan to come here and see if Bobby and Becky could like me before they know who I am." Zoe hesitated when the impatience smoothed from J.D.'s face and she realized how excruciatingly intense his attention was suddenly. His expression was neutral, but Zoe interpreted it as the calm before the storm. The rest of her confession babbled out with unvarnished candor.

"I didn't want them to know who I was. I wanted to see if they could like me for me, not because of the Sedgewicks or because they felt they had to 'cause I'm their sister. I was going to win them over. I thought I had plenty of time before the book was released. I wanted them to like me before things got crazy. I didn't want them to know me the way Dillon Casey will tell about me. I—"

It was as much the increasingly grim look on J.D.'s face as it was hearing herself repeat the "I" word so many times that silenced Zoe. And made her feel ashamed to her soul. God, what a shallow, self-centered twit she was!

J.D.'s silence seemed to confirm everything she believed about herself. His somber expression was some sort of pronouncement on her. It felt just as shattering as Jess's, just as devastating as the Sedgewicks'.

Zoe gave him a wry, humorless smile as she thought how unanimous the consensus about her was. She didn't need to wait to find out what Bobby and Becky and everyone else on Hayes would decide about her. Some decisions didn't require much deliberation.

J.D. was still looking over at her, his expression as unreadable to her as hieroglyphics. But Zoe was suddenly weary of trying to read anyone, tired of looking for what she ached to see.

The drugging fatigue that suddenly swept her made the room spin and her body feel like it weighed a thousand pounds. Her eyelids were impossible to keep open, and she felt consciousness slip from her grasp as smoothly as a kite string.

J.D. caught Zoe easily as she slumped forward. She didn't so much as twitch as he shifted her to pick her up and stood slowly to his feet. Zoe was dead to the world, oblivious to everything, including the soft snores that might have made him smile at another time.

He'd known she was packing a load of secrets, but he thought he'd figured out most of them. He'd sensed the pain and brokenness behind her good fairy facade, but he realized now he'd glimpsed only a shadow of it.

Something had happened to her today. Something she hadn't admitted. There'd been nothing in what she'd told him that she couldn't have already known. She'd known about the book and that she had to warn Jess. She'd known her twisted-up reasons for coming here as she had, and she'd apparently already speculated about the book's effect on the kids.

For her to suddenly want to sell out then get rip-roaring drunk was some sort of reaction. Her sudden refusal to talk to Jess and warn him didn't make sense once she'd admitted that one of her reasons for coming to Hayes had been to do just that.

Unless she'd already tried. The more he considered it, the more the idea made sense. If she'd tried to talk to Jess and things had gone wrong, it could account for her raid on his whiskey and her refusal to talk to Jess now.

J.D. carried Zoe into her room and paused at the side

of her bed. He might have let her sleep in her clothes, if not for the healing wasp stings. Because of those, he had to flirt with the torture of undressing her. He laid her gently on one side of the bed and methodically stripped off her clothes down to her underwear as he chivalrously tried to ignore her small, perfect body. He yanked down the bedspread and sheet on the other side of the bed, then lifted her over and tugged the covers up to her chin.

J.D. stared down into her sleep-soft features for a long time, thinking about what she'd said, more certain by the moment that his golden good fairy had got her wings crushed.

If she'd come here as she had because she'd wanted to see if Bobby and Becky would like her for herself, it had been a useless exercise. Everyone liked Zoe Yahzoo, everyone fell in love with her sparkle and fun. How could she not know that? What kind of upbringing did you have to have to even think up such bizarre shenanigans? Why had she thought she had to bribe him not to hate her?

J.D. grappled with the elemental difference between them, stunned that they seemed more starkly opposite than ever. It was this clearer sense of how vast their differences were that made him realize what a wild mismatch he and Zoe would make if either of them ever took Carmelita's marriage advice seriously. He didn't want to dwell on the reason for the unhappiness that suddenly blossomed in his chest.

He was turning to leave the room when his boot caught on the corner of a stack of magazines that peeped out from beneath the bed. He leaned down to push them out of harm's way, then caught sight of the inset photo near the corner of the top one.

It was a picture of Zoe, and she was dressed in a daringly cut black gown that fit like it had been painted on. Curiosity made him drag it out.

As he sorted through the stack, he saw that almost every cover featured some picture of Zoe with the Sedgewicks. That the headline article in each one was about the unauthorized biography sent a surprising flash of anger through him.

So this was what had brought Zoe to Hayes. J.D. scanned one or two of the articles as he crouched there by the bed, but was too disgusted to glance through them all. The outrageous invasion of privacy and the tawdry sensationalism of the articles made him furious. As he shoved the magazines back under the bed and straightened, he couldn't help but look over at Zoe.

Deeply asleep, her soft cheeks flushed and her short wedge of platinum curls sparkling on the pillow, she looked too vulnerable and fragile and pure to be the subject for the cheap tripe of scandal sheets.

The astonishing idea that she was anyway jarred him.

Zoe awoke sometime near ten that next morning. Her head was pounding, and the foul taste in her mouth made her nauseous. It took several moments for her to figure out why she felt so awful. It took no time at all for her to pronounce a heartfelt curse on Jim Beam and his ilk. She carefully rolled to her side and slid off the bed, teetering as she tried to get upright and stay that way.

It dawned on her as she navigated from the bed to the bathroom and the shower, that she'd neglected to remove her underwear and put on her pajamas the night before. The reason she'd somehow foregone her normal routine escaped her. Which gave her faint alarm. She hadn't realized before now how much she relied on her wits to deal with the world. The fact that her mind felt dull and slow gave her the disturbing sense that she was off kilter and vulnerable.

The sharp needles of hot spray peppered through her hair to her scalp as she washed her hair and showered. She waited until the hot water ran lukewarm, then stepped out and grabbed a towel. She managed to dress and take dreary note of the time before memory kicked in. When it did, the resulting plunge of her heart made her wish she'd stayed in bed.

"The *señor* told me to tell you it has hair of the dog that bit you."

Carmelita plunked a tall glass before her as she sat in her chair at the breakfast table. Zoe stared suspiciously at the chilled concoction that bore shades of color from yellow to deep orange to red. As she picked it up and gave the liquid a testing swirl, she noted sickly that some of it clotted together with the consistency of lumpy slime. Her stomach pitched and she quickly set it down.

"It is the *señor*'s family remedy for hangovers."

At the stern thread in Carmelita's tone, Zoe glanced up, then felt her face warm. "What's in it?"

Carmelita's dark brows winged up in an arch. "You could drink half a bottle of whiskey, but are worried about this?" She gave a wry chuckle and waved her hand. "Drink it all. And remember with regret what you did that made you have to drink this."

Carmelita's clear disapproval was softened by the sparkle of humor in her dark eyes. That the woman was amused at Zoe's self-inflicted predicament—and the glass of what was plainly as much punishment as cure— stirred

Zoe's sense of humor and lifted her dismal spirits. Carmelita still liked her. For now.

Zoe stared at the horrid concoction, then gamely picked it up under Carmelita's watchful eye. At her last-second hesitation, the woman crossed her arms over her chest and gave her a stern look to prompt her. Zoe scrunched her eyes closed and forced the contents of the glass down, having no problem at all remembering with regret why she had to drink the awful mixture that bore the thick taste of raw egg, cayenne and tabasco. That it also carried the strong taste of whiskey must have been what Carmelita had meant by "hair of the dog that bit you."

Zoe thumped the glass down with a gusty sigh of relief. Carmelita whisked it away, returning in a moment with a small stack of dry toast and a bottle of aspirin.

Her stomach went into near-public revolt. Zoe was halfway off her chair for a mad dash to the bathroom before the wave of nausea magically calmed. She eased back down, beginning to feel better. By the time she downed some aspirin, finished the toast and dared a cup of coffee, Zoe felt almost human.

But without the physical misery of a hangover to distract her, the events of the day and night before began a ghastly parade through her thoughts.

Had she really failed so utterly with Jess and made such a fool of herself with J.D.? She remembered most of what she'd confessed to J.D., but she remembered every expression on his stern face with aching clarity. Particularly his terrible grimness once he'd known the extent of her self-centered folly.

She agonized over that and almost reached a private vow to never face J.D. again when she heard a boot-step on the porch. The back door swung wide and he walked in.

"Hungover?" His big voice boomed good-naturedly as his dark eyes homed in on hers.

Zoe's gaze fled his. She couldn't bear to see how disgusted he must be with her. The fear that he might also make her face Jess and subject herself to further agony was stronger still.

She wasn't surprised at all when J.D. told her, "Jess is coming to the house. You can have that talk with him."

Zoe sprang to her feet and shook her head. "I can't now, J.D. You know what he has to be told so he can prepare the kids."

"You want me to tell him?"

The question made her send him a grateful look. "Yes, please. And a million thanks for doing it."

J.D. shook his head, his expression more grim and purposeful than she'd ever seen. Anxiety gave her a painful jolt. "I'm not going to do it for you, Hollywood. You've got to face this."

Her small, "I can't," made no impression.

"Do you love those kids?" The blunt question was a reproach.

Zoe nodded faintly. Her weak, "You know I do," was choked.

"Then you've got to do it." The stern statement thrust at her.

Zoe couldn't look away from the dark solemn eyes that silently warned he would be disappointed in her if she didn't. It struck her then that J.D.'s good character wouldn't have allowed him a moment's thought or hesitation if there was some moral right he felt he had to do.

Cowardice or the threat of emotional devastation wouldn't give him even a second's pause.

But it gave Zoe hours of pause. She was a coward to the core and she didn't have enough good character to push through a buttonhole. Coming here in the sneaky way she had to play her foolish little like-me-for-me game was irrefutable proof. J.D. didn't seem to understand that his expectations of her were lofty, and about as difficult for her to meet as height requirements for a model.

And yet, as she looked over into his implacable expression, Zoe realized she valued this man's approval too much not to try. She loved J.D. precisely because he was the man he was and, though the coward in her was screaming in protest, she also loved that he was leaning heavily on her to do the right thing. She'd needed someone her whole life to set a moral parameter, someone to rein in her natural exuberance and set a fair, clearly defined standard for her to live up to.

J.D.'s hard work and good character measuring stick was fair, down-to-earth, and eminently practical. Zoe realized with some surprise that she'd do almost anything to meet it. Whether she ever had a chance to win J.D.'s love or not, and even if the Everdines never accepted her as kin, she'd never be able to live with herself after this if she didn't make the effort.

"I'll do it." The words didn't come out very strongly, but then, Zoe didn't consider that she should waste what little strength and resolve she had on any definitive statements to J.D. Not when she needed it all to face Jess again.

Once she'd agreed, it took almost no time at all for J.D. to bustle her to his office. It was astonishing how quickly Jess showed up, but it wasn't surprising at all to see that he appeared less than thrilled to be present in the same room as her. Because she'd not known the best way to begin, she'd dashed upstairs moments before Jess's arrival and grabbed her stash of magazines.

When J.D. abruptly exited the room and closed the door behind him, Zoe almost lost her nerve.

The two times she dared to glance Jess's way, she noted his expression was as hard as a brick, and that he wasn't looking her way at all.

Nervously, she crossed to him and held the stack of magazines out. "A popular author who specializes in scandalous, tell-all, unauthorized biographies of celebrities is doing a book on my adoptive parents." For a dizzying few moments, she thought Jess wouldn't take the magazines.

"I saw your picture on some of those in Ft. Worth. That's how I found out who you really are." Jess's brusque tone was little more than an accusation and Zoe's heart fell.

He finally took the magazines. She passed him the last one separately and called his attention to the line that promised the next issue would print a detailed excerpt from the book on Zoe's life with the Sedgewicks.

"That's the one I'm worried about. I hired investigators to find S-Sarah, but none of them ever came up with anything. When I realized Jason and Angela had regularly gone behind my back to buy them off so they would conveniently fail, I hired someone out of state. He found Sarah, but—" Zoe couldn't bring herself to say the words "but she'd died." "But he found out that she had two other children who lived here."

Jess's restless shift in the wing chair made her foreshorten most of the other details about buying into Hayes and coming here to get to know the kids before she disclosed who she was. Zoe acknowledged that she was still too cowardly to confess everything to Jess. She rushed on before he became too impatient and cut her off.

"Someone who worked for the investigator heard about the author's latest writing project and sold him the information about Bobby and Becky."

That at last earned her Jess's full attention, but the harsh gleam in his eyes was livid with accusation.

"I-I went to the author—Dillon Casey is his name— and tried to get him to leave Bobby's and Becky's names out of his book and not to reveal their location on Hayes. But the hallmark of his books are the details. He has no fear of lawsuits, since he considers them nothing more than pricey publicity."

Zoe paused for a horrifying moment because of the killing intensity in Jess's eyes. "So I failed to persuade him to leave the kids' names and location out of print. The huge popularity of Jason and Angela and the widespread public attention toward anything or anyone connected with them will—"

Jess's furious swear word, and his near launch from the wing chair, made Zoe spring back.

"So what you're telling me is, my kids are gonna be hounded by the press and have their mamma and daddy's private history laid out in public."

Zoe found a shred of courage as he leaned aggressively toward her. "T-that's what I'm telling you. And that it's my fault."

Her soft words seemed to take a fraction of the aggression from his belligerent stance. But her equally soft, "I'm so sorry," seemed to rile him all over again.

His eyes blazed down into hers. Zoe imagined she saw

the blue fire waver a moment and go out. But the moment was so quick, she must have imagined it, because the next second it rekindled and forced her gaze to flee his.

His low, ''Stay away from my kids,'' seared her soul. She almost fainted when he charged from the room and let the door swing wide. Through blurred eyes, she gazed stupidly at the stack of magazines that had somehow scattered to the floor. Numb, she bent and picked them up. She hefted the lot into the small garbage can next to J.D.'s big desk before she quietly exited the room.

CHAPTER EIGHT

ZOE hadn't been able to find the courage to face J.D. She hadn't been able to even look at Carmelita on her way out the back door. She felt restless and wild inside, and more than a little betrayed by the disheartening reward of doing the right thing—however belatedly.

She ended up at the garage, and went through the side door to where her car was parked. The bright red color glowed even in the shade and Zoe opened the door to get behind the wheel. She reached for the garage door opener on the dash, aimed it, then listened to the sound of the big door motoring up. She slipped the key into the ignition when the door reached the end of the track and thumped to a stop.

Moments later she backed out and turned around, rocketing down the graveled drive to leave an enormous rooster tail of Texas dust in her wake. She slowed to turn onto the highway, then hit the accelerator again.

The hot wind that buffeted the car and raked through her bright curls seemed to blow her miserable thoughts away to a safe distance. The hard pressure of her small foot on the accelerator pushed the car to the limits she'd guessed at, but heretofore had had too much sense to explore.

But the sun was bright, the sky was blue, and the strip of Texas highway before her was as empty as she felt. The mirages she chased on the pavement drew her inexorably forward.

Just like all the other mirages, she reflected bitterly.

* * *

It was hours before Zoe's wide, whirlwind tour of Texas highways put her on the highway back to town and the Hayes Ranch beyond. The state trooper who'd clocked her doing a hundred and ten through his speed trap in another county had threatened to arrest her on the spot, but he'd caved quickly to Zoe Yahzoo charm.

She hadn't been able to charm him out of a traffic ticket with a godawful fine, however, but her close encounter with Texas law enforcement had instantly converted her into a law-abiding citizen. She'd driven no more than the speed limit after that and felt her wild emotions calm in proportion to the discipline of adherence.

She'd driven through town and was almost halfway to Hayes when she saw a car off to the side of a rise ahead. She automatically slowed when she saw that the driver already had the car on a jack. Her heart gave a painful twinge when she recognized the car and the young blonde who stepped out from behind.

Becky Everdine had caught sight of her red convertible, because she was suddenly waving her arms to get Zoe to pull over. Leery of disregarding Jess's demand for her to stay away from his kids, Zoe slowed her car, turned it around, then pulled up behind the Everdines' car. Becky bounded over to her before she could get out.

"I gotta flat, Zoe. I got the tire off, but the spare is flat, too. Can you give me a ride into town to fix it?"

Zoe had instant misgivings, but a quick glance in the rearview mirror showed the highway to Hayes was as empty as the highway into town. The midafternoon sun was hot along the pavement. There was no way she could refuse to give Becky a ride.

She made herself grin up at Becky, glad for the sunglasses that would conceal the effort. "Toss the tire in the trunk. We might as well get air in the spare while we're at it,'' she said, then popped the trunk release and got out to help. Once both tires were in the trunk and they were strapped into their seat belts, Zoe checked the mirrors and pulled out.

''Thanks, Zoe. I was afraid I'd have to walk.''

Zoe's, ''No problem,'' was light but, she hoped, not an invitation for more conversation. She didn't want to know if Jess had told the kids anything yet, and she certainly didn't want to know what he'd told them.

She'd already decided during her long drive to pack her things and move to a motel in town until the papers for the sale of Hayes were ready to be signed. She needed to break as swiftly and cleanly from Hayes as possible since she knew Jess would want her gone.

Her family was unattainable. She didn't think she could stand to know for sure that J.D. was, too. It helped her dismal expectations of the future to believe J.D. would always be here on Hayes, and that perhaps there was a sliver of something wonderful possible at some future time too distant to calculate.

The whole idea gave her another mirage to chase, but she reckoned she'd survived too much of her life on mirages to break the habit.

They reached town a few minutes later, and Zoe slowed the car. She turned into the full-service gas station and pulled off to the side. She popped the trunk release and Becky got out to get one of the attendants. Zoe took off her sunglasses and got out, too. She waited until the attendant got the tires from the trunk to take them into the service area before she called Becky over to the soft drink machines.

''How about a soda?'' Zoe invited. ''My treat.'' They

made their selections, then took them over to a bench in the shade of the station.

"Can I ask you something, Zoe?"

Becky's hesitant tone sent a charge of dread across Zoe's nerve endings. She hoped her pretended distraction as she glanced down the street and her vague-sounding "What?" would discourage Becky from asking anything too serious. She'd felt Becky's close scrutiny more than once on their short trip to town. She'd sensed then what was coming, known it with queasy certainty. When Becky fidgeted tensely beside her, Zoe braced herself.

"Are you really my...sister?"

The words landed on Zoe's battered heart like a knock-out punch. She glanced down, gave her soda can a swirl that stirred the contents, then had a quick sip.

"Are you, Zoe?"

Becky's soft prompting pushed at her. Zoe lowered the can, then gave in. She glanced over into Becky's earnest expression.

"Yes." Zoe looked away, then leaned back on the bench with a sigh. "I'm selling out to J.D." She gave a shrug. "I was on my way back to pack my things when I picked you up. I'll be leaving as soon as the papers that sell back my percentage of Hayes are ready to sign."

Becky touched her arm. "But you can't leave now. Bobby and I want to get to know you."

Zoe shook her head to that. "Not now, honey. Maybe when the two of you are older—" She swiftly amended it to, "Definitely then," and gave Becky a small smile.

Becky's face crumpled a bit. "Daddy will get over being mad," she said urgently. "I told him you must be sorry about what you wrote in that letter, or you wouldn't have come all the way here."

Zoe's attention fixed instantly on the mention of a letter. "What letter?"

"The letter you wrote Mama and Daddy." Becky frowned.

Zoe turned more fully toward her and reached over to grip her hand. "What letter?"

"You know about the letter," Becky chided. "You wrote it."

Something twisted sickly in Zoe and she shook her head. "I never wrote a letter. I *should* have before I came here, but I didn't." Zoe didn't realize the frown of confusion on her face so closely mirrored her sister's. "What do you know about a letter?"

Becky was looking at her strangely, but she complied. It was quickly evident to Zoe that Becky was still young enough that the details babbled out with a youthful lack of tact.

"Mama and Daddy hired an investigator to find you after you turned eighteen. He found out you were adopted by movie stars, who you were, and where you were. Mama and Daddy wrote you a letter—Daddy says he thinks they might have rewritten it a dozen times so they wouldn't sound like hicks from Texas to you, since you lived in Beverly Hills and all that."

Zoe's breathing went ragged as she listened to what Becky was saying. Jess and Sarah had sent her a letter? Had that been what Jess was talking about yesterday when he'd told her that a better time to talk to him had come and gone five years ago?

It hurt to hear Becky's little aside—that she'd seen their mother make a tiny, barely visible mark on the kitchen calendar for every day that passed between the day they'd mailed their letter, and the day Sarah found a letter from

California in the mailbox. It had arrived four weeks to the day, typewritten on elegant paper in a chic, lined envelope.

But the gist of the message was that Ms. Spenser Trevyn Sedgewick, who felt a ranch foreman's family had nothing to offer her, wouldn't much appreciate being bothered by further contact from the Everdines. *You said everything then that there was to say, and you were damned final about it,* Jess had said.

Zoe lifted a trembling hand to her head, heartsick at the stark cruelty of the letter—the letter she'd never, ever, have written. The horrible suspicion that flashed to life made her head spin as Becky chattered on.

"Mama refused to throw the letter away. It's still in her keepsake box. She made all kinds of excuses to Daddy for you—Spenser is young, her life is probably filled with so many glamorous, exciting things, we'll give her time to mature…"

Becky's voice trailed off abruptly. Zoe was alert to the idea that Becky had just realized how distressing this all was for Zoe and that she suddenly regretted giving so much detail. Zoe lowered her hand and looked over somberly at the upset on her sister's face. Her instincts told her there was a bit more to the story.

"What else?"

That there was something more was evident by the tremor of Becky's lips and the way her worried gaze flinched from Zoe's. Zoe gripped her hand. "Please. Tell me the rest, Becky."

Becky shook her head and Zoe tried again. "I swear to you, honey, if I had ever gotten a letter from them, I would have come to them right away. I looked for our mother—" Zoe broke off, reluctant to confess the details of the pitiful search she'd made during her childhood. "Let's just say I always, *always* tried to find her."

"Then who sent the letter?"

The answer to Becky's question roused the rage and frustration Zoe had felt for as long as she could remember. Rage at the Sedgewicks' power to control and manipulate the life of a child they barely cared for, frustration that they still practiced their manipulations at more levels than she was aware of, despite her efforts to thwart them. Nevertheless, to actually tell her young sister who she suspected of writing the cruel letter was difficult.

"Probably Angela." The words were low, but she looked over into her sister's face and persisted softly, "Tell me the rest."

Becky bit her lip in indecision and Zoe hazarded her most painful guess. "They never got over the letter, did they? Especially Sarah."

Becky's eyes filled with tears and several shot down her cheeks. "She wouldn't throw the letter away. Sometimes, she'd have nightmares and I'd hear her crying. She'd tell Daddy she'd dreamed you were hurt somehow or that you needed her, but she could never do anything to help you. Then Daddy'd get upset and tell her that she'd done the best she'd known how to do at the time and that giving you up was *his* fault, not hers."

Zoe couldn't bear another word and sprang to her feet to gulp in air as she drove her fingers through her bright curls in agony. The whirlwind of rage and pain and heartache was so profound that she suddenly felt faint.

"Oh, Zoe—sit down—please!" Becky was at her side, trying to take her arm.

Zoe shook her head and moved shakily toward the outside entrance of the small women's rest room. Becky let her go and Zoe shut herself in.

The terrible knowledge that Sarah Everdine's emotional suffering over her lost child had been so acute made what Zoe had suffered in her growing up years suddenly seem so much less important. Whatever pain and loss Zoe had weathered, at least it hadn't been compounded by the crushing guilt Sarah had clearly borne for giving her up. That theirs had been a companion pain which could have found solace five years before while Sarah was still alive left Zoe breathless with anguish.

But their one precious opportunity to find each other had been stolen away. The all-important letter so carefully written by Sarah and Jess because they feared they might sound like hicks from Texas to their materially privileged child had fallen into merciless hands. Cruel hands that had penned a reply which had caused Sarah agony for the rest of her life.

It was no wonder Jess had been so harsh with her, she realized dizzily.

Zoe bent her head, her slim body shaking as the knowledge of the bitter tragedy impacted her more deeply. She was too shocked to cry, the pain was so profound. She didn't know how long she stood there with her arms wrapped tightly around herself before the worst of the tremors passed and her stunned emotions struggled sluggishly to adjust. At last, she stepped forward to the small sink and shakily twisted on the cold water tap. Mindful now of how long Becky had been kept waiting, she dashed her hot face with water and dried off with a wad of paper towels. She made a last effort to collect herself.

The knowledge that nothing could ever undo this terrible wrong for Sarah left her desolate inside. As she stepped outside and rejoined her teary-eyed sister, Zoe wished with all her heart there was.

Desperate to function, Zoe offered her sister as much of a normal smile as she could. "Do you suppose those tires are ready?"

Becky nodded. "They just put them in your trunk. Are you all right?"

Zoe reached out and wrapped an arm around her sister's shoulders to walk with her to the car. Her soft, "Please don't worry about me," was choked, and she tried to smile.

"Do you think your father would believe me if I tried to tell him that I didn't write that letter? Without any proof other than my word?"

Even if she could somehow convince Jess, she wasn't certain it would make anyone but her feel better. And even that would be marginal now. Still, she didn't want Angela's cruelty to continue to be credited to her.

Becky frowned anxiously. "I don't know. I'll tell him I believe you."

Zoe shook her head. "No, honey. Please don't intervene for me. I don't want to come between the two of you." She couldn't bear to be the cause of a rift between her sister and father. From all she'd seen so far, Jess had a loving relationship with both kids, and she didn't want to hurt that.

They reached the car and Zoe dropped her arm as they parted to go to their separate sides to get in. Becky suddenly caught her hand.

"Would you stay, Zoe? Please? At least for a few days?"

"I don't know," she answered softly. "It's probably better to go."

"No—that can't be better," Becky urged. "Maybe J.D. could talk to him for you."

Zoe's heart was dealt fresh pain at the mention of J.D. Leaving Hayes and her family was a reminder that she was also leaving him. The instinctive knowledge that J.D. was one of a kind, and somehow the only man she could ever feature loving and wanting to be with for the rest of her life made the future seem unbearably bleak.

"No," she said quietly. "I don't want to put J.D. in the middle, either."

"But, Zoe, you can't just—"

The loud blare of a horn and the roar of a pickup engine as it swung off the street and barreled into the service station lot startled them both. The pickup tires squalled as Jess hit the brakes and slid to a stop beside Zoe's convertible. He was out of the truck in an instant, his face flushed with anger. He was shouting before he'd gone two steps.

"Becky—get in the truck."

Zoe's low, "Hurry, Becky," and the panicked look she sent her made Becky rush to comply with her father's order. Becky's quick compliance didn't deter Jess, who came around to the back of Zoe's car and towered over her.

"When I told you to stay away from my kids, what the hell did you think I meant?"

Zoe couldn't look away from the tight anger on his face. Oh, God, this was her father. He was crushing her, destroying her hope and making it impossible to imagine there was any way to get through to him. Her gaze faltered, and she leaned briefly toward her trunk to key it open and lift the trunk lid.

She looked up into her father's face. "I know what you

meant, Mr. Everdine. You'll need to get Becky's tires out of my trunk.''

Jess couldn't seem to stop glaring down at her those next ominous moments. In those moments, what Becky had told her about Sarah's nightmares came back to Zoe on a thread of intuition that blazed like lightning.

Daddy'd get upset and tell her that she'd done the best she'd known how to do at the time, and that giving you up was his *fault, not hers*. His *fault, not hers*. The words speared into the fresh wound of his relentless rejection. The idea that this man had somehow initiated the chain of events that had devastated Sarah's life and her own, yet was laying the blame on Zoe, made it impossible not to strike back.

The wild pain in Zoe surged up. She gave him a bitter smile as the tormented self-doubts and insecurities of a lifetime spewed forth.

''So, how did it happen, Mr. Everdine? Did you take one look at me and tell Sarah, 'Nope. Let's not keep this one'? Was my arrival not convenient for you, or did you get a good look at me and see some terrible flaw that didn't make me worth keeping?''

Jess's hard face flushed and the harsh intensity in his eyes was livid with pain. The knowledge that she'd dealt him a bit of the crushing pain in her own heart was not nearly as satisfying as she'd hoped.

Not even her equally bitter ''It appears you were something of a prophet,'' as she turned from him and stalked to her car door, gave her a glimmer of the satisfaction she'd grabbed for.

The moment she felt the weight of the tires lifted from her trunk, she started the engine. The sound of the lid slammed shut set off her roiling emotions like a starter pistol. She shoved her foot down on the accelerator and shot out of the service station lot, the volatile emotions she could barely control speeding her toward Hayes.

The overwhelming need to be with J.D., to hear his gruff drawl and somehow try to soak up a bit more of his granite steadiness came over her in a wave that made her hurt. She suddenly craved the feel of his big arms crushing her against his hard body. She was starved for another taste of him, for one rough male kiss that would imprint him forever on her heart and mind. Somehow, she had to have that from him—something from him—something she could carry with her when she left Hayes.

She had to leave Hayes. Tonight. She considered she was, after all, just as gutless and shallow as ever, because she'd reached the limit of what she could take from Jess. The knowledge that he was tough and virtually heartless would make him an absolute nightmare for any reporter who might try to hound Bobby and Becky. No one in the area would ever dare give the kids grief about their parents' youthful indiscretion. Because of their formidable father, the Everdine children would weather whatever was ahead with ease.

There was no reason for her to stay. Her continued presence would either drive a wedge between the kids and their only parent, or compel them to side with their father and spoil any chance Zoe might have for a relationship with them when they were grown.

Though the prospect of a future relationship with Bobby and Becky was probably just another mirage, for Zoe, it was just about the only thing she could see in the distance.

CHAPTER NINE

"YOU have been gone such a long time!" Carmelita exclaimed as Zoe let herself in the back door. When Carmelita came her way with a look of care and concern on her sweet face, Zoe almost broke down. "We were worried."

Zoe's crooked smile was the best she could do. "My apologies, *señora*. I didn't mean to worry you." She shakily reached out to the Mexican woman and touched her arm. "I hope you won't be offended if I don't have some of that wonderful supper I smell. I'm not hungry tonight. I'm going…upstairs."

She couldn't seem to put together the words that would tell Carmelita she meant to pack her things and clear out. Not when Carmelita's soft brown eyes were searching her pale features for the details of the upset she'd sensed—and genuinely seemed concerned about.

It was a relief when Carmelita allowed her a quick escape. Once she reached her room, she crossed to a small closet where she'd stashed her boxes and luggage. She dragged out one of the larger pieces and opened it on the bed, then turned to start with the clothing in her dresser drawer.

The sound of J.D.'s heavy tread coming down the hall made her glance toward her open door just as he came into sight.

His imposing height filled the doorway. "You worried

hell out of me, Hollywood." He came her way and Zoe flinched from his stern expression.

She struggled mightily to reclaim the lighthearted personality that played off J.D.'s prickly gruffness like magic. She needed something of J.D., some last something special, some last opportunity to experience what made him profoundly irresistible to her.

She looked at him and tried a Zoe Yahzoo smile that fell as abysmally flat as her desperate intentions.

"Does that mean you like me, John Dalton?"

"It means you worried hell out of me," he repeated gruffly.

Zoe's smile widened to cover the fresh jab of pain to her chaotic emotions. "Oh, that's right," she said lightly. "I haven't signed the papers yet, have I?" She gave his arm a pat and crossed the last steps to her dresser to yank open a drawer. "Don't worry, J.D. Before I came to Texas, I added a few lines to my will that ensure my interest in Hayes will return to you immediately in the event of my death or diminished capacity."

She gasped when J.D. grabbed her arm and swung her toward him. "That's a hell of a thing to say."

Zoe rallied. "It's a hell of a fact, John Dalton. Who I know, what I own, and the size of my bank balance is everyone else's prime concern. Why wouldn't it be yours, particularly since Hayes is your birthright?"

J.D.'s expression was thunderous. All at once, Zoe felt ashamed for the insult she'd dealt him and her gaze fled his. She made a slight move to free her arm, then turned away and covered her burning face with her hands.

"Oh, I'm sorry, John Dalton." Her whispered words caught on a hitch of delayed reaction. She dropped her hands and wrapped her arms tightly around herself. "You didn't deserve that.'' The sob of despair that jerked out made her bite her lip to hold back the others. Her soft, ''Is there any way you can forgive me?'' was barely audible.

She was badly startled by the warm, hard fingers that closed over her narrow shoulders and gripped gently. She squeezed her eyes closed, both to contain the hot tears that were blinding her, and to focus on the wonderful comfort of his strong, sure hands.

''I'd like us to part friends,'' she whispered, hating the faint hint of desperation in her soft voice.

J.D.'s voice was equally soft, but with the gravelly texture Zoe loved. ''Why? Are you going somewhere, Hollywood?''

Zoe couldn't suppress the violent shaking that quaked through her as she summoned as light a tone as she could manage. ''Yeah, I think I've pretty much worn out my welcome in this part of Texas.''

The violent shaking became more pronounced as J.D. stepped close and his big arms came around her from behind to lash her firmly against him. ''Who says?''

Zoe gave a shrug. ''Oh, I can pretty much tell.'' Of their own volition, Zoe's fingers sought the hard-muscled definition of J.D.'s thick forearms and closed over them greedily.

His hard jaw settled against her cheek. ''Jess gave you a hard time?''

''No more than I deserve,'' she said quietly, then took a wavering breath. ''You should have heard the appalling things I said to him. I had no idea I'd picked up any of Angela's capacity for bitchiness.'' She turned her face toward his. ''I didn't mean to inflict any of that on you, John Dalton, honest. I really do…admire you, you know." A brief smile touched her lips. "I wish I was half the man you are."

J.D. groaned at that. "If you were, we'd make a hell of a picture standing here like this." He turned her in his arms, his dark eyes serious as he looked down into her pale face. His big hand came up and lifted her chin when she tried to evade his close scrutiny.

"I don't give a damn what kind of tangle you and Jess got into, aside from the fact that you're hurting over it. I don't give a damn who thinks you've worn out your welcome at Hayes. You're my partner, Zoe Yahzoo, and as long as you are, you need to stay on Hayes and live up to your one third of the partnership."

Zoe's heart was squeezing madly with tenderness and gratitude for J.D.'s gruff words. How she loved this big man. She gave him a crooked smile, unaware of the sad little bend to it as she reminded him, "But we're about to sign papers and you're going to transfer a whopping fortune into my bank account that will dissolve that partnership, John Dalton."

J.D.'s stern features relaxed the tiniest bit. "Hell, Hollywood, you know lawyers and how they like to gum up the works haggling over which i's to dot and how many t's to cross. No telling how long it'll take 'em to come up with something we can sign."

Zoe did get teary then. "Why are you doing this?"

"Maybe I'm trying to return the favor."

His statement made no sense to Zoe and she blinked hard to get a clearer look up into his dark eyes. "What favor?"

J.D. reached up and tugged gently on a bright curl. "That little favor you did me by outbidding those environmentalists."

Zoe's gaze fled his self-consciously. "When did you find out about that?"

"Yesterday." His hand caught her chin and redirected her gaze back to his. "So I owe you a big one, Zoe."

She shook her head emphatically. "You don't owe me a thing. I bought into Hayes for my own selfish reasons, not because I meant to do anything particularly noble," she said hastily. "Please don't credit me with any golden character traits, John Dalton. I don't have very many."

J.D. glared down at her, but the glimmer of tenderness in his dark eyes softened it. "I'll do whatever I damned well please, since I own the majority of this partnership—how about something to eat? I'm hungry as hell."

His quick change of subject caught her by surprise. She shook her head, about to tell him she wasn't very hungry, when he suddenly started her toward the door.

"You'll feel better once we get a hot meal in you. Carmelita's gone off to her sister's for the evening, so you can tell me all about what's going on between you and Jess."

Zoe allowed him to usher her along with his big hand firmly on the back of her waist, until they were partway down the stairs and she had second thoughts. She glanced J.D.'s way.

"I'm not sure you should know any details, J.D. I don't want to involve you in any more than I already have."

"Too late for that, darlin'. I'm in up to my tan line," he declared as he kept her moving down the stairs. The surprising fact that he didn't appear at all annoyed confused her.

She let him shepherd her to the kitchen and sat down without protest when he pulled her chair out for her. It touched her that he gamely picked up a pair of pot-holders and got their supper out of the oven. She stared down at her plate as he sat the platter and bowls on the table, tossed down the pot holders, then took his usual place across from her.

His gruff, "Better get something on that plate and eat up," was so bossy it made her smile. She reluctantly complied, cut into her steak and had a first bite. The rich flavor stirred her appetite and before long she'd managed to get down a full supper.

It amazed her a little when, after they finished eating, rinsed their dishes and loaded them in the dishwasher, J.D. didn't press her to talk. Instead, he escorted her down to the cook house for a bowl of Coley's ice cream and her usual cut-throat game of checkers with the cook. It was dark by the time they walked back to the house.

Zoe felt better after their meal and a bit of her normal routine at the cook house. Her emotions didn't feel nearly as volatile, but she was suddenly weary beyond belief.

All of that changed the moment they stepped into the ranch kitchen. On their way out, J.D. had switched off every light but the one on the range hood, so the mood of the big house was quiet and soothing. The coward in Zoe hoped she could get by with simply crossing the kitchen to the hall door and make a casual escape upstairs to bed. But J.D. caught her arm the moment he'd closed the porch door.

Having recovered a bit of her Zoe sparkle, she let him turn her toward him and gave him a smile. The determined line of his mouth was clear, even in the soft light.

"Uh-oh, John Dalton. Why do I suddenly think you're about to do an impression of an old time Texas Ranger

who would ride into hell—or at least as far as Mexico—
to get his man?''

The line between J.D.'s dark brows deepened. ''Why
do I suddenly think you're about to throw sand in my
eyes and make a run for the border?'' he answered softly.

His big hand came up and he settled his hard palm
against her cheek. Zoe couldn't keep herself from reaching up to press it tighter to her pale skin. The compulsion
to turn her head and place a kiss on his calloused palm was
too strong to resist. Her lashes drifted closed as she did.
After a moment she slid her lips away and rubbed her
cheek against his palm. The patience she sensed in him
made her dare a look up into his dark eyes.

''How big is that front porch you mentioned the other
night?'' she asked softly, but the off-hand smile she tried
wobbled a little.

J.D.'s deep voice was a gravelly rasp. ''As big as it
needs to be, darlin'.''

Zoe put up a hand to stifle a sound that was part
chuckle, part sob. J.D. turned her toward the doorway to
the hall and wrapped his arm around her shoulders. They
walked to the darkened living room and sat down together
on the sofa.

Before she knew it, the details of her encounters with
Jess flowed out, along with a pained repeat of what Becky
had told her about the letter and its tragic impact. When
she finished, she was so appalled by the wracking sobs
she could no longer keep back, that she abruptly pulled
away from J.D. She leaned forward with her elbows
propped on her knees and her hands pressed over her face
in a vain attempt to muffle her anguish.

J.D. leaned forward himself and placed a hand on her

shoulder to give it a bracing squeeze. She tried desperately to recover.

"S-sorry. I'll stop in a moment. I don't have a habit of doing this, you know." The spasm of sobs that followed thwarted her intentions. J.D.'s hand slid off her shoulder and Zoe suddenly found herself across his lap, facing him, cradled tightly in his arms. Her arms went around his neck.

Despite her effort not to, she finally gave in to the deluge of tears. It didn't help her control at all that J.D. whispered gruff encouragement to her to let it out as he kept her firmly on his lap. The worst of the tears passed, but still J.D. held her, his big hand moving up and down her back in a slow, soothing motion. He took his hand away only long enough to shift them both and dig a handkerchief from his back pocket.

Zoe took it gratefully, then hurriedly unfolded it and put it to enough use to reduce it to a damp ball. She subsided against him, her cheek snuggled against his wide shoulder.

J.D. let out a slow breath. "This is going to come out all right, Zoe." His big hand smoothed gently over her curls.

Zoe didn't agree. But the hallmark of Zoe Yahzoo had always been her ability to appear unfazed by the things that would give normal mortals pain. Coming to Texas had thrown her performance off badly, but it was time to reclaim the image. Zoe leaned back a bit and grinned tiredly at J.D.

"You aren't one of those annoying optimists, are you, John Dalton?"

"I don't need to be an optimist. All it takes is knowing the people involved. Jess Everdine would no more let his own flesh and blood go down the road never to be heard from again than I would. He'll come around.''

J.D.'s opinion gave her heart a sharp pang. She had difficulty maintaining her smile. ''That's probably true with Bobby and Becky.''

''It'll be true with you, too, Zoe.''

Zoe shook her head and looked away as her smile faded. ''Please don't say that, John Dalton.'' She felt J.D.'s solemn scrutiny. His voice was thoughtful and low.

''You don't understand much about what blood relation means to some people, do you?''

She didn't need to think about her answer. ''I know what it means to me. I always believed it might have made a difference with Jason and Angela if I had been their natural child.'' She shrugged. ''I know what it will mean to me when I have children—if I do.'' Zoe stopped there. ''If'' had more to do with J.D. than she wanted him to guess.

J.D.'s voice was just as thoughtful and low as it had been, but it was somehow softer and quieter. ''What will it mean to you, Zoe?''

The emotion that overwhelmed her at his unexpected question made it difficult to speak. The surprising fact that she wanted to answer helped, and she looked at him in the dimness. ''It will mean that there's nothing I wouldn't do for that child.'' Her gaze shifted away and she tried to moderate the fierceness of her declaration. ''I had a lot of years to make vows about how I would raise a child, how I would make him or her, or—even better—them, feel secure and loved and wanted. I'd be careful not to spoil them too much, I'd hope—''

Zoe cut herself off, suddenly self-conscious. Lord, what would she know about raising a child? Given the

Sedgewicks' horrid example, her theories about raising children were based on what she'd fantasized about as a child, what she'd seen on the family-run ranches she'd lived on and what she'd read in books.

Her voice was quiet and a little choked as she subsided against his shoulder. "I can't talk about that anymore."

J.D.'s arms tightened. She took a quick breath and forced a lighter tone to change the subject. "Anyway, Bobby and Becky are great. They know about me now. I think someday—"

To her dismay, she couldn't put her hope for someday into words, either. It was a surprise to find she had a superstitious reluctance to jinx the possibilities by speaking them aloud. Besides, to her it sounded pitiable to declare any particular hope for the future where the kids were concerned after things had gone so terribly wrong with their father.

"I'm sorry. I don't mean to chatter on and on." She leaned away from J.D. to give him a small smile. "Like I said, I think I've worn out my welcome in this part of Texas. And, though I appreciate that you're trying to do me a favor by holding up the sale, I think it's best for everyone to get the papers signed right away."

Zoe couldn't maintain eye contact with the intensity in J.D.'s gaze and looked away. She made a small move to signal she meant to get off his lap, but his arm tightened. He reached up to turn her face.

"Right now, I don't much care for what's best for everyone else, Hollywood," he said as he made her look at him.

In the next instant his lips seized hers, the pressure of his big hand on the back of her head forcing her mouth hard against his. Zoe's initial surprise vanished, and she was suddenly kissing him back with a wild enthusiasm that took no account of tenderness or propriety.

This was what she'd craved, a rough male kiss to dominate her senses. A kiss and a taste so compelling and hard-driving that it made mush of every thought and reduced her to a mass of nerve endings and sensations. Zoe gave herself wholeheartedly, soaking in every electric tingle, not wanting to miss even a heartbeat of the sensual delight she wanted to remember forever.

Sometime in those fevered moments, J.D. worked open more than half the buttons on her blouse. His bold fingers edged beneath the lace of her bra to her breast, toying with its sensitive peak delicately, but with devastating expertise. She was so overwhelmed with sensation that she gasped for breath and clutched at him.

Her breathless "Make love to me, John Dalton," was little more than a mouthing of the words, but J.D. heard. She was dismayed when his fingers began to ease away. Her quick move to place her hand over his to keep it where it was thwarted his retreat by only a quick scattering of seconds.

Then, despite her clear signal, J.D. slipped his hand from beneath hers. That his kiss became more urgent was an apology of sorts—a kind of consolation prize, Zoe reckoned dizzily as frustration stormed through her.

Her frustration was so acute as the kiss began to mellow that she found herself on the verge of begging for more. She managed not to shame herself by actually doing so. When he finally moved his lips from hers and crushed her tightly against him, Zoe battled the sting of tears as the sensual whirlwind began to ebb.

Zoe realized then that she wasn't the only one trembling with desire and disappointment. J.D.'s big body was practically quaking with it.

But the fact that her passionate request had spoiled everything sent Zoe's heart into an inevitable plunge. The worst thing she could imagine—asking for love and being denied—was once again terribly routine for her. Her emotional jinx appeared to have already seized the high ground in sexual matters, and Zoe felt a new kind of hopelessness.

Suddenly restless, possessed of the unbearable need to escape, Zoe straightened, her face flushed with shame and useless effort as J.D. stubbornly kept her where she was. She was grateful the room was too dim for him to see the extent of her upset as she put everything she had into speaking.

"Does this mean you've reconsidered?" she asked, striving for a light, flirting tone, relieved that she'd managed it.

"I'm not going to take advantage of you, Zoe." J.D.'s low words were calm and resolute.

Zoe leaned toward him in the dimness and planted a quick kiss on his mouth. "I'd take advantage of you in a minute, John Dalton," she joked, but her heart was aching. J.D. would have been the first man she'd ever allowed that close. Not that anyone would believe Zoe Yahzoo had never lost her virginity, not when Jason and Angela's sexual exploits were frequent and modern morality so lax. She'd been offering J.D. Hayes a lot, but he didn't want it. The idea that she couldn't get close enough to him for even a quick fling was another hard punch to her wounded heart.

"Well, since that hot little kiss has fizzled for you already, I'd like to get on up to bed. I've had a hell of a day, John Dalton. I could use a good night's sleep.'' She felt his hold relax and she slid off his lap, wavering a moment when she came to her feet before she got her bearings in the dim room. J.D.'s big hand caught hers, delaying her new attempt to escape.

"That hot little kiss is going to play hell with my good night's sleep, Hollywood,'' he grumbled. "Just because I'm not going to take advantage of you tonight when you're stirred up about your family, doesn't mean there won't come a time when I'll take everything you've got.''

J.D.'s words were an iron-clad vow. That was Zoe's first impression. An instant later she took them as kind words from a man who, underneath his gruffness, was compassionate and generous.

And that made her feel pitiful and needy. Her light, "Another time then,'' carried a hint of melancholy she couldn't help. Zoe slowly pulled her hand from his and made her way around the sofa to the stairs. There'd never be another time and J.D. knew it. Zoe hated that she knew it, too.

Zoe tiredly prepared for bed and crawled beneath the covers, worn out, but unable to forget the very best of her time with J.D. that night.

For a tough, blunt Texan who spent his days working with dangerous, contrary animals in the brutal Texas heat, J.D. was an astonishingly gentle man. In spite of his sexual rejection of her, everything she'd sensed about him was somehow much deeper and wider and truer than she'd suspected.

How did you win a man like John Dalton? How did you make a place in the life of a man who was so secure in himself, so strong and self-sufficient? Zoe desperately took stock of the things she had to offer.

Money, property, celebrity connections, looks and an entertaining, never-met-a-stranger personality. The liabilities that came with the package included troubles with his foreman, the celebrity and notoriety of the Sedgewicks, Zoe's damaged upbringing and a history of eccentric pursuits that ran the gamut from wildly speculative stock investments to her role as a sought-after pseudo-star on the edges of the Sedgewicks' phenomenal success.

Hardly the traits a solid, down-to-earth man like John Dalton Hayes could tolerate in any woman for long.

Zoe had already come to the conclusion that she'd not actually lost anything she'd already had by coming to Texas to find her family. She'd never had much of a family with the Sedgewicks, she probably never would with the Everdines. The fact that she had hope for a future relationship with Bobby and Becky was actually a plus on the gains side of her personal ledger, something that should have made this whole traumatic trip to Texas worthwhile.

But J.D. had skewered her tally sheet of gains and losses. He'd scrawled his name across the top of a new sheet, his very existence altering her focus and redirecting her emotional goals. Despite her dismal assessment of the things she had to offer and her chances of winning J.D., Zoe wasn't surprised to realize that when the time came to put the final mark in one of the columns beneath his name, she still hoped with all her heart the mark would land in that wide, pristine space beneath the gains side.

*   *   *

"How are you, Zoe?" J.D.'s gentle question as she took her usual place across the breakfast table from him that next morning gave her worn heart a soft lift. The bright smile she gave him won a cautious half smile from him that deepened the creases on one lean cheek.

"Much better, thank you." Zoe glanced Carmelita's way. "What's for breakfast, *señora*? I'm starved."

"That is good," Carmelita nodded approvingly. "You will have steak and eggs and the shredded potatoes very brown as you like them, but I have also made your favorite."

Zoe's light brows shot up with delight. "I was hoping those were cinnamon rolls I smelled. I hope you made lots."

The rest of breakfast went as Zoe intended. She beat J.D. to the comic section of the Sunday paper and read it aloud to him between bites as he tried to read through the business section. She thoroughly enjoyed the leisurely Sunday morning meal, as usual, chiding J.D. for his early morning grumpiness and trying a mild flirtation or two. Despite her crushing disappointments, particularly the one with him the night before, she meant to make the most of as many more mornings and days and nights as she had left on Hayes.

The last thing she wanted was to leave Hayes like a whipped dog with its tail between its legs. Pride dictated she leave with as much dignity as she could summon. When it came time to load her things in the car, she wanted to be every bit the playfully flamboyant, tin-foil-shallow Zoe Yahzoo who'd arrived that first day.

CHAPTER TEN

JESS Everdine had spent another hellish night. Sunday had dawned too early for him. He was in too black a mood for church, though he imagined Sarah would have gently chastened him with the reminder that spending the morning in the Lord's house could fix that. He'd sent the kids off to Sunday School without him, his conscience nettled by their somber faces. That they both were upset and disappointed in their daddy was no secret.

Neither of his children could resist championing Zoe. They'd managed to force everything they knew about her on him, chronicling every minute they'd spent with her as well as making it clear that they meant to keep in touch with her. His small family was in an uproar, but it was nothing compared to the uproar in his own heart.

So, how did it happen, Mr. Everdine? Did you take one look at me and tell Sarah, 'Nope. Let's not keep this one'? Was my arrival not convenient for you, or did you get a good look at me and see some terrible flaw that didn't make me worth keeping?

Zoe's bitter words haunted him. The pain he'd seen in her eyes was still vivid in his memory.

It appears you were something of a prophet. Those last words had hammered home the strong impression that for all Zoe's remarkable good looks and wealth, there was something wrong about the way she saw herself.

He regretted his words to her when she'd first tried to talk to her. *Look Zoe, or Spenser, whoever you feel like being today…* If Zoe was half as insecure about herself as he now feared, those words must have devastated her.

Jess knew he was a prideful, stubborn man. He hadn't realized his capacity for cruelty.

Sometime during his long, restless night, the letter Spenser Sedgewick had written five years ago had ceased to matter. She'd been given away at birth. If she'd thought her mama and daddy hadn't wanted her as an infant when she'd needed them most, then she'd probably resented that they'd suddenly decided to barge in on her rich Hollywood life when she was grown. Jess regretted that he hadn't understood that. He regretted being so harsh.

Jess bent his head and dug his finger and thumb into the corners of his eyes as he tried to contain the powerful emotions that churned in his gut.

Zoe Yahzoo was his child, his and Sarah's. The cock-eyed way she'd tried to enter their lives no longer mattered, either. The fact that she'd finally tried made all the difference. It was past time to let her know.

Zoe's morning ride was soothing. Because the routine on Sunday was quite lax on Hayes compared to the rest of the week, she'd packed her saddlebags and gone off on Brute. This might be her last chance to have the run of Hayes and enjoy it, so she meant to make the most of the opportunity.

J.D. was in his office bringing his paperwork up to date, so to avoid making herself a total pest, Zoe had elected to go riding. She still meant to seize every minute with him she could, but later, after he was finished.

The day promised to be a hot one, so she rode Brute on a route that would parallel one of the creeks. By the time the sun got high enough to get really hot, she and

Brute could return to the headquarters, making full use of the shade from the long line of cottonwoods along the creek bank.

Zoe needed the peaceful ride. She hoped it would restore her in some way, heal her from all the other needs that seemed doomed to be forever thwarted. She was already feeling better. Thinking about Sarah still pained her, but the knowledge that there was nothing she could do about her birth mother now dampened a bit of the restlessness in her. Sarah must have wanted her, even if she had given her up. Zoe might never know the exact reason, but the idea that Sarah had searched for her consoled her in some mysterious way. She didn't let herself think about Jess. There were still some things too distressing to think about.

She drew Brute to a halt on a ridge that overlooked the creek and gave her a panoramic view of the wide, empty range land that surrounded her. The wind was blowing hot, but strong enough to relieve the bright heat of the sun.

She'd finally looked her fill at the vast expanse before her, exhilarated by the mammoth size and distance, awed by its overwhelming size. She turned Brute toward the creek before she saw the rider who waited on the opposite bank below.

Zoe's father was a big man. He sat his horse easily, confidently, and she recognized him instantly. The impression Zoe got—that he had sought her out—gave her as much hope as terror. It was too late to pretend she didn't see him.

The impatient toss of Brute's head made her aware that she'd pulled back on the reins. The bay must have picked up her sudden tension, because he pranced restlessly and worked at the bit as he waited for her to signal her next command.

She couldn't move, and didn't know if she was dismayed or relieved when Jess made it for her. His lanky buckskin stepped forward, walking sedately through the creek as he crossed to Zoe's side. The buckskin continued up the gentle slope toward her, his unhurried pace giving her emotions time to crank to full throttle. She was certain she'd faint by the time Jess eased back on the reins to halt his horse beside Brute.

"You weren't given up because there was anything wrong with you, Zoe." Jess's low words were rough, but the harshness she expected to see on his face was remarkably absent. "The wrong was with your daddy and mama. It's a story you need to hear. If you want."

Zoe stared at her father. There was a tenderness about him that caught her off guard. She couldn't mistake the weary pain in his eyes, or the tiny glint of hope and anxiety she saw there.

She dug up a panicked dose of Zoe sparkle to mask the dread that persisted. "Will this be a new version of 'Go away, kid, ya bother me'?" The quirky little smile she gave to cover her distress trembled despite her best effort.

The choked breath Jess took in startled her, but the thick tears that deepened the blue of his eyes did not. "No, baby." He reached over a bit awkwardly to touch her hand. "Not again, not ever."

Zoe couldn't help that she turned her hand over and gripped his. She was so overwhelmed she couldn't speak.

"Your daddy has a history of stupidity when it comes to recognizing the best things that come along in his life. The good Lord has always had to work a little overtime to bring me around to another chance." Jess appeared

overcome for those next seconds before he could go on.
''I'm hoping He's gonna give me that second chance one
more time.''

The tears that tumbled over Zoe's lashes to splash down
her cheeks gave Jess the only answer she was capable of.

Jess Everdine and Sarah McCauley had been sweethearts
since the seventh grade. Sarah dreamed of a wedding after
high school graduation, a home and children. Jess had
rodeo fever. He'd wanted the wedding, the home and the
children, but later, after he'd won the money to finance
the life he'd wanted to give Sarah. As the son of a poor
rancher, he'd wanted more for Sarah than his father had
been able to give his mother. He'd also wanted the thrill
and cowboy glory that went with being a champion bronc
rider.

By their senior year of high school, he'd competed locally and won enough times to show promise. The itin-
erant life-style that would enable him to travel and see
the country greatly appealed to a boy who'd grown up
with the hardscrabble drudgery of working a broken-down
spread with a father who'd grown old and sick before his
time. Plagued by hard luck, an unreliable water source
and enough bad markets and poor health to break his
spirit, Sam Everdine had encouraged Jess's rodeo ambitions.

Sarah had been born into a prosperous ranch family.
She'd wanted Jess to work for her father. They could have
the old homestead house, and when her parents passed on,
he could work for her older brother. Jess's pride wouldn't
allow him to marry into money and live as a hired hand
to his rich inlaws.

They'd finally come to an outright argument the day

after graduation. Sarah declared that she never wanted to see him again. He'd been happy to oblige her.

She'd change her mind when he won the buckle and the money, he'd reasoned. She'd be glad later when he could buy them a nice place of their own.

Jess didn't call her at all the first year he was away. When he finally did, it had been Independence Day more than a year later. But Sarah had been cool on the phone, sounding more distant than the eight hundred miles that had separated them. She didn't take his calls after that.

Meanwhile, he won the National Finals in bronc riding. He'd won the buckle and the prize money he'd wanted, but he'd given up on Sarah. And, his daddy had been dying. The cost of keeping the ranch going for his mother and paying for the experimental cancer treatments the insurance wouldn't cover ate away at his winnings. In the end, his father succumbed and their debt-ridden ranch had to be sold. The money they cleared from the sale and what was left of Jess's winnings went to buy his mother a nice house in town and provide her with a modest nest egg.

He'd returned to the rodeo circuit for another year, but never made it to the national finals again. He finally burned out on rodeo. He came back to Texas, but only as far as the next county north of where he'd grown up. He wasn't broke, but with only a few thousand dollars in the bank, he had nowhere near what he'd need to buy a place of his own.

He'd hired on as foreman on a midsize ranch. He'd worked there several months by the time he'd gone to a Saturday night dance. To his surprise, Sarah McCauley had been there with some friends. Still unmarried and unable to completely ignore him, she'd given in to his request to dance. He promptly dominated her time on the dance floor.

Jess had thought of her nearly every day of the five years since their breakup, but had long ago given up on the idea of a second chance with her. But now she was at last in his arms, and the old feelings came back for them both. He'd not wanted to squander the unexpected opportunity to win her back. At least as a ranch foreman, he had something to offer. It was less than what he'd wanted to give her, but it would be a decent life, and they could raise a family.

To his dismay, his quick proposal was met with a sad little refusal from Sarah. That's when he'd learned about the baby she'd given up—his baby. She'd figured he'd never forgive her for not being able to withstand her family and that the news would make him change his mind about wanting to marry her.

Jess had been torn apart by the story, further humbled by the fact that he'd left Sarah pregnant and alone while he'd pursued his selfish dream of rodeo glory. Knowing their firstborn daughter was long gone, they'd married and had two more children. They'd saved money over the years so they'd be ready to hire a good private investigator to find her when she turned eighteen.

As Becky had told Zoe, once they found her and tried to make contact, the letter they'd received for their efforts had broken their hearts. Sarah had initially suffered a hard bout of depression. But, Jess was careful to emphasize to Zoe, the year before the car accident that had taken Sarah's life, her sunny disposition had reappeared. Her optimism about one day hearing from Spenser when she had children of her own and experienced motherhood for herself had been as strong as her vastly restored good spirits. There'd been no more nightmares that last year of her life, no more tears. Sarah had found peace, and Jess had found a measure of peace himself.

Until he realized Spenser Sedgewick had come to Texas with a new name....

''John Dalton! Are you here?'' Zoe's excited call as she entered the kitchen from the back porch went unanswered. ''J.D.?''

She quickly hung up her hat and started for his office. The late afternoon silence of the big house didn't bother her at first. Carmelita spent most Sundays with her family, so she hadn't expected her to be around.

The profound happiness Zoe felt was about to burst out of her chest, but a bit of it ebbed when she reached the den and saw J.D. wasn't there. A hurried trip upstairs told her he wasn't in the house at all. Undaunted, she rushed back out through the kitchen and hurried to the long garage. J.D.'s pickup was gone.

Zoe went back to the house feeling a little deflated. J.D. had predicted that Jess wouldn't let her go down the road never to be heard from again. He'd been right and she was eager to tell him so. She stepped into the kitchen and closed the door, then sagged against it, delirious with happiness.

Jess had answered the questions she'd carried for a lifetime. Knowing how she'd been given up and why had made a deep impression on her. The ill-defined perceptions she'd held about herself her whole life had shifted somehow and refocused. She hadn't been flawed or unlovable; she'd not been given up because Sarah and Jess hadn't wanted her. For the first time in her life, she began to feel settled inside, rooted, real.

She'd been the product of young love that had lost its way, but never quite died. Jess and Sarah's story had been sad, tragic in parts, but underlain by the kind of enduring love and tenderness Zoe greatly envied.

And hoped to have with J.D.

Zoe felt a new rush of happiness and thrust herself from the door to cross the kitchen and head upstairs for a quick shower. Perhaps it was just as well that she'd have some time alone. Once she and Jess had talked things out and gone to his house for lunch, Bobby and Becky were back from church. Becky had been putting the finishing touches on the meal.

After their happy reunion, they'd eaten, then Jess brought out the family photo albums. Zoe's head was still spinning from the number of people she'd seen in the albums. Though Jess was an only child, his family of aunts, uncles and cousins was enormous. Zoe had no idea how she'd ever figure out who was who and how they were all related, but Jess promised she'd have a dandy chance to make a start when she attended the Everdine family reunion planned for early August.

Zoe Yahzoo was on top of the world.

J.D. Hayes had rarely experienced true misery. Even Raylene's dramatic exit from his life, their pitched court battle and the partial loss of Hayes in the divorce hadn't produced this boot-dragging, heart-heavy ache.

But now that Zoe's fun and sparkle had been centered almost exclusively at the Everdine's house these past three days, J.D. was feeling a letdown he'd never felt before. The lion's share of her time was now spent with her father, sister and brother. Jess's mother, Agnes, had come over from Keswick two days ago to meet her long-lost grandchild, further dominating Zoe's attention.

J.D. was happy for Zoe. The brief time they did spend together over breakfast and the few minutes they had when she came back to the house late in the evenings just before bed, had shown him clearly that what he'd sensed about Zoe before had changed.

Zoe was no longer so melancholy and broken inside. She seemed surer about herself somehow, less fragile. She still smiled her megawatt smiles, she still sparkled and she was the same fun, flirtatious Zoe he'd found so irresistible. But the sparkle and fun now went deeper than her carefully projected surface image. Zoe was truly becoming the smile-spangled, irrepressible imp she'd pretended to be, and J.D. was more powerfully taken with her than ever.

He didn't know what he'd do once the papers were signed and she finally went back to California. He wasn't sure he could stand knowing his future connection with her would be solely through the Everdines. Besides, Jess was interested in a small, successful ranch over in the next county that would come on the market by spring. If Jess bought it as he planned, J.D.'s hope of seeing Zoe when she came to visit her family would be much less certain.

J.D. had rarely experienced true misery, but the notion that Zoe had lost interest in him was one of the sharpest disappointments of his life. The knowledge that she would take a huge hunk of his heart with her when she packed up her sparkle and fun and left Texas, made him feel every bit the grim, humorless, *lonely* man he'd been before she'd shown up and waved her magic wand.

He had no idea how to reclaim her attention and see if

he could tell whether all her past flirtations meant anything now. He wasn't sure he should even try.

Zoe received a package on Thursday. It had been lying on the table by the front door when she'd come in and she'd noticed that it was addressed to her. The weight and shape she felt through the padded mailer sent her high spirits down several notches as she inspected it for a return address.

Glad that Carmelita was in the kitchen preparing supper and hadn't heard her come in, Zoe hurried upstairs for privacy. She closed the door to her room and crossed to the bed, her knees suddenly shaky as she sat down on the edge of the mattress.

She'd all but forgotten the biography. The past few days had been the most wonderful of her life. Her only regret was that she'd not spent much time with J.D. and she missed him terribly. She'd come back before supper today to begin to remedy that, but the package delayed her plan.

Zoe's hands shook as she dug her short nails under the flap and pulled it open. She took a deep breath, slipped her fingers in to grip the edge of the hardcover book, then pulled it out. Zoe didn't let herself look at the book jacket until she checked to see if there was a letter in the mailer. When she didn't find one, or any other indication of what had sent it, she set the mailer aside.

The Sedgewicks Offstage: Behind the Lights and the Legend by Dillon Casey. The words flashed up from raised gold-foil lettering against a shiny-black book jacket.

She stared down at the dreaded tell-all book. Suddenly filled with the anxiety that had been so blessedly absent these past days, she forced herself to open it. Beginning with the first page, she began to scan for the words Becky, Bobby, Everdine, Hayes Ranch or Texas.

Somewhere in those first pages, the other words Dillon Casey had written began to penetrate. Gripped by a terrible combination of curiosity and mortification, Zoe went back to the first page, unable to keep from reading every word.

She never heard J.D. come in downstairs, was too absorbed to remember to let anyone know she was in the house or to go down to supper. As she worked off her boots and scooted up to sit on the bed with her pillows wedged between her back and the brass scrollwork of the headboard, she kept reading.

It was hours before she finished, hours before she was absolutely certain of everything Casey had put into print about Bobby and Becky. That he'd changed their names to Danny and Sherry Anderson was as shocking a surprise as the fact that he'd named the state they lived in as Montana instead of Texas.

The horrors she'd anticipated him writing about the Sedgewicks were worse than she'd imagined. That Casey had found out about the letter Jess and Sarah had written her and had printed a copy of the cruel response was another stunner. He'd named Angela as the one who'd written it and emphasized that her malicious interference had prevented Zoe from meeting her biological mother while she was still alive.

The fact that he'd guessed that Spenser's summers of migrating from one dude ranch to another had been a secret, desperate search to find her real mother caused Zoe the only real pang of embarrassment. He'd got nearly everything he'd disclosed about her upbringing and her relationship with her adoptive parents right. What astonished her was that he'd done so in such a way that would make the reader strongly sympathetic to Spenser/Zoe.

She felt a little better about it, particularly since he'd not made her sound too pitiful. And if changing the kids' names and location and giving her a fair portrayal in his book hadn't been enough, Dillon Casey had gone easy on any predictions of doom and gloom for her future.

Zoe realized her face was wet when she finally set the book aside. The unexpected pity she felt for Jason and Angela, however much they might deserve having the details of their lives so brutally exposed, kept her in her room until well past time to make it down to the cook house for ice cream.

She considered calling the Sedgewicks to express some sort of sympathy for the chaos and upset the book would cause them. She gave up the idea when she realized that anything she said to them now on the subject would provoke a bitter accusation of blame. A simple, vague note that said something along the lines of "I hope you are well and weathering it all with your usual aplomb" would be sufficient.

Zoe took a few moments to call Jess on the phone extension in her room. He was relieved that Casey had changed the kids names to throw off the media. She elected to wait to tell him that Casey had named Angela as the author of the cruel letter. Jess already believed she hadn't written it herself. The whole subject was now unimportant to him.

Besides, everything was going wonderfully for them all. *Almost* everything, Zoe amended as she glanced at the clock on her bedside table and realized how late it was.

She wouldn't get much of a start on making up for lost time with J.D. tonight.

She did need to let him know she was in the house, however, and got up to do so. She'd opened her door to step into the hall when she heard him come up the stairs.

"Hey there, J.D.," she called to him. He glanced her way, his harsh expression softening.

"Hey there, yourself, Zoe. Things going well for you?" The tired half smile he gave her as he walked down the hall toward her did great things for the long cheek creases she liked so much.

Zoe gave him a smile. "Very well, J.D. How about you?"

"Good enough."

She suddenly wanted to touch him, to somehow banish the weariness she sensed about him. But J.D. reached up to tug gently on a bright curl beside her cheek and went on walking down the long hall.

Her soft, "Good night, John Dalton," was answered with a low, "'Night, Hollywood," before J.D. stepped into his room.

CHAPTER ELEVEN

"THE lawyers have the papers ready to sign," J.D. told her that next morning at breakfast. "Any time you're ready."

Zoe frowned at the information and finished chewing her bite of steak. His low, "If you still want to go through with it," made her hurry.

"I certainly do want to go through with it, John Dalton," she hastily assured him. "Hayes is your inheritance. It's not right that anyone but your children should have a piece of it. Let's sign today. You name the time."

That Zoe was still in an almighty hurry to sell was clear to J.D. He didn't want to examine too closely the disappointment he felt. Zoe gave him a sparkling look and one of her imp smiles.

"So, how many children do you plan to pass Hayes on to, John Dalton?"

He grunted and took a last bite of steak so he wouldn't have to answer that. Zoe chattered right on.

"I hope you don't do the usual and only consider leaving it for your firstborn son to run. You might have a daughter or two who'd do a dandy job of it."

J.D. grunted again, but Zoe barely hesitated.

"You should have at least one daughter who can ride and rope and run the place. Send all your kids to college for degrees in agriculture." She aimed her fork at him. "But make sure you raise them to keep as many of the old ways as possible. Stay traditional. No helicopters, motorcycles or feedlots. Send at least one child to law school so there can be a potential state legislator, or maybe even a congressman or U.S. senator in the family to influence legislation that benefits ranching interests.''

She took a last bite of breakfast and watched J.D.'s grumpy expression darken.

''You've got my kids raised, planned their college, and mapped out their careers before five-thirty in the morning, Hollywood,'' he groused.

Zoe gave him a chiding smile. ''You're what? Thirty-four?'' She shook her head and gave a wave of her fork. ''You have a *lot*—'' she rounded her eyes for emphasis ''—of time to make up for, John Dalton. You need to make some ambitious plans and dedicate yourself to getting a few of them going. Life's not all sweat and hard work.''

Zoe sprang up from her chair and flitted away from the table before he could recover. By then, she was at the sink filling her thermos and complimenting Carmelita on another breakfast ''well done.'' Carmelita was tittering over what she'd heard of their exchange. Zoe turned back to him and slung her saddlebags over her shoulder. Her light brows crinkled as she took obvious note of the fact that he still sat at the table.

''I thought you were done eating, J.D. Come on, shake a leg. Vacation's over for the summer.'' With that, she was at the door, had her hat on and was reaching for the doorknob. She practically vanished, leaving J.D. halfway out of his chair, a heartfelt snarl of frustration rising from his chest.

That Carmelita stood at the sink grinning at him, gave J.D. the distinct feeling that he was the butt of some female joke he couldn't begin to get.

He got his hat and charged out the back before he realized he was all but running to catch up.

Zoe rushed them both along so fast with her energetic enthusiasm for anything to do with ranch work that she fairly wore J.D. out. She fidgeted her way through his meeting with the hands to discuss what needed to be done that day and who would do it. She'd gone with him to check cattle, doctor a few, and herd three yearlings who'd got tangled in barbed wire to the headquarters for stitches and antibiotics. She helped him repair the section of fence that had caused the injuries, checked three of the windmills, and insisted they spray for wasps under the eaves of one of the smaller barns later. "To thwart temptation," she'd declared, jerking a thumb in the direction of the Everdine house to indicate it was Bobby's temptation she meant to thwart.

They were riding back to the house for the noon meal when Zoe told him about receiving a copy of the biography in the mail the day before. When she finished giving him a brief rundown, she looked over at him.

"On the whole, it's a pretty brutal book, but in addition to leaving the kids' names out, Casey was much nicer to me than I expected."

J.D. appeared to be thinking that over. Irritation darkened his features. "Nicer?"

"Well, sure, J.D. He didn't once mention the words self-destruct, overdose, or the Betty Ford Center," she joked.

J.D.'s gaze shot to hers. He saw her grin and frowned mightily. "Hellfire, Hollywood, take the sneaky viper to lunch. What the hell kind of nice is that? He invaded your privacy, tormented you with worry about the kids, and wrote things about your personal life without your per mission. That book'll have the media on you like fuzz on a peach. But, just because he didn't mention suicide or the Betty Ford Center, you think he treated you nice?'' J.D. gave a harsh bark of laughter.

''We're talking comparatively nice here, J.D.,'' she insisted. ''Compared to what he could have written—more in the form of speculation about how I'll end up rather than anything particularly scandalous, I'll have you know—Casey managed to stick fairly close to the facts and not make me sound like a pitiful neurotic. I've handled the media lots of times. Now that they won't be targeting the kids, I won't worry much until I see if anyone shows up here.''

J.D. faced forward and shook his head. ''Are you ever going to be able to live without some author or reporter digging into your private life and trying to make money on a story about you?''

His dark gaze swung back to hers and Zoe was rocked by the grimness she saw there. But then, she'd known J.D. wasn't the type to tolerate notoriety in a potential mate.

''I don't need to have media attention to be happy, John Dalton. But because of Jason and Angela, there will always be that potential.'' She shrugged and looked ahead of them to the headquarters in the distance. ''I'll just have to hope it doesn't get out of hand before people lose interest.''

J.D. was silent for a time, and Zoe was, too. His silence worried her, so she decided to divert them both.

''So, have you thought about your plan?''

J.D. glanced her way. ''What plan is that?''

Zoe gave him a stern look and scolded, ''No wonder you're thirty-four and have no heirs to Hayes, John

Dalton. I'm talking about your plan to find a wife and get an heir going.''

J.D. gave a cranky sigh, but Zoe grinned mischievously. ''I've heard men can still father children when they're in their seventies or eighties.''

J.D.'s prickly ''Oh you have?'' made her grin widen.

''But other than serving themselves a last bit of male vanity, what's the point—aside from proving it's possible?'' She gave a wave of her hand as she expanded on the subject with relish.

''The old geezer dies before the kid's out of diapers, and the kid's mom either raises him alone or hopes to find a new husband to help her raise the child. A waste—not to mention that in your case, it would also be a matter of someone other than a Hayes in charge of running the Hayes Ranch. And how would you know if your young wife would make a good choice with another husband? He might turn out to be a gold digger or a con man who'd pick Hayes clean, run it into the ground, or sell it to someone who'd divide it up. He'd abandon your wife, take the money, and your child would end up without a penny to his name, living in a big city somewhere in a cheap apartment, without a clue about what you'd meant him to have or the history behind the Hayes name.''

Zoe reached over and gripped his thick wrist to give him an urgent shake. ''Daylight's burnin', partner.''

J.D.'s formidable expression cracked and the glint of reluctant humor in his dark eyes delighted her.

''Bull.'' His one-word opinion made Zoe giggle and pull her hand away.

''So don't listen to me, John Dalton. By the time this horrid little scenario plays itself out, we'll both be planted somewhere, and we'll never know.''

With that, Zoe touched a heel to Brute. The bay moved into an easy canter that carried them ahead of J.D.'s sorrel. J.D. didn't rush to catch up, letting her reach the stable far ahead of him.

It was two o'clock by the time they got to town for their appointment at the lawyer's office. They'd both cleaned up and changed their clothes. J.D. had settled on a white shirt and a newer pair of jeans, but Zoe had clearly dressed to express a bit of her flamboyant taste.

J.D. had seen the huge, silver belt buckle and black dress Stetson the day she'd arrived at Hayes, but the lively, multicolored paisley blouse and pink jeans she wore with them was a complete surprise. The red western boots she had on drew out the reds in the blouse and matched her red silk neckerchief. And yet Zoe looked chic, refined, and every bit a socialite playing cowgirl dress-up. He had a hard time keeping his eyes off her.

He didn't have a prayer. Common sense had been pounding him with that prediction for hours now. As he pulled into a parking space and switched off the engine, J.D. felt his mood sour. He'd wanted to get close to Zoe that whole day. He'd wanted to see if he could engineer something that would put them both in a position to follow up on that kiss the other night on the sofa. But Zoe, full of fun and teasing and a dozen little hit-and-run touches, had kept a careful distance.

J.D. got out of the car and walked around it to open her door for her. As she stepped out, he closed the door. He took her elbow, doing his best to make the move look casual rather than the necessity to touch her it suddenly was. When she pulled her arm from his gentle grip to slip her hand through the crook of his arm in a subtly posses-sive way, his heart was given another nudge.

Just walking next to Zoe made him feel awkward and oversize, hopelessly earthbound. Zoe didn't just walk, he noted for the umpteenth time. She floated, skipped and danced along, like a golden good fairy with gossamer wings, magic slippers and a shiny silver wand to grant wishes to the deserving. J.D. no longer objected to the whimsical notions that Zoe seemed to inspire. She was both the genuine article and a fake; a bright hunk of gold covered with sparkling pyrite. In most ways, she was a gleaming enigma to him and might always be. Ethereal, illusive, rare. Zoe Yahzoo was too special for a rough country man like him, too delicate for his harsh, blunt ways.

But he wanted her. During the short time she'd been on Hayes—perhaps from that very first day he'd met her at the fence when she'd given him that brazen smack on the knee—he'd become addicted to the fairy dust she'd sprinkled over his harsh, humorless life. He'd not realized how much he'd let himself settle for sweat, hard work and the subtle bleakness of solitude. Until Zoe.

But happily-ever-after with Zoe was a chancy prospect. It wasn't her background or celebrity or anything about her that made it so. It was him. He was a no-fuss, no-frills, square-toed man—well on his way to fossilhood, if Zoe's teasing that day was any indication. And even J.D. knew the good fairy never mated with the troll. As pow-erful as her magic was, Zoe would never turn him into a handsome prince with elegant manners, or refine him enough to fit easily into the high society part of her life.

As J.D. reached ahead of them and opened the office door, Zoe glanced up at him, her neon eyes as bright and deep as he'd ever seen them. Her megawatt smile warmed him like a shaft of hot sunlight. She didn't seem to see he was a troll. Or that he was troll enough to hope she wouldn't for a long time to come.

Zoe did her best to appear as sunny as usual. It upset her more than she wanted anyone to guess that selling her one third of Hayes back to J.D. would cut an important tie between them.

Lord, she didn't want to leave Hayes; she didn't care if she ever left Texas or set foot in California again. Yet despite making up for lost time with her family, she couldn't hang around indefinitely. Now that she would no longer be J.D.'s co-owner, she wasn't comfortable taking up space in his home as a mere houseguest.

Perhaps she'd overdone it that day, needling him about marriage and heirs to Hayes. It had been all she could do to keep from proposing marriage herself, but in the end, she'd chickened out. She would have been devastated if he'd refused her.

And now she regretted pushing him to consider marriage at all. She couldn't bear the idea that she might have got him thinking strongly about it, only to leave Texas and find out later that he'd taken her advice and married someone else.

Zoe managed to cover her glum thoughts well behind her smiles to the receptionist, then to J.D.'s lawyer, Mr. Blake. Her personal lawyer was already waiting on the phone line by the time they were seated in the inner office. Mr. Blake switched the call from California onto the speaker phone, and once the pleasantries were out of the way, he started passing them the first of the papers they were to sign.

J.D. began to scan the top page of the papers, but Zoe addressed a question to her attorney. "Bianca, do you have any ideas about who might have sent me a copy of the bio? There was no letter with it and no return address. Oh—and you can speak freely, unless it's something awful."

"I certainly do know, Zoe. I got a call from Mr. Casey not more than a half hour ago on that very subject. It came from him, and you should be getting a letter." Bianca gave a knowing chuckle. "It sounded to me as if he has a crush on you. He'll probably mention lunch. He wanted me to convey his offer to do a book on you, but only with your permission. Or so he claimed."

J.D. made a sound that was little more than a snarl.

Bianca heard. "What was that? You aren't in a barn, are you?"

Zoe laughed at her attorney's appalled tone. "No, Bianca. That was my soon-to-be-former co-owner, Mr. Hayes. He's quite formidable and opinionated, and I'm…quite taken with him," she finished quickly. She'd not been able to resist getting that in before she changed the subject. "Are these papers safe to sign?"

"Of course, but you need to read them through anyway," Bianca counseled, and Zoe made herself do so. The room went silent for several minutes. As she began signing her share of paperwork, Zoe was aware that J.D. was still only flipping through his own. By the time she finished signing, J.D. had stopped reading and was simply watching her. The intensity of his dark gaze suddenly made her breathless.

Her soft, "Is something wrong?" made him glance at his lawyer.

"Give us a minute, Blake," he said gruffly. The attor

ney looked surprised, but he spoke a quick, "Hayes wants a minute alone with your client," to Bianca before he pressed the button that would take the call off the speaker phone. He got up and exited the room.

J.D.'s dark gaze pierced hers and Zoe had to resist the strong urge to glance away. He looked every bit as formidable as she'd told Bianca a few minutes ago.

"Are you aware that you have a pretty scary look on your face, John Dalton?" she asked softly. The restlessness she felt made her get up to place her sheaf of papers on the big desk before she turned back to J.D. and sat on its front edge.

J.D.'s gaze had followed her every move, but now it took a slow journey from her eyes to the toes of her red boots, which were now just a hand span from the toes of his big black ones. Zoe suppressed a tingle when his dark eyes made an unhurried return trip to fix on hers.

"What were you getting at this morning, Hollywood?"

J.D.'s utter seriousness was intimidating. Her soft voice was a little squeaky as she asked, "You mean about your plan?"

When he didn't shake his head to that, she answered with a stiff little wave of her hand. "Oh, I was doing the usual, John Dalton." His gaze was relentless, prompting her to be more candid than she had the courage to be.

"Actually, I was teasing you, but…" she hesitated, "I think you know me well enough by now to know I sometimes have a bit of a hidden agenda when I do that."

J.D.'s hard expression eased slightly. "What do you suppose became of that hot little kiss the other night?"

Zoe's heart shot into a wild, tripping rhythm as she watched him slowly come to his feet to tower over her. He tossed his papers to her empty chair.

"It seemed to fizzle pretty quick, J.D.," she said, a half smile sneaking over her lips as he frowned. "For you it seemed to." She let her smile widen. J.D. smiled then, too, but it was faintly predatory.

"How about for you?" he questioned next. Zoe slowly eased off the desk and came to her feet.

"It was...pretty good," she admitted with playful reluctance. "Of course, now that I'm starting to remember a bit more of it, I seem to recall that it had a kind of a..." She paused, then snapped her fingers a couple of times as if trying to think of the right words. She brightened, then pointed up at him to declare, "A legendary, comes-along-once-in-a-lifetime sort of feel to it." She grinned impishly. "But I'd have to have another one like it to tell for sure. You know, something a bit more up to date to compare it to."

Her breath caught when he stepped toe-to-toe with her. It made her dizzy to look up so far and she automatically inched backward. J.D. moved with her until she was backed against the desk.

"Then let's do a comparison." J.D. swept her up so swiftly and kissed her that Zoe's smile was more squashed curve than pucker. Her arms came up and lashed around his neck as her red boots dangled well above the black shine of his. Zoe gave back every bit as good as she got, somehow managing to be both the conqueror and the vanquished as J.D. urged, demanded and coaxed her to a wild frenzy of sensation and profound emotion. He didn't ease his lips from hers until they were both struggling for breath.

Zoe pressed a few small kisses to the long creases on his cheek. She got out a breathless, "Have you...made any plans yet, John Dalton?"

"As a matter of fact," he rumbled, but his mouth found hers and he kissed her again until they needed to breathe.

"I'm in love with you, Zoe Yahzoo," he whispered hoarsely as he kept her crushed against him. His dark gaze blazed into hers. He brought up a trembling hand and ran a knuckle down her flushed cheek. "Stay with me, baby, please. Be my wife and have children with me."

Zoe stared into his harsh face. The raw earnestness she saw on his proud, rugged features made her eyes sting. His dark eyes were gentle, and the contrast between his innate toughness and his equally impressive tenderness made her heart burst with profound affection. She pulled her arm from around his neck and placed her small palm on his hard jaw.

"I love you forever, John Dalton, but do you mean it? Are you sure?" Her eyes were almost impossible to keep clear of tears. She placed a finger over his lips to keep him silent. The insecurities she'd struggled with her whole life were making themselves felt, and she couldn't ignore them.

"I can't change who I am, and I don't think I can change very many of the things that come with that. There will always be the potential for media attention that you might not appreciate. I will always be connected somehow to Hollywood. Wouldn't all that bother you?" She slipped her finger from his lips.

J.D. opened his mouth to speak, but Zoe hastily put her finger back on his lips as other thoughts occurred to her. They tumbled out on a swift torrent of nervousness.

"I'm kinda flighty, John Dalton. I don't always go about things the way other people might, and I have some character flaws. Besides which, I'm headstrong, I'm used to doing what I please, and I'm way too silly sometimes.

In spite of what Casey didn't write in his book, I have an occasional neurotic moment that might make you crazy, but…''

Her voice lowered to a shaky whisper. "I love you dearly, John Dalton. I love it that you're tough, but you're always gentle with me. I love it that you have integrity and strong ideas and that you're down-to-earth. I love it that you're blunt, that you aren't afraid to sweat and swear and act the way you feel and say exactly what you mean. I love you forever and I want to have at least six of your heirs—'' She tapped her finger on his lips as she switched the subject back. "But you've got to think seriously about what you're getting into with me."

For all her attempts to let J.D. know exactly what he was getting, Zoe prayed he wouldn't think about any of her warnings too seriously.

"And then there's Jason and Angela," she added, and rolled her eyes. She didn't want to elaborate on them at all. Besides, she doubted they'd trifle with J.D. once they met him. He was probably one of the few people she'd ever known who was tough enough to blow them off like dandelion fuzz.

Zoe moved her finger, her worried little "Okay, that's it," was followed by a small smile that trembled.

J.D. was watching her face, his dark eyes probing hers. "That's it?" he asked tersely.

Zoe nodded and took a quick breath. "As much as I can think of while I'm rattled."

J.D. grinned, the suddenness of it startling her. "*I'm* naming our kids."

Zoe's brow crinkled in a faint frown that was pure play-acting as she felt love surge in her heart. "Oh, you are?

You think John Dalton, Jr., Nick, Victoria, Julia, Henry, Flip and Gomer are too bizarre for Hayes kids?''

His deep rumbling chuckle shook them both. "No J.D., Jr. I won't have any son of mine nicknamed Junior. Henry is a middle name, Flip and Gomer are for horses. I love you, Zoe. Will you be my wife?''

Zoe couldn't help the happy tears that shot down her cheeks as she gave him a huge smile. "I'll always love you, J.D., with all my heart, and I'll be your wife." She hugged him tightly as she struggled to get control over her jubilant emotions. When she finally did, she kissed him, doing her best to express a part of the love she felt for him. It was a while before she reluctantly broke off the kiss and gave him a teary smile.

"Your Mr. Blake probably won't appreciate that we took over his office and left him waiting so long. Bianca hates being left on hold.''

"They're getting paid for their time, Hollywood. They can wait," he said gruffly.

"Well, I don't think I can, J.D. Let's get these papers signed and find the place where they hand out marriage licenses. I want to get my ZY brand on your hide before you start having second thoughts.''

J.D. chuckled and shook his head. "There won't be any second thoughts, Zoe, not for me. And I'm not going to sign any of Blake's papers.''

"Why not?" Zoe had already signed hers. Had J.D. seen something in his copies that he didn't like or wanted to have changed?

"Because I like having a partner, Hollywood. I like having *you* for a partner. We can both pass Hayes on to our kids when the time comes.''

Zoe brought a hand to his lean cheek, overcome again with emotion. "I know how much Hayes means to you."

He nodded. "So maybe you have a better idea of what you mean to me, Zoe. Let's get out of here. We can be married the minute it's legal, unless you'd like to wait for a big wedding."

"Any wedding at Hayes will be a big wedding, J.D.," Zoe declared. "Carmelita, Coley and Gus—everyone will have to come. And I have a family that will be there, and a father to give me away." The reminder sent a few more happy tears skittering down her cheeks. "We can have the ceremony on the front porch. I'll get a really good photographer, I can get a caterer here in three days so Carmelita and Coley can relax—I've even got a really old white wedding gown I bought at a costume auction a year ago, I—"

J.D. halted the excited torrent with a kiss. When he finally released her and set her gently on her feet, Zoe swayed in weak-kneed happiness. In moments, he'd swept her from the office, tossed his lawyer a brusque, "Deal's off," and hustled her out the front door of the law office into the Texas heat.

A group of reporters, flanked by a handful of photographers, charged up the sidewalk at them. It was then that J.D. noticed the cars and vans that now cluttered both sides of the small town street.

Zoe's panicked, "Uh-oh, John Dalton, here it comes," and her anxious glance into his face to gauge his reaction made him press her tighter against his side and hurry them toward his car.

"Give them a big smile and tell them whatever you want, Hollywood." He answered her quick little "You're sure?" with a growling "Yes."

J.D. managed to open Zoe's door and get her shielded behind it before the reporters reached them. He escaped to the driver's side and got in to start the engine by the time the chorus of "Miss Yahzoo!" came to a crescendo.

He heard one bold lady's, "What comment do you have about Dillon Casey's Sedgewick biography?" as Zoe put her foot in the car and eased in to close the door. She pressed a button to lower the window partway, then held up a hand to halt the babble of questions that followed. Her light touch on J.D.'s arm was a signal for him to start the big car forward.

Zoe gave a laugh to go with the thousand-watt smile she flashed them all. The click and whir of cameras picked up pace. Two video cameras were aimed at an angle through the wide windshield to film them both. The cameras kept up as the car rolled forward.

"You know I can't comment," Zoe called to them, and gave a playful shake of her head. She turned to smile at the rugged, stern-faced man beside her who was taking it all in with grim patience.

She didn't answer the next question, "Who's the cowboy?" or the new frenzy for attention it stirred. J.D. pulled the big car onto the street and sped away from the swarm of reporters who chased after them on foot for a half block.

Zoe took a nervous breath. "That's just a taste. If they don't already know who you are or where the Hayes Ranch is, they will very soon."

J.D. reached over and gripped her trembling hand. He laced her small, slim fingers between his big ones before he looked over at her. "Blake warned me there were reporters in town snooping around before we came in for our appointment. Jess and the men are moving some of the cattle to the front pastures by the highway. Once we're through the gate, wire goes up and we'll run a few head of cattle in to graze along the ranch road. Our biggest, nastiest bull will be in that bunch. I doubt he'll give those reporters anything but second thoughts.'' J.D.'s big smile made Zoe laugh.

"Lets get to the courthouse and see about that license,'' he said gruffly. Zoe smiled happily and gave his big hand a squeeze.

Zoe Yahzoo became Mrs. John Dalton Hayes in a private ceremony on the big front porch of the Hayes ranch house. It took a bit of vigilance to keep the cattle assigned to the ranch drive from overrunning the tree-shaded festivities in the huge yard. J.D.'s biggest, nastiest bull, Bodacious, much preferred his assigned task near the wired-over front entrance to the ranch. Zoe reckoned it was the activity of the reporters themselves as they tried to find a way past the cattle that kept the surly bull's attention. The only helicopter that showed up was the one J.D. hired to ferry in a few guests. He'd also hired it to fly the two of them away once the reception was over and Zoe had tossed her bright bouquet.

They spent their honeymoon at a secluded cabin on a small lake in the Ozarks. J.D. learned his bride could bait a hook and catch fish. Zoe learned that her tough Texas rancher was even more thrilling in bed than he was out of it. They changed each other's lives.

So much so, that the dark-haired son they conceived before their first wedding anniversary was named John Dalton, Jr. The fact that no one dared call the boy Junior was because the boy's daddy was so formidable—and his adoring mother referred to the boy as Johnny D. Their second son, Nick's, middle name was Henry, but the next four children were all blue-eyed blondes: Victoria, Julia, Sarah and Theresa Jane, who could ride and rope as well as their brothers.

The vast Hayes Ranch had heirs aplenty, but the most impressive legacy Zoe and John Dalton left their children was a legacy of love, laughter and tender devotion. The precarious match between the good fairy and the troll was exactly right.

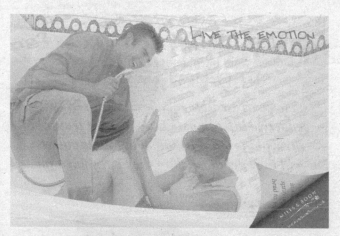

Don't miss *Book Twelve* of this BRAND-NEW 12 book collection 'Bachelor Auction'.

Who says money can't buy love?

On sale 1st August

Available at most branches of WH Smith, Tesco, Martins, Borders, Eason, Sainsbury's, and all good paperback bookshops.

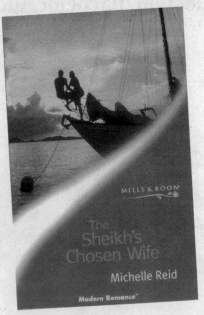

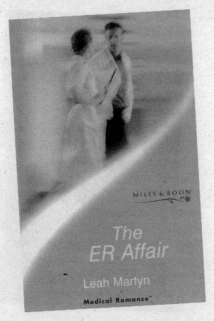